Ask These People About
THE KINGMAKER

Jeff Jefferson, the actor who let himself be
molded into a political idol . . . Joanne West,
raised to the Hollywood heights, then left to
fall into an abyss of sex and self-destruction . . .
"Cat's Eye" Bastione, the Chicago "Godfather"
who adopted a hungry kid, and lived to
regret it . . .

Or the famous singer with his mellow voice
and bottomless thirst . . . the beautiful
actor's agent whose body was used to sweeten
a deal . . . the campaign chief of a major
party who opened up terrifying new vistas
of power . . .

They all could tell you about the Kingmaker
—if they dared. . . .

"SUPERB!" —*Pittsburgh Press*

THE
KINGMAKER

HENRY DENKER

A DELL BOOK

Published by
DELL PUBLISHING CO., INC.
1 Dag Hammarskjold Plaza
New York, New York 10017

Reprinted by arrangement with
David McKay Company, Inc.
New York, New York 10017

Printed in the United States of America

First Dell printing—April 1973

To Edith, my wife

PROLOGUE

The clock tower showed six minutes to midnight as the last black limousine pulled up at the State Capitol. The back door opened. A man climbed out, stared up at the impressive building, its dome aglow from the inside. He glanced at the two California Highway Patrol troopers on guard at the top of the broad stone steps and started toward them.

He was a small, dignified man, tightly built, with graying hair, dressed tonight, as always, in the height of restrained fashion. With his pince-nez glasses, he often startled those of his own generation by resembling so closely the late Supreme Court Justice, Felix Frankfurter. Thus he succeeded in giving a reserved and an almost elegant appearance to the profession of being a Hollywood agent, in itself no small accomplishment.

He shuddered a bit now. The air was cool but not cold for a New Year's Eve. Yet his silk dinner jacket and his luxurious black vicuña dress coat felt insufficient to protect him. He wondered, was it age? Or was it damnable local pride about the weather which demanded that everyone underdress as if to prove it was always sunny and mild in California, even on cool, damp nights?

Or, he asked himself, was it the occasion?

He had reached the top step as one of the Highway patrolmen, in full uniform and holding a clipboard, moved to confront him.

"Name, sir?"

"Cone," the little man said.

The trooper consulted his list, on which almost all the names had been checked off, found the name CONE, DR. IRWIN.

"Very well, Doctor. The ceremony will be in the rotunda. Straight ahead."

The second trooper opened the large heavy door for
him. Cone nodded in appreciation and moved into the
Capitol building.

Once inside, the exaggerated hum of voices sounded as
if it had been fed through an echo chamber, gaining
resonance and richness from the sheer size and emptiness
of the place.

It struck him how much this was like the old days. The
early days, when, if a band was too small or a singer's
voice too thin, he would insist on having it fed through
an echo chamber to make the band seem twice as large or
give the singer's modest voice pretensions to operatic
quality.

They damned well might need an echo chamber in this
place tonight, he thought, and from now on.

The guests were all gathered in a small area in the
center of the rotunda, some standing, most of them seated
in the few rows of temporary seats which had been arranged to accommodate the select audience invited to this
august ceremony.

The Doctor spied Spencer Gould and Freddie Feig.
They were both neatly attired, nice-looking, tough, self-
centered men and completely without conscience. Which
was precisely why he had hired them years ago.

Then he saw Walter Craig, to whom must go the greatest share of the credit for tonight.

The others, The Doctor wondered now, where were all
the others? Buddy Black, though also his employee, could
not be here, of course. That would be bad politics. But
the others, at least some of them, might have shown up.
All those who intentionally or unintentionally, knowingly
or unknowingly, had played a part in making this night
and this ceremony possible.

Spencer and Freddie were coming toward him to greet
him, smiling their congratulations at his achievement. It
was exactly the same smile he had seen on their faces at
the opening of a picture that they all expected would be a
hit. Or on nights when one of TCA's clients had a big
opening on Broadway. Or when they had just launched a
TV series that promised a long, healthy, profitable run for
TCA. To Spence and Freddie even an inaugural was merely like putting another show on the road. Another hit.

The Doctor accepted their greetings with a nod. He

sat down feeling tired. Not from the activities of the long, hectic week. All his weeks were hectic. He was tired in the lifetime sense of being tired. He was more depressed at this moment than he had been on election night.

Now, Walter Craig came over to shake his hand. For once The Doctor permitted the contact.

"Soon as the clock strikes midnight they can start," Craig said.

The Doctor nodded again. As if his permission were necessary to commence the ceremony. Having done that, he leaned back and realized that his chair had no arms. He hated chairs without arms. Now he would not relax at all. His mind started groping to recapture his unfinished thought, as minds do. What the hell had he been thinking about, just before Spence and Freddie . . . ? Oh, yes. The others. Where were the others? Of course, he couldn't expect some of them to turn up tonight. Certainly not Joanne. Or that girl . . . what was her name? Charlene, Charlene Rashbaum. Or Lee Mandell who practiced law in Washington. But at least some of the others. . . . Where were they, what were they doing that kept them away?

The huge bell in the nearby tower began to toll midnight. The sound carried into and vibrated around the empty rotunda. It was midnight in Sacramento. Two o'clock in Chicago. Three o'clock on the Atlantic Coast. Nine o'clock in the morning on the Riviera.

At Cap d'Antibes, in a huge villa overlooking the Mediterranean, Doris Martinson, an eyemask protecting her from the world, was snoring unevenly while sleeping off the effects of the lavish New Year's Eve party she had given for two hundred guests. To the far side of the giant round bed lay her too-young husband, irritated beyond sleeping by her gurgling snore. Yet he was relieved that she was asleep. The damned bitch was more demanding drunk than sober, and even less enjoyable. If his friends who envied him only knew the truth.

She moved now. He came alert, stopped breathing. But she had only shifted position, allowing one copious breast to free itself from her Dior nightgown. One thing he could say for her, she still had a good body, great breasts. She resumed her light but irritating snore.

Just before she had launched into her serious drinking for the evening she had instructed him, "Don't forget, Jacques! I've got to send a cable to California! Remind me!" He had reminded her. Twice. But whether she had sent it or not, he did not know. Nor care. His problem now was to try to get some sleep finally.

In Bronxville, New York, where it was three o'clock in the morning, Carl Brewster, Vice President in Charge of Television at S.S.D. & O., was leaning over the toilet bowl in the master bedroom of his large old house in one of the finest and most restricted communities on the entire East Coast. He was vomiting.

From the bedroom came the voice of his irate wife. "I begged you to stop drinking!"

"It wasn't the booze! It was that damned Chinese food! You know, there's a whole Chinese food syndrome! Doctors have been discovering . . ."

But the burning sensation in his throat was hot acid once more and he had to throw up again. He recovered, continuing as if he had never been interrupted.

"Some people just can't take all that sodium whatever-the-hell it is."

"Monosodium glutamate," she called back. "Especially after seven double scotches, which I counted myself! And I'll bet you never sent that wire!"

"Wire? What wire?"

"There! See!" she taunted.

"So what?" Brewster said, coming halfway out of the bathroom to argue. "I gave that sonofabitch his start on TV. He owes his whole career to me. Without me he never gets to be governor. *He* ought to be sending *me* wires!"

Before his wife could answer, the acid was up in his throat again, burning bitterly. He had to turn and race back to the toilet bowl.

In a Washington, D.C. apartment, a stocky white-haired man with the thick, knobby hands of an old-time football player, and the persuasive manner of a skillful lawyer, was carrying on early morning negotiations with a Western Union operator as he sat on the side of his bed in his pajamas.

"Look, young lady, I'll spell it for you. *S-h-m-u-c-k!* Never mind what it means! *I* know. And *he'll* know. That's all that matters. Now spell it back. Good! Good!" the white-haired man said.

From the other side of the bed, the diminutive woman who was his wife warned, "Lee, they won't deliver it."

He quieted her with a gesture of his huge hand and continued speaking into the phone. "Okay, let's get this straight, young lady. From the top. 'The Honorable Jeff Jefferson, Governor of the State of California, State Capitol, Sacramento, California . . .' "

She interrupted him, but he exploded, "Look! *I'm* paying for this! *I'll* count the words! 'Sacramento, California.' The message: 'Dear Jeff, I hope you remember the old days when I explained the difference between a *shmuck* and a prick. Don't be either one and you'll be okay. Congratulations. Affectionately, Lee Mandell.' That's it."

The Western Union girl made one last effort at protest.

"Young lady," Mandell roared, "I am one of the most important lawyers in this city! And I am warning you that if you don't send that wire as I dictated it, you're abridging my right of free speech! And I will sue Western Union for five million dollars!"

"Lee!" his wife admonished. "What kind of nonsense . . ."

"Okay, young lady. Just send it! And we won't mention this incident to anyone!" Lee Mandell hung up.

He turned out the light, slipped back into bed and took a deep breath.

Timidly, from her side of the bed, his wife said, "Lee, that was not very nice language to send to a governor."

"He'll understand. He's really a very nice guy. I always liked him. Of course, if this is the beginning of a trend . . . I mean actors, TV personalities becoming a serious element in political life . . . I don't know."

He seemed suddenly older and more worried as he stared into the darkness.

"First time he was ever on TV was alongside me during those hearings . . . In a way I feel responsible."

At North Oaks Country Club, a non-restricted, totally Jewish institution, the annual formal New Year's Eve dinner-dance and buffet was beginning to wind down. The waiters were bringing out huge stainless steel steam table pans full of pre-toasted bagels, scrambled eggs, bacon and ham, as well as large platters of lox and smoked white-fish, this for the early morning New Year's Day break-fast which was a North Oaks tradition. Now everyone could eat, go home, tired, over-alcoholed, overfed and get some sleep before having to get up and watch the endless football bowl games on television.

Marvin Berg, attorney, and President of Rashbaum Theatres, Inc., was suddenly missing his wife. After in-quiring about her, he decided she must be in the ladies' room. Fearing she might be ill, he went in search of her. But he spied her in the phone booth just outside the ladies' room. She saw him, waved through the closed glass door to indicate that she was fine and would join him for the buffet in a moment.

She turned back to the phone to complete her con-versation.

"Straight wire. 'Honorable Jeff Jefferson, Governor of the State of California. Sacramento.' Yes, yes it's in California. The message reads: 'Among all the pet names I ever dreamed of, His Excellency was not one. Con-gratulations. And love.' Sign it . . . just sign it . . . 'Char-lene.' Would you read it back, please?"

The Western Union operator read back the message, asking, "Is that all?"

"Yes," Charlene said. "Charge it to the telephone num-ber I gave you. And . . . and Happy New Year."

She hung up, opened the door, started toward her hus-band. She was a tall young woman, striking because of it, and because of her defiant black hair, her emerald green satin gown and her body which she carried with the grace of an athlete. When she joined her husband, she ex-plained, "Just checking to see if everything's okay at home."

"Kids okay?"

"Both asleep. Let's . . . let's get some food. I'm fam-ished."

She took his hand and led him toward the large walnut-paneled dining room which had been converted to simulate a night club for New Year's Eve. An impossibly loud band was still beating out Caribbean rhythms for some of

Chicago's best Jewish families.

In Palm Springs, the bar and the Terrace Room at the Racquet Club were so jammed and noisy with drinkers that the music being piped in from the dining room could hardly be heard. A blonde who was a little too blonde and too puffy under the chin and eyes, expensively dressed and obviously drunk sat crushed against the bar next to an extremely tanned young man who was trying to attract the bartender's attention so he could order her another straight gin on the rocks with lemon peel.

When he had failed in four attempts, she turned to him.

"Let's screw this joint! We can't get a drink around here! We'll go back to the house."

"The party's just beginning," the young man protested.

"What do you want to do, look around for younger stuff? Is that it?" she accused loudly.

"Joanne, sweetie," he tried to quiet her, becoming aware that those close around them were beginning to listen.

"I said, we go!" She bolted off her stool fully intending to be indignant but only succeeded in betraying the fact that she was drunk. She made it to the door, stepped out into the night air.

It was cool. The dark blue sky had a prodigal splash of stars across it. She did not notice. She was too drunk, too angry. The young man pursued her. He almost caught up with her when she was past the pool and on the dewy lawn.

"Joanne! Joie!"

She didn't stop or turn. He overtook her, seized her arm.

"You let go of me . . . you . . . you . . ." And because she couldn't think of any worse epithet she called him what he was, "You tennis pro!" making it sound like the lowest of professions.

"Joie . . . take it easy . . . honey . . ."

He pulled her to him, embraced her; then, despite the heavy stench of gin on her breath, he kissed her with an open mouth. That calmed her anger but aroused her sexuality. She kissed back, tightened her embrace, ground her pelvis against him till she could feel him coming erect against her.

"Let's go back to the house," he whispered.

She laughed, close in his ear. "What's wrong with the lawn?"

"People might pass by," he pleaded.

"Let 'em!"

"We'll go back to the house," he insisted.

She turned furious. "You ashamed of me?"

"No, honey, honest!"

"Because I haven't made a picture in two years? Or do you think I'm too old for you? Well, you just remember one thing, Mr. Tennis Pro! I could have been fucking the Governor of the State of California tonight if I'd wanted to!"

She broke away. He chased her. Caught up with her. And behind the protective shield of an elephantine tamarisk tree on the cool damp grass of the Racquet Club lawn he had her. While the noise, the shouting, the singing from inside the bar informed him that another Happy New Year had just arrived.

In Sacramento the bell across from the Capitol building had finished tolling twelve.

Doctor Irwin Cone was suddenly brought back to the reality of the moment when Spencer Gould and Walter Craig occupied the seats on either side of him in anticipation of the ceremony that was about to begin.

Now the high, thick oak door leading to a room off the rotunda opened. In the doorway appeared the Chief Justice of the State Supreme Court, draped in his black judicial robes, to endow the occasion with deserving solemnity. Behind the Justice walked a tall man, his hair blond but graying, his face lean, strong, handsome in its outlines but, despite its fresh tan, creased with the tiredness that political campaigning leaves as its ineradicable residue. Alongside him walked a blonde woman with a face too strong to be called merely pretty. Somberly dressed in a simple dark gown, she walked as awed as if she were approaching the altar of some ancient cathedral.

As the small procession moved, the fireflies of the news media danced around them taking hundreds of shots.

The principals gathered before the small audience. When the photographers had taken up their positions so

they could record the ceremony for posterity, the Chief
Justice raised the Bible he carried. His look invited the
man to place his left hand on it and raise his right.

"Repeat after me this oath for the office of Governor,"
the Chief Justice pontificated, "I . . ."

"I, Jeffry Jefferson . . ." the man said gravely.

"do solemnly swear that I will support and defend . . ."

"do solemnly swear that I will support and defend . . ."

"the Constitution of the United States and the Constitution of the State of California . . ."

"the Constitution of the United States and the Constitution of the State of California . . ."

"against all enemies, foreign and domestic . . ."

"against all enemies, foreign and domestic . . ."

All enemies, foreign and domestic . . . the phrase echoed
in The Doctor's mind so that he became oblivious of the
rest. It seemed unreal, the entire scene. Even as he heard
the words enunciated so gravely by the Chief Justice,
echoed with equal gravity by the duly elected Governor,
Jeff Jefferson, The Doctor found it difficult to believe.
This could more rightly be a scene from one of Jeff's TV
films. The Chief Justice might well have been sent over
from Central Casting. And Jeff might be playing a governor because this week that was what the script called for.

Suddenly The Doctor knew what had made the night
seem so cold. What made him feel so weary now. It was
uneasiness. A deep sense of uneasiness.

Not guilt, he protested. He had no reason to feel any
personal guilt.

To take a man who had been an actor, a man without
a single day's experience in government and catapult him
to the highest office in the state was an achievement. And
nothing to feel guilty about.

If there had to be blame, place it where it belonged.
On the system which sanctioned it. On the people who
permitted it. On the media which allowed themselves to be
manipulated so easily.

All The Doctor had done was to apply the same
basic rule to politics as he had to developing TCA into
the leading power in the entertainment industry.

A lifetime ago he had been instructed by an expert, a

man of primitive but deep insight: "Never waste your
muscle. Find out where the weakness is and put your
muscle there."

That was all he had done. And it had worked. If he
had made it work better than anyone else, that was no
crime. No crime. . . .

PART ONE

"Never waste your muscle. Find out where the weakness is and put your muscle there."

It was the soundest piece of advice The Doctor had ever been given by anyone. That it came from Angelo "Cat's Eye" Bastione, did not diminish its value. It enhanced it. For Bastione was a man who controlled an empire that had long ago been spawned in Chicago but had since metastasized throughout the nation. A man of no education, with only an animal need to survive, conquer, and rule, Bastione stood like a giant in a world where to lose meant to die an untimely death.

The Doctor had built his career on that simple precept. As the entertainment industry grew larger, and picture companies turned into big business while radio and television networks became giant monopolies, Irwin Cone never wasted his muscle.

The bigger the entities grew, the more vulnerable they became to pressure, particularly when it was applied with a total absence of emotion or conscience.

The Doctor's real education had begun at that point when, as a young man, his medical education had almost been completed. His years in medical school had been a frantic race between finishing the required courses and helping in his father's desperate effort to maintain his small grocery business on Maxwell Street in a Chicago ghetto.

It seemed that his father had lived only for the day when he could see his son, Isidore Cohen, receive the degree, Doctor of Medicine. For two months thereafter, pressing creditors had forced the old man into bankruptcy. With bankruptcy came his first heart attack. So that young Isidore Cohen, his name as yet unAnglicized, was suddenly

confronted with an invalid father and no means of support beyond his twenty-four-dollar-a-month intern's salary.

There were only two choices open to him. He could go
back to selling shoes part time as he had in college. Or
he could reassemble his old band to play at small fraternity dances, Italian or Jewish weddings, and bar mitz-
vahs. Selling shoes was more certain than random band
bookings. But the hours demanded in shoe departments
did not fit easily into an intern's schedule. He had decided in favor of the band.

Fortunately, it being the early thirties, the other members of the band were facing hard times, too. Even those
who were employed had been delighted to earn five dollars for a night of playing college medleys or Yiddish
kazatkahs.

He didn't like it, mainly because in his mind he had
thankfully relegated that kind of work to the past. It was
not seemly for a doctor to stand up and play before a
mob that was gorging itself on food.

But it was a living, not only for himself, but, more important, for his father, Samuel. Some nights after an especially good affair Izzy would net fifteen dollars for himself after giving each of his sidemen their five dollars.
Other nights, when the host was particularly argumenta-
tive or forthrightly dishonest, Izzy had barely enough to
pay off his boys. The next morning he would go on duty
at the hospital, sleepy, hungry, disgruntled, wondering
whether it was worth it. One thing he knew, he must never
let his father suspect how bad things were. As far as the
old man was concerned everything was fine. Money was,
if not plentiful, certainly adequate. So Papa could sit in
the park during the day, go to synagogue Friday night
and Saturday morning, and never have to work again as
long as he lived.

On the bad nights, Isidore Cohen thanked God that his
mother hadn't lived to see her "brilliant" son still up there
on the bandstand playing for people who had no appreciation of the fact that they were listening to a real honest-
to-God medical doctor. But he sustained himself with the
promise that once his internship was over, he would
find a residency in a good hospital, which would enable
him to get along without outside income. Then later,

there would come practice, an office in a good upper-middle-class neighborhood, perhaps even marriage to a nice Jewish girl with a rich father, and finally his financial worries would be over forever.

The girls he had courted during his high school and college days had long ago given up on him. In times like those, unless the girl's father was rich to start with, and could finance a young doctor until he established a practice, she didn't waste her time on a medical student. Not if she wanted to marry and have children before she was thirty.

So each of the girls Izzy might have married ended up marrying someone else. Not that Izzy minded too much. If he could catch a feel of a young pretty nurse in the floor kitchen at the hospital, or maybe even get laid by one of them in the small hours of the morning when things were slow in Emergency, his sex life was taken care of without any great concern of involvement.

His main object was to get through his internship, secure the right residency and hold his breath long enough to get out into practice.

That's the way things would have gone for Isidore Cohen, M.D., except for a chance meeting one night in Emergency Receiving. In the neighborhood where Sinai Hospital was located, late admissions were mainly of two types: Negroes who had wounded one another in street fights or girls hemorrhaging with all manner of projectiles in their vaginas from having tried to abort themselves.

But on this night there came to Emergency a young man, white, obviously Jewish, bleeding severely and dangerously from several long slash wounds on his face. With him was a stocky older man, wearing a large felt hat and a tan camel's hair polo coat which was stained with fresh red blood. His swarthy face was set.

"Doc, you save this guy!" he commanded. And he stood back watching with black intense eyes as Izzy estimated the loss of blood, called for an infusion of saline and glucose, and began to stitch up the most severe cuts.

Once the worst of it was over the stocky man moved closer, his attitude more relaxed and admiring. As Izzy

tied stitch after stitch with great dexterity the man said,
"You got good hands, Doc. I mean, your fingers, they're
fast! You going to be a great doctor."

"That isn't something you learn in medical school. You
learn that playing a violin," Izzy said, half jokingly.

"You play the violin?" the man asked, with increased
admiration. At the same time he fingered a small ring on
his little finger, rubbing its golden cat's-eye gem like a
talisman.

"Yeah," Izzy said, turning away to get a better view of
the patient's face. "I have a little combo. We play nights
. . . for laughs mainly."

The man seemed impressed. "That's nice. I mean someone working hard like you do, still keeping up with music. Nice."

"It isn't all so nice," Izzy conceded, then relating suddenly to his work, he pointed out, "See that? If that blade
had gone in another millimeter or two and hit the carotid
artery, that would have been it."

"Curtains?"

"Curtains."

Izzy kept inserting the suture needle, pulling the gut
through, tying it into neat small stitches. Suddenly the
man asked, "What ya mean it ain't all nice?"

"Interns don't get paid much. So I play the fiddle to . . .
to fill in. . . ."

"You need bucks?"

Izzy nodded, turning away again to work, followed by
the stocky man who leaned over to watch. All the while
he kept rubbing the gem in his pinky ring.

When Izzy had finished the last of the eighty-four
stitches, and assured himself that the patient's blood pressure was starting to climb back to normal, he turned to
the waiting nurse, "Continue saline and glucose. Just in
case shock sets in. Find him a bed. Must be one in Ward
B."

The nurse got behind the stretcher to push it out of
Emergency but it would not move. Izzy bent to free the
wheels. He found the stocky man's foot firmly planted in
front of one wheel.

"I'm taking him home," the man said blandly.

"I don't think that's a good idea," Izzy disagreed.

"It's a good idea," the man insisted, losing his smile.

"We have regulations and routine. . . ."

"That's exactly what I don't like. Routines. And regulations."

"I'm sorry about that . . ." Izzy began.

The man interrupted sharply, "Hey, Doc, c'mere!" He gestured with his head to draw the young doctor into the corner of the room near the Emergency entrance. "If you worryin' about the patient's condition, he gonna get the best care." He indicated with his head the huge dark limousine parked alongside the ambulance dock. "We brang him here. We gonna take him away. He gonna be very comfortable. Very safe. Safer than here. Take my word."

"Sorry. Besides, I have to get the whole history from him to file the police report. . . ."

"There ain't gonna be no report!" the man said flatly.

"That's the law when obvious violence is involved."

"Hey, kid! You know who you're talking to?" the dark man demanded, suddenly angry. When Izzy didn't answer, the man held up his right hand, making a fist so that his little finger rode higher than the others, then slowly he turned his hand back and forth displaying his ring. "You never heard the name Cat's Eye?" he asked with bruised vanity and great intolerance for stupidity.

Cat's Eye . . . Izzy said to himself; there was only one man of note named Cat's Eye. Cat's Eye Bastione. Suddenly the young doctor felt both surprise and fear, great fear. He was glad he hadn't known before, else his fingers would not have been so steady or so nimble.

"Now, kid, don't get nervous. I ain't going to hurt you. Here, look, if I was going to put the muscle on you, would I give you this?"

Bastione held out a crisp new hundred dollar bill.

"Interns can't accept gifts."

"Then let me put it another way. You want to save this guy's life?"

"He'll be safer here than if you move him," Izzy said.

"Long as he's in Chicago he ain't safe." Izzy raised his eyebrows. "Take my word," said Bastione. "This kid ain't part of no mob. He's a comic. He's working for me in the Chez Paree on the near North Side. You heard of that?"

"Of course."

"Okay. He is a nice young Jew boy, coming up as a real big-time comic. And he is drawing the people. Until the Irishman decides it is hurting his Shamrock Club. So he sends two of his cutters up to the kid's hotel and they do this job on him. Now, if he died that'd be the end of it. But since he didn't, and he saw who done it, they know they can't let him stay in Chicago, alive. They come right in here, right in your goddamned Ward B and finish him! Now you want that to happen?"

"No."

"So, no police report. And we take him with us."

"He should be seen by a doctor. Every day for the next week."

"You want to do it yourself, we can make a deal."

"No. Thanks. Just remember to have those stitches taken out in four days. Any longer, they can become infected."

"Okay. Four days. But remember, no reports. Right? I don't give a damn. They can't touch me. It's him I'm worried about."

Izzy hesitated a moment, then nodded.

"Okay, kid! I don't forget." The stocky man gave a signal through the glass part of the door. Two men leaped out of the limousine, came in to lift the patient, carry him out and place him on the back seat. The car pulled away into the night.

The young nurse, a pretty blonde girl from nearby dairy country in Wisconsin, waited till the door had closed before she asked, "Was that really him? Cat's Eye Bastione?"

"I certainly wasn't going to stand there and argue with him about it," Izzy said.

"Here. Have a cup of coffee. You need it," she said, pouring from the sooted-over white porcelain coffee pot that always sat on the Bunsen burner. He took the cup and tried to sip, but it was blistering hot. So he put it aside saying, "I better let this cool." He turned to her, put his arms out to embrace her. He liked to nuzzle against her because of her good-sized breasts and because she never resisted him too strongly. But tonight she announced, "Don't get yourself overheated!"

"What's the matter? Your period?" he asked, trying to remember.

"Mrs. Ryan."

"What did she say?"

"Her standard speech. About interns. Except this time she specifically mentioned you."

"She's jealous!" he accused. "Did I ever tell you how she tried to corner me in the linen closet?"

"Old Lady Ryan?" the young nurse asked, astounded. Then realizing he was joking, she relented and laughed. He took that as his cue to try again. He started to work his fingers coyly between the two top buttons of her starched white uniform to get a feel of her breasts, which were reputed to be the firmest in the hospital.

"Don't!" she protested. But when he was about to give up, she explained softly, "This uniform has to last two more days." And she unbuttoned the top button so he could have easy access to her.

He slid his hand in, fingered his way down the shoulder strap of her slip and found a familiar resting place against her large warm breast, for she never had need to wear a bra. Her nipple was already reacting to him. When he kissed her, and his tongue began playing inside her mouth, her nipples came fully erect, and yet remained soft to his touch. He gentled her breast out of her stiff uniform, began to kiss it and soon she was pressing his head so tight against her that he had difficulty breathing.

By now his other hand was unbuttoning the rest of her uniform till she could slide out of it one shoulder at a time without interrupting him.

Now the moment came when, from habit, they both knew what must be done. It was accomplished without words.

He released her, his emotions a mingling of momentary regret and eventual expectation. She pulled the uniform about her shoulders, glanced out the door to make sure no one was coming down the hall and then darted three doors down and disappeared. He waited only seconds, then repeated the same furtive maneuver.

In the totally dark, aseptic-smelling linen closet, surrounded by shelves of fresh clean pillowcases, sheets, and towels, he resumed kissing her breasts, sliding down the shoulder straps of her slip one at a time till she was naked from the waist up. His only regret was that it was dark and he could not feast his eyes on her magnificent breasts which delighted his hands and his mouth so completely.

Secluded in the closet, he had no need to confine himself. He reached down and gradually slid her slip below her hips until it fell to the floor. She reached for his fly, finding the buttons, undoing them one by one. He knew from experience he had no need to assist her. She reached in, her hand stealing around him and lifting him out.

Now came the most delicate part of the action. He had to back her gently toward one of the shelves so that her solid buttocks could rest on it just enough to enable her to spread her young thighs and afford him entrance. It required the utmost of cooperation for the danger was always present that if he failed to make proper contact quickly he would come prematurely ruining the entire affair.

Moments like these were the only times he had reason to be thankful that he was short. For taller interns had a sad backbreaking history of linen-closet love-making. But young Cohen was a perfect height for her. And she helped him in. She was very tight for a girl with such good hips and thighs but it only made the venture more exciting. Once he was safely in, he helped her lift her legs so that soon she was locked around him so powerfully that it hurt, but it was an ecstatic kind of hurt. Thus balanced, they began to move in the time-honored rhythm of lovers, until he could tell from the grip of her thighs that she was at the peak of her intensity. Then he drove home in shorter and swifter strokes bringing them both to a climax of delight and relief.

Only when he began to regain his breath did young Cohen realize how much he had needed her as an antidote to his terror over having confronted Cat's Eye Bastione. Then he heard the floor loudspeaker insistently summoning, "Dr. Cohen . . . Dr. Isidore Cohen . . . Dr. Cohen . . ."

Less than two weeks had gone by, in fact it was the eleventh day after he had sutured the young comic, when

Dr. Isidore Cohen found a message waiting for him in his box at the hospital. "Please call NO. 4772."

The number was not familiar. But when he had a break he called. The voice that answered was instantly recognizable.

"Hey, Doc. You been botherin' me. In my business I don't like no open accounts. You do something for me. I do something for you. Even. Now, you don't take money, that I know. If you was one of the boys then I could ask you, you want me to make a hit on somebody, and I get 'em hit for you. But with you it got to be somethin' different. Okay. I finally figured out. You play the fiddle. You got a combo. You work a few nights a week. Whatever job comes along. Okay. Well, something just came along. I got a job for you. Two night a week. Friday and Saturday. In a little joint I got on Clark Street. Easy work. Good money. You could clear yourself, thirty, forty clams a week. Every week. What do you say?"

"Well, I . . . I'm on duty every other Saturday," Izzy said.

"So you make a deal with one of the other interns."

"Well, I . . ."

"Look, kid, I am only asking you to do what you're doing. Only do it for good dollars. What's wrong?"

"I'll think about it."

"While you're thinking the world's turning and you ain't gettin' younger. Say yes! Okay?"

Izzy said nothing.

It took two more calls from Bastione before Izzy finally agreed. Then Bastione said, "Good! Somehow I feel lucky with Jews!"

So Dr. Isidore Cohen made arrangements with two other interns to cover for him on Friday and Saturday nights. Five days and nights he was a doctor at Sinai Hospital. But on the sixth and seventh nights he was a band leader at one of Bastione's clubs, which was really a little clip joint frequented by B-girls and out-of-towners. Still, he no longer ran the risk of not being paid or of having to pay out more to his sidemen than he earned himself.

It was a good set-up, it even allowed him to have a woman in three times a week to clean and take Papa out for air when the weather was nice. As for Bastione and playing in a mob club, Izzy Cohen did what needy men have always done. He said to himself, there is nothing dishonest about playing music. I do my job the best I can, I take my money, and I leave without asking any questions.

Besides, he consoled himself, it wouldn't go on too much longer. Once he started his residency, hopefully at a good hospital, possibly even Rush Memorial, he could quit the music business forever. He had no illusions, though. A Jew, no matter what medical school he came from, didn't just walk into an internship or a residency at a good gentile hospital. But his medical school record was excellent, and his chief at Sinai had said he would put in a good word with an old classmate of his at Rush. So it was possible.

The goal of becoming a successful doctor with an office in a good Jewish neighborhood loomed large and real now. He was already promising himself that when he made the move he would not only quit music but would exchange his stolid heavy-framed glasses for pince-nez, like the newly appointed Supreme Court Justice Felix Frankfurter, whom some people said he resembled.

So it would have gone. Into the residency at Rush, out of the music business and on his way finally to a lucrative practice.

Except that one day while facing a serious labor problem, Cat's Eye Bastione ordered thoughtfully, "Get me the little Jew!" When his lieutenant hesitated, confused, Bastione exclaimed impatiently, "The little Jew! Who has the band in the clip joint over on Clark Street!"

"Oh, him? Yeah!"

"Get him!"

His lieutenant went off, nodding like a stolid animal. Bastione sat back in his office at the garage distillery, shoved his hat back on his head, began to finger his cat's-eye ring, polishing the stone with the thumb of his other hand.

In due time, after he had been called at the hospital, had a chance to get off duty and change from his whites, Dr. Isidore Cohen, the little Jew, arrived.

Bastione began pleasantly enough. Had he lived up to his word? Provided a steady job? Good money? And no trouble? Yes, Izzy agreed, gingerly. Okay, now it was Bastione who needed a favor. He spelled it out plainly.

Some dumb nervy dago without enough brains to be scared for his life, was trying to organize the Chicago night club musicians into a union! Bastione wanted to kill the union before it even began. He wanted to starve those wops into submission.

"Stupido! Stupido!," Bastione kept repeating, all the while the fury in him building up. Except that occasionally he broke off to say, "We let a union live here in Chicago, next thing they move into New York, Philly, L.A. And my friends will be calling me, saying, 'Hey, you stupid wop, what did you start there in Chicago?' We got to stop it now! Tonight!"

Bastione turned on Izzy suddenly. "This is what you're going to do. You going to take your combo into my Chez Paree. For a lot more than what you're getting now. You're going to play seven nights a week. If I got to square it with the hospital, or we got to pay off some interns to take your place, okay, but you got to work seven nights a week. . . ."

"I can't do that," Izzy started to say.

"For three times what you're getting now, you can do it," Bastione said.

The little doctor was taken aback. Three times what he was getting, when he was already being overpaid.

"Look, Mr. Bastione," he said softly, reasonably, "for three times what I'm getting you could pay those men so well they wouldn't want a union."

"That's not the point!" Bastione exploded. "When I think they should get more, they'll get more! But nobody puts the muscle on Bastione and gets away with it! I'm waiting to hear, kid. Well?"

"I'll . . . I'll think about it. . . ." Dr. Isidore Cohen said softly.

"Okay. But don't think forever. I got to know by morning. Okay, kid?"

"Okay. By morning."

Cohen left. Bastione watched him, confident. When a needy man said he was going to think something over, the

answer was always yes. All that the man was really thinking over was the way he could justify that yes.

There were several factors of importance to Dr. Isidore
Cohen. The money was staggeringly good. More than he
had ever earned. And the chance of that residency at
Rush was still not certain.

So all the real pressures of his everyday life militated in
favor of his saying yes to Bastione. But there was still a
part of him that said no, and strongly. His was an old
Jewish liberal background. His father was more a so-
cialist than a Jew. If Norman Thomas had ever come to
town on Yom Kippur there would be no question where
Samuel Cohen would be found. Not in *schul*, but at the
Jewish People's Institute where Thomas would speak
whenever he was in Chicago. No, Samuel Cohen would
not like his son acting as a strike-breaker.

Yet, look at his father. Old now, worn out, defeated.
All his principles, all his theories, all his concern about
his fellow man had availed both him and mankind nothing.
Maybe the best way, the shrewdest way, was to play the
system as well as you could, make your bundle, then with
security behind you, become a really effective liberal.

As Bastione had known from the beginning, Dr. Isidore
Cohen decided to accept the offer.

The whole first week, each time Izzy passed the picket
line he felt like a traitor. But that first week's pay was
more cash than he had ever held in his skillful delicate
hands. When Bastione noted his pleasure, he said, "Not
bad, ha, kid? What I promised you. I don't cop out on a
deal. Never!"

More to conceal his avarice than to complain, Izzy said,
"Yeah. It's great. But the look in the eyes of those poor
guys picketing out there. . . ."

"It's their own fault, dumb dagoes!" Bastione exploded
bitterly.

The very next night when Izzy reported for work there
was no picket line to pass through. He discovered later
that a few brass knuckles, a little blood on the right
mouths, a few bucks in the right police hands and picketing had become a dangerous activity outside the Chez
Paree.

When Izzy went to Bastione to complain, the stocky

man seemed genuinely hurt. "Jesus, kid! I did it for you! You said you didn't like them faces they was making at you every night. Christ! Make up your mind, kid!"

By the end of the second week, Cat's Eye asked Izzy Cohen to assemble a second combo for another of his clubs in Chicago. Then a third for his club in Cicero. And later a fourth combo for a club across the state line in Hammond.

By the end of three months, the strike was over; the incipient union was destroyed. The musicians, broke and in debt, came back to work, begging for jobs on any terms, jobs that were no longer there. Cat's Eye had decided against them.

Izzy couldn't accept that. However he had excused his previous behavior, he could not bear making a profit at the expense of family men who were being put out of work forever. So he went to Cat's Eye to plead for them. The beefy man played with his cat's-eye tie pin and he smiled. The more he smiled, the more hesitant Izzy became.

When he finished, Cat's Eye leaned forward and said, "Kid, that was a nice speech. Someday when I am in a fix, I would like somebody to make such a speech for me. I been moved. So this is what I will do. You want those dumb dagoes to go back to work, okay! They'll go to work for you!"

At first Izzy didn't understand. He thought it was one of Bastione's cruel jokes, that now he was being fired along with the recalcitrant musicians. Not so. For Bastione continued, "I had a meet with the boys. One thing we don't forget is a favor. Because of what you done here in Chicago, there is no union in no night club across the country. To show how they feel about you, the boys decided that from now on you are going to book the bands into all of their clubs from coast to coast!"

Bastione laid it out in precise terms. He and his "friends" owned or controlled every night club of importance in the country. In Chicago, New York, Baltimore, Boston, Detroit, Los Angeles, Washington, Cleveland, and Frisco, it came to a total of forty-two clubs. Booking bands into forty-two major nightclubs could throw off an income of at least four or five grand a week. Sure, Izzy would have to hire men to scout talent, supervise the engagements, collect the money and distribute it, but Bastione was sure that The Doctor was a smart enough Jew to walk away from the office every Saturday night with two grand net.

"And, kid, there ain't no doctor in Chicago, not even the best, nets that kind of dough," Bastione said with great assurance.

Izzy thought for a moment, while Bastione waited, smiling, proud of having delivered such a gift of gratitude. Then Izzy dared to say, hoping he could get the words out without faltering, "Okay, Mr. Bastione. But . . ."

"Sonofabitch!" Bastione exploded. "Can't anyone make a deal with a Jew without buts?" Finally he calmed a bit. "All right! What's the but?"

"The men . . . when they come back, they got to get a raise."

Instead of the vehemence Izzy had anticipated, Bastione took the suggestion quietly, but with the same thoughtful look that he had worn when Izzy complained about the pickets. So now Izzy felt the floor under his feet become soft and unstable. After an uncomfortable silence, the Italian spoke.

"Kid, you disappoint me. I always figure no matter how smart a wop is, a Jew is smarter. But you ain't. And you went to college." Bastione seemed truly disappointed. Then as though he were talking to his young brother, he said, " 'Course we give 'em more dough. But no gift. We got to make them dumb guinea bastards think they won it. So the first thing you do is get on their side. Form a union. Demand increases. Then I'll give 'em to you. That way *you'll* be a hero instead of a scab. And *I'll* control the union."

"I didn't agree to you controlling any union," Izzy demurred.

But Cat's Eye cut him off. "I wouldn't trust any union to any Jew! You're all too fucking soft about things like that!" He polished the cat's-eye in his cufflink, then said, "We got to clean you up a little after the way you broke that strike. So *you'll* form the union. *You'll* get 'em the raise. But after that, the union'll be nationwide and I'll put in my own wop to control it!"

Bastione was contemplative again. "Dumb wops! And I'm the dumbest! *I* shoulda had them in a union before they ever *wanted* one! Why didn't I think of that before! Dumb wop, that's all!"

He turned his fierce gaze on Izzy. "You're a doctor. You know about such things. You was the one pointed out them arteries to me . . . here . . ." Bastione leaned forward, placed his thick thumb against Izzy's throat to press on his carotid.

"Carotid arteries . . . yeah . . ." Izzy said, not daring to draw back.

"After you told me that, I tried it out. If I want to control a man, I don't have to do nothing but grab him around the throat like this." He swiftly slipped his arm around Izzy's throat, exerted some pressure, making Izzy feel faint. "I hold my arm like this, and he's out cold. I keep holding it there a few minutes he's dead. Nice and quiet, and clean. Just put your muscle in the right place, and you can control any man. Any organization.

"That's the way it is, specially with this world getting bigger and bigger. Find the right place and put your muscle there. You can control more and more with less and less. But never waste your muscle on the wrong place," he declared.

"I shoulda remembered that. I shoulda *give* 'em a union. *My* union. Then I don't have no trouble. Okay, so *you'll* give 'em a union."

2

"Doctor Irwin Cone of Talent Corporation of America, calling!" his secretary Bertha announced crisply to the secretary of Donald Balding, account executive in one of Chicago's leading advertising agencies.

"I'm sorry, but Mr. Balding is not in," the secretary evaded. For the names Irwin Cone and Talent Corporation of America were completely unknown to her. "Can you tell me the nature of Dr. Cohen's business with Mr. Balding?"

"Cone!" the fleshy, dark-haired Bertha persisted, "C . . . o . . . n . . . e." She spelled it out meticulously.

"I have that," Balding's secretary responded a bit impatiently. "And the nature of his call?"

"Dr. Cone would like Mr. and Mrs. Balding to be his guests for the dinner show in the Lake Shore Room tomorrow night."

"I'll . . . I'll speak to Mr. Balding as soon as he returns and we'll get back to you."

Once Bertha left the number with Balding's secretary, she made eight other calls to eight other advertising agencies, with exactly the same results. Within the hour, five of the nine men called back to speak to Dr. Cone directly. And Isidore Cohen, M.D. who in the past year had legally become Irwin Cone, T.C.A. took those calls himself, standing at his new desk in his new office just off North Michigan Avenue. Around him painters were still decorating the office for his use. And, except for his own desk and Bertha's, the furniture was still to be moved in.

For after only one year in the band business, Dr. Isidore Cohen had decided to incorporate under the broad, impressive, all-inclusive name of Talent Corporation of

America and to change his own name as well. Since he could not bring himself to depart radically from his origins, he rationalized anglicizing his name from Cohen to Cone by saying that his father would have less trouble with a new name if it were not too vastly different.

Not that Cohen had to change his name to do business with Cat's Eye Bastione and his friends. It was the business into which he was now venturing that demanded it. For early in his first year of band-booking he had decided that radio, which had at first evolved as a novelty, might now well become a substantial business. No one knew quite what to do with it yet, but The Doctor was sure that controlling bands and singers as he did, would make him a part of the new industry. So with a view to doing business with the large gentile advertising agencies and national advertisers he had decided to change his own name and had adopted a corporate name as impressive as his most optimistic ambitions.

With his new name, his impressive corporate front and his new office being assembled around him, he was ready for his big move into the radio business. The first step had just been taken. And evidently it was producing results, as he took the callback from Donald Balding.

"Dr. Cohen?" Balding's voice reached him cautiously and tentatively.

Bertha, who was on the extension across the room, put her hand over the instrument and apologized, "I spelled it out!" But Cone put her irritation at rest with a slight wave of his hand as he applied himself to Balding.

"Cone . . . C-o-n-e, Mr. Balding, Cone. I was calling to ask if you and your missus would like to be my guests for dinner tomorrow night."

"So I understand. But I don't get it. . . ."

"What's there to get, Mr. Balding? A nice dinner in very pleasant surroundings." Then Cone added very casually, "And possibly the chance to get the first look at a new piece of talent you might want to present to one of your clients. Especially a client whom you might want to induce to go into radio."

"Oh. Yes, yes, of course. In the interest of our clients we can't afford to pass up any opportunities," Balding declared. "Not in times like these."

"Good!" The Doctor responded heartily. Then he added, "But don't forget, we'll be expecting Mrs. Balding, too."

"Of course!" Balding responded. "Tomorrow night. The Lake Shore Room."

"At seven!" Cone sealed the arrangement.

When Balding arrived at the Lake Shore Room next evening he found to his surprise that he was not the only invitee. For when the little man who introduced himself as Dr. Cone greeted him, he led the Baldings to a table where four other account executives from four other agencies were already seated with their wives. Dinner passed easily if a bit tenuously for no executive wished to betray either his curiosity or his ignorance.

Once coffee had been served, the floor show began. It featured a young man from Yale who, like The Doctor, had organized a band to pay his way through college. But, instead of turning to other pursuits, this young man, Ronnie Dale, had persisted with his band and had begun to play engagements in hotel dining rooms. When his presence had been mentioned to The Doctor, the little man had visited the Lake Shore Room not once but twice. The second time to reconfirm what he only thought he saw the first time. And the second time he took Bertha with him.

Yes, it was true. This tall, thin, unprepossessing young man from Yale, with a nasal voice which he projected through a small megaphone definitely did appeal to women. For himself, The Doctor preferred more robust voices, more obvious talent. But women liked this young man. As Bertha said, "What's not to like? A nice clean-cut chap. And a college man besides. How could you not like him?"

By now The Doctor had learned enough about entertainment not to be governed by his own preferences. While other agents watched the talent, The Doctor watched the audience. If women liked this boy, that was enough for him.

This night, at The Doctor's large table, the effect was precisely what he had hoped. The account executives were pleased, yet not greatly impressed. But their wives sat staring, involved, completely oblivious to anything but the nasal young singer.

The Doctor leaned back from the table, gesturing Balding and several other men to lean back with him as he whispered, "That, gentlemen, is what we call a phenomenon. *You* don't understand it. *I* don't understand it. But there it is. And there *they* are." He pointed to their wives.

"Tonight," he continued, "I am only going to ask one question. Who buys what your clients sell? Men? Or women? Think it over. Oh, by the way, I represent that boy. Exclusive!"

Once he said that, he slipped away from the table, paid the entire check on his way out and disappeared.

Before noon the next day every man who had been at dinner the previous night called The Doctor's office. Bertha, as she had been instructed, took a message and promised that Doctor Cone would call back when he returned. All the while Cone sat at his desk and only when he had the five message slips in his hand, did he instruct Bertha to get Ronnie Dale at the hotel. When the switchboard operator proclaimed protectively that Ronnie Dale was never to be disturbed so early after doing a supper show, The Doctor himself picked up his extension and said firmly, "Operator! You listen to me! Unless you want to rob that boy of the greatest opportunity of his life, wake him up! Right now!"

He knew that the same motherly instinct that had caused her to protect the young man would also force her to wake him now. It did.

Within an hour The Doctor met Ronnie Dale for the first time. Over breakfast, Cone described a whole new career starting with radio and ending in nationwide exposure in theaters and possibly even motion pictures. Before he left the table, The Doctor had signed Ronnie Dale to an exclusive agency contract.

So armed, he returned to his office and only then began to return the calls which he had refused to take during the morning.

Two hours later, Irwin Cone was sitting in the office of Donald Balding. Balding, his feet up on his huge mahogany desk, was admitting, "Frankly, I don't get it. But last night, and this morning at breakfast, that's all my wife talked about. That kid. You ask me, I think he's fun-

ny looking. And without that megaphone, his voice
couldn't reach across this desk."

As Balding spoke, Cone nodded and proceeded to make
a gesture which consisted of holding out his hand, palm
down, and fluttering his four fingers against his thumb.

"And it wasn't only my wife . . . but when they went
to the ladies' room, my wife said, that was all the other
women could talk about. . . ." Balding interrupted himself
to demand, "What the hell are you doing?"

"This, my dear man," Cone said, continuing his fluttering gesture, "this is the power that boy has over women."

"What?" Balding demanded.

"In medicine this is what we call vaginal contractions.
It's what happens to every woman when she has an orgasm."

Balding was obviously disturbed by what he deemed a
tasteless analogy, but The Doctor was not deterred.
"With young girls who haven't yet had an orgasm, and
with older women who've forgotten about such things,
this boy creates flutters in the right place. Let him sing to
enough women long enough and he'll have them coming
right in their chairs."

Cone paused for an instant. "He will also be able to
sell them anything your clients wish. If women should
buy it, he can sell it. Right through their vaginas. There's
only one name for what this boy has: cunt power!"

The Doctor allowed the phrase to sink in.

"Now, I have four other calls just like yours. I'll hold
them off if you pick out one of your advertisers and set
up a meeting right now. One of your big advertisers, who
sells his product to women!"

Balding pursed his lips thoughtfully, then said, "The
client I have in mind is a very strict Episcopalian. He demands that all our advertising be tasteful. It doesn't have
to be honest, as long as it's in good taste. So, I hope it
won't be necessary to say all those things . . . I mean,
about vaginal flutters . . . and cunts . . . will it?"

"Not as long as he gets the point!" Cone said.

Balding reached for the phone.

The sponsor was a man in his late sixties, dressed in
a plain drab gray suit and antiseptically smelling of bay
rum. A stern-looking Episcopalian, he seemed either

deaf or grimly disinterested. He stared through his office window at the dreary winter afternoon as Cone spoke to him. But, with occasional furtive gestures of encouragement from Balding, Cone continued with his presentation. When Cone finished, the client continued staring out the window for a few moments. Then he turned, not to Cone, but to Balding.

"I like that idea, having a college boy advertise my product. When can I see him?"

"Tonight," The Doctor said quickly. "The Lake Shore Room. I'll arrange a table."

But the client continued to address himself to Balding, "Yes, we'll go, Marjorie and I." Then he added, suddenly, "By the way, what's his name?"

Balding answered this time, "Ronnie Dale."

"Dale . . . Ronnie Dale . . ." the client evaluated. "That always been his name?"

Balding looked to Cone. "Far as I know," Cone said.

"Well, make sure. I don't want it to come out later that he's some Jewboy with a changed name!"

Irwin Cone's face became tense, pale, then it began to flush. It was obvious that the client had not made an unwitting error.

For he said, "Look, Mr. Cohen . . ." enunciating each syllable clearly, "personally I have nothing against Jews. But some of our customers do. And I don't see any need to antagonize them. Myself, I do business with all sorts of people."

"I understand," Cone said, regretful for the first time that he had ever changed his name. "I've never asked him but I'm sure that Dale isn't Jewish. Still, I wouldn't want you to run the risk of having a 'Jewboy' advertising your product. So I will ask Dale. I will make absolutely sure of his background. And if he's not Jewish I will call you back."

The client smiled drily, nodded.

"And," Cone continued, "I will tell you to go fuck yourself!"

Balding reddened apoplectically, but Cone concluded, "I don't know if nice God-fearing Episcopalians do that kind of thing. But you'll have plenty of time to learn before you get a chance at that boy again! You couldn't buy him now for all the money in the world!"

Irwin Cone, the little Jew, strode out of that room like a fierce giant, passing Balding who stood silent, red-faced, and suddenly sick with fear that he had jeopardized, if not lost, his largest account. Cone would never forget the look of fear on Balding's face.

But the client sat immobile behind his desk, grim, self-justified. "Now you know why I never like to do business with Jews. Rude, arrogant people!"

Late that afternoon, Irwin Cone, of T.C.A., sold Ronnie Dale to a manufacturer of cereals. Ronnie and his Varsity-men would appear an hour each week on radio for a trial period of three months to advertise an entire line of break-fast foods.

At the end of the day, just before five o'clock, Irwin Cone returned to his freshly painted, newly decorated of-fice, and placed a call to Balding's client. He was quick to answer, for Cone heard his voice only seconds after he had announced himself to the secretary.

"Ah, Mr. Cohen . . . so you decided to call back after all. . . ." the man greeted him smugly. "Well, I want you to know that I am not one to harbor grudges. . . ."

"Well," Cone interrupted, "I want *you* to know that *I am!* I have sold Ronnie Dale to Quaker Flakes Foods. If you like good music, tune in on the tenth. That's when he starts!"

Before the old bastard could answer, Cone hung up. It was the day he initiated a practice that would become his telephone trademark. When Irwin Cone had had his say all conversation was over.

It felt good, as he sat there, his fingers dancing nervous-ly and vindictively on the telephone. But his satisfaction was short-lived. For in minutes he realized that if he hadn't been so eager to tell the old bastard off, he would not have made the deal that day but would have played off one sponsor against another and made a far richer deal.

So that evening he made two firm resolutions which would become TCA policy for the future.

Never make a deal when you're angry.

And if TCA's future business was going to take him or his employees into *goyisheh* offices to confront such vi-cious prejudiced sponsors they had better be carefully selected and properly prepared for it. TCA would hire only college men, with nice names, their own or newly acquired, men who could wear Ivy League clothes and hold their own in the gentile jungle of advertising, where those in power, though more polished, and more subtle, could also be more vicious than Cat's Eye Bastione.

From the start of their relationship, Irwin Cone not only doted on Ronnie Dale, he practically adopted him. Probably because Dale was Cone's first real discovery. The band business was just that, a business. Handed to him, no, thrust on him by Cat's Eye out of gratitude as well as for the Italian bear's own future purposes. But Dale was Irwin Cone's own first personal production. He had heard about him, scouted him, carefully planned his sale and exploitation. There was a sense of power in that achievement, as well as the satisfaction of accomplishment.

Cone selected all Ronnie's songs, screening the thousands that were submitted. He sat in on every rehearsal, approved every word the scriptwriter wrote for Dale to deliver on the air. He supervised and even re-wrote some of the orchestrations and changed the instrumentation of the Varsitymen to add more strings and mellow saxophones to produce a more melodic and romantic background for Dale's voice which always ran the risk of becoming monotonous. Cone insisted on proper microphone balance so that Dale's voice, thin as it was, would not be drowned out by the orchestra. He even insisted on echo-chamber reinforcement, over the agonized protests of studio engineers, so Dale's voice would seem richer and fuller than it naturally was.

He was such a tyrant on Dale's behalf that, behind his back, people called him Little Napoleon, and some even hinted that he had an unnatural affection for the younger singer. But all of them agreed that, in the end, Cone had found and produced a national personality, a miracle in fact, out of a young man who sang fairly well, knew music somewhat and was so undistinguished in his appearance that you could pass him on the street and never look twice.

It was not without price, however. For there were stretches, long stretches when the band business was carried on by his secretary, Bertha, that fleshy girl, with the dark hair and the slight mustache on her upper lip. Always Cone was promising her that soon, very soon, he would begin to hire those bright, well-educated, well-named young men to pick up the load. But he was too busy with Dale even to do that. Those who accused him of showering on Dale the devotion of a stage mother were not wrong.

As for Dale, he was easy to work with. Pliable, accommodating, hungry to learn. He had a sharp mind, especially when it came to figures. The Doctor could explain the most complicated set of circumstances and if it involved money Dale would grasp it at once. And, unlike other performers, he was quick to make decisions. He was a joy to work with, The Doctor always maintained to those who cautioned him against putting so much of his time into any one client.

It turned out that Dale had his own problems, too.

The phone was ringing when The Doctor unlocked the door to his apartment at three in the morning. It had the sound of trouble. But how could that be? He had already seen Ronnie Dale through tonight's air show and his repeat for the Coast, had made his usual weekly rounds of the clubs to make sure that everything was okay. Who the hell could be looking for him at this hour?

Tired, The Doctor felt inclined not to answer. Good news never comes at three o'clock in the morning. Bad news will always be back first thing in the morning. But, conscientiously, he lifted the phone.

"Doctor . . . Where you been? I've been calling and calling!" It was Ronnie Dale, breathless not from exertion but from fear. He spoke softly, tensely, in a highly confidential tone, as if he were being overheard.

"What's wrong, kid?"

"Look . . . I'm . . . I'm in some trouble. . . ."

"What kind? Not police trouble?" The Doctor asked.

Finally Ronnie answered, "Yeah."

"How bad? You locked up?"

"Yeah. . . ."

"What for?" No answer was forthcoming immediately. "Kid, if I don't know, I can't help. *What for?*" The Doctor demanded.

"It has to do with a girl. . . ."

"Yeah?" The Doctor urged impatiently.

"A fifteen-year-old girl," Ronnie admitted finally.

"Christ!" The Doctor said. "Sit still! Don't say a word! You didn't get any lawyer mixed up in this yet, did you?"

"I kept calling you, that's all," Ronnie said.

"Okay. You talking on the desk phone at the station house?"

"Uh huh," Ronnie said.

"Get me the desk man's name!" He waited and in a moment Ronnie was back with the sergeant's name. "Okay! Now shut up! Don't say another word. And wait till you hear from me!"

The Doctor hung up. Agitated as he was, he couldn't pretend to himself that he had not expected this. Perhaps even sooner than it had occurred. For he had long noticed that Dale, for all his nice, clean, bland Ivy League looks and manners, had this special weakness.

Besieged as he was by mature women and girls in their twenties who were eager to make his sex life interesting, exciting and more varied than any reasonable man might expect, Dale still preferred young girls. Budding breasts made him more passionate than full sensuous ones. His desire for seduction was far stronger than his desire to mate with a willing woman. He could lose himself with infinitely more abandon in the wispy pubic hair of a tense young virgin than in that of a full-bloomed woman. Only the fact that Dale was hard-working, meticulous about his performance and conscientious about his career had persuaded The Doctor to ignore this weakness.

No, The Doctor couldn't pretend that he was shocked, or even surprised. But now action was needed. The right action. And the proper degree of secrecy. For Ronnie Dale and his Varsitymen had just been renewed for their second year on the air, a full year this time, no thirteen-week options. Part of that renewal deal had been a morals clause, making the contract cancellable immediately if Ronnie Dale engaged in any activity that would bring scandal or public disapproval upon his sponsor or the product.

The Doctor knew only too well there was one thing to do now. Reluctantly, he searched in his little black book, found the number, placed the call. He realized at once when his ring was answered that he had awakened Cat's Eye Bastione from a deep sleep.

"Cat's Eye? Doc Cone."

"Yeah? What's up? What'sa matter?" Bastione asked irritably.

"I need help! Big help. My singer . . . Ronnie Dale. . . . He's in a jam with the Law."

"Drunk driving?" Bastione asked.

"Morals. A fifteen-year-old girl."

"A fifteen-year-old kid? Fuck 'im! I got a fifteen-year-old daughter myself! Let the bastard burn!"

"Cat's Eye . . . listen to me. Please?" He hated to humble himself to anyone, hated to become indebted to anyone, but this was a time to do all the things he hated to do. "Cat's Eye, this kid means too much to me. I got too much time, too much money wrapped up in him to just let him burn."

"I know!" the gravelly Italian voice came back. "Maybe this is the best thing. You know what people are saying behind your back? You're a regular Yiddishe Mama with that kid. He don't say a word, sing a note, or go to the bathroom without you okaying it. There's even some beefs from the clubs. You're paying more attention to that kid than the rest of your business put together!"

"We can argue that out some other time. He's in jail right now. I've got to do something before it hits the papers!"

"Well," Bastione grumbled, as he usually did when he was about to concede to Cone. "Give me ten minutes. Call you back."

Only after he had hung up did Cone realize that he hadn't given the old Italian any information as to where Dale was being held. But within ten minutes Cone's phone rang.

"Doc?" It was Bastione's voice, less gruff now and more businesslike. "A rap like this they don't talk less than big ones."

"A thousand?" Cone asked. "Okay!"

"Wait a minute, wait a minute, Doc. *Five* big ones!"

"Five?" Cone repeated, the amount far larger than he had expected.

"For five big ones you get back his file and his prints, everything! There's no record at all."

"Okay," Cone answered, relieved, though the price was stiff. "Call them back and say okay."

"I already made the deal for you," Bastione said.

"What about the money?"

"I give my word," Bastione said. "Go pick up your boy." He hung up before Cone could even thank him.

They were in the cab on the way back to Cone's apartment. Disheveled and shaken, Ronnie kept repeating over and over, "I won't forget this, Doctor. I won't ever forget what you did for me."

"It's okay, kid," The Doctor kept repeating, but all the while he was thinking. With one such episode on his record, with Bastione's reluctance to intercede, it might be wisest in the long run to get Ronnie out of Chicago. A repetition of this rap couldn't be squared for five thousand, if it could be squared at all.

Besides, The Doctor kept telling himself, it was time for both of them, he and Ronnie, to extend their horizons beyond Chicago. Chicago was fine as an origination point for a radio program, but in Show Business as in any business there was only one city that really counted. New York. It was the goal he had dreamed of for the future. But the events of this night had brought the future much closer far sooner than he had envisioned.

While Ronnie was eating the breakfast that Cone himself had cooked, the little man sat across the table and talked.

"New York, kid. That's the place! New York is the capital of the world! Sure, we could go there, hat in hand, shake our fists at the tall buildings and shout 'New York, we're going to lick you one day!' But that's the way failures start out.

"We got to come in strong. With a hit. A big hit. I've even thought about you doing a musical on Broadway. But a good musical is hard to find. And why take a chance on being a flop? You don't have to do that, not with your reputation.

"No, there's a better way. A safer way. A way I know all about. Clubs!"

Ronnie looked up from his breakfast.

"That's right. We could move into New York by opening your own club. Instead of Ronnie Dale and the Varsitymen it becomes Ronnie Dale's Frat House! And we
decorate it to look like a regular fraternity house.
Trophies. Tennis rackets. Footballs used in famous games.
A whole new slant on night clubs. They'll love it! That's
the way we go into New York! Okay, kid?"

"Okay!" Dale said, as eager as Cone to leave Chicago
in view of the events of the past night.

"Good! Now get some sleep. Soon as I can, I'll go to
New York and find a spot. With real estate going begging
it shouldn't be hard," Cone said.

As Dale started toward Cone's bedroom, he turned back
to say, "It won't happen again. I give you my word!"

"Okay, kid," The Doctor answered.

"And I'll never forget this. Never!" Dale promised.

Cone nodded, accepting Dale's gratitude, but all the
while suspecting that this was the kind of trouble that a
man never got into only once. It would be best to get
Dale out of Chicago as soon as possible.

It took another favor from Cat's Eye to get permission
to even open a club in New York. But Cone humbled himself, asked for it, and received it. Knowing that one day he
would have to repay Bastione in some form. That
done, Cone spent days in New York till he found a large
whitestone house in the East Sixties. It had been on the
market ever since the Crash. With only a little cash
down to pay off the taxes and assuming a large mortgage,
he was able to take possession. He set about at once re-
building the lower two floors into a luxurious entrance,
club and kitchens. The upper two floors The Doctor decided to turn into a duplex apartment for Dale's living
quarters. Partly for purposes of economy, as he explained
to Dale. Mostly because it would be easier for him to
keep track of Dale and his private life. Perhaps he could
prevent a repetition of the Chicago trouble that way.

The work took only a few months. And by the arrival
of the spring season the club was ready for its opening.

The night that Ronnie Dale's Frat House opened to a
black-tie and evening-gown audience, Irwin Cone knew he

had his hit. His big hit. He was in New York in the way he'd always dreamed. Chicago was behind him. And the recent events there were part of a forgotten history.

Everything worked. The motif The Doctor had selected, the whole concept of a college fraternity, with college shields and pennants, football scenes, trophy cases with old autographed footballs, crossed tennis rackets on the paneled walls, it all worked. Tables accommodating four hundred people could be packed onto the second floor and still leave a bit of room for dancing. Even the tiny dance floor worked for them. Girls and women loved being forced to dance so close to Ronnie Dale while he crooned at them.

In what were frankly acknowledged to be deep Depression times, The Frat House did excellent business, turnaway business on most nights. And when fall came, on football weekends like Army-Notre Dame and Army-Navy, even limousines couldn't force their way into that block in the East Sixties.

For the first half year everything worked not only as well as The Doctor had dreamed but even better. He was even seriously considering giving up the band business and devoting all his time to Ronnie Dale and perhaps one or two other specialized acts.

Then Winchell made his first column reference to the club not as the Frat House but "The Cat House." And The Doctor had to acknowledge to himself what he had been trying to ignore again. Ronnie had fallen back into his old habit by luring very young fans, of whom there were many, up to his convenient apartment in the late afternoons or for an all night stay after his late show. The practice had not gone unobserved. Gossip even went so far as to include the names of young girls from some of New York's best society families.

Within days Mark Hellinger in his column in the *News* not only used the term "The Cat House" but even hinted at certain perversions which seriously threatened Dale's image as the nice, clean-cut, all-American college boy. Winchell went even further the next week.

Now, much as he wished to avoid a direct confrontation with Dale, The Doctor felt impelled to take a stand. To introduce the subject, he had first mapped out a per-

sonal appearance tour spanning the country and to begin
in the late spring when club business normally fell off anyway. The tour would cover all the large cities, coast to
coast, except for Chicago. And Dale and his Frat House
Revue would play only the largest theaters, fairs and
auditoria with a substantial guaranteed base and a large
share of the gross receipts as well.

It was not the first time that the theater circuits had
been after Dale to go on tour. But no tour was as promising and profitable as this one which The Doctor had
worked out. So that this time, unlike all previous times, he
was sure Dale would say yes.

The Doctor touched on the idea lightly and left with
Dale a detailed typed estimate of the gross takes and the
net monies that Dale might expect. For The Doctor knew
if there was one thing this thrifty young man loved even
more than virginal girls it was money. Having placed the
itinerary and the enormous estimated take before Dale,
Cone now sought some way to broach the other and more
dominant subject, hoping that the tour would make the
other subject less distasteful.

"Ronnie-baby . . . you . . . you see Winchell last night?"

"No. Was he here?" Ronnie asked, studying the figures.

"I meant his column," Cone persisted.

"What did he say this time?" Ronnie demanded, his irritation already evident.

"The same as he said last time. And the time before
that."

"Some day somebody is going to shut that bastard up
for good!" Ronnie replied angrily. "I might even see a
lawyer about him!"

"That wouldn't be such a good idea," Cone suggested.

"There might be other ways," Dale countered. "You
know, he's made a lot of enemies in the Mob!"

"And a lot of friends, too. Some of them in Chicago,"
The Doctor warned.

"I was wondering when you were going to bring that
up!" Dale accused, turning so fast that the sheaf of figures slid to the floor.

As Cone stooped to pick them up he said, "I didn't
bring up Winchell for any other purpose but to point out
that might be another reason to go on tour now. To get

away from here for a while. You know how I feel, all an artist owes his audience is a good show. For the rest, it's none of their goddamned business what he does."

"Is that what it is? Or are you pushing this tour," and Ronnie snatched the papers out of The Doctor's hand, "because you can't resist the grosses and your commissions?"

Suddenly the balance of power between the two men had shifted. For the first time in their relationship Dale had become the aggressor and Cone the victim.

"You know, Irwin-baby . . ." Dale imitated The Doctor's tone, "you know what I've been thinking? Here I am, I own this club. Most of it. And I am paying you a commission. To book me into my own club. That's a laugh, isn't it? And on the radio show, how long am I going to go on paying you for something you sold just once? You know how much commission you've screwed out of me in the last year and a half on radio alone? Thirty thousand dollars, my accountant tells me. For one day's work! That's all you ever did! Sold it just once! Why should I continue to pay you now?"

"For one thing, because we have a deal. In addition to my share of the club, ten percent of all your earnings." Dale didn't answer, just stood there smiling in a way that irritated Cone. "I took you from a four hundred dollar a week band in a little room on the Lake Shore and built you into a national personality!"

"And for that you expect to own me for the rest of my life?" Dale demanded. "Own me, run me, run my private life, make me go on tour when I don't want to, don't have to!"

"Not *own* . . . *represent*. For instance, when your radio contract comes up for renewal next month . . ."

"It's come up," Dale said, "and it's been renewed."

"By whom?" the surprised little man demanded.

"By my lawyer."

"But we have a contract . . ." The Doctor started to say.

"*Had,* Irwin-baby . . . *had.* I repudiated that contract."

"On what grounds?" The Doctor demanded.

"On whatever grounds my lawyer figures out I have," Dale countered. "From now on I work through my attorney and my accountant. I go on tour, if *I* feel like it.

And I don't feel like it! I like it here in New York. And with the radio show and the club what the hell do I need a tour for? Or an agent? Or a psychiatrist! Or a house mother! If I want to go down on a different kid each night that's *my* business! Not Winchell's! Not yours! At least not anymore. My lawyer'll call you to make a deal to buy out your interest in the club."

" 'Buy out'? I'll sue! I'll get an injunction. I'll keep you from working anywhere in the world, for the rest of our deal!" The Doctor threatened.

"My lawyer said you wouldn't be that stupid," Dale answered smugly. "He said you wouldn't want to get a bad reputation with talent. Or with the Advertising Agency and my Sponsor. You'll be wanting to make other deals with them in the future. No, my lawyer says, when you think it all over you'll decide that the smartest thing you can do is just pick up your marbles and go home."

"We'll see about that!" The Doctor warned and left the club for the last time. He walked west and into Central Park. The fury was seething in him so intensely that he knew he could not contain it in any office.

Yes, he goddamned well would get an injunction! But, what Dale had said was true. He would alienate the Agency and the Sponsor in the process. So perhaps an injunction would not be the wisest course.

He could break the whole sordid story about Dale and his teen-age girls. But how would he explain his own silence for so long?

Of course, he could put in a call to Cat's Eye. That's all it would take. One call. And they would hit Dale and that would be the final payoff—that young arrogant ungrateful bastard!

But The Doctor knew he could never do that. Pressure, yes. Muscle, when required. But to ask for a hit on any human being, no matter how treacherous, no, he could never do that.

He had reached the park lake by that time, was watching the rowers propel their rented boats across the green water. His fury had calmed somewhat. Sufficiently for him to realize that in the heat of such confrontations certain basic truths are always spoken and a man was a fool to ignore them.

Of course it was a mistake to devote so much time to any one client. He promised himself—he would never become that involved again. A client was only a client, not a son, not a brother. It was a business relationship. You could pretend to worry about them, but always you must keep aloof. Must never become emotionally involved. Talent must serve your purposes or screw it! *Use* talent, don't let *it* use *you!* Cold. Cold as a surgeon. Otherwise you get your balls caught in a wringer—as he had this time.

However bad a reputation agents had for being flesh peddlers and exploiters, when the chips were down, clients like Ronnie Dale had fewer scruples than any agent.

So The Doctor had best wipe the whole bitter disillusioning experience out of his mind. What the hell, some men had done that with their own flesh-and-blood sons.

There was one thing Dale had said which remained with The Doctor, even now as he was resigned to forgetting the rest of it.

"With the radio show and the club, what the hell do I need a tour for?"

That demanded pondering. Dale had made an important point. Show Business was changing. Network radio was the cause of it all. The vaudeville houses, all except the biggest, were beginning to suffer. The clubs, too, were showing the effect of radio on certain nights so band bookings were suffering. But, most of all, radio was changing the attitude of performers. Book an act like Ronnie Dale on a long-term radio contract and he didn't want to do fairs and one-nighters any more. Living in New York or Hollywood was easier, pleasanter. Vaudevillians had spent their entire professional lives traveling ten months a year. Traveling and complaining. But traveling nevertheless. Because they had no choice.

Now, The Doctor was forced to realize, they were discovering they didn't have to travel any more. If a star was signed to a radio series he could have a home in Westchester or Beverly Hills and live like everyone else, seeing his wife and kids every day, instead of spasmodically during layoffs and between bookings.

Radio was doing one other thing. It was threatening to make the agent a less necessary part of the business.

Once someone like Ronnie Dale had ingratiated himself with his sponsor he decided that he didn't need an agent any longer. Only an attorney and an accountant, as Dale himself had said. Yes, radio was endowing stars with an independence which might make Ronnie Dale's rebellion only the beginning.

So, standing there at the lake edge, oblivious of the rowers by now, The Doctor reassured himself that the entire experience with Ronnie Dale, frustrating as it was, could turn out to be an event of tremendous importance in his own career if he capitalized on it.

Of course, there was one problem still unsolved. If radio was going to cannibalize the clubs, the vaudeville houses and even motion pictures, there could be less and less of TCA's kind of business to be had. In order for TCA to survive and prosper, its ten percent had to attach to more and more. The future of TCA and Doctor Irwin Cone lay not only in stronger contracts that bound stars closer to him, not only in digging deeper roots in radio, but in enlarging the base to which his ten percent attached.

Ten percent, yes. But ten percent of *what?*

He walked away from the Central Park lake that day not knowing the answer but resolved to go back to Chicago and find it.

All the way back to Chicago on the Twentieth Century Limited, The Doctor could not sleep. Not because of the galling frustration over Ronnie Dale. That night it was the face of Donald Balding that kept invading his thoughts, Balding's red face, his apoplectic look when The Doctor had said to Balding's refined Episcopalian client, "And if he's not Jewish, I will call you back and tell you to go fuck yourself!"

Why Balding's face kept coming back that night The Doctor didn't know. But it would become clear to him very soon.

3

Irwin Cone, The Doctor, was sitting in the orchestra of
one of the few remaining large presentation houses in Chicago. The band onstage was reaching the brassy crescendo
of what was known in those days as a Paramount finish.

But this time The Doctor was not here to listen to any
band. He was scouting new talent. A singer, preferably.
A singer who could be developed into another Ronnie
Dale. That was what it would take to make his plan work.

For he knew now why Balding's embarrassed apoplectic
face had pursued him that night on the Century. Just as
he knew why Balding had been so appalled that day. By
making his rude remark to Balding's client, The Doctor
had jeopardized Balding's two-million-dollar advertising account. And on that two-million-dollar account hung a fifteen percent commission for Balding's agency, a cool three
hundred thousand dollars a year. Quite a racket those
Agencies had. They got fifteen percent of every dollar
they spent on behalf of the advertiser.

Gentiles could say what they liked about Jews being
shrewd and grasping in business. They could endow
them with brains beyond average, or with mystical luck
as Bastione did. Gentiles could pick Jewish lawyers and
accountants and feel sure they had the best brains on their
side, but what Jew in the world would have had the
chutzpah to figure out that the more of a man's money
you spent the more you were entitled to keep for yourself?

Yes, the principle that one took a percentage of the action, all the action, fascinated The Doctor now. It would
be the answer to his problem of how to earn more commissions for TCA in a shrinking entertainment market.
But arriving at that conclusion was far from being able to
enforce it.

No, initiating such a policy would not be easy. He would have to resort to his first commandment. He would have to use muscle. Muscle applied to the right place, to the proper weakness.

Balding's red stunned face indicated clearly where the weakness was. The fifteen percent. The agency's fifteen percent. It was the carotid artery of their business. Put your muscle there, maneuver an agency into a spot where its fifteen percent was threatened, where its account was jeopardized, and the rest would be simple.

But to carry out his plan The Doctor had to find a new act, a new piece of talent, a new Ronnie Dale. And he had to possess that unique quality of appealing enormously by voice and voice alone to millions of people listening in their homes.

Finding that talent had not been easy. In the weeks since he had been back in Chicago, The Doctor had assiduously scouted every night club, large or small, every presentation house in and around the city, and had come up dry.

So here he was again, on an afternoon when he would rather be elsewhere, listening to yet another band doing yet another Paramount finish and not feeling very hopeful about his prospects of picking up that new piece of talent today.

The applause for the band was dying away. The lights came down to flood the area around the center stage microphone. A trio of scat singers called the Joy Boys stepped into the pool of light. Oceans of cloth seemed to move with them, for they were dressed in the popular conception of the style known as "collegian." They wore gray flannel oxford bags many inches too wide for their legs, striped blazers of red, white and blue and large bow ties. The width of their bags, the flash of their blazers made the three seem even smaller than they were, and the shortest of them seemed comically small, and might have been pathetic if he were not so impish. All one noticed of him were his smile, his clothes and his large protruding ears. But in his favor, The Doctor noted that he carried the melody in a clean, pleasant baritone. His phrasing was good and although his diction was slurred it was pleasant to the ear. His interpolations and scat breaks consisted of improvised meaningless sounds which reminded The Doctor of the word he used to call his old grandmother, *bubbah*, except that this young man had lengthened it into *bubbaboo*. But the audience responded strongly, they loved him, smiled all the while they listened to him. If he was not yet a finished performer, he had style, warmth and definite personality appeal. Above all, The Doctor felt, he had potential. His short stature, plain face and large ears wouldn't matter on radio.

The Doctor was already waiting in their dressing room by the time the Joy Boys came off. They were surprised to see him, more surprised when he said to his candidate, "Got a minute?"

"Sure. Why? Who are you?"

"Doctor Irwin Cone."

"I don't need any doctor," the young man started to say, but suddenly the name meant something. "The Doctor? The man who books all the clubs?"

"The man who books all the clubs," The Doctor repeated.

The singer looked him over skeptically, exchanging glances with his two colleagues, obviously dubious that anyone as young as The Doctor could be so powerful.

"Look, I haven't got all day. I want to talk to you. Come out for a drink."

The young man started to remove his blazer. The Doctor intervened, "Leave it on. Leave your makeup on too. I've got no time!"

So, in costume and makeup, the young man accompanied The Doctor to a small ex-speakeasy down the block from the theater. One of Bastione's places, The Doctor was known there. He asked for a quiet corner, and got it. The Doctor ordered drinks. As soon as the waiter left, The Doctor began.

"What's your name?"

"Leslie McIlhaine," the young man said, defensively, expecting some rejoinder.

"We can change that," was all The Doctor said. "The Joy Boys, who does that name belong to?"

"I don't know," Leslie said. "All three of us, I guess. Why?"

The waiter was back with straight rye and water chasers on the side. The Doctor fingered his shot glass and didn't drink. But the young man downed his in two gulps.

The Doctor tended to dismiss that. The shot glasses were small here. When the young man eyed The Doctor's glass, he shoved it across the table gently, the gesture not entailing any opinion.

"Where do you come from? How long you been singing?"

"LA. Three years."

"Before that?" The Doctor interrupted Leslie's second gulp of his second drink.

"College." Young McIlhaine laughed, "though we didn't go around dressed like this."

"I know."

"You a college man, too?"

"College. Medical School," Cone said.

"You mean it's true? You're not just called The Doctor? You really are?"

Cone nodded. "Work your way through school?" Now McIlhaine nodded. "Singing with a band?" Again he nodded and he began toying with the empty shot glass. Cone snapped at the waiter, held up two fingers. Soon two more drinks appeared.

Drink by drink, The Doctor found out about young Leslie McIlhaine, including how much he hated his name, which his mother had given him after a character in a book she'd read, that he had no ambition more singular or defined than being a "big star," that he was actually a nice young man, but without that relentless hunger which usually motivated those ambitious for stardom. It struck The Doctor that this niceness itself was his distinguishing characteristic onstage. It was the thing that the Audience and The Doctor found so ingratiating about him.

One thing more The Doctor discovered, how much young Leslie McIlhaine could drink. That could prove a problem. He had to evaluate very carefully whether Leslie McIlhaine was worth the risk.

By the time they had talked for two hours McIlhaine had put away eight drinks and was eager for a ninth. The Doctor glanced at his watch. "What time's your next show?"

"Next show?" McIlhaine repeated vaguely, a next show or any show being the furthest thing from his mind.

The Doctor had to help him up from his chair, assist him out, down the block to the stage entrance, then into the alley where he turned him over to the stage doorman. The Doctor started back down the alley, hit the street where the crowds were lining up to buy tickets for the seven-thirty show. His first inclination was to walk away, forget the whole thing, especially young Leslie McIlhaine. But curiosity prevented him. How would the other two perform without McIlhaine? How much difference would it make to the act? Or if, indeed, the Joy Boys would appear at all.

He bought a ticket and went in. Impatient about seeing any of the routine show over again, he stood in the back of the house, then went down to the elaborate lounge, smoked several cigarettes, finally when he heard the faint strains of the orchestral introduction to the Joy Boys he went back up. All three Joy Boys were in the spotlight, singing as they had sung before. From the back of the house Cone couldn't make out Leslie McIlhaine's condition, so he slipped down the side aisle of the darkened house, searching for a single in the first few rows. He found one in the second row, dropped into it to look straight up at the three Joy Boys.

There in the middle was Leslie McIlhaine, as warm, relaxed, ingratiating and amusing as he had been in the early show. Whatever booze did to his ability to walk, talk, or operate in general, one thing it did not do, inhibit his ability to sing in that easy, boyish, charming manner that endeared him to audiences.

He did not possess the sexuality of Russ Columbo, the flair of Harry Richman or the magnificent sell of Al Jolson. He had none of those qualities, which was exactly the quality that The Doctor decided would make him a perfect personality to enter thirty million American homes by way of radio. In a way, Leslie McIlhaine was a warmer, less stiff, non-nasal Ronnie Dale. And he had a sense of humor besides.

As for his drinking, The Doctor would take care of that in his own way when the time came. The first problem was cutting him loose from the Joy Boys and the band. He could handle that easily enough. No band leader who envisioned playing any big night club in America would refuse The Doctor such a simple request as cutting loose a piece of talent.

As for McIlhaine himself, The Doctor planned a cam-

paign to develop him from obscurity as a single till he
could present him as a featured act in the Chez Paree. Immediately he put him under contract, paying the young
man's weekly salary out of his own pocket. He hired Milt
Hammer, a top vocal coach, to select his songs, supervise
his arrangements and meticulously guide him through their
delivery. Then he hired a director to stage an act for him.
And he changed the young man's name from McIlhaine to
Barrie. Bobbie Barrie.

After four weeks of intensive work, The Doctor decided
to expose him to an audience, as a single, for the first
time. Perhaps out of sentiment, he chose the small club
where his own combo had played its first engagement for
Cat's Eye Bastione.

Bobbie Barrie opened in the Clark Street club to an
audience that consisted of fifty-three people, six waiters,
and Doctor Irwin Cone.

The Doctor took a table to one side of the audience,
yet close enough to the bandstand to study Bobbie very
closely. As he had ordered, the lights went down to
black, followed by a drum roll. The voice of Master of
Ceremonies-Comedian announced in a ringing tone, "the
Chicago debut" of that "great new American crooner imported from the West Coast . . . Bobbie Barrie!"

The spotlight hit a corner of the piano. Dressed in a
black dinner jacket, Bobbie Barrie stepped into the light,
seized the mike stand with both hands, waited for his orchestral introduction. Then he moved into his song, but
more stiffly than The Doctor had expected, even for a
debut. The ease was gone, and with it Barrie's warmth,
charm and humor.

His first reaction, prompted mainly by Bobbie's two-
handed clutch on the mike stand, was, "That fucking kid
got himself *too* drunk this time!" Now The Doctor
turned his gaze, somewhat unwillingly, from the bandstand
toward the audience.

He studied the faces of the women. They were watching,
listening, and, though uneasy, they were involved with
Bobbie Barrie, worried about him, sharing in his stiffness
and his nervousness. They liked him. Not loved him. He
wasn't that good. Whether Barrie could ever create the
vaginal flutters that Ronnie Dale induced was highly questionable. But they had become involved with him, they

worried about him, they adopted him. Yes, that was the word, adopted him.

When the act was over, there was only one call for an encore. And that seemed more polite than insistent. Something had happened. Somewhere, in the booze, or the choice of songs, or in just being a single, stiffness and lack of ease had corrupted this boy's style.

As one of the anonymous Joy Boys, supported and assisted by two other boys, wearing that outlandish college boy's masquerade he could go out, relax and charm an audience. Alone, on his own, as Bobbie Barrie, with that spot tight on him, wearing a dinner jacket, it all seemed to disappear.

By the time the show was over, The Doctor knew he had to make a decision. The whole month, the coach, the director, the arrangements, the four weeks salary, all of it was either lost or would have to be desperately justified.

As he was pondering that the Manager, sensing his disappointment, said encouragingly, "He's a nice kid. At least the broads seem to like him."

"In this business there are two words I hate," The Doctor said. " 'Like' and 'nice.' They're the kiss of death. In show business they got to love you and you got to score. Big! Anything short of that is disaster."

"Look, Doc, I'd sign that kid for another two weeks right now," the Manager said, to mollify him.

"Well, I wouldn't!" The Doctor said. "I want the club cleared! Right now!"

"But the waiters and the cleaning women . . ." the Manager said, pointing to the waiters who had started to clear the tables so they could stack the chairs.

"They can do that tomorrow! Out! All of them! I want this place empty and quiet. Everybody out except the pianist!" The Doctor ordered.

The club was quiet. And dark, except for a worklight on the bandstand which made the empty tables and chairs seem grotesque and depressing. The Doctor waited. When Bobbie Barrie didn't emerge from his dressing room, The Doctor went to find him. Barrie was taking a drink, had his back to the door when The Doctor entered. The Doctor moved into the room, stepped around to confront Barrie, whipped the drink out of his hand with a single back-handed blow.

"Now what the hell happened out there?" The Doctor demanded.

Barrie turned away, saying, "You're going to tell me I stank. I know. But I can't tell you why."

"You can't, eh? It couldn't have been ten drinks instead of six?"

"Five belts, five was all I had. I swear!"

"Was it being out there alone? Do you need those two clowns alongside you all the time? Is that what the rest of your career is going to be like, a nameless kid with two other nameless kids, under a phony title like the Joy Boys? Just how long do you think people are going to consider you a Joy Boy? Suppose the style changes tomorrow, college boys are out, then where the hell are you?

"Now you are either a singer," The Doctor seized him by the lapels and held him tight, "or you're not. And if you're not, then you better quit. The hell with the money I have invested in you! Quit now! Tonight! I'll just write the whole thing off. What do you say?"

"I could go back to the band, I could rejoin the group."

"NO!" The Doctor shouted. "How long do you think you'd last knowing you had your big chance and blew it? The rest of your life you'd know you were a second-rater. Well, this business is no place for second-raters! Now, get out there!"

"Where?"

"Out there! You're going to do this act till I find out what's wrong!" The Doctor commanded. He turned and walked out, not even considering the possibility that Barrie would refuse to follow.

The Doctor took his place at a table in the center of the room. He gestured the pianist to his seat and he waited. In moments Bobbie Barrie came out. His hair hastily combed, glistening from all the water he had applied to put it back in place. His tie was tied, his dinner jacket buttoned and as unwrinkled as it could be, following the brusque way The Doctor had handled it.

Barrie took his place at the mike, the worklight casting harsh and uncontrolled lights and shadows on his face. The Doctor cued the pianist. At the first notes, Barrie seized the mike with both hands and waited for his first entrance.

"Take your hands off that thing!" The Doctor shouted from the darkness.

"But, I'm supposed . . ."

"Let go of that mike!" The Doctor ordered, putting out less voice and more anger.

Barrie pulled his hands away from the mike stand as if he'd been suddenly shocked by a short in the wire. He leaned back from it, started into his first few bars.

"Lean in closer!" The Doctor ordered. But as Barrie leaned in and his hands went instinctively to the shiny mike stand The Doctor interrupted, "Don't touch that thing!"

Once Barrie started singing it became discouragingly obvious to The Doctor. All ease and warmth had deserted the young man. The thing The Doctor loved so when he saw him in the theater was gone. He was phrasing differently, attacking words in the lyric in a way he hadn't done before. He was trying to be strong where before he had been gentle. He was trying to make love where before he had been content to be loved.

"No, no, no!" The Doctor finally interrupted. "Hold it! Hold it!"

Barrie stopped abruptly. The Doctor left his place at the table, came forward, asked the pianist, "Just what the hell are you playing?"

"The kid's arrangements. Like they were handed to me." He picked up the music to show it to The Doctor. The Doctor scanned the lead sheet. Yes, this was the arrangement, all right. He turned on Barrie.

"Did you screw around with these arrangements?"

"No, sir!" Barrie said.

"Okay," The Doctor said reflectively. He stared at Barrie for a moment, then reached out to unbutton his dinner jacket. He pulled at Barrie's tie till the ends came loose and hung open. Then he ran his fingers through Barrie's damp hair and mussed it. He handed the arrangement back to the pianist saying, "Eliminate all that crap. Just give me the melody, with one finger. I want this to sound impromptu. Not too polished and glossy. Just a guy standing up there singing. A guy who really hates the idea of pretentious arrangements or wearing a stiff dinner jacket or a tie. A guy who really doesn't want his hair combed.

There's only one thing this kid loves. To sing! With an ac-
companiment or without! He just loves to sing! Got it?"

They both nodded, the pianist and Barrie, though
Barrie seemed lost, hurt, about to cry. But The Doctor
did not indulge him, he merely turned, went back to his
seat at the table.

The pianist played Barrie into his first number again.
The kid began to sing. Better, softer, more relaxed. Yet
still accenting the words in a stiff, strange way unnatural
to him.

The Doctor interrupted, "Hold it, kid! What is that
phrasing? I told you, don't work at it! Let it flow!"

"But that's what he said. . . ."

"Who? Who said?" The Doctor demanded.

"Milt."

"Milt? He told you to do that? Some vocal coach! I'll
get after him in the morning. For right now, give it to
me, easy, natural. Let it flow, kid, let it flow."

Barrie nodded, motioned to the pianist, who started to
play him in again. This time when he moved in close to
the mike and he seized it in both hands, The Doctor did
not object. It was easy, natural, it looked graceful, intimate, friendly, not staged. The Doctor found that now
he could lean back and listen. The false phrasing was
gone. The tension was going out of the boy. The disorder
of his dress and hair relaxed him, or else made him seem
relaxed. The stiffness was dissipating. The warmth had
begun to return. He even interpolated a few *bubbaboos*
on his own.

The Doctor let him go through his entire act, from
number to number, without any applause. At the end,
The Doctor stood and applauded, alone in the empty
echoing place. He walked up to mount the bandstand
where the boy stood, his back to the room. When The
Doctor turned him around he discovered that, whether
from relief, fear, or sheer exhaustion, Barrie was crying.

The Doctor wiped the tears from the boy's cheeks with
his fingers. Then he said, "Kid, from now on, if anybody
asks you to do anything that doesn't come natural to you,
don't do it. If they insist, you come to me. You got good
instincts. Be loyal to them. We'll get these arrangements
rescored. You go back to your own phrasing. And
we'll see how it goes tomorrow night."

Barrie nodded. "Now go back and change," The Doctor said. As Barrie started back toward the dressing room, The Doctor called out, "Just for tonight, wear that tuxedo again. After that, we'll see. And no drinking! You hear?"

In the darkness, Barrie nodded and went on into the dressing room. The Doctor turned to the pianist, "Tonight fake it. Nice, simple, clean. Give him all the room he needs. After that, we'll see if he justifies getting his arrangements rewritten."

That evening at the first show it went better. Not great but better. Barrie was more relaxed. The women listened more intently. The applause grew from polite to almost enthusiastic and urged Barrie into two of his encore numbers. When he left the bandstand there was a wave of applause. Not the torrent that The Doctor would have liked but more, by far, than he had earned the night before.

Between the first and second show, The Doctor went to Barrie's tiny dressing room, squeezed in, was barely able to close the door.

"Kid, that was better. In the second show if you feel like holding that mike, hold it. But only if you feel like it. Now when you get into your fourth number I want you to resent that tuxedo and tie. Unbutton the jacket. Rip the tie open. As if they get in the way of your singing. You want to be free to sing for the ladies. Don't make love to them. Let them do that. You just live to sing. They'll do the rest. Okay?"

Barrie nodded. Then said, "It's still lousy, isn't it?"

"Kid, just do this second show the way I said. It'll work. I know it'll work."

Because the boy needed it, and The Doctor felt sorry for him, he patted Barrie gently on the cheek. "Just try it. One more time." As he left the dressing room, Cone had to remind himself, *He's only talent. Use him. Don't become involved with him.*

The audience for the second show was smaller than the first. That was a bad sign. Nobody had stayed around to see the second show. But The Doctor consoled himself, for tryouts better a small audience than a big one. If it didn't work, why fail before a large house?

When Barrie's turn came, the lights went down, the spot

hit the piano, the voice of the Master of Ceremonies came through the auxiliary mike and after some polite applause Barrie came on, moved into the spotlight. The Doctor thought he suspected fear, not fear of an audience but fear of failing. He was a young boy, terrified and alone, in a field of unfriendly blue light, stiffly attired and ill at ease. But when he began to sing, he did so easily, gently, not having to fight a complicated arrangement.

Barrie took them through three songs and then, as The Doctor instructed, he suddenly unbuttoned his jacket, ripped impatiently at his tie, till the ends hung loose. He unbuttoned his collar and jerked his head and neck free in a gesture of defiance that amused the audience. They seemed to share his sense of freedom.

Then, smiling, and as if to include the audience in his little boy's prank, he rumpled his own hair in a gesture of defiance against form and propriety. A few in the audience applauded. Most of them women, The Doctor noted.

After that, Barrie sang more freely, more intimately, the audience reacting with growing enthusiasm, mounting higher and higher with each song. He was forced to do all of his three encores. Before they would let him leave the stand, Barrie had to repeat one of his regular numbers. When he left, some were on their feet applauding him. On his way toward his dressing room two women tried to kiss him.

The Doctor stood there watching, saying to himself, "If Dale gave them vaginal flutters, one day this kid'll give them instant orgasm!"

He helped the kid wipe the perspiration off his neck and back. He peeled the wet shirt from him, covered him with the old robe that hung on the hook on the door.

"Okay, kid. That's it. You did it once, you can do it again. Better. Easier the next time than this time. You'll do four weeks here. Then I'll move you into the Chez Paree."

The kid's face lit up, half desire, half fear.

"That's right. Chez Paree!"

"Then New York?" Barrie asked.

"Then? Then, maybe, radio," The Doctor said, sounding very vague and casual. He was never going to let Barrie know that he was merely an instrument in a carefully worked out plan to create a good solid broad base to which TCA would attach its ten percent commission for a long long time.

By the time Bobbie Barrie's four-week engagement at the Clark Street club was finished, parties were coming down from the North Side to see the new young singing sensation. Even Cat's Eye Bastione came down one night. The Doctor spotted him, went to greet him. Cat's Eye shook hands coolly, and asked, "What's doing, Doc? I heard you got some great kid down here and you never tell me? How come?"

"I've got him in training down here. When he's ready I'm moving him up to the Chez Paree."

"Good. Good," Bastione said, but he started to polish the cat's eye gem in his gold tie pin.

Barrie went on, did his show, which had now been expanded by four numbers and two more encores. He came on with the air of a winner, fattened on three whole weeks of ovations. He came on to the kind of applause that had been conditioned by reputation and by those in the audience who had come back to see him for a second or third time. Now they were calling for him to loosen his tie, open his jacket and unbutton his shirt. This time when he went off finally, he ripped the bow tie from under his collar and tossed it out at the crowd, which set off a scramble among the women.

When the second show was over, Cat's Eye Bastione came back to find The Doctor in the kid's dressing room. Barrie was hunched over, breathing hard, sweating profusely. The Doctor was drying him like a handler mopping a fighter after a tough bout. Bastione poked his head into the tiny dressing room.

"This kid is ready. He could open at the Chez Paree tomorrow night," Bastione said.

"Tuesday," The Doctor said. "He'll finish out the week here, as per contract. Then he's off Sunday night and Monday."

"Okay, you're The Doctor," Bastione said, smiling to indicate he was making a joke. Then in a transparent effort to give his words an impromptu air, he continued, "If you got a minute, Doc, I like to talk to you."

Though he disliked the sound of it, The Doctor dropped

the towel protectively around Barrie's shoulders and
stepped outside. When they were head to head, Bastione
said in a husky whisper, "Doc, I like to own a piece of
this kid. He's got it. He's got it big." The Doctor paused a
moment, then decided finally to risk it. He shook his head,
slightly, but very perceptibly. "I mean buy," Bastione persisted. "I mean I'm going to pay. Cash."

"I can't sell what I don't own," The Doctor said. Bas-
tione eyed him dubiously. "That's right. I have a contract.
I represent him. Everything he does. But I don't own him.
So, sorry."

Bastione was visibly distressed. But he did not push it.
It was a sign of his respect and affection for Irwin Cone.
From The Doctor's point of view, he was not going to
compromise or endanger a plan too long laid and too
long pursued by taking a quick profit now.

"Well," Bastione compromised, "bring him into the
Chez Paree starting Tuesday. We'll do big with him there."

The bulky bear of an Italian turned and started down
the narrow hallway to the stage door. The Doctor
squeezed back into Barrie's tiny dressing room and found
he was already getting dressed. He noticed, too, the glass
half full of rye, a glass which had been full when he left
the room.

When Barrie was dressed, he turned, picked up his little bag, was ready to exit, but The Doctor did not yield
the door to him. Instead he said, "Look around, kid." Puzzled, Barrie stood there. "Look good!" The Doctor ordered. "And remember this place. This stinking, dingy
dressing room. The little toilet out there, with the rust in
the bowl, the broken chain and the leaking box overhead.
The cold water in the wash basin. The roaches that cross
your dressing table whenever they feel like it. Remember
all that! Because from here on it's up to you. You can go
all the way. Or you can wind up here again. If you listen
to me, you'll make it. Right to the top. If you think
you're too smart to listen, if you start thinking on your
own, you can wind up back here so quick it'll numb you
for life. Now the first thing *is this*."

The Doctor snatched up the empty glass. "If you can't
drink a little don't drink at all!" He hurled the glass
against the dirty streaked wall at the far end of the room.

It hit, exploded, and Barrie had to pull back to protect his face from the fragments.

"Now, come on!"

The Bobbie Barrie opening at the Chez Paree was a great success. Because of the advance publicity which The Doctor had planted, most of the Chicago papers sent critics to cover the opening. And Barrie scored with every one of them. After that, The Doctor arranged a careful continuous stream of publicity that even found its way into the New York papers.

By the end of Bobbie Barrie's second week at the Chez Paree, The Doctor was ready for the next move in his overall plan. He had an item planted in the *Tribune* hinting that Bobbie Barrie was playing his last week in Chicago because he was heading for New York and discussions that would lead to a network radio series of his own, under the sponsorship of a national food company. That night and for the next two nights, executives of the important Chicago-based advertising agencies showed up at the club. Some of them brought their clients with them. By the morning of the third day, The Doctor had received four calls at his office. Four agencies had clients who might be interested enough in Bobbie Barrie to talk a radio deal. The Doctor had Bertha call back in each instance and say that Doctor Cone was sorry, that the deal in New York was so close to closing that he couldn't in good conscience open serious discussions in Chicago.

Then Cone waited twenty-four hours. The next day, three of the agencies called back and left messages with Bertha. They might make it worth Barrie's while to discuss the matter, as long as the New York deal wasn't definitely closed.

At that point, The Doctor finally deigned to call back in person. He made an appointment with each of the three agencies. At each he had a long meeting in which he maintained the cool, distant attitude of someone who was making a courtesy call and had not the slightest interest in selling what was already sold in New York.

In each meeting he was able to work up a substantial bid for Barrie's salary for a one-hour network radio show. Whereupon, The Doctor indicated in a vague and general way, there would naturally have to be more to the show. Barrie couldn't just stand up at the mike and sing for one hour. Of course, of course, the anxious agencies hastily agreed. So The Doctor finally pretended to let himself be persuaded to invite the various sponsors to the Chez Paree with their wives, families and friends to see and hear Bobbie Barrie in person.

Sponsors came, their wives and daughters came, some nights more than one sponsor appeared. Each suspected the reason the other was there, which only added fever to the competition.

By the end of the week, The Doctor had before him three firm offers of fifteen hundred dollars a week as a starting fee for Bobbie Barrie's services, with escalations every thirteen weeks. Of course, as always, The Doctor was careful to mention in his casual way, there would have to be more to the show. And, of course, representing eager sponsors, the agencies were quick to agree.

In the company of the agency executive, The Doctor went to visit each of the three sponsors interested and came away with an agreement on Bobbie Barrie. In every instance, The Doctor raised the question of the rest of the show and the sponsor agreed that his agency would work out the details. But the offer was firm.

Once he had reached that point, The Doctor felt safe in sitting down with the three agency people, one at a time of course, and "working out the details."

In the offices of Starr, Brook & Cordrey, The Doctor sat in the office of Vice President and Account Executive Steven Cordrey. When invited to give his view of what the Bobbie Barrie Show should consist of, The Doctor itemized: Bobbie, of course, at fifteen hundred, the band at seven hundred and fifty, a writer for continuity at two hundred and fifty, an MC and a comic at five hundred a week, a director at five hundred, and a guest star at a thousand dollars a week.

That would come to forty-five hundred dollars a week. Quite a bit for a weekly show which had not yet proved itself, Cordrey observed. But, he conceded, with the sponsor so eager for Barrie and with the agency so sure of his success, it was worth the risk. At least for a thirteen-week trial period.

The Doctor corrected him immediately. "For a twenty-six-week period!"

Cordrey stiffened, then finally nodded, giving The Doctor the one vital clue he sought. Cordrey had obviously been instructed to try to hold out for only thirteen weeks. But, if he had to, in order to make the deal, to commit for twenty-six weeks. That meant the sponsor was really hot for Barrie. Now, The Doctor felt he was ready for the ultimate prize in the entire game. He made a pretense at writing down the figures hastily, adding them up not once but twice to make sure he was right. Then he drew a line at the bottom. Through all this Cordrey sat in his chair attempting on the one hand to see what The Doctor was writing, while trying not to give the impression that he was curious.

Finally The Doctor said, "That leaves one last item."

"One . . . last item?" Cordrey echoed warily.

"TCA is not in business for its health," The Doctor said. "We have our commission to figure."

"Your ten percent is part of Barrie's fifteen hundred. That's the way it's always done," Cordrey said, quite sure of his ground.

"Well, if all we were selling you was Bobbie Barrie you'd be right. We'd take our ten percent out of his fee. But we're selling you the whole package. We'll be responsible for the entire show. Barrie, the band, MC, writer, director, guest, the works. Even so, for all that work, we're willing to settle for our usual ten percent."

"Ten percent . . . of *everything?*" Cordrey rose up from his chair. "That's outrageous! We won't pay it! Ten percent of everything? Why that's . . . that's . . ."

"That's four hundred and fifty dollars a week," The Doctor supplied quickly.

"We'll never pay a commission that high!" Cordrey declared flatly.

"I didn't say *you* had to pay it. Just say we're selling you a package of entertainment that costs five thousand dollars a week."

"Our client will ask for a breakdown."

"Don't give it to him."

"But we have to!" Cordrey insisted.

"In that case . . ." The Doctor got up, picked up his piece of yellow paper, folded it neatly, deliberately slipped it into his pocket before leaving.

"Wait a minute!" Cordrey asked desperately.

"Yes?" Cone said, half turning, but still indicating his intention to leave.

"You made a deal to deliver Barrie for fifteen hundred a week!" Cordrey challenged.

"I'm ready to deliver," The Doctor said. "Subject to 'working out the details.' Now, unless you want to go back to your sponsor and tell him that you couldn't work it out, and that you can't deliver Barrie, you'd better think over what I said. The whole package of entertainment for five grand. Or forget it!"

The Doctor walked out. He didn't have to watch Cordrey's face. It would be precisely the same as Balding's face the day The Doctor had jeopardized Balding's fifteen percent by telling his anti-Semitic client to go screw. All agency men seem to have the same face under the same set of pressures and circumstances. Oh, those nice, cool, calm, well-tailored, neatly turned out *goyim*, who can be so uppity and superior when they are in command. Well, let the bastard suffer a little now.

The Doctor went straight back to his office. There he simply waited. Right after lunch, which he calculated gave Cordrey a chance to have three martinis and a sandwich with Starr and Brook, The Doctor received a phone call. Cordrey was on the line. He tried to sound grave, and hurt, but he only sounded like three martinis.

"We've talked it over, here at the shop," he said, "and we can see the justice of your position. After all, you *are* furnishing a whole package of entertainment."

Which Irwin Cone translated to mean "Okay, you Jew bastard, you have us by the balls. We don't dare tell the client he can't have Barrie. Because if we do we'll lose the account and our fifteen percent. So we're going to swallow your line of shit and say yes, and call it 'the justice of your position.' "

But to Irwin Cone it didn't matter what they said, or what they thought. Inside him, he felt a pounding exultation. They had bought it! Hated it, but bought it!

When he hung up the phone he felt an excitement and an elation which had only been equaled twice before in his life. The afternoon he received his degree as a Doctor of Medicine. And the night he was laid for the first time.

But this victory not only equaled those experiences, it exceeded them. For it had the combined jubilation of both a personal accomplishment and a sexual triumph.

As he sat there with his hand still resting on the phone, he wondered, was part of his satisfaction because he had evened a bitter score with Ronnie Dale, because he had turned the betrayal into a victory? Or was it that he had made an important discovery about himself? To him, more exciting, more satisfying even than sex was creating and engineering a deal that no one else would have dared. Or if they had, they would not have been able to plan and execute it in the skillful, devious and meticulous manner that he had.

Whatever his feelings, one thing he knew. He had this day established a precedent from which TCA would benefit in the millions in years to come. Ten percent of the action! Of all the action! Right off the top! And, from now on, off the top of every situation in which TCA had enough muscle to make it stick.

Cat's Eye Bastione was right. Find the other guy's weakness, his pressure point, and put your muscle there. You could control more and more with less and less. That was power!

This excitement over making a deal would never leave Irwin Cone. Each deal would be a fresh, all-consuming challenge. Sometimes in the midst of having sex with one of the aspiring young singers or actresses who were always available to him now, a new angle on some deal would occur to him and he would hasten to achieve his climax so that he could reach for the bedside phone.

In the years to come when radio packages would be sold for as high as twenty-five thousand a week and more, TCA commissions would rise to twenty-five hundred a week, three thousand, four, five! One day TCA would receive weekly commissions larger than the entire budget of that original Bobbie Barrie show. And when television would arrive and packages would sell for a hundred thousand and more, TCA commissions on a single show could amount to twenty-five thousand dollars a week!

Till, years later, one agency man would remark, facetiously but bitterly, "The Doctor wasn't sorry to see World War Two begin. He knew that somehow he'd wind up with ten percent of it."

4

In the years that followed, The Doctor expanded TCA's activities into many other complete packages of radio entertainment built around singers or comics and later around dramatic stars. As each cycle came and went, The Doctor changed his emphasis, always keeping abreast of the newest trends and in many cases starting them.

When he felt that singers and bands were beginning to slip, he pioneered the trend toward shows built around comics. When comics began to glut the market, he started to seduce the finest dramatic stars from the stage into radio. Under his guidance TCA packaged costly hour-long shows for sponsors who coveted the aura of the stars to help sell commonplace products like soap or soup.

Always TCA operated on the same basis, furnishing the complete package and taking ten percent off the top. Some times TCA stole a bit off the bottom too, by padding costs, or inflating the salaries of stars for budget purposes above what they were actually receiving.

The number of packages The Doctor organized, sold and manipulated yielded other benefits besides. Once TCA controlled a package, The Doctor would insert into that show budding TCA talent, thereby developing new stars for himself. Or when TCA was in danger of losing a star because of some dissatisfaction, he could offer the rebellious client a profitable guest appearance on a TCA-controlled package and thus delay the crisis a while longer.

A radio package had other uses too. When The Doctor wanted to steal a valued client away from another agent, he could hold out a group of guaranteed guest appearances on TCA-controlled shows as a lure.

But the guiding principle of the business remained The Doctor's resolution never to engage in any situation in which TCA did not receive ten percent of all the action. He came to believe in that principle more strongly than in Judaism, which was the only legacy his poor father had left him. Judaism he practiced only on the two High Holy days, and those Saturdays when the sons of his most important Jewish clients were being *Bar Mitzvahed*. But ten percentism he practiced every day of the year, rigidly, without ceasing, and with a steadfastness that would put his ancestral defenders at Masada to shame.

Of course, as the years passed, The Doctor did not originate or accomplish all deals and strategies by himself. TCA began to grow so swiftly that to service its clients effectively in nightclubs, radio, the stage, and eventually, most important of all, in motion pictures, he had to establish offices in New York, Beverly Hills, and London.

He also had to surround himself with young assistants, each of whom he selected and trained to be capable of eventually taking over the extensive TCA operations.

As The Doctor had promised himself following his early anti-Semitic encounters with the advertising business, his employees were all Jewish; bright, college-educated, and above all, polished. Madison Avenue—and Michigan Avenue too—were going to accept, and even be dependent on Jews, if only to even the score for those early insults.

The Doctor's first acquisition had been Spencer Gould, fresh from Harvard Business School. Gould, whose father was named Goldenberg and who still manufactured syrups for little soda fountains in Brooklyn, was a tall thin young man. Sedately dressed in the Ivy manner. He didn't *look* Jewish, whatever that meant, but he was given to using his handkerchief very frequently due to a chronic sinus condition which flared up seriously twice a year and resulted in his being confined to bed for a week or ten days.

With The Doctor's training and experience it had been easy for him to diagnose Gould's condition at their first interview. But somehow the satisfaction he had derived from having an associate whom he could call "Spence" appealed to him more than the periodic disadvantages of Gould's sinuses.

Spence . . . Spence . . . The name had a nice classy *goyish* ring to it. "I'll have Spence call you with the details and firm up the deal. . . ." "I can't make it to Detroit

for the presentation of the show, but Spence will go. . . ."
"Spence will be at NBC first thing in the morning and he'll
get the right time slot! You can always rely on Spence!"

It sounded impressive. Nice, clean, highly reliable.
Spence, it was a name far removed from the one the rab-
bi had used to bless him years ago at his Bar Mitzvah.
On that day he was called to the Torah as *Shlomo ben
Yitzhak*.

Spence Gould proved himself to The Doctor in many
ways. He had a keen, sound mind. He learned early that
he could not allow his own taste to interfere with selling
any show or any piece of talent. He learned, too, that in
a business where a deal could last thirteen weeks or thirteen years you did not overlook a single advantage, no
matter how minor. You made every deal on the basis that
it would last forever and you figured every penny and
every fraction of a percentage point on that basis.

Another lesson Spence learned swiftly from The Doctor, never let the performer's interest supersede TCA's.
Sometimes it was painful to blow a deal when the client
desperately needed work, but Irwin Cone was determined
never to establish any precedent unfavorable to TCA and
its future dealings. As far as the unfortunate client was
concerned, the deal fell through because of "a sudden
change of marketing plans by the advertising agency . . ."
or "an outrageously bad deal, for your own self-respect,
we couldn't let you take it. . . ." or "The sponsor's wife
just didn't like the show. You know how sponsors' wives
are. . . ."

Eventually, Spence Gould was joined by two other
young men. Buddy Black, who had started life as Her-
man Schwartz. And Freddie Feig, whose name had been
shortened from Feigenbaum.

Soon, all three became devout practitioners of The Doctor's basic rules, prime of which was, of course: find out
where the weakness is, then put your muscle there.

And the corollary to that rule. The Doctor's own invention: where there is no weakness, create one.

Eventually, Spence, Buddy and Freddie became known
in the industry as Cone's Cobras.

At the same time that he was laying the groundwork

for his extensive show business empire, The Doctor was also concerned with establishing a family dynasty. When he chose a wife, he chose her as much to give him sons as for reasons of affection and personal regard.

He had determined early in his career that the one kind of girl he would not choose for a wife was someone in show business. It disgusted him, the kinds of things that ambitious singers, dancers and actresses were willing to do to further their careers. It even disgusted him how often he took advantage of those opportunities. But at that stage of his early career, as when he was an intern, he had little time for pursuit and seduction, so he had relieved himself with what was available.

When it came time to look for a wife, he searched and found a more conventional girl. Her parents had named her Molly, but midway through high school she had switched to Melba. In high school she had been a bright student and went on to Hunter College where she majored in Art. She was working in an antique shop on Madison Avenue when The Doctor first met her. He had stopped in to price a desk that was displayed in the window and had been highly impressed by the shy, dark-haired, diminutive girl who was even shorter than he was. She blushed easily, which somehow convinced him that she was a virgin. As their conversation progressed and he learned that she was waiting for her appointment to teach art in one of the city high schools, he had a feeling that she might well be the kind of cultured girl in whom he could be seriously interested.

She was not too fleshy, a tendency he disliked in many Jewish girls. Nor did she give his practiced doctor's eye reason to believe that she would become so as time went by. All things considered, she might make an excellent mother for his sons.

He took her out several times before she invited him to her home on Mosholu Parkway. Her parents, whose Jewish hearts quickened at the thought of their daughter being courted by a doctor, were openly disappointed when they discovered that he was actually an agent. They had hoped for better for their Melba. But, in her own persistent, studious way, Melba had made inquiries and discovered the true potential of the little man and she had decided, long before he had, that they would marry.

His father came to New York for the wedding. After old Samuel met his son's bride-to-be for the first time he observed, "She reminds me of your mother." Which young Cone took to be a compliment, but which the old man had intended as an expression of his disappointment.

The occasion was in all respects a conventional Jewish wedding. Each family went through with it feeling that their prized offspring could have done better. Much better.

Once they were married, Melba Cone put her mind and energies to becoming a helpful wife, which, in The Doctor's business, meant being an excellent hostess and a woman deeply involved in charities of all sorts, at least to the extent of lending her name. But mainly she devoted herself to living up to the standard expected from the wife of a very powerful man.

For years she had carefully concealed her Bronx intonation so that she could pass her teachers' orals. As Mrs. Irwin Cone she began to sound positively British. She always dressed in the best of taste, wearing her hair and her clothes in the style of Wallis Simpson Windsor whom she liked to believe she resembled. In the circles in which she traveled, being The Doctor's wife made her royalty and she lived the part to the hilt. For that, he was proud of her, though after a while he realized that playing his wife became more important to her than being his wife. Nor did he mind, as long as she functioned as a valuable adjunct of his business.

A TCA client once remarked of her that not since the dark and beautiful Princess Berenice of the Macabbean dynasty has such a princess as Melba Cone ruled over all of Jewry.

There was, however, one important area in which Melba finally disappointed her husband. He had married her for sons. But, to the relief of almost everyone in show business, she gave him two daughters. No one outside the family could contemplate with calm the thought that there might be a lineal succession of Cones.

The first time that it became known Melba Cone was pregnant, people in the business speculated on whether she would deliver or hatch out eggs, like a cobra. The second time, when she was overdue, the same people who joked that The Doctor had married only to file a joint income tax return, kept saying that he would not let Melba deliver until he had exacted the right deal from her obstetrician.

The time came when the Cones had to move to California so that The Doctor could personally supervise TCA's now extensive film talent. There Melba Cone achieved the very pinnacle of Hollywood social success. No one ever spoke well of her behind her back and no one ever refused an invitation to one of her parties. And she gave the most lavish, elegant, tax-deductible parties in the Western Hemisphere.

Eventually The Doctor even developed a way of capitalizing on Melba's degree in Art, though she never did go on to teach the subject. As TCA's offices proliferated from Chicago and New York to Beverly Hills, London, Paris and Rome, Melba Cone personally decorated them all with fine old English and French antique furniture.

Even on that furniture, The Doctor had had an angle, a bit of what Cat's Eye Bastione called "the vigorish." Cone felt it was sheer waste to lay out hundreds of thousands of dollars for furniture and then settle for only a small annual tax depreciation. So, after considerable thought and legal consultation, The Doctor had decided that Melba would tour England, buying almost a million dollars worth of antiques to completely outfit all TCA offices. But she would buy them for herself. And then rent them to TCA on an annual basis. Thus each year TCA would have tax-deductible expenses for furniture rental of some three hundred thousand dollars a year, which meant, of course, that each year the government absorbed at least one hundred and fifty thousand dollars of that amount. Which meant in turn that each year Melba Cone had an income of three hundred thousand dollars, half of which came from that same United States Government. It also meant that each year most of the money she laid out for travel and entertainment could be written off as business expenses.

That was the kind of extra vigorish that excited The Doctor. Some top Hollywood executives thirsted for the sexual pleasures to be derived from fleshy young starlets, but Irwin Cone derived his most intense pleasures from his business. More satisfying and exciting to him than being laid by an over-endowed, ambitious seventeen-year-old girl was the opportunity to wangle some extra edge where money was concerned.

PART TWO

PART TWO

1

As the years went by, as motion pictures became the dominant medium of entertainment, The Doctor settled more and more deeply into the Hollywood phase of TCA's operation, though a phone call of sufficient gravity could, on an hour's notice, send him flying to New York, London, Paris, Rome or anywhere that a picture was in difficulty. Others might cringe at the mention of trouble, but The Doctor thrived on it. In an industry where any change was always viewed as disastrous, Irwin Cone capitalized on upheavals.

As long as TCA had ten percent of the action—all the action—he welcomed change for good or bad. Even such an emergent disaster as the threat of a congressional investigation of Hollywood politics did not alarm The Doctor. In fact, it was precisely such a threat that caused him to take a renewed interest in the waning career of one TCA client, Jeff Jefferson.

An all-American-looking star of middling talent and middling success for almost a decade, Jeff Jefferson had begun to lose his ready saleability at the same time that pictures about World War II lost theirs. Had it not been for the investigation, Jeff Jefferson would probably have slipped into that limbo reserved for second-rank stars and from which there is no returning.

The threat of a congressional investigation of un-American activities in Hollywood couldn't have come at a worse time. With the industry already staggering from a court decree forcing all studios to sell off their theaters, thus losing their monopolistic outlets, and with the added fear of a new competitor, television, the motion picture business was not ready to face a hostile committee eager to brand the whole town Red!

At first the committee, under the chairmanship of a florid, bald, and righteous Vermont congressman named Colby, had contented itself with subpoenaing a few writers and actors from Broadway to appear in Washington. But as soon as Colby realized the space-grabbing potentiality of show-business names in the press, he and his equally ambitious colleagues decided to "broaden the scope" of their inquiry.

Maintaining that it would enable them to function more effectively, they decided to hold their hearings at what they believed to be the focus of the Red infection, Hollywood. What seemed at first to be only unsettling rumor turned into hard, unhappy fact when subpoenas were served throughout the city.

As the head of one studio moaned when three of his stars were served, "Disaster! That's all we need now! It should come out we're a front for a Red spy ring! It's the end of the picture business! Might as well cut your throat and bleed to death!"

But since he had predicted the same fate and prescribed the same course of treatment when he had had to sign the government's consent decree to sell their theaters, no one paid much attention to him. Instead, all the studio heads and their lawyers met together to decide on the proper strategy to employ in confronting Chairman Colby and his committee.

In the course of that all-industry meeting the name of Lee Mandell was first mentioned by the chief counsel to MGM.

Lee Mandell was a highly regarded labor lawyer in Washington. A one-time White House aide and confidant of FDR, Mandell had been extremely successful in private practice after he resigned from government.

Because of his political affiliations, as well as his intimate knowledge of the various federal boards and administrations, many of which he had helped set up, he was considered an expert in all matters governmental. His work before the National Labor Relations Board was highly respected and well paid for by both employers and unions alike. And his volunteer work with the American Civil Liberties Union had gained him the profound respect of intelligent conservatives as well as liberals.

Mandell's services would be extremely costly, but since the pending investigation threatened many of their most valuable stars, directors and writers, the studios decided to combine legal forces and retain him.

Once Mandell agreed to accept the job the studios furtively flew him to Hollywood, where he was installed in a secluded hundred-and-fifty-dollar-a-day bungalow at the Beverly Hills Hotel. They placed a Cadillac and a chauffeur at his disposal. Because he had come out alone, they even offered, quite delicately of course, a few choice starlets on the side if he were so inclined. But he was not so inclined. Instead he puffed on his pipe, smiled benignly, and that crisis passed.

His first few days were spent quietly summoning subpoenaed subjects to his bungalow patio. There, in the warmth of the Beverly Hills sun, he gently probed into their political affiliations, contributions, and memberships in various groups which on the surface seemed not to be political. He even questioned them about their subscriptions to magazines and other periodicals.

Like a well-trained psychoanalyst, Mandell never betrayed any personal reaction of his own, no matter what his potential witnesses admitted. He reflected neither displeasure nor concern. Instead, with his thick graying mustache and his curved-stem pipe, he seemed more fatherly than any father, more benign even than God. Though if one studied his technique carefully one realized that the frequency with which he re-lit his pipe indicated concern. Also that he asked his most incriminating questions between striking the match and applying it to the tobacco. The flaming match, the suspense as to whether Mandell would burn himself before he used it, so intrigued the witness that he gave less guarded and more frank answers.

After several days of such quiet probing, Lee Mandell was ready to meet in secret session with the combined committee of lawyers representing all the studios.

The meeting was at midday in the private executive dining room at Metro-Goldwyn-Mayer. Lunch was served and disposed of quickly for everyone was waiting to hear Mandell's opinion.

Once coffee had been served, the lawyer gave an unspoken signal to clear the room of waiters or anyone not intimately involved in the business at hand.

When they were secluded, with the door not only closed but locked, Mandell lit up his pipe again, took a puff and allowed the smoke to trickle freely from his nostrils. Then he sighed and, finally delivered his considered verdict.

"Gentlemen," he pronounced gravely, "you are up to your ass in trouble. Bad trouble."

It was hardly the judicial rendering of their situation they had expected. But if Mandell had wanted to alarm them he succeeded admirably. Having set the tone of the meeting, he continued:

"It stinks! Like a dead fish! In fact, I am sorry you gentlemen called me in!"

A deadly pall replaced the alarm which he had generated, for this seemed the preamble to Mandell's resignation.

Gerald Gainsburgh, senior in years, chief counsel to Metro, leaned forward, and said, "Mr. Mandell, if you feel that the matter is more involved, more time-consuming, more demanding than you originally thought, we can always adjust the fee upward." Gainsburgh felt proud of himself for having sized up the situation, anticipated Mandell, and given him a basis on which to ask for a larger fee without having to go through any embarrassing preliminaries.

Mandell turned on him sharply, "Mr. Gainsburgh, if I wanted more money I would simply have said, 'Gentlemen, I want more money.' I don't have to beat about the bush when I want to charge a higher fee. I am talking about the case."

Now Mandell dropped his calm, pipe-smoking pose. He was on his feet exhibiting far more vigor than anyone suspected he had.

"I am an old-timer at this game. I was a Communist myself."

There was a gasp of surprise too strong to be suppressed. But Mandell went on.

"One of the cells down in Washington. So I know this game backwards and forwards. And I can talk this way because I'm not a Communist any longer. But neither am I one of those who ran right to the church to confess. I was there. I saw it in operation. I finally decided it was not a good thing. Not for me. Not for the country. Not for the human race. So I quit.

"Now, I don't hate myself either for what I was or what I am now. I am a realist about it. Young people are always going to be hooked by idealism. I don't blame them. But once they find out that the idealism is a fraud and still they hold on, then I *do* blame them. But even when I blame them, that does not mean that I think they should be hounded. Or that they should be deprived of legal defense. Or that they should be treated like criminals, *unless* . . . remember this . . . *unless* they actually *are* criminals.

"Now, I don't think we are dealing with any criminals here."

A series of relieved exhalations ran around the table.

"I may find out otherwise. But up to this moment, no. So what *are* we dealing with? I would say you have a small knot of hard-core Communists. And the rest . . . *shmucks*.

"Oh, but what a lot of *shmucks!*" Mandell moaned. "Now that presents a double problem. A *shmuck* who joins the Party because he is a *shmuck* is also a very bad risk when it comes to testifying. He hasn't been trained. He doesn't know how you handle yourself in an investigation.

"I wouldn't put your hard-core Communists on the stand if I could help it, no matter what the pressure. On the other hand, among your *shmucks*, I haven't found one yet whom I think smart enough to face the committee."

He hesitated just long enough to light his curved-stem pipe. Then looking across the flickering match he said, "What we need is a *shabbos goy*. For you gentlemen who don't understand Yiddish, a *shabbos goy* is the gentile whom Orthodox Jews hire to light the lights and do the chores they are forbidden to do on the Sabbath.

"So, gentlemen, that's the problem. I need a front man! A nice, clean, unassailable Hollywood personality whom I can put on the stand or use as an exhibit. About whom I can say to the whole country, 'This is the real typical Hollywood citizen.' That's the only way we can counter-act some of the testimony that's bound to come out. So I want suggestions. Now! Or at least by tomorrow!"

With that, the meeting was over. But no one left the room. Instead, the crowd broke up into small groups debating as to who might be the best candidate.

After almost an hour, one of the lawyers, Wesley Freeman, said in exasperation, "This is tougher than casting the lead in a big picture!"

"Precisely," shouted Lee Mandell. "If you had to choose an actor to represent the whole motion picture industry before the committee, what characteristics would you ask for? Nice looks, innocent expression, bland manner, yet a man full of sincere convictions. The right convictions! Find me such an actor and I think we can swing it. Each of you approach your casting people, discreetly, of course. Then give me a list of the five best candidates you can suggest. I want them in twenty-four hours! We don't have much time!"

Seven lists were presented to Lee Mandell the next day, delivered by hand in unmarked envelopes. Of the thirty-five names there were a number of duplications. Jimmy Stewart appeared on every list, but Mandell ruled him out at once. Stewart had all the qualities he was seeking except one: he was too intelligent. He would always say what he honestly believed and that was not what Mandell wanted.

One other name appeared five times: Jeff Jefferson. For a moment, Mandell had trouble conjuring up Jeff's face, which he noted, subconsciously, was a favorable sign. That meant the man had not distinguished himself too strongly on the screen. Good! People have a tendency to resent the too-successful, the too-handsome, the too-wealthy. And, in this instance, the press and the nation at large were going to be the jury, so Mandell did not want to risk their jealousy.

Jefferson . . . Jeff Jefferson . . . Mandell finally remembered him. He had a good face, a nice, clean, earnest gentile face. Most of all, you could believe him. He decided to ask Jeff in for an interview.

He called Gerald Gainsburgh at Metro, explained his desire to meet with Jefferson as soon as possible. Gainsburgh promised to produce him.

As soon as Gainsburgh had hung up the phone, even before he removed his hand from it, he began to think, how to make the approach? To call Jefferson directly as chief counsel to Metro, would obligate him and the studio. There might even be some implied promise of a picture commitment. So the approach could not be direct. Who then was the best contact? Jefferson was represented by TCA. The answer was obvious.

The Doctor. Naturally, The Doctor.

Within minutes Gainsburgh succeeded in getting through to Cone, not because of Gainsburgh's prestige but because one of TCA's most prominent stars had her contract up for renewal at Metro and The Doctor was anxious to close, conditions in the industry being as unstable as they were.

The minute The Doctor realized what Gainsburgh wanted to discuss, he refused to continue the conversation by phone. Instead he made a lunch date at Hillcrest for that same day.

At a table close by the windows that looked out on the golf course, away from the usual noisy actor-producer-writer-infested tables in the men's dining room at Hillcrest, Cone and Gainsburgh had their meeting.

The Doctor listened carefully, allowing Gainsburgh to fill him in on Mandell, though The Doctor had heard all about the lawyer and yesterday's meeting. Still he always made it a practice to listen patiently. The more the other man talked the more he revealed of himself, his inner stresses, his weaknesses, most importantly, his pressure points.

So The Doctor waited while Gainburgh expounded on the challenge the industry faced, Lee Mandell's opinion of what to do, how to do it, and who was needed to carry out his strategy. Which brought Gainsburgh finally to Mandell's interest in Jeff Jefferson.

Now The Doctor leaned forward for the first time. So, for the good of the industry, Mandell wanted Jefferson as a front man? Never one to allow a tactical advantage to escape him, Cone remarked sadly, "And just what has the movie business done for the good of Jeff Jefferson in the past eighteen months?" It was disposed of as a throwaway line, a lament for his client, but Cone knew it could serve as the basis for some future advantage.

Feeling a little guilty about the industry's shabby treatment of Jeff Jefferson among a host of other second rank stars, Gainsburgh protested, "Irwin, I don't have to tell you the pressure we're under. Everybody is being squeezed." The Doctor was polite enough not to point out that lawyers and executives for motion picture companies were surviving nicely on their regular full salaries.

Instead The Doctor mused, "Jeff Jefferson? He could do the job. Oh, yes, he could do it. But whether he would *want* to, that I can't promise. . . ." Cone always entered any potential negotiating situation by hinting that he represented a reluctant client who would have to be lured, enticed, entreated, to do what was being asked of him. And of course, the implication was that only The Doctor or one of his black-suited cobras could lure, entice, and entreat successfully.

Gainsburgh, who over the years had dealt with Cone in important negotiations knew exactly the flattering response that was required of him at this point, "Irwin, if it was easy would I have bothered you?"

The Doctor made a small deprecating gesture, as if he were thoughtfully planning how he might convince Jeff to meet with Mandell. Finally, he said, "Give me a few days."

"A few days?" Gainsburgh was visibly upset. "The hearings begin next week, Irwin!"

"Gerald, I didn't set the hearings. And I don't like my client being called in at the last minute. After all, this is serious business. It could wreck Jefferson's whole career, if the public takes the wrong attitude."

Gainsburgh was tempted to reply, "Career? What career? Jefferson's over the hill right now!" Instead, adopting the same grave air as Cone, Gainsburgh said grimly, "Of course, there's risk. Don't think we in the industry don't realize that, or will ever forget it. But I feel sure it will help his career. In the long run, it might help us all— Jefferson, the industry, TCA, all of us."

With that subtle promise of a payoff, Cone felt he could proceed to end the luncheon. "I'll talk to him today. It won't be easy. After all, he's being asked to front for a lot of studios who've been giving him the brush for a year now. But I'll talk to him."

The Doctor always made it a policy never to promise

much, never to appear optimistic, and never to attempt to do anything that was easy.

On the drive back to TCA's impressive imitation colonial building on Santa Monica, the dapper little man came to the conclusion that in some way, a way that he had not yet clearly discerned, it would be a potentially profitable move for him to bring Jeff Jefferson and Lee Mandell together.

Having decided that, he reached at once for his car phone to call his secretary Alise, the English girl whom he had imported to Beverly Hills because it was such a chi-chi thing to do.

"Alise?"

"Yes, sir!" she answered and commenced at once to read off the many messages which had accumulated in his brief absence.

"Hold them! Get Jeff Jefferson on another line and patch me in! At once!"

"Yes, sir!" Alise responded with military efficiency. "I'll put you on hold, sir."

As he held on to the lifeless phone, he pondered his approach to Jefferson. This could be tricky. It was like asking a star who'd gone jobless for months to play a benefit. He heard his phone come alive.

"Jeff-baby?"

But it was Alise. "I'm sorry, sir, but Mr. Jefferson is not at home."

"Then find out where the hell he is and get him!" The Doctor exploded impatiently.

"I'm afraid that won't be possible."

"What do you mean 'that won't be possible'?" he demanded.

"According to Buddy, Mr. Jefferson is in Amarillo today. And possibly tomorrow, too."

"Amarillo? Well, get him at his hotel!"

"I'm sorry, Doctor, but the booking slip doesn't show any hotel."

"Booking slip?" The Doctor repeated, puzzled. A booking slip meant Jefferson was working. But in Amarillo? At what? Vaguely, it came to him.

Of course. Jeff Jefferson must be doing one of his personal appearances. Jefferson hated them. He did them, but it was a struggle each time to get him to say yes.

Alise was talking again. "Shall I leave a message, sir?"

"Yes . . . tell him to call as soon as he gets back . . . no, no!"

"Sir?"

"No message. We'll try again tomorrow."

"Yes, sir!"

He hung up. Better not to let Jefferson know that he had called. He might think that The Doctor had finally gotten him a good part in a picture. Then the whole Lee Mandell gambit would be a terrible letdown and he would refuse to do it.

When The Doctor wanted anyone to do something of questionable personal value he always liked to take them by surprise. So he would wait till Jefferson returned from Amarillo.

2

Jeff Jefferson could see they were waiting to greet him even before the limousine pulled up at the gate of the arena. The rodeo officials flaunted their big red, white and blue badges of privilege and authority, and their bronzed faces glowed under broad, white, spotless Stetsons.

Jefferson peered ahead through the tinted glass, thinking to himself, Oh Christ! Here we go again! Damn TCA! Damn The Doctor! Damn that bastard Buddy Black whom The Doctor had sent to talk him into doing yet another rodeo guest shot. A hell of a job for a movie star. And not just any movie star. President of the whole damned Screen Actors Guild!

True, he hadn't had a decent picture offer for many months now. Just a few personal appearances, mainly at rodeos. The money wasn't bad, especially today. Ten grand just to put on a phony all-white and silver Western rig, the kind no self-respecting cowboy would be caught dead in. Then he would mount the palomino. His deal always specified a palomino. The golden coloring went with his own blond hair and fair skin. He would wait just inside the dark runway, hear the fanfare, his introduction on the loudspeakers . . . "direct from Hollywood . . . great American movie star . . . in person . . . one and only . . . Jeff Jefferson!"

With a deep dig into its flanks he would send the animal charging into the daylight. Then he would circle the entire arena, his own white Stetson held high and stiff in the breeze. As always there would be that surge of applause, the whistles, cheers and voices which greeted him, helping him through the ordeal.

Fake. It was all fake. He liked horses, but hated West-

erns. Maybe because he had never been as good on a
horse as he would have liked to be. Once, at his peak,
he'd had a clause inserted into his contract which provided
he couldn't be required to do more than two Westerns a
year. Now, he could secretly admit to himself, he'd grab
a Western if it were offered.

The part of the rodeo he hated most was the "Star
Spangled Banner." Soon he would be at the mike again,
singing in that untrained off-key voice of his, hoping that
the band, bad as it was, would be loud enough to cover
him. Especially on that one high phrase . . . "and the
rockets' red glare . . ." He had never quite made that one.

No more time for thinking or self-reproach, for there
they were. The committee waited to greet him.

Let's hope this time there are no wives, no daughters,
he thought wearily. He was tired, too tired even for the
uninvolved catch-as-catch-can screwing indigenous to these
events. Somehow the wives and daughters of the great
American Southwest were more prone to drinking and
screwing than any women he knew, even ambitious starlets in Hollywood.

He could fend off most of them. Yet at every rodeo
somehow there was always one woman, or one girl, who
attached herself to him and it always seemed easier to lay
her than go through the trouble of getting rid of her.
Noblesse oblige, he thought bitterly.

Strangely, it never led to any difficulty with husbands or
other male relatives. It seemed to be an accepted part of
hospitality here in cow country. Or did the men feel it was
an honor to have their wives or sisters serviced by a real
movie star from Hollywood? Maybe it improved the breed.

Who knows, next Christmas Neiman-Marcus might have
a new offering in its catalog, "Surprise your wife for
Christmas! Give her a weekend with the Movie Star of
her Choice! On a sable rug! Twenty-five thousand dollars!"

The car had stopped. The crowd surged so close it was
difficult to open the door. Yet for all his previous distaste,
he felt a moment of comfort at being besieged. It offset all
the weeks of waiting around at home for the phone to
ring. Especially those days when Joanne was away working at the studio.

Responding to their eagerness, he gave them his familiar smile. Big, broad, natural, warm, it had that all-American quality which audiences had loved, though the critics, especially in New York, accused him of smiling his way through every picture. Every time he thought of that, he would silently retort: Yeah? What about that amputation scene in *End of Glory?*

The crowd's welcome routed his fantasies, his smile having evoked another wave of greeting. This time he could hear the shrill female voices overriding the men. He could sense it, even now. Tonight, if he couldn't make that last plane, he would not wind up alone. He was already resigned.

He stepped from the car, looked around, smiling, and at the same time sizing up the candidates. There were two tall blondes with good, robust figures deliciously fitted in dresses cut very low for so early in the day. Then his eye caught one tall brunette—glistening black hair, deep black eyes, a small smile. She didn't cheer, didn't join the others in the confusion of the greeting. She just stood off, looked, smiled, with all the assurance of a regular charge customer at Neiman-Marcus who had already received her catalog and was doing her Christmas shopping early.

It was rare to find a woman with that kind of sexual assurance. But she had it. She never even followed when the committee propelled him into the dark runway of the arena. Suddenly he found himself looking back at her. From afar, she saw and smiled, a little more broadly this time. When their eyes made contact it gave him the same kind of charge he usually felt when he entered a woman he really wanted. He could feel her right down to his balls. Some woman.

Now that he had moved into the shadows under the stands of the arena, the smell of horses and cattle assailed him. He didn't mind. Farm-born, this part was like coming home. But out in the Midwest, there were no cowboys, no rodeos.

There was a bar set up in his dressing room, but Jeff refused a drink. One thing he had always believed, give the audience what it paid for, what it expected. He had a basic sense of integrity about that, at least.

That, and his work for the Guild, he kept reassuring

himself, as he changed from his slacks and jacket into the despised white-and-silver cowboy outfit. There had been times in recent months, in the small hours of the morning while Joanne was sleeping after a hard day's shooting at the studio, he lay in bed wishing there were some graceful way of retiring from pictures and just devoting himself to the work of the Screen Actors Guild.

But there was no money in that. Nor did he have enough now to live on, not on the scale to which he'd been accustomed. And he would not live off Joanne.

Yes, it was a bad time for any just-below-top-rank movie star facing forty-five in two years. Especially stars like himself, who had been cradled, protected, and enslaved by long-term studio contracts. All stars hated them. But they all depended on them. Especially when those contracts ran out and were not renewed.

He was so depressed that the knock on the door was welcome. The parade was all shaped up and ready to go if he was.

In the deep shadows of the tunnel his palomino was waiting. The flagbearers, one carrying the Stars and Stripes, the other carrying the Lone Star flag of Texas were already saddled up.

Jeff reached his palomino, looked it over. A fine animal. He seized the reins, swept his right leg up and over, settled into the deep welcoming Western saddle. He tested the reins then signaled the parade master.

The word was transmitted. From outside in the arena came a strong, deep, husky voice on the public address system.

"And now, the highlight of our rodeo, the appearance, in person, of the Grand Marshal and Judge of this year's Amarillo All-Time All-American Rodeo. . . ."

Then on the signal from the parade master, Jeff spurred his palomino. It bolted forward into the bright sunlight.

The roar came at him in a great rolling wave. He smiled bigger, brighter, raised his white Stetson high. With his other hand he turned the magnificent blond beast sharply to his left and started his circle of the stands, no more than ten feet from rows and rows of clapping, shouting spectators.

Their cheers always comforted him. Except when he

passed the pens. There the riders and busters leaned against the fence, each with one boot up on a slat, an old stained Stetson pushed back on his head. And they just smiled. Which always made him feel self-conscious.

He reached the center of the arena where the mike had been placed for him to start the "Star Spangled Banner." He looked over the Sam Houston High School Band, knowing they would be no good, but hoping they would at least be loud enough to cover him. The conductor gave them their downbeat, at the same moment someone handed Jeff the mike. He rose up in his stirrups and he was singing. "Oh, say can you see . . ." For better or worse, he was into it.

Actually, it went off not too badly. And the applause forgave him everything. While it was still vibrating, he reined his palomino toward the judges' box where the entire committee was standing to greet him.

Still wearing his big fixed smile, he dismounted, surrendering the animal to ready hands. He started into the welcome shade of the judges' box, with the committee members reaching across each other to slap him on the back, congratulating him as though he'd just accomplished some extraordinary feat.

When he turned to smile at the occupants in the box behind his seat, he saw her again—the tall, black-haired young woman with the small smile. Her eyes were fixed on him appraising, approving, yet somehow mocking as if she were daring him, testing him. He felt that same surging in his groin.

He turned back to face the arena. For the next five hours he would have to smile, observe, applaud, vote, with an expert's eye, on innumerable rodeo events all of which bored him completely.

He thought he had masked his disinterest well until, sometime during the second hour, someone handed him a tall, icy glass of bourbon and branch.

The drink didn't surprise him; it was welcome. But the voice, a woman's voice, with that same half-smiling, mocking quality in it made him turn sharply.

"Man, you need this!" she said, as if she were fully aware of his discontent. Their hands touched when he took the glass. Frosty as her fingers were, they gave him that feeling again, deep down in his balls.

He turned back to judge the events.

The sun was low in the west, igniting a long swath of cloud into a brilliant flaming streak against the deepening blue sky. In moments, the topmost fringes of the cloud bank would begin turning a dark purpling gray.

Jeff glanced at the clouds from time to time, wondering how long before it would be over. There was only the last event to complete, the final scores to tally, the prizes, the closing ceremonies. He stole a glance at his wrist watch. It would be tight, very tight, to make that last plane. At that, there were four stops between Amarillo and L.A. He wouldn't be home before midnight, possibly later.

Then he thought grimly, What was there to hurry *for?* Joanne would have got home by then, had her five or six drinks, her ever-so-carefully planned and measured dinner, and gone to bed. She was very vain about her body, went to great lengths to stay on a diet during a picture or while waiting for her next picture. It would never occur to her that if she had one drink a night instead of five she might eat more and still not gain weight.

But Joanne was like that, the perfect, planned, closed mind. It saved thinking. And it protected her against any arguments based on common sense, particularly when they suggested something she didn't want to do. In that way, she had the perfect Hollywood mentality. She accepted or created pet theories and pat phrases which gave her the pretense of thoughtful intelligence. She read little, knew less, was genuinely enthusiastic only about two things, making pictures and drinking gin.

It was her gin, the damned smell of it, that led to the decreasing frequency of their sexual contacts. That was the word for it, contacts. It was no longer a coupling in love, or a meeting of man and woman in passionate sexual union, or even an encounter. It lacked both great desire and great hostility. Their sex was like her meals, enough to keep life going but never enough to gain on. That, plus the odor of gin which she seemed to exude from her easy flowing pores, not only made it difficult to have sex with her, it gave him a good and reasonable justification for his own affairs, which had become more frequent in the past few years.

He needed justification because he had never been able to shake his severe Methodist upbringing. He had been raised to know what sin was. When he didn't hear about it at church, he heard about it from his mother who was a very strict woman. Music, unless it was a hymn, was suspect. His mother rarely held him close even when he was little. The only time he remembered her doing so was when he'd been ill with pneumonia and the doctor had given him up.

When he grew older, from the time he was eleven and on, he used to wonder if she ever allowed his father to come close to her. Times, late at night, he would lie awake eavesdropping. But he never heard any suggestive sounds.

Her Methodist puritanism and the strong alkali smell of soap, the two things he remembered most about her, remained with him even now, so that he always had to have a rationale for any sexual escapade outside his marriage.

One defense he could plead in all truth: his philandering did not start till Joanne had begun to drink heavily. Why she had he never could discover. Yet the ironic fact was, despite it, she had gained on him professionally, gained, overtaken and surpassed him. She was moving up into the rank of top stars. While he couldn't get himself arrested these days.

The judges were interrupting him suddenly to cast his vote for the last time. Now all that remained was the final tally so that he could award the check for the grand prize.

While he was waiting, he glanced back toward the dark-haired girl. This time she was not there. Using the need to stretch as a pretext, he stood up, turned around fully to take a good look. No, she was not in her seat. She was nowhere in the box, nor even in the section. She had simply gone.

Sonofabitch, he said to himself, the whole damn afternoon went on too long! She must have tired of waiting and left! He didn't even know her name or have any graceful way to learn it. He looked at his watch again. He could still make that last plane.

The final scores were announced. The winner came to the judges' stand, Jeff handed over the check. Now, his last duty accomplished, he was free.

He changed back into his traveling clothes, grabbed his suitcase, raced to the parking lot to await his limousine. Instead a huge white Rolls Royce pulled up. Not one of the Beverly Hills Silver Cloud model that he was so used to seeing in supermarket parking lots, but a huge one, long, graceful, white with dark, dark windows protecting the rear compartment from the strong Texas sun and from onlookers as well. He was about to turn away when the door opened. The tall, smiling, black-haired young woman was inside, leaning forward from the back seat.

"Get in," she invited.

"I have to get to the airport in a hurry," he countered, feeling foolish even as he said it.

"I'll take you," she said, smiling in a way that let him know she was enjoying not only his awkwardness but her own boldness.

Irritated, he shoved his suitcase in and climbed aboard. The door slammed, the car took off. When he turned to her, he found her staring at him, still smiling. It annoyed him. Indicating the chauffeur, Jeff asked, "Does he know where to go?"

"He knows."

"I don't have much time," he said, glancing at his wrist watch.

"That depends," she said.

"It's the last plane out."

"The last *scheduled* plane out," she corrected. "And a milk run at that. You could have dinner here and still beat that plane into L.A."

"How?"

"My plane," she said. His skepticism made her add, "It's a DC 6. You can be in L.A. before midnight. *If* you want to." She said the last making it quite obvious that she did not expect he would want to.

"You're pretty sure of yourself."

"When you have a billion dollars you'd be surprised how sure you can be."

She said it softly, but with a firmness that convinced him of two things. She meant billion, not million. And she had it. There was no answer to that, so he rested back in the soft glove-leather seat with a distinct awareness of being gently but definitely overwhelmed.

"I don't even know your name."

"Will you stay?" Then she added, as casually as she could, "For dinner, I mean."

"Long as I can get back tonight," he answered.

"Good. We'll eat at my place."

"Okay."

She smiled and leaned forward, pulled down a retractable walnut panel which raised into easy reach a caddy of bottles, glasses and ice.

"Bourbon?"

"Don't you have to tell him we're not going to the airport?"

"He knows," she said. "Bourbon?"

"Scotch, with ice and a touch of water." He leaned back, saying to himself, maybe it takes a billion dollars to be this sure. She handed him his drink. At the same time she suddenly picked up their conversation.

"Doris. Doris Martinson."

He'd almost forgotten that he had asked her name. He lifted his glass. Usually, he drank slowly, a sip at a time, almost in defiance of Joanne. But this time, because he was dry or uneasy, he took a good long gulp. Then, "Martinson. That's oil, isn't it?"

"Oil. Cotton. Copper. Publishing. Canning. Shipping. Mining . . ." She left it unfinished, as though vaguely but unsuccessfully trying to recall what all the other Martinson holdings were.

"Which must keep *Mr.* Martinson very busy," he said. But his reading of the line was actually a comment on her complete personal freedom, her defiant lack of concern about gossip or convention.

"Which is what made Mr. Martinson very *dead*," she corrected.

"Oh?"

It was a single syllable, not even a word, only a sound. But it said everything. The sudden fact of her widowhood changed the entire game, like turning up a spade in gin rummy and instantly doubling the stakes. She had said it to put him at ease; instead it troubled him. Now, for a reason he could not supply, she had become dangerous.

Still it did permit him to ease back and make a more leisurely appraisal of her. Her features lacked Joanne's delicacy. Her bone structure would not make her particularly photogenic by Hollywood standards. Some women are too strong, too beautiful for a camera. Doris Martinson's was a beauty of strength, not weakness. Her body was a good, mature body, with full breasts swelling slightly above the casual opening of her silk blouse.

She was leaning back, the honey sable coat around her shoulders contrasting with the black silk of her blouse and skirt, both expertly tailored with a designer's touch of Western flair. Black was obviously her best color. It dramatized her white skin, enhanced her own black hair. Most of all it made her red lips brighter and moister.

Now she was taking his glass to refill it.

"How long? Mr. Martinson, I mean?" Jeff asked.

"Three years. Venezuela. Plane crash."

That sparked his memory. It showed on his face. She continued.

"Yes. *That* Martinson."

He was truly impressed now. "That" Martinson had been one of the wealthiest men in the world. Though Jeff had never been aware of any Mrs. Martinson.

"He must have been in his late fifties . . ." he ventured.

"Sixty-four," she corrected and went on to answer his other question before he could ask it. "I was his second wife. He never would have married again if it hadn't been for Jackie." She added quickly, "His son. One and only."

"Needed a mother for him," Jeff supplied, explaining the age difference to her advantage. But she laughed quite heartily making her breasts heave against the opening of her blouse.

"By the time we married Jackie was twenty-six. No, the only reason he married me was to prove to the world that even if his dear sweet Jackie had turned out to be a fag, Cleat Martinson was still a man. And he had enough gism in his pecker to get laid every day of his life 'til he took off on that last flight. I'll say that much for him. He wasn't very good at it. Not much fun. But he was strong, he had plenty, and he had the ass to swing it, too."

She admired the dead man in a way, but she resented every animal act of sex he had inflicted on her. She made that very clear. Then suddenly she added:

"Must have been another reason, too. To cut off Jackie, he had to have someone to leave his fortune to. Just giving it to charity wasn't his idea of how to do it. You can't go 'round hating a charity. But this way, he hoped Jackie would spend the rest of his life hating me and cursing his father. It was the perfect revenge."

"What happened to him?"

"I think old Cleat would turn in his grave if he knew how little Jackie cared. He just opened up a boutique and bookshop in downtown Dallas, took a young commercial artist in to live with him. They're both very happy I hear."

She said it with a glow of satisfaction. Anything that thwarted old Cleat Martinson evened the score for her somehow.

The Rolls was just turning off the straight, monotonously level blacktop road to start through the gates of what seemed private, cultivated land, though there was no house in sight.

Jeff stared out at the well-kept lawns, the bordering trees, regular in size and shape. Then he noticed it, ahead, at the end of the driveway. The house was huge, white, quite southern in its architecture. There were tall, graceful columns, high windows, wide veranda, an ornate balcony across the second story. He was impressed.

"Look familiar?" she asked.

"Yes. Yes, it does." But he was puzzled.

"Tara," she said simply.

"Tara? *Gone With the Wind* Tara?"

"You're goddamn right!" Doris Martinson said, considerably amused. "While they were considering building a new house they saw *Gone With the Wind*. Jenny Martinson was still alive in those days. She said, 'Cleat, why don't we have one like that?' So that's what he did. Ordered a house that was a copy of Tara, only larger, completely air conditioned. Got as big an air conditioning plant as the Music Hall in New York. The day we got married we had sixteen hundred guests, and they hardly filled the place. Of course, now, it gets lonesome. I'd sell it, if anyone in the world could afford to buy it. I think maybe I'll just turn it over to some school or orphanage when I get married again."

"You're planning on getting married again," he said, asking more than stating.

"Oh, yes," she said.

They were pulling up at the house. The Rolls came to a stop gently and with such ease that it was barely notice-

able. A Negro in butler's livery came out to open the
door.

"Just leave Mr. Jefferson's bag in the coat room. He
may be flying out right after dinner."

She entered. Jeff watched her, still working on her "He
may be flying out."

They had dinner in the banquet-huge dining room, a
room most tastefully and authentically furnished to fit
precisely with the architecture. English and American
antiques, innumerable graceful antique-silver sconces set
off a wide Colonial fireplace, walls done in rich, deep
green. Every color of every room he had seen thus far
served as a flattering background for her dark beauty.

Later they were served coffee in the huge drawing room
before the high white wood and red-brick plantation fireplace. As she poured more coffee for Jeff she leaned forward so he could see that she had nothing on under her
red-velvet hostess gown. She needed nothing either. Her
breasts, reflecting the red of the gown, seemed pinker
than her white face, and fuller than they had in the
car. If she had done it deliberately to stir him, she succeeded.

When she handed back his coffee cup Jeff felt that
same surge as when she had handed him the bourbon in
the arena. She was saying:

"Actually, aside from business, Cleat was a bore. A
crude bore. Might as well have climbed into bed with
his boots and spurs on. All the finesse of a ranch hand
buggering a sheep. There was nothing easy about him,
nothing slow or relaxed. He did it the same way he bought
land, sold oil, built buildings, took over factories. In the
most efficient, least verbal way possible. He didn't know
the first thing about making love. I was his woman and
that gave him the right. All it was, was plain, primitive
fucking."

The word, in the context of that elegant room coming
from that beautiful face, startled Jeff visibly. She smiled.
"The servants are in their own part of the house. So don't
worry, unless of course . . ." She leaned forward, smiling,
looking into his eyes, at the same time exposing more of
her pink-white breasts. "Good God, after all I went
through, don't tell me I picked a puritan." She laughed.

It angered him. Perhaps because she was close to the

truth. Hardly a time he'd ever had a woman that he didn't think about his mother and sin. Even Joanne had sensed it, without having any idea of what it was. Once she'd said, "Who sits on the edge of the bed when you're making love to me? Why can't it be just the two of us?" He had got out of their bed and slept in the den that night.

Now he demanded sharply, "What did you mean, 'after all you went through'?"

Doris only laughed again. Angrily, as if to punish her, he reached out, seized her hand, pulled her close to him in a single violent jerk. If he hurt her, he pleased her more. She didn't object or resist. When he kissed her, her mouth was open for him. When his hands thrust upward toward her breasts, her gown was already parted. Her breasts were firm and they filled his hands to overflowing, like a rich warm harvest. When he pressed them, she pressed back and upward, thrusting not only her breasts against him but her entire body as well.

The cool, controlled, sophisticated woman was suddenly quite savage. When he breathed something about going to her bedroom, she whispered hoarsely, "Right in this room!" It was important to her that he take her here, now, in Cleat Martinson's huge fine living room. And he did. On the rug. Before the fireplace. Neiman-Marcus or no, Christmas was early this year.

She recovered her breath slowly, in deep spasms. Then in shallower, contented inhalations. It was finally over when her hand crabbed up the side of the table, found cigarettes and a lighter, came down again. She lit two, inhaled twice on both, then handed him one.

"I don't smoke."

"You don't have to," she said. "Sweetie, you don't have to do anything but what you do." She threw one cigarette into the fire, drew on the other one, short takes, spitting out the smoke.

"You will stay!" she said suddenly and intensely.

"Your plane's supposed to fly me back. Tonight. Remember?"

"You must stay," she said, and it was the end of all discussion.

She rose up, her gown still open, her white body startling against the flaring red, her black hair loose and hanging down over her shoulders. She took one last puff

on her cigarette, flipped it into the fire. She reached out,
seized his hand and pulled. If he hadn't sprung up, she
would have lifted him.

They went up the wide staircase and along the hall toward the corner of the house and her suite. She led him
into a bedroom with a large round bed. It was a woman's
suite, the furniture, the frills, the fragrance of it. She led
him to the bed, let her gown drop off her shoulders and
fall to the floor. Then she started to undress him.

"If I don't leave, I have to call."

"Call," she said, continuing to take off his clothes.

Trying to concentrate, he dialed long distance, asked
for his own home. Finally Martha, the maid answered.
Mrs. Jefferson was in the tub. Get her. In a few moments, Joanne was on the line.

"Jeff?"

"Joie?"

"Where are you?"

"Amarillo. Missed the last plane."

"Probably shacked up in some motel with a waitress!"
she accused.

"Joie!"

By now Doris had undressed him completely. She came
around behind him. He could feel her breasts and the rest
of her warm body pressing into him.

"Don't 'Joie' me! You said you'd be home."

Doris was so close she could hear the entire conversation. When he turned to keep the phone from her, she
moved with him, her body hot and moist against him.

"Why, something wrong?" he asked.

"No, nothing wrong. Just tonight I . . . I wanted to talk
to you." She almost sounded wistful, a young girl again,
as though she really needed him. But he knew that couldn't
be true.

"Well, I'm sorry. I missed the plane!" he said curtly.

Doris was running her long fingernails lightly across his
shoulders, down his chest. He could feel his flesh rise to
them. She came around to face him, staring right into his
eyes, smiling, enjoying completely his harassing and frustrating encounter with Joanne.

"I can just see you chasing that plane down the runway," Joanne was saying, "and not quite catching it!"

"I think you've had a few too many."

"I think *you've* had a few too many! Broads, I mean!"

"Joie!"

Doris was running her thumbnail down his hard, flat gut. When he started to recoil, she took him in her hand. He came erect almost at once. He started to turn, leaning away with the phone pressed against his ear. But she reached out with both hands and brought him back sharply. Then she pressed her face against him, bit him with a sharp, stinging bite just below his navel. It made him cringe. But only momentarily. For now she started to work her way down, with tiny tantalizing bites of her teeth, skillful convolutions of her tongue.

Joanne's voice was there, he could hear it saying something about tonight, about it being somewhat special.

But by that time Doris was at him. He couldn't resist her. Her hands held him too fiercely. Her tongue and mouth continued to work their way down with a practiced finesse that belied her intensity and her strength. Gradually he surrendered himself completely, unaware of anything but her. Till there was nothing in the world but her agile tongue, her moist mouth and the fierce desire in his loins. Then came the sudden explosion within him and the ecstasy that accompanied its release.

When it was over, he slumped forward onto the silk sheets, panting and empty. As he lay there, two things came back to him. Somehow, during it all, he had hung up the phone. And just before doing so, Joanne had said something about a nomination.

Doris slipped down beside him as content as if he had fulfilled her.

Jeff rolled away from her and reached for the phone again. Her hand snaked out to take it from him but he turned swiftly and dialed the operator.

"Person to person, Irwin Cone! Beverly Hills. Crestview 4-2244. If he's not there, find out where he is and get him! Tell him Jeff Jefferson is calling. I'll hold!"

Doris made no effort to intrude now. She reached back and found a cigarette. In the dark room its glow was the only light. Yet her eyes seemed brighter, more piercing. She pulled up her legs, clasping them tight against her breasts like a schoolgirl.

She studied him so intently that now for the first time Jeff was self-conscious about being naked. Then he heard

Cone's voice, calm and professional as always.

"Yes, Jeff? Something wrong?" The Doctor asked gingerly, wondering if Jeff had any inkling about his own fruitless attempt to find him early in the day. It could completely destroy the element of surprise.

"Doctor, I'm here in Amarillo. Missed the last plane. Just talked to Joanne. She got all excited and then hung up on me. But just before she did, she said something about a nomination . . ."

Relieved that his own strategy was still intact, The Doctor was delighted to respond, "Didn't you hear on the radio? Came out this afternoon. She got an Oscar nomination!"

"For *Hills of Silence?*"

"Right! And we think . . . at the office, we think she has one hell of a chance! One hell of a chance!"

"Terrific!" Jeff tried to enthuse, but it was a lousy reading. He knew it. Doris knew it. "I'll call her right back!"

"Right!" The Doctor encouraged. Then making it seem casual, almost inconsequential, he asked, "Be back in town tomorrow, kid?"

"Tomorrow."

"Good. Good," The Doctor said, pretending to seem no more than politely interested. Then just before he hung up, he said casually, "Give me a buzz when you get a minute."

Give him a buzz, Jeff thought. The Doctor never said that to anyone without a reason, yet if there'd been a reason he would have said so. Before Jeff had time to dwell on it, Doris took the receiver from his hand and replaced it.

"Christ, I should have congratulated her at least. . . ."

"About what?"

"She just got nominated."

"*You* just got nominated," Doris corrected.

He turned to her. She reached to pull him down beside her on the bed. But he didn't yield. His attitude, his resentment demanded an explanation. She paused, inhaled, causing her cigarette to glow more brightly and highlight her face and her naked breasts.

"You know what it's going to mean, her winning?" Doris asked.

"She'll be tougher to live with than ever," Jeff said.

"She'll drink more, screw more. Yes, that's right. Regardless of what you see on the screen, that sweet, fine innocent girl whom audiences and critics adore. . . . Man, she can resent me and my playing around . . . but she does her share!"

He hadn't meant to discuss Joanne. Somehow discussing her with another woman was a worse betrayal than committing adultery.

"If I were you, I'd get out now," Doris said simply.

He turned sharply to glare at her, eyes narrow, angry. One of the rare times he lost that all-American-boy look was when his eyes focused that way, expressing deep hostility, suspicion, or fear.

Doris reached out to him, not intending to arouse him this time. She took his hand, held it hard.

"I had my eye on you a long time ago. Long before Cleat died. It made him bearable. In the whole seven years of our marriage, getting laid every night that we were together, I never once came. Not that I let him know. It would have destroyed his image of himself. But I endured all that because of the money.

"And then I would get to thinking, when the money was all mine, what would I do with it? That's when I decided on you."

He looked down at her, trying in the darkness to see if she were serious. As the glow of the cigarette lit up her face he could see that she was. More, she was quite intent on telling him.

"I must have been fourteen the first time I saw you in a picture. It was a small part, but I noticed you. *Sierra Sunset.*"

"Oh, Christ, not that one! I only had two scenes, both bad. I thought I'd never get another part."

"*I* liked you. I kept looking for you after that. Every time I saw your picture in a magazine I'd cut it out. Every time you were in a movie I went to see it. My dates used to hate it. But I didn't care. I would sit there in the theater and let them feel my tits, just so I could watch you. It got to be a joke with the boys. If you wanted to muzzle the hell out of Doris, just take her to a Jeff Jefferson movie. And having the kind of tits I have, you just know I went to lots of movies. All because of you."

She wasn't smiling. She was totally serious.

"Of course, I never thought I had a chance until I met Cleat. I was almost eighteen when we moved here. My father had failed again. He opened and closed more diners than anyone in the West. Then he decided on Amarillo, a boom town—oil, cattle, millionaires. So we moved here, opened the Chuck Wagon. Every lousy greasy spoon in Texas thinks it gets color by calling itself the Chuck Wagon. I was the waitress.

"That's the way I met Cleat Martinson. Just before his wife died. After she died, he would come back at least once a day whenever he was in town, usually on his way to or from the airport where he kept his planes.

"I played it cool. It was 'Good morning, Mr. Martinson' with a nice big smile. Or 'Hi' or 'Good afternoon.' But nothing more. I was waiting for him to make his play. Funny the way he finally did. Never asked me for a date for himself. Said he had a son about my age. That we would make a good couple together. Why didn't I come out to the house of a Sunday. Go riding. Have some lunch. Spend the rest of the day around the pool. Just a nice Sunday for the young folks at the Martinson place.

"Soon as I saw Jackie I said to myself, the old man didn't bring me out here to make any match for his son. I was right.

"It happened when I went into the poolhouse to change. I was stepping out of my wet suit with my bare ass to the door when I heard it open. Then I felt his hands come around, grab my breasts and press me tight. I thought he would come right then and there, he was so hot.

"Pretending as much surprise and hurt as I could, I screamed, 'Mr. Martinson!'

"Then he started talking. Fast. How he'd been crazy about me even before his wife died. How he thought about me, dreamed about me, about my tits, my black hair, my behind, the way it looked in that tight waitress's uniform. He had to have me. Had to. After that it was easy to get him to propose. I had the biggest wedding there'd ever been in the State of Texas. And I wouldn't let him touch me until it was over.

"Afterwards I figure on a per screw basis I got about five hundred and fifty thousand dollars a time. I don't think any woman in the world ever matched that. And I promised myself, for all the sacrifices I'd made, I was going to do something nice for myself."

She sat up in the dark, her eyes level with Jeff's. "You're what I decided I was going to do for myself."

"Just what the hell do you mean by that?" he demanded.

"I wanted you. I wanted you here. I wanted to find out if you were what I used to dream about. You are. Man, you are good. I don't know who taught you. Whether it was your wife, or some other woman, or all the other women. But just one time with you is worth two thousand times of being used by Cleat Martinson.

"Now you can get angry. Or you can just listen. And think. Because you've got a lot to think about. Especially after your wife's nomination. It hasn't been going too well, I know. Even if I didn't do a check on you, I'd know. I could tell when your name showed up on the list of available stars that TCA sent down for the job."

"Job?" he asked, furious.

"What do *you* call it? A 'personal appearance'? We haggled over the price, settled on it. You agreed, you came here, did your act and you'll get paid. Down here, Mister, we call that a job. I suspected you were in trouble when it became tough to get your pictures to screen. I have a standing order with a distributor in Dallas. I get the first print of any Jeff Jefferson film as soon as it arrives. Lately there haven't been any. And your name doesn't show up much in the columns, except as President of the Actors Guild. So I said, they can't be getting along. If she's doing so well and he's slipping, they can't be getting along. Now, with her getting nominated . . ." Doris didn't complete the sentence. She was waiting for him to react.

"So you thought . . . Why you conniving, presumptuous bitch! Who the hell gave you the right to assume that even if I wasn't doing well, I'd . . . just what the hell do you think I am?"

Softly, but with that small, sure smile returning to her face, she said, "Well, you're here, aren't you?"

He had a strong urge to hit her hard across the mouth, beautiful as it was. But she didn't flinch.

"It wouldn't be bad," she continued softly. "Think about

it. And you wouldn't have to worry. About anything. Your career. Your age."

He stared hard at that one, but she stared back.

"We're good together. For looks. For age. In bed. We could grow old together gracefully. Comfortably. I could have what I've always dreamed of. And you could have security. In your business when you get past forty that's a mighty big word."

Her hand reached out to his thigh, moved upward. His first impulse was to evade her. But, more than her money, her sexuality appealed to him. What Joanne rejected, this woman wanted, wanted hungrily. It was good to be wanted. So he yielded, letting her touch him, letting her draw him close until he slipped easily into her again, more easily than the first time.

There was something feverish about the way she made love. Hot, moist, all-encompassing. Was it just with him? Or was she that way with any man who took her fancy? It didn't matter right now. She wanted him. He wanted to be wanted. That was always sufficient justification for sex.

When he awoke, he was alone. He sat up, startled to be in a round, strange bed. Then he saw her across the room, in the red-velvet gown again. She had parted the draperies slightly and was staring out at the dawn. He got out of bed, went to her. Though she was aware of him, she did not turn. He put his arms around her. She seized his hands, held them tight against her breasts. Her large nipples rose and puckered to the touch of his fingers, but she kept staring out.

"I hate Texas. The heat and the dust. The wind and the snow. But I think I will miss the Texas dawns forever."

He realized suddenly that she was speaking as though he was going with her and he stiffened with resistance.

"Think about it," she said, quite secure in her feeling that eventually his decision must favor her. When he didn't answer she said, "Instead of a hustling actor you could be one of the world's most independent gentlemen. You wouldn't have to wait for the telephone to ring. Or scout the trade papers to see what new films are being planned. Or call The Doctor to find out if you're being considered. And later why weren't you considered. None of that anymore. That's something to think about."

She knew she'd scored when she felt his fingers tighten against her breasts. But she knew too that sometimes the worst thing a woman can do is score against a man, especially with the truth.

"That's the best pitch for becoming a gigolo I ever heard," he said.

She turned to face him. "I'm talking about marriage, Mister!"

She was so sincere, so hurt, that he was sorry for what he had said.

"Whatever you call it, it would be the same thing."

"I don't care what you call it, as long as you say yes."

He turned from her, made his way back to the bed in the darkness, found his clothes and was about to get dressed when she said, "There's shaving equipment in the bathroom. Everything you need."

He started toward the bathroom, but she called out, "Not that one." He found a second door, entered and discovered a bath completely equipped and decorated for a man in navy tile with red for relief. The motif was carried out in the towels and the fittings in the medicine chest. He selected a safety razor, lathered up with an expensive, imported, highly perfumed shaving cream, started drawing the razor carefully across his skin.

His eyes were fixed on their reflection in the mirror. The mild, gentle blue which was so disarmingly boyish when he was younger, seemed ineffectual now that he was more mature. Around the eyes, wrinkles were starting, some deep, the beginnings of pouches. There were operations that eliminated pouches like those. And the lines in his face could be lifted away, almost as easily as tightening a violin string. Hair was simple, frequent touch-ups, or a dye job every month or so.

Except that none of those measures lasted. Soon you got to look like a fifty-year-old juvenile, with a stiff handmade face, hair that wasn't blond but a hokey yellow that called the rest of you a liar. The best thing, the ideal thing was to age, as she said, gracefully. Grow into older parts, little by little. He decided that when he got back to L.A. this afternoon, he'd call The Doctor, set up a good long conference away from the TCA office and discuss with him the new, mature approach to Jeff Jefferson's career.

He had reached that conclusion when he was stepping out of the shower. He felt for a towel, but Doris handed it to him. Her hair was up again, not neatly coiffed, but only casually swept up and pinned back. She looked even better that way.

She sat on the ledge of the clothes caddy, her chin resting in her hands. Like a schoolgirl, she admired him as he dried himself.

"You always angry when you take a shower?"

He interrupted toweling to look at her.

"The way you soap up, the way you turn, the way you close your eyes and face up into the spray. Angry. Was it what I said?"

When he tossed the towel onto the rack and looked about for his clothes, she said, "There're fresh shorts in the cabinet."

He looked to the navy blue door where she pointed, opened it, found neatly stacked piles of shorts and silk undershirts on convenient shelves.

"Thirty-two?" she asked.

"How did you know?"

She didn't answer but went to the closet, pulled out first a pair of shorts, then a silk undershirt asking, "Forty-two?" He nodded. She handed them to him.

As he took them, he smiled. "Quite an inventory."

"Not really. Undershirts from forty to forty-six. Shorts from twenty-eight to thirty-six. Any smaller than that, not enough man. Any bigger than that, not worth the trouble. So my men always come in those sizes."

He started to slip into the shorts, noticed the label, *Countess Mara.*

"Shirt?" she asked.

"Sixteen, thirty-four."

She opened the second door of the closet, selected a light blue shirt of fine English broadcloth, checked the size and handed it to him. "My favorite color in men's shirts. And it will look great on you, because of your eyes and your blond hair."

He put it on. It felt as soft and light as silk. He was buttoning the shirt, looking into the mirror. She was right, it was a good color for him. He used the comb and brush to put his damp hair in place, took one last look and was ready to go.

"We'll have breakfast out on the terrace," she said.

"I have to get back," he insisted firmly.

"I suppose you'd rather I didn't fly with you."

"It would be better if you didn't."

"I guess I know the answer now," she admitted. "And the reason. I asked a year before you're ready. Well, I can wait. One thing I want to know, though! It *was* good the two of us? That *could* work, couldn't it?"

"It was better than good. You're great. You would be, even without the money, maybe even greater."

"I'll wait. It may take a year. Maybe a little longer. I can wait."

She started out of the bathroom. He followed, found his slacks and shoes at bedside, slipped into them. Now that the draperies were drawn, he could see a breakfast table had been set up on the balcony against the rail, overlooking the wide, circular driveway. She had indeed planned everything, right down to breakfast with a view.

He was ready to go. She kissed him, not passionately this time, but thankfully, in friendly fashion and with the full expectation of seeing him again. He kissed back strongly, deliberately, because he knew how much it meant to her. It was the least he could do, and it seemed to satisfy and encourage her. Then he started out and down the wide stairs.

It did not trouble him till the plane was passing over the Mojave Desert and starting its descent into Los Angeles—had he kissed Doris back to thank her and let her down easy? Or had he done it to make it easier for himself, less awkward to go back if he and Joanne did break up? Or if no picture showed up? Or if he just grew tired of the endless battle, the frustration, the completely helpless feeling that afflicts actors, especially stars, as they wait between jobs.

Such waiting had a desperate quality. There was no good place for an out-of-work star to go, nothing for him to do, no one for him to associate with. Worst of all, he was completely unprepared for this sudden solitude.

Working on a picture, his every moment used to be planned by others, his director, producer, agent, studio publicity man. A hundred different people were intimately devoted to, involved and intensely interested in everything Jeff Jefferson did.

When he was unemployed, or more politely "between pictures," it was the complete reverse. No one cared, no one gave a damn. Some actors at liberty for long stretches took up hobbies. But that was a fraud, Jeff knew, to give the impression of being industriously devoted to some worthwhile activity, when all the time the only thing of any personal consequence to a star was his next role, his scheduled time to report on the lot in the morning, so he could pull into his own special parking spot, appear for early makeup, all with some apparent resentment for "the old grind." Yet nothing pleased a star more. And, if the truth were told, nothing else pleased a star at all.

Of course, there was always tennis and golf, the two favorite refuges of the unemployed actor who could afford it. Jeff was better than merely good at both. In fact, after he had straightened out his drive, and learned how to make skillful, controlled approach shots, the club pro told him that if he applied himself he might even become a pro himself. His handicap was down to three by that time. And he quit.

He quit because he found the game had become a narcotic, easing his pain and concern about his career. He needed more pain, more discontent, not less. He would have been better off, he told himself, if he were home more, brooding more, perhaps creating or finding ideas for pictures which The Doctor might sell to some studio with Jeff in the starring role.

Once he had even bought a typewriter, harboring the secret hope that he might turn into a writer. Other actors had progressed from acting to directing. Why not to writing? But every plot that he brought to The Doctor reminded the little man of some picture that Jeff had made before. So he gave up writing as he had given up golf.

There were days now when he suffered almost physical agony from sheer lack of activity.

Now that the plane had lost altitude, the desert and the mountains passing swiftly beneath him brought reality back with a disheartening rush. Yes, he admitted to himself, the real reason he had kissed Doris back was to leave the latchstring out.

3

When the limousine dropped him in his own driveway he would not let the chauffeur carry his bag to the door. As the car drew away, sweeping majestically down the circular incline, the door opened to his ring. It was Martha, the large handsome Negro woman who did all their cleaning and cooking, except on party occasions when Joanne hired a great deal of additional help. But in the main, with Martha, the gardeners and the pool man, everything ran smoothly in the Jefferson household.

Jeff put down his bag, crossed the marble floor to the telephone table that stood just off the foyer inside the library. He flipped through the messages. All of them were for Joanne, who had already left for the studio, obviously without looking at her messages of the night before. Too tired, from a long day of shooting. Or what followed after the shooting.

Attempting to appear casual, Jeff asked Martha, "Mrs. Jefferson eat in last night?"

"Must have ate out. Called and said I could leave early," Martha said, lifting Jeff's suitcase.

"Never mind, Martha, I'll do that!" Whatever else she might do for him, he did not like to see her, or any woman, do anything as strenuous as lifting his suitcase or hauling his golf bag. Perhaps it was because he remembered his mother's thin, drawn face when she had to do heavy chores at home, lifting the butter churn or dragging a sack of flour from the storeroom when he was still too young to help. He had a strict sense of what women were supposed to do, and not do.

Besides, to take the bag up and unpack would help him conceal the fact that he was disappointed at receiving no messages.

Martha followed, waiting to take his soiled laundry.

115

Oh, yes, she remembered there had been two calls for him: One, was a secretary who left no message. The other had come when she was in the kitchen so she had left the note on the grocery pad.

Jeff finished putting his rodeo outfit away and tried to seem disinterested about going downstairs. But he headed right for the kitchen. There he found it, written under the grocery list, in Martha's primitive half scrawl. "Mr. Abe Heller say to call. *Imp.*" Imp. was underlined.

No message from anyone at TCA. That meant still no offers, no possibilities to discuss, not even the kind of vague promises which TCA invented to keep important clients on the hook, especially when their agency contracts were due to run out as his soon was.

Of course last evening The Doctor did say something about Jeff giving him a buzz when he got back to town. It might not mean anything, but there was nothing to be lost. So, figuring that anything Abe Heller might have to say could wait, Jeff dialed TCA first. He asked for The Doctor, was put through to Alise who always seemed cheerful and happy to hear his voice.

"Alise, honey, I spoke to The Doctor at home last night. He asked me to give him a buzz today," Jeff said, hoping that with that preamble she would put him right on.

Instead, Alise said in her most fretful voice, "Oh, dear, I *am* sorry, but the Doctor had to fly out early this morning. Some emergency came up in New York with a new dramatic TV series, and he had to meet with the Vice President of S.S.D. & O."

"Oh, well, when he gets back. . . ." Jeff said, trying to make it sound like a trivial bit of mistiming.

But to himself, he accused, Emergency, shit! The bastard knew last night that he'd be on his way to New York this morning! That "give me a buzz" was nothing but pure bullshit!

Actually, this was one time when Jeff judged The Doctor unfairly. For the little man had indeed been summoned to New York to attend to an emergency. But Jeff would never believe that. Not anymore than he believed Alise when she said, "I'll have him get back to you the moment he returns!"

He knew Alise said that to every caller whom The

Doctor was avoiding. He hung up, started to dial again. Now, even a call to Abe Heller was something to help fill the morning.

Abe was executive secretary of the Screen Actors Guild, which meant that he was Jeff's man-of-all-work, as he had been to every Guild president for the last twelve years.

Abe did the real work, made the calls, arranged the agenda for meetings of the Executive Council and for the Annual Membership meeting. He also wrote all the speeches Jeff delivered in his capacity as president. Abe's only weakness was that once a week, he discovered a full-blown crisis. Whenever he did, he left a message of which the last word was always "important" and which Martha always underlined.

"Oy! Am I glad you called!" Abe said as soon as he heard Jeff's voice.

"Trouble?" Jeff asked. "What now?"

"I can't say over the phone."

This was a most unusual response from Abe who was always willing, in fact delighted, to describe any trouble instantly and in its worst aspects.

"Why not, Abe?"

"I'll come right over to see you. Better still, can you meet me at the drive-in on La Cienega and Wilshire? *Dolores*. We have to go to a meeting right after." Then Abe appended the proviso, always demanded by Hollywood etiquette, particularly if one were talking to an unemployed star, "That is, if you're not busy."

Jeff always resented it. But in this case because it did sound like an unusual emergency he swallowed his annoyance and lied, "I'll cancel my lunch date and make it."

"Half an hour?" Abe persisted.

"Half an hour," Jeff agreed.

He arrived at *Dolores Drive-In and Chili Heaven* to find that Abe had already had one cup of coffee, one piece of cheese Danish and was ready for seconds. Jeff could always tell when Abe was nervous: his large bites, his enormous gulps of coffee, the catlike way he licked the sticky syrup of the Danish off his stubby fingers.

"Trouble!" Abe moaned. "Things aren't bad enough, with television, with falling grosses, unemployment, now we got trouble with the government!"

"How can we be in government trouble?" Jeff demanded. "We're no monopoly. We're a guild. A union of employees. So we earn more than other people. But the principle is still the same, as you always keep telling me," Jeff reminded him.

"Not that kind of trouble."

"Then what kind?" Jeff demanded, completely puzzled.

"Red!"

"Oh, that," Jeff said, relieved. "Rumors. That committee is never coming out here."

"Oh, no?" Abe moaned. "Subpoenas are flying around this town like shit in a fertilizer factory! In the last twenty-four hours fourteen writers got pinned. Seven of our members! Some rumors!"

"Who?"

"Eddie Robinson. John Garfield. Frederic March. Florence. Larry Parks . . ."

"Ridiculous!" Jeff responded.

"Ridiculous? When the whole industry secretly flies a big lawyer out from Washington to handle the whole *schmear* it is no longer ridiculous."

More coffee, more Danish, came in answer to Abe's single gesture to the waitress.

"You're right," Jeff said thoughtfully. Then because he felt called on to say it in defense of his own members, he added, "We've got to do something about that!"

"I was waiting for you to come back to town. There's a meeting over at Dalton's house. Started about . . ." Abe consulted his watch. "Started about an hour ago. All the Guild presidents are there. We got to put up a united front! I tell you, it's a *pogrom!*"

There it was, one of those folksy Jewish words that could suddenly make Jeff feel like an intruder. Show business was his business, had been almost all his adult life. Yet the Jews in the industry could always make him feel like a rank outsider with a single word.

Several times he had sat in The Doctor's office when the little man had reverted to Yiddish on the phone while discussing a deal which he didn't want Jeff to understand.

Some actors and writers, as Midwestern and gentile in their origins as Jeff, had made it a practice to add Yiddish expressions to their vocabularies to give them closer kinship with their Jewish colleagues. Many of them had even adopted ethnic dietary habits, serving lox and bagels at Sunday morning brunches, or dropping by at Linny's for hot corned beef or pastrami.

On that score, Jeff had always maintained an integrity of his own, though some called it aloofness.

But this was no time for small personal idiosyncrasies. If the entire industry was under attack, it was a serious matter for them all.

He paid for Abe's Danish and coffee. They left, each in his own car, to join up at Dalton's place in Coldwater Canyon.

Outside the house the street was lined on both sides with Jaguars, Rollses, convertible Caddys, and a few low-slung Italian sports cars. The meeting was already in progress when Jeff and Abe entered. There were more than fifty people, actors, writers, directors, mostly men.

Carl Freidman, president of the Screenwriters Guild, was just finishing speaking. Spotting Jeff, Carl beckoned him down front to take his place along side the president of the Directors Guild.

Once Jeff was seated, Carl concluded,

"I say that this is a fascist-type attack on this community called Hollywood, starting first with the Jews! After they have weeded them out then it will be anyone who does not subscribe to the fascist political line of that damned congressional committee. No, this is not merely a Jewish fight, but an all-industry fight, a screenwriters' fight, an actors' fight. It involves us all!

"So I say, our first order of business is to establish a united front!"

Jeff felt many eyes in the room turn toward him. He rose to speak, not because of any inner compulsion but because he felt it was demanded of him. There were other gentiles here, but none with his official status as a Guild president. He knew he would have to give the appearance of being involved, at the least.

"I want you to know one thing," he began slowly. "My Guild is going to stand behind its members."

There was great applause, shouts of approval, looks of appreciation from the audience.

"God knows, we've had enough trouble in this industry in the last few years. Enough actors going without work. We can't stand a blow like this."

Again, more applause. The encouragement was more militant, less defensive now.

"Of course . . ." and here he sensed a noticeable letdown among his listeners, "as a Guild we have to consult our charter, and our counsel, before I know exactly how far I can go without compromising my office. But within those limitations I can assure you of my entire cooperation and the complete backing of the Screen Actors Guild and its membership!"

This last, conditional as it was, Jeff delivered in the same tone that he usually reserved for his climactic scene in a picture. But the effect was less than he had hoped for. At the end he was greeted not with an ovation, but with polite applause which told him that he had failed again.

His foot off the gas pedal, Jeff was coasting down Coldwater Canyon, following the winding street, braking only rarely, when the sharp downhill curves made his tires squeal.

He was thinking about the meeting, about his own resistance to involvement, his own speech which had started out so strongly and ended up so lamely. Perhaps if the truth be told, and whom could he tell it to better than himself, he had backed off because there was enormous personal risk in becoming involved right now. Sure, he knew that there were Communists around him. How many, he never had attempted to assess. He had a number in his own membership. And they tried from time to time to get resolutions passed to put the Guild on record endorsing one political cause or another. But most times they failed. Some of his scripts had carried too much "message," but it had usually been deleted before shooting. So how many Communists there were, or how effective they were, he did not know. In fact, he hadn't wanted to know.

One thing he did know. With his career in the precarious state it was, self-preservation, not political causes, had to be his prime concern.

As he reached the foot of Beverly he decided that he really should discuss the problem with The Doctor. Instead of turning left and going east on Sunset toward his home, he considered continuing on to Santa Monica and

TCA's large colonial-style mansion.

But he knew that the one thing an actor did *not* do, especially a star, was to drop in on his agent without making an appointment. For it was possible that the agent was not there or, even worse, that he was, but for one reason or another was not available. Waiting around to see an agent damaged a star's standing with receptionists, private secretaries and the entire agency personnel.

The Doctor usually turned away all stars who came in unexpectedly. In fact, Jeff had always joked that in dealing with The Doctor it would be very helpful to have an agent represent him with his agent. He wasn't the first to say it, and as with many jokes, it had a kernel of hard truth in it.

So, after hesitating until impatient drivers behind him began honking their horns, Jeff flipped on his directional signal, turned left and headed back toward his house.

He parked the car and went inside. After checking that there had been no calls while he was gone, he went out back to lie near the pool and catch the fading sun while he pondered the entire situation concerning committees, investigations, Guilds and the wisest course for him to follow.

He was still at poolside when the sound of Joanne's car told him she was finally home from the studio. He got up quickly to greet her, especially to congratulate her on her Oscar nomination. Whatever their disagreements, their personal frictions, he owed her that much. An actress isn't nominated for an Oscar often, most of them not even once in a lifetime. Look at himself, always good, steady, reliable, always giving them a solid Jeff Jefferson performance yet he had never received a nomination, not even for his great amputation scene in *End of Glory*. Though the director had told him after the take: "Jeff-sweetie, that's the Oscar! Right there in that one scene! I'll stake my career on it!"

Nevertheless, Joanne had received a nomination and worked hard for it. And last night he should have listened long enough to hear her news and congratulate her, regardless of what happened afterwards between him and Doris. Well, he would greet her now and make up for it.

As he came through the fence gate between the pool

area and the garage he heard her brake the car suddenly. Then she backed up, went forward again, moving into the garage. He could see now that she'd parked badly, too close to the left wall, so that she would have to slide over to get out on the passenger side. As she did, her door nicked the paint of his spotless Caddy. But he said nothing.

She turned to find herself pinned between her open door and his car. When she caught sight of him, her face became tense and angry.

"Oh, shit! Do you have to come out and spy on me every time I park the car! I am *not* drunk!"

He knew that line well. He could play back the whole scene. She'd had a few drinks at the studio with her leading man and her director to relax her after shooting. After that, maybe a little screwing around with her director, Gary. Jeff had never had any definite proof of it. He had not even heard a strong rumor in a city that existed on rumors, confirmed or otherwise. Still he suspected. No, actually he knew. The less frequent their own lovemaking, the more he knew. But there'd been no proof. Thus far.

One thing he had learned, though, was not to provoke her when she was in this condition, not in restaurants, at parties or out in the open driveway where all of Beverly Hills could hear. As she became more successful she became more vocal, more given to rages which were liberally endowed with words quite foreign to her sweet-young-girl image. If she didn't look so innocent perhaps he would have minded her coarse language less.

He held the gate open to let her slip through. As she passed him he could smell very strong perfume, and even stronger gin. Of the two, the perfume was more disturbing. Once she entered the pool area, he let the gate close and moved back to the garage. Before he could even inspect for damage, he heard her call out, "I did not bruise your fucking precious Cadillac!"

He turned to find her glaring at him over the fence. Instead of remonstrating with her, he said softly, "I want to apologize about last night. I never did give you a chance to tell me about the nomination. I'm happy. Very happy."

"I'll bet!" she said, contemptuously implying that he was jealous. She turned, went into the house. He could hear her give Martha a great, warm, and affectionate hello.

By the time he entered, she was upstairs. He could hear her tub running. That was usual, working or nervous tension made her perspire profusely, and what an odor she gave off. She was slamming closet doors and moving clothes hangers violently in her slacks and sweater closet.

That was a bad sign. When she was trying to be as virginal as a nun with him she always signaled it, intentionally or otherwise, by wearing slacks and a sweater. Very homey, very informal, very nice for having her picture taken for a fan magazine or *House and Garden*, but also very keep-your-horny-hands-off-me-tonight. Something must have happened after shooting at the studio this afternoon. He was sure because of the gin and especially all that perfume to cover up her body smell. Maybe she was so steamed about his not saying anything about her nomination that she deliberately screwed Gary to get even with him. Sweet, innocent, lovely, blond girl-next-door Joanne West Jefferson was capable of exactly that.

Someday, he threatened silently, someday he would just chance by the studio at the end of shooting and confront her. But in his heart he knew he never would. First, because unemployed stars did not go to a studio during the working day unless it was to discuss an important part in an important picture.

The other reason he wouldn't spy on her was because that kind of confrontation, if it did happen, would have been too painful for him. He despised her drinking and her screwing, but in his way he loved her. And because he did, it was necessary to keep up the pretense of the happily married Hollywood couple, the exception to the commonly accepted canard that all Hollywood marriages end badly.

Seven years ago when he and Joanne had married, they went home together, back to Iowa. The studio had arranged for photographers to be waiting because it was good publicity, good for his image as the all-American boy, and for her image as the girl next door. They had had to pose incessantly in the hatchway of the plane, on the steps of the gangway, and then with his mother and father. Jeff figured by actual count that his mother kissed him more times that one day than she had in all his life before that.

Though she seemed skeptical of Joanne at first, as she would have been about any girl who was an actress, she accepted her before the four long somber days of their visit were over. On the afternoon of the third day, Jeff went out into the barn to help his mother gather the eggs. Without interrupting her work, she said, "That's a nice girl, Jeff. Sweet. Be good to her." He nodded. He had never intended to be anything but good to her. Then his mother had added, "And don't force her."

When he stared at his mother, she avoided his eyes by searching more diligently for eggs among the chicken roosts.

"There's times a woman doesn't have the feeling. A woman is no cow. She can't be mounted and mated just because someone else is in heat. That's why you had no brothers and sisters. I tried. I just couldn't bring myself. So don't force her."

She didn't wish an answer, or wait for one. She just swung her basket over her arm, started back to the house. The subject was never mentioned again, not when his father died two years later or the few times he went back to visit her, alone. Both times Joanne was working, and he was between pictures. By that time Joanne had begun to drink and he didn't like to discuss her with his mother, beyond her asking, "How is dear Joannie?" and his replying, "She's fine, Ma. Fine. Sent you her love."

He was relieved that his mother was dead, that she did not live to see Joanne eclipse him in his career, or to see their marriage end up this way. Although it would not have surprised or distressed her too much, he was sure. Marriages, as long as they did not erupt in public scandal, were not intended to be happy.

They did not have dinner together that night. Joanne claimed to be too tired. She had Martha bring a tray up to the bedroom. He was relieved to eat alone, in the informal dinette that looked out on the pool. He had much thinking to do. The situation that had presented itself today was serious, the congressional investigation posed a threat of great dimensions, not only to those accused, but to himself if he took a strong stand on the wrong side. In arguments with Joanne, or in discussions with The Doctor or Buddy Black, he could make much of his career and his standing in the industry. But to himself, alone, he could not pretend. He was a star, but not a great star. He didn't have the depth of Tracy, not the eloquent and empathetic warmth of Cooper, to whom people the world over responded with such loyalty and devotion. He was not the male sex symbol Gable was. Nor was he a consummate actor, certainly not Ronald Colman, by a long shot.

At his best he was a pretty fair actor, a good Western hero or football player type. But his kind of picture had become less and less popular in recent years.

The more he contemplated his standing and his chances the more he realized the bitter wisdom of one of The Doctor's sayings: "When stars die, they die fast and forever." Like John Gilbert whose career ended in just three months, between the advent of talkies and the day the studio heads decided that Gilbert could never talk well enough to match his visual image. True, they paid him his fantastic salary for two more years, ten thousand dollars a week, but they never let him make another foot of film.

For second rank stars death came somewhat more slowly, as it was coming to Jeff. Few calls, fewer parts, no scripts delivered to the house by anxious producers, directors or writers for him to read and "consider."

What to do? What to do when you are lying out back at your own pool, behind your own house that is worth a hundred thousand dollars and costs almost a thousand a week to keep up? What to do when your price used to be three hundred thousand a picture and has been cut to a hundred and fifty thousand and still no offers? What to do when your wife is nominated for an Oscar and you can't even get a part?"

Doris Martinson had said only this morning, "I guess I asked a year too soon."

Alone, Jeff could say to himself, "Or did she ask a year too late?"

It would have been far easier and more graceful to quit near his peak than to admit defeat now. Yes, defeat. Failure. The thought shriveled his stomach, tightened his scrotum.

4

It was the end of The Doctor's office day, and he had only one chore left to do. He pressed down the button on his intercom.

"Alise . . ."

"Yes, sir!" She was always as fresh and bright at six o'clock as she had been at nine. But when The Doctor instructed her to phone Jeff, and set an appointment with him for ten the next morning at the Jefferson house, her enthusiasm suddenly ebbed. She repeated a bit anxiously, "At the Jefferson house, Doctor?"

"Yes, at the Jefferson house."

She sounded sad as she said, "Yes, sir." Because, unaware of The Doctor's mission, she assumed that there could be only one reason why he would make a personal journey to Jeff's home: to tell Jeff, as gently as he could, that TCA wished to be relieved of the burden of representing him. Agents did that. And it was a development to be feared if one was a middling star and hadn't worked in some time.

She called Jeff and asked if he would be available for a meeting at ten next morning with The Doctor. Jeff's first response was a hearty, "Yes, yes. I'll be free," assuming that TCA had finally come up with a deal for him, a good deal, if The Doctor himself wanted to discuss it. He was suddenly deflated when he heard Alise say, "Very good, sir. Doctor Cone will be there at ten, then."

"Here?"

"Yes, sir," she answered, trying to shield him from the obvious hurt by giving the phrase a swift, casual reading.

"Okay . . ." Jeff said, suspecting as Alise had that The Doctor was coming with termination news. Now he was sure. Doris Martinson *had* asked a year too late.

Next morning when The Doctor arrived, Jeff invited him out to the patio. But The Doctor suggested softly, "No, Jeff, a quieter place, more confidential."

Jeff felt a sudden stab of abdominal pain which was nothing less than fear. For an instant it even crossed his mind that somehow Joanne was involved. That she knew and she had given her permission for TCA to drop him. Joanne was capable of that.

They went into the library. Rejecting all offers of alcohol, The Doctor perched forward in his chair, holding himself erect, his glasses riding authoritatively on his nose.

"Jeff, when I ask you what I'm going to ask, you have a perfect right to get up, show me the door, even boot me in the ass if I'm slow getting through it."

With that opening Jeff relaxed a bit. For some reason Jeff couldn't understand, The Doctor was requesting a favor.

"Jeff, what I'm asking I'm not asking on my own behalf. Or for TCA. This is on behalf of the whole industry. To which, and I say this as your agent, to which you owe not a fucking thing!"

It was not like The Doctor to resort to such language except to indicate intense feelings of outrage, anger, desperation or frustration. And, then, only in critical moments of bargaining, when he wished to indicate to the other side that he was thinking of breaking off negotiations. He would signal his personal outrage by resorting to vulgarities and his opponent would know that The Doctor was genuinely angry or hurt. Thereafter the opponent usually backed off and The Doctor made the deal his way. So now, Jeff knew that what The Doctor wished to discuss was truly of enormous importance. Having signaled that, having been assured that his signal had been received, The Doctor felt free to broach the business at hand.

"I don't have to tell you about what's happened in this town since you went to Austin."

"Amarillo," Jeff corrected.

"Oh, yes, of course, Amarillo. By the way, how did it go there?"

"Okay. Another rodeo, another personal appearance."

There was a rebuke in Jeff's tone.

"They certainly wanted you badly. Soon as Buddy indicated that the usual five thousand might not be enough, they came right back with an offer of ten."

That tripped a little register in Jeff's mind. The high price, better than he'd received before, that must have been Doris Martinson. She probably put up the extra five thousand herself. But Jeff said nothing, nor did he relax his thoughtful pose.

"What I'm saying is, this industry which has made it necessary for you to go out on those personal appearances you hate, this industry has sent me hat in hand to ask you a big favor."

The Doctor paused, expecting that Jeff would respond. But he didn't, just sat there, quietly waiting.

"In the last few days a congressional committee has indicated they are ready to blow this town wide open. I understand they have names, dates of meetings, contributions. And they are going to smear us all with a big broad Red brush.

"Now, true, you are the president of the Screen Actors Guild and you have a certain duty to your members. But the duty I am going to ask you to assume is greater than that. The studios want you to represent the entire industry at the congressional hearings!"

The Doctor made the statement with the same vigor and enthusiasm with which one presents an Academy Award. He fully expected from Jeff the same fumbling, surprised, hokey kind of shit-kicking acceptance. Instead, Jeff sat there, waiting to hear more before he committed himself.

The Doctor rose and began pacing the Spanish-tile floor, his built-up leather heels clicking with staccato military sharpness.

"There's a lot to be said for heading that committee. The photographs alone would be worth it. Just picture coming up the steps to the hearing. John Huston, Gregory Peck, Greer Garson, Billy Wilder, Errol Flynn, Humphrey Bogart, Spence, Coop, and then you, Chairman of the Talent Committee of the entire industry. It would do wonders for your image."

The Doctor lowered his voice somewhat and sounded more fatherly now. "And it would help in another way,

Jeff. It would put the industry in your debt forever. Producers and studio heads, who have been acting like the lice they are, would be coming up with pictures and parts that really fit your talent. They all know about our meeting this morning. In fact, right now, they're all waiting, more than a little anxious about what you're going to say to me."

There it was, the threat, just as Jeff had expected from The Doctor at this stage of the game. So they were waiting for his reply, with either undying gratitude if he said yes, or unending resentment if he said no.

Having issued his threat, The Doctor could now dwell on the altruistic reasons which would make it possible for Jeff to say yes gracefully.

"Of course, Jeff, there is one thing bigger than any man's career right now. The industry. With television giving away entertainment, with employment down, productions down, this investigation could be the death blow. Even if you decided never to make another picture again, I don't think you'd want to see this industry close its doors forever. Not an industry that's been as good to you as this one has."

He made a small, discreet, but very expressive gesture indicating that this elegant room, this great house, and everything in it testified to what Jeff owed to the picture business.

"Now, the studio heads do not intend to let you go unprotected. And I don't just mean the committee that escorts you to the hearings. I mean we have retained the very best counsel available. He will be with you every moment, throughout your interviews, speeches, or testimony, if that's what it takes. Though I doubt that.

"Mainly, you will just be lending your presence to exemplify the kind of fine decent people who make up this industry. And you will be the focus of more publicity than you've ever had on any picture."

The Doctor paused to let that sink in. Then he added, "You could become the most important actor in America in the space of a few weeks! Now, if you don't want to answer the big question today, I can understand that. But at least do yourself the favor of talking with Lee Mandell. . . ."

At the mention of Mandell's name, Jeff looked up

sharply, revealing more than he had intended of how impressed he was.

"Yes, Lee Mandell. I told you, you would be advised by the best. He's at the Beverly Hills. Waiting for your call. He asked for you himself. Out of all the actors in Hollywood, he asked for *you*."

The Doctor paused before he said softly, "I leave it up to you, Jeff." He held out his hand, something he was always loath to do. For the first time since he'd been represented by TCA, Jeff Jefferson was privileged to shake it.

The Doctor was gone. The house was empty, or seemed to be, since Martha was in the kitchen preparing dinner and might as well have been in the next house or the next county so silent and removed was she.

Jeff turned to drop into his big leather chair again, but instead decided to go out to the pool. He pushed back the huge glass door, crossed the lanai and stepped out into the pool area. The warmth of the day was giving way to evening. The water of the pool, blue because the concrete was painted blue, rippled slightly from the force of the circulator. For the rest nothing moved.

He lay down on one of the chaises to think it all out. The most significant fact was The Doctor's personal interest. True, there were a number of TCA clients involved, and the little man might be seeking to protect his own interests by protecting theirs. But his eagerness seemed to signify more. Perhaps what he said was true, it was an industry-wide crisis. They had picked Jeff, partly because he was president of Actors Guild, of course, but there must have been other reasons as well.

Not the least of those could be that if a sacrificial lamb was needed, Jeff Jefferson was more expendable than Coop, Tracy, or any of the other names The Doctor had mentioned. Maybe that's all they needed, one Christian to throw to the lions, while the rest escaped.

When engaged in crisis situations Jeff often found his thoughts reverting to his mother's religious images. Sacrificial lambs, Christians and lions were one thing. The realities were another. There was a core of truth in one thing The Doctor had said. If Jeff carried it off it could mean a whole new career. If he failed, his failure would be only little more complete and final than it was right now.

Certainly he risked very little by calling Lee Mandell. He reached for the poolside phone, dialed Crestview 6-2251. When the hotel answered he asked for Mandell, was connected with his bungalow. He introduced himself. The lawyer was most anxious to get together and they arranged a meeting at Mandell's bungalow for breakfast.

The next morning Jeff was greeted by pipe-smoking, open-shirted Lee Mandell who clasped Jeff's hand with a surprisingly strong grip. Mandell offered him a chair, thrust a menu at him. "Order up!" Jeff settled for coffee, toast and orange juice. When Mandell got on the phone to order breakfast Jeff discovered that the man, for all his bulk, ate little. Just coffee, lots of it.

As he hung up Mandell said, "People eat too goddamned much! In a world full of starving people, overeating kills more Americans than anything else. How does that strike your sense of justice?"

Jeff didn't comment, just smiled. Mandell turned on him, seemed about to growl but then relented and said, "That was a ploy. I wanted to see if you'd launch into a nice liberal tirade against the injustices of this world."

Without waiting for any reaction, Mandell went on.

"A fascinating state you have here. You are first in the nation in the production of wine, lemons and avocados. By a wide margin! You also lead the nation in the production of one other commodity—*shmucks!* Now, mind you, I don't condemn all *shmucks.* I feel sorry for them. I feel sorry for any victim.

"It must be my Jewishness. Because you'll notice that when gentiles play this genital game they choose the word prick. What does that word connote? A prick is mean, nasty, aggressive. On the other hand take the Jewish word *shmuck.* Referring to precisely the same part of the male anatomy. What does *shmuck* signify? Foolish, susceptible, an eternal victim. Perhaps because of our long sad history, we think first about the victims.

"Now as it relates to the case in hand, we have both species. The pricks are the hard-core Communists. You have some of those here. But the *shmucks,* oh, you have a bumper crop of those. Well, I have to protect them from the consequences of their own stupidity. And you have to help me.

"So it is very important that we understand each other

completely. Because you and I . . ." and he looked straight into Jeff's eyes, leaning halfway out of his chair to do so, "you and I hold this whole damn city, this whole *meshuganeh* industry right in the palms of our hands." Palm upward, he held out his thick hand, the fingers of which were not only stubby and thick but bore testimony to numerous injuries.

Mandell seemed conscious of them suddenly, held up his right hand to exhibit two healed breaks, on the thumb and the middle finger. "Blocked punts. Both of them. Played tackle at CCNY. You?"

"End," Jeff said, wondering if Mandell knew or if he was making a blind stab.

"Iowa State?" the lawyer asked, confirming that he knew quite a bit about Jeff's background and was only pretending to be vague.

"No. Iowa Southern."

"And then?"

"Became a sports announcer, doing the college games. Then the Tri-State League baseball games. Until I got interested in pictures and decided to come out and take a chance here."

"And became a star," Mandell said, nodding in a gesture that Jeff took to be admiration. "Maybe if I didn't go to Law School I could have become Edward G. Robinson." Mandell laughed. There was a knock on the door. He rose to admit the waiter with their breakfast.

Over coffee Mandell asked suddenly, "Do you know why so many people out here permit themselves to be *shmucks?*" When Jeff did not answer at once, Mandell persisted. "Do you at least have a theory?"

"I think it's the money," Jeff said finally. "There's more money made here than almost anywhere else in the world. And by people who never really expected to make it. People who don't even feel they're entitled to it. That sets up feelings of guilt. They want to share, they want to help. They feel responsible for the less fortunate."

"You feel that way, too?"

"I guess so," Jeff said finally.

"A thing like that you don't know? You just 'guess'?" Mandell asked, a bit more sharply.

"Yes, I feel that way."

"Okay, then." Suddenly Mandell launched into an explanation. "Look, Jefferson, let's get one thing straight. I don't necessarily want you to testify. I want you on my team as a symbol, a fine, clean-cut American symbol. You've heard about guilt by association? Well, I want innocence by association. From you.

"However, *my* decision about your testifying may not be the controlling factor. The committee might serve you with a subpoena while you're sitting alongside me. So I have to prepare you as I would if I were intending to use you as a witness. Clear?"

Jeff nodded, more uncertain now that he knew the committee could take the matter out of Mandell's hands.

"The point I am making is this: If you *should* have to testify, never 'guess,' never 'reckon,' never say 'possibly.' "You know or you don't know. And there's no crime in either. As long as you're definite."

Mandell started to pace, and Jeff forgot his toast and coffee. He followed the man closely, though Mandell was unaware that he was being stared at.

"A man who 'guesses so' or 'reckons' is a man who seems to be covering up. And there is nothing that some headline-hungry congressman likes better than running off a dozen tricky questions against someone who isn't a professional witness. He will take your 'guess so' and turn it into an evasion. He'll make you look like a liar. He'll disparage the rest of your testimony by tripping you up on one little inconsequential expression."

Mandell turned on Jeff. "After all, what did I ask you? Did you have a theory about something? There's nothing wrong in having a theory about anything. Or *not* having a theory. So if you have one, say yes! And if you don't, say no. That's that and can't be subject to attack!"

Mandell started to relight his pipe; over the lit match he asked, "Unless, of course, there is some area in which you *are* subject to attack. And if you are, *tell me now!*"

Jeff thought a moment, wondering whether to mention the various affairs he'd had in the past two years. While he was pondering, Mandell asked, "Okay. What are you thinking about?"

"When you say 'anything' what does that mean?"

Mandell smiled and said, "I don't think they're going to

ask you who you're screwing this week. Or last week. Or last month. Though a couple of those horny Southern Baptists might, just for headline value."

"And suppose I do testify and they *do* ask?"

"Why I expect you to become indignant! To consider it a slur on you, on your wife, and on the whole home-loving Hollywood community. It is a mere extension of the slander under which all Hollywood people are forced to live, the belief that they are sexually loose and depraved."

"You expect me to say all that?" Jeff asked.

"No, *I'm* going to say all that for you. You are just going to look so goddamned righteous and hurt that the rest of the committee will feel ashamed of the member who asked."

"And after you finish, then what?"

"*Before* I say that, I am going to know in detail if any committee members who come out here have been screwing around with any young starlets themselves."

"You mean that you're going to . . ."

Swiftly, angrily, Mandell said, "No, I'm not! But if they are received out here by the studios in the same way I was received, with every 'courtesy' extended to them, they'll get their share of offers and temptations. And one of them, or all of them, may possibly fall into bed with some pretty young piece of ass. *When* they do, *if* they do, I'll want to know about it. But not one second before. I have my ethics. I'll take every edge I can legally get, but I won't frame anyone. Any more questions?"

Jeff shook his head, impressed by the chunky man who peered over his pipe with eyes strong and sharply focused. Mandell paused a moment, then launched into the more delicate phase of his explanation.

"Now, I want *you* to do the talking."

"About what?" Jeff asked.

"About you. About what you think, what you believe. What are your views, politically, socially? Not that they'll ask, but if you have the right answers it might be good to volunteer."

"You think it'd help to say I'm a Democrat?"

"For this purpose Republican would be better. Now are you a New Deal Democrat? A Roosevelt-Truman man?"

"Yes."

"Why?"

"You said they weren't going to ask me questions like that."

"*I'm* asking!" Mandell said.

"It really has nothing to do with his . . ."

"I'd like to know!" Mandell persisted.

"Okay," Jeff said, but he hesitated before beginning. "I come from a little town in northeastern Iowa. I was in my second year of college when the worst of the Depression hit the farming country. Banks were foreclosing mortgages. Then the banks themselves were closing down, leaving everyone hung without enough cash to buy feed, or even flour to bake bread. Of course, there was no money for tuition, so I had to come home, hitching my way.

"The day I got home was one of those gray Iowa days, low, thick, heavy clouds, a strong wind blowing. When the truck I had hitched dropped me off, I started walking up toward the house. I could see my father outside the barn on the old tractor. Just sitting there, like a statue. His eyes were open but he wasn't seeing me or anything. He was the most defeated man I ever saw in my life. He looked as if his time was over but he hadn't yet learned how to die.

"He said nothing. Nor did I. I just walked on toward the house. It looked grayer than I ever remember it looking. I stepped up onto the porch. I heard Ma call out, 'Jeff?' She always knew my step by the creak of the porch boards. I went inside. She was sitting there in the kitchen, the room cold and dark. It was strange not to find something boiling on the stove, even if it was just coffee.

" 'Did you see him?' she asked me. I nodded. 'He just give up. Soon as we heard the word about the bank. And how there'd be no loan for seed corn this year, he just give up. I said, "Let's use the last of the savings." But he wouldn't. Said it was for your education. His son wasn't going to be no ignorant dirt-farmer. He was going to be a college-educated man, who'd know how to compete with the cooperatives. So he wouldn't touch the tuition money even for seed.' She shook her head.

"And I had to say, 'That's why I'm home, Ma. The tuition money never got to me.' She turned to look up into my face, that small thin little woman, and she said,

'Course not. The bank closed. People say it'll never open up again.'

" 'And all the money? The two thousand dollars?' "

" 'Fourteen hundred. All gone. Just gone. When he heard, he went out there, walking the fields, then sat there on the old tractor and never said a word. And I . . . I just been waiting. What for, I don't know. But waiting. Now that you're here, I do know. We're going down to that bank. We're going to get that money out!'

" 'How, Ma?' I asked her.

" 'We're just going to get it out!' she said. She rose up and seemed about a foot taller than she was, took my hand as she used to when I was just a kid and she was taking me off to church of a Sunday. We started out of that cold, gray house.

"We passed him but he never saw us. We reached the barn, she got into the passenger seat of the old Model A and I climbed in behind the wheel. As we drove out I noticed the gas gauge was way down. I made it to the road, turned right and started toward town. That gas needle kept flickering between empty and hopeful. Just outside of town we came to Parker's garage and filling station. I pulled in.

"Parker was standing outside, between the two pumps. It struck me he wasn't smiling. It looked as if he were standing guard rather than welcoming customers. When I pulled up and said, 'Hi, Mr. Parker,' he gave me a grudging, wary kind of 'Hi,' and waited. 'Fill it up,' I said. He stared at me, then at Ma, then back at me and asked, 'Got the money?' I turned to Ma but she didn't say a word. Her mouth was just pursed tight, deep little lines running from her lips like dried-out streams in dead summer. So I reached into my pocket, found nineteen cents, and handed it over. Parker pumped out a gallon of gas, and not one drop more. As I started up the motor again, he came round to my side, and said, 'The Company won't leave any, 'less I pay cash for every drop.' Not a word about being sorry to treat old friends that way. But we knew.

"I drove into town. Still having no idea of what Ma intended to do. The main street was crowded with people for a weekday. They stood around in little knots of fives and sixes. The men smoked burned-down cigarettes, the women, most of them, watched their kids and tried to keep them from fighting or crying just as they would at a funeral.

"I kept saying to myself, this is the grayest sky and the grayest day I can ever remember. It was getting real cold because it was late afternoon by now. I turned to Ma and asked, 'What are we going to do?'

" 'Drive to the bank!'

" 'What good'll it do?'

" 'Just drive to the bank!'

"So I did. The crowd was bigger there. I parked the car and we got out. We moved into the crowd, pressed up close against the bank window trying to see in. There were more than a few men inside. I recognized some, the Sheriff, Mayor Christensen, a few others, like Dr. Brainard. But it was dark in there. And with everyone blocking the view, it was hard to see anything.

"Ma said to those around, 'How long we going to stand outside and wait? If he don't want to lend us seed money that's one thing! But we got our own money in there. Let's get it!' Nobody moved and Ma drew herself up and said, 'When it comes to demanding my own I'm not going to be like all you men, helpless and silent. I don't know about any of you, but I'm demanding mine!' Her voice was very shrill. I knew she was going to yell or cry, one or the other.

"Then Old Bridger, the hardware man, said, 'Min, ain't you heard? He put a thirty-thirty in his mouth and pulled the trigger.'

" 'Who?' she asked.

" 'Henry. Henry Thorne. When he couldn't open the bank he just . . .'

She gasped, a sucked-in painful breath. Then she did start to cry. Whether she was crying for Henry Thorne, or for all the rest of us waiting out there in the gray and the cold I never knew. I took her hand, led her back to the car. We drove all the way home without a word.

"When we got back to the farm, I turned off the paved road onto the dirt. It was so dark I could barely make out the tractor. But I knew Pa wasn't sitting there anymore. She knew it too. I could tell by the way her body stiffened. She and I both had the same thought. I speeded up, pulled up at the tractor and got out calling, 'Pa! Pa!' There was no answer. So I jumped out of the car and raced for the barn. I don't know why the barn, except that far back in my mind somehow I knew if he was going to do something it wouldn't be in her very clean house but out here.

"Calling, 'Pa! Pa!' I made it to the barn. There I found him. I don't know what he was doing before I shouted, but by the time I got there he was pitching some hay into the stalls for the two work horses. I felt better, much better. Until I turned to leave. Then I saw it, his double barrel hunting gun standing in the corner, muzzle up. I couldn't help it. I turned from it to stare at him. He noticed, but just pitched more hay over into the stalls. When he thought it was enough, he quit, carried the pitchfork to the corner, leaned it there, and took up the gun saying, 'Things being what they are, thought I would try to get us a few pheasant for supper.'

"He started out, loading shells as he went. I never asked, he never said, if that was what he'd really had in mind. Or whether we had got back just in time to stop him from doing something else. But from that time on he was like a man who had survived a long bad illness. He recovered. But he was never the same again.

"Before he died, things got better. The bank reopened. People gradually collected their money. Confidence began to return. The government began to take an interest in farmers. Pa made it back. He was never rich, never even well-to-do, but he came back to better than he was. And that was good, because he didn't live much longer. And it is no good for a man to die on the heels of failure. A man should die going up, not coming down."

Mandell was silent after Jeff finished. He had heard more than he bargained for. And Jeff had said far more than he had ever intended.

"I never told that to anyone before," he said apologetically and Mandell realized that Jeff's story had revealed as much about himself now as about his father long ago.

"Your mother, she still alive?"

"No. Gone. Four years now."

Mandell thought a moment, then asked suddenly, "So

that's why you became a Democrat? A New Deal Democrat?"

"That's why."

Mandell lit another match, held it over his pipe. Looking just beyond the flame, he asked, "Can you understand then, why some people became Communists?"

"*I* didn't become one, and it happened to me," Jeff countered.

"How do you know if you wouldn't have under that kind of pressure, if someone had made the right approach to you at the right time? How do you know?"

"I *don't* know," Jeff countered. "But is it so important what I think?"

"I want you to be aware of one thing, Jefferson. Each man has his own wounds. His own scars. And chooses his own medicine. And if he doesn't choose the same way you do, or I do, that shouldn't condemn him," Mandell said looking very concerned.

Which caused Jeff to ask, "What do you expect is going to come out at those hearings?"

"Nothing," Mandell said, then amended it quickly. "Nothing, if I can help it."

"*Can* you help it?"

"There's a Constitution. And a Fifth Amendment that keeps a man from incriminating himself in a possible criminal case. That'll be enough to go on. Of course, what the public will do to people who won't talk I can't guarantee. But then I'm a lawyer, not a public relations man. Jefferson, I will be depending on you. Depending on you very heavily. I hope you decide to do it."

Mandell held out his hand. They shook. Jeff left the bungalow and started down the red-concrete, shrub-lined walk of the Beverly Hills Hotel, past fat-trunked tamarisks and tall, slender palms. When Mandell was sure Jeff was out of hearing, he picked up the phone and asked the operator for Dr. Irwin Cone.

She rang back when The Doctor was on the line.

"Cone? Mandell. I just finished with your client Jefferson. He'll do fine. *If* I can rely on him."

"You can rely on him."

"Few things I have to know. Does he drink much?"

"No. He keeps in good condition."

"Does he screw around?"

"A man is not made from wood," The Doctor quoted from the old Yiddish joke.

"I mean dangerous screwing. Such as other men's wives? Or very, very young girls? Or . . . or boys? I'm not judging. But I have to know."

"Just women. All over jail-bait age."

"Good. Because in all other respects he is fine. Good American boy, from a farm in Iowa. Nice looking. Well-spoken, if he has to speak. Every mother would want him for a son. Of course, in a strange way, what's best about him is that he's nondescript. Handsome but nondescript. He's nobody, so he can be anybody."

"Is that bad for an actor, who spends his life being somebody else?" The Doctor asked.

"I didn't say it was bad. I said it was good. Yes, he can be anybody. And for us he's going to be Mr. America U.S.A."

"Thank God, there's *some* value in being blond," The Doctor said.

"What do you mean?"

"For a leading man, blond is a curse. They don't register. And with blue eyes it's even worse. They wash out on film. No big leading man has ever made it being blond. Juveniles, some. But a real big star, like Bogart, Gable, Powell, Gilbert, must be dark!"

"Is that why he never really made it big?"

"I think so," The Doctor said sadly.

"Interesting," Mandell said. "I wonder what Negroes would say about that? Anyhow for what I want, blond and blue-eyed couldn't be improved on!"

"Right!" And The Doctor hung up.

5

Lee Mandell was also right about one other thing. The industry turned itself inside out to welcome, entertain and host the congressional committee. It almost created the impression that to be investigated was an honor rather than a dread threat that kept many Beverly Hills residents up through the nights wondering what to say if asked, or what not to say, or whether even to appear if subpoenaed.

By the time the day arrived for the opening of the hearings, Mandell was completely prepared, which meant that he knew the strengths of his case. And the weaknesses. He knew which of the subpoenaed stars and writers and directors were Communists and which weren't. Which had been and no longer were. He also knew which ones had been advised, mainly by himself, to reply on their constitutional right to remain silent.

The danger in asserting constitutional rights was that the public at large, as well as those immediately involved in the proceedings, always assumed that only a guilty person would take refuge in such rights. Most of the high brass at the studios felt that way too, only more so, for they were paying out two, three, five thousand dollars a week to writers, directors and actors who were going to besmirch the entire industry and blacken its product by refusing to tell all.

This dissatisfaction reached such proportions that a special meeting had to be called at which Lee Mandell and Irwin Cone tried to explain and mollify the executives. But the prevalent feeling was expressed by an executive from Fox, "Suspicions can do us more harm than the truth. After all, what is the worst that could come out— that twenty, thirty, forty, a hundred guys were Communists? Good! Let's have it out in the open! Then let's

141

get rid of those bastards and prove to the world that the industry itself is clean again. It's certainly better than letting the whole country think we're all deliberately harboring Communists!"

The logic was so powerful that it almost stampeded the meeting and there was the imminent possibility that on the very eve of the first hearing Lee Mandell might lose control of the situation and his meticulously prepared strategy might disintegrate at the last moment. It was not the first time that on the eve of trial his client's emotions had led to such a crisis.

It was fortunate for him that The Doctor was present. For Cone stood up, and by that simple action brought the entire meeting to a sudden expectant silence. Relieved, Mandell could smile to himself at such a simple but complete exercise in total power.

"All right! All right, gentlemen!" The Doctor began. "Let's discuss 'telling them the truth.' Let's have an old-time revival meeting. Right here and now! Let's have everybody confess in public. I would like to be first!

"Three days ago, one of my most eminent clients came to me, a star of note, a nice, fine, intelligent man known to you all. I could see that he was in trouble. More trouble than would be indicated merely by his receiving a subpoena. He would not speak to me in the office. We had to drive way out into the valley. And then I had to ask my chauffeur to get out of the car before he would talk.

"Then he told me the truth that you men are so hungry for. One night, back during the war, he gave a party at his house for Russian War Relief. Now, is there any man in this room who didn't give a donation to Russian War Relief or a dozen other similar causes? So, like you, I took this man by the arm and said, 'Get hold of yourself. Just tell the truth. There's no need to be so worried. No need to tremble. No need to cry.' Yes, gentlemen, he was crying. Not actor's tears. But the tears of a terrified man, a man whose whole career was going down the drain.

"But I couldn't calm him. He kept saying, 'You don't understand, you don't understand. . . .' So I let him cry until he was able to talk. What he had to say was quite interesting. For at that party at his house that night there appeared, without an invitation, but in the company of another guest, a high Russian military officer, a general in full dress uniform."

"So what?" the man from Warners called out. "During the war those things happened. And everybody accepted it!"

"So what?" The Doctor echoed. "So this! Five years later, when they began to investigate the Rosenbergs and the atom bomb secrets, it came out in the newspapers that the man who smuggled those papers out of the country to Russia was that same Soviet general!"

The Doctor paused for a long moment to let his words sink in. Then he continued, "Gentlemen, I think we have more to lose by full disclosure than by following the advice of our very capable counsel. I, for one, am certainly not going to turn in an innocent man for something that, damaging as it might seem, was not his fault."

There was some desultory grumbling among the executives, but finally one of them made a motion to allow all strategy to be dictated by Mandell.

Left alone after the meeting, the attorney turned to Cone. "That really true?" The Doctor nodded gravely.

"Who?"

"I can't tell you. I have *my* ethics, too. But the nicest man in the world, believe me."

Mandell did not pursue the subject further. Instead, he turned his inquiry to matters of tactics. "Shall I put Jefferson on? I can't make up my mind."

The little man laughed. "I'm a doctor, not a lawyer, but if you want my advice, knowing what I know about this town and its *meshuganeh* inmates, I'd save him. You don't know what's going to come. So keep Jeff for dessert. After a bad meal, sometimes all you can remember is the dessert, if it was good."

Mandell nodded. If Jeff testified at all, he would testify last.

In the main, the hearings went as Mandell had expected. Several of the congressmen spent most of their time asking questions of the kind that would elicit little information but would provide good headlines. Bald, feisty, plump Chairman Colby, the New England puritan, insisted on re-

ferring extensively to the Bible, even interspersing quotations in his questions, especially when confronting a reluctant witness. He kept urging confession as being good
for the soul.

He kept saying, "Make a clean breast of it, son. You'll
feel better. And you'll discover this is a mighty forgiving
country." One felt that he might take the witness by the
hand, drop down to his knees with him, and sing a psalm.
But Colby stopped short of that.

Through it all Mandell remained calm, as did Jeff, following Mandell's example. Whenever Jeff was tempted to
lean across Mandell's associate to make a comment, he restrained himself, even during the harrowing hours when
the first screenwriter refused to testify. More than once
the writer exceeded Mandell's advice and traded diatribes
with committee members, thereby jeopardizing his constitutional right to silence. Still Mandell, his associate,
and Jeff appeared composed.

But the toughest battle Mandell faced involved bringing television cameras into the hearing room. Sanctimo-
niously cloaking their personal motives behind "the People's right to know," Colby and his colleagues wanted to
televise the entire proceedings. The networks and local stations supported them, making their demand in the name
of freedom of the press. But everyone knew that such
open hearings, spiced with well-known movie names, were
an excellent way to attract TV audiences and build ratings, and all at practically no cost.

As for Colby and his colleagues, what better way for a
congressman to appear in public, nationwide, day after
day, and in what better cause than to ferret out the nation's enemies?

Mandell remained dogged in his refusal. There would
be no television cameras, no public circus! Or else there
would be no witnesses! He was willing to go to the Supreme Court on that issue.

For the first few days Mandell had prevailed. However,
once that first uncooperative screenwriter resorted to the
Fifth Amendment and the congressmen realized fully the
opportunity such stubborn silence afforded them for patriotic filibusters, their appetite for exposure on television
increased to uncontrollable proportions.

Mandell remained unmoved, both in his public and private debates on the subject. In public he assiduously pursued one line; that the introduction of television cameras, lights, and crews constituted such a bizarre and terrifying distraction that the witnesses would be deprived of their right to a fair hearing.

Privately, Mandell's strategy was more practical than legal. All the while the legal debate raged between himself and Colby, the most reluctant witnesses were being called. They appeared in untelevised hearings, refused to testify, and were excoriated by committee members in long, bitter harangues, of which only a very small part actually found its way into the newspapers.

If Mandell could drag out the legal debate until the last reluctant witness was used up, he would score an enormous triumph. And no one knew that better than Chairman Colby.

By the time the eighth writer to take the Fifth had left the stand, the issue of television coverage was brought to a sudden and surprising head. Mandell and Jeff found out about it only as they were leaving the hearing room at the end of the session. Outside the room, Gainsburgh, house counsel for Metro, was waiting. As soon as he could separate Mandell from the newspapermen who pursued him, he pulled him aside.

"What's up?" asked Mandell.

"The sonofabitch went to court!" Gainsburgh said.

"Colby went to court? What for?"

"Got an order permitting the introduction of television cameras and lights into the hearings. 'The public has a right to be informed in matters pertaining to the nation's security.'"

"So now he's going to have a field day parading a string of unwilling witnesses on national TV."

Gainsburgh nodded.

"I don't think the order's legal. It can be upset on appeal," Mandell said.

"By the time you appeal or get a stay from the Federal Court out here, the damage is done. It'll ruin the industry. They'll treat us like Kefauver treated the Mafia. Anybody who appears on that screen is a criminal in the eyes of the public. When that sanctimonious bastard gets done sermonizing and saluting the flag we'll all look like Russian spies. The public can be very fickle. They'll forget the service we did for the country in time of war and national emergency. . . ."

But Mandell hadn't been listening to Gainsburgh since his first word about the court order. He had been thinking. He interrupted Gainsburgh sharply. "I need two days, three maybe."

"What for?"

"I want three days to run through the witnesses planning to stand on their constitutional rights before I let those cameras come into the hearing room. Get it for me!"

"How?" Gainsburgh asked.

"You know more about that kind of thing than I do. Get me three days!" Mandell commanded.

6

When the Chairman of the House UnAmerican Activities Committee entered Romanoff's that evening in response to an invitation from Robert Kilzer, adviser, representative, and censor to the entire motion picture industry, Colby was aware that in a luxurious room full of the world's most famous celebrities, he was himself a celebrity.

As the short, beefy chairman approached his table, Kilzer rose, extended his hand in greeting and smiled that kindly, intelligent smile which alone justified half his huge salary. The other half he earned by just such moments as this, winning favor or favorable consideration for the industry from men in high government places. Having served under Roosevelt and Truman, his connections were excellent. When the government sought to increase entertainment taxes at the box office, Kilzer intervened. When a scandal was about to erupt or had erupted as in the case of Ingrid Bergman, it was Kilzer's job as "Czar" of the industry to ease public clamor and governmental demands for censorship. At hearings before government committees on industry practices, Kilzer was the ideal witness. He could read a prepared statement with great conviction. He could avoid answering embarrassing questions with a considered torrent of obfuscating language which lent dignity to confusion.

Tonight Kilzer was earning his hundred and fifty thousand dollars a year, plus expenses, by entertaining the Chairman of the House Committee. He knew it. And more, Chairman Colby knew it.

He set the tone of the dinner by stating at the outset, "Kilzer, I know why you called me. Nevertheless, I am delighted to have dinner with you, provided that we dispose

147

of the television issue right away and promise not to discuss it during the rest of the evening."

It was a forthright statement, spoken as by a man of principle, and quite in keeping with the impression which Colby always radiated.

Kilzer smiled, a willing concession to Colby that he had read Kilzer's mind. "Yes, I was going to talk to you about that court order."

"Well, let me tell you. Tomorrow or as soon as we can move the lights and the cameras into that room, we're going to be on the TV! Nationwide! I've already cleared it with all three networks. We'll have at least three hours a day on the air."

"Do you think it's fair to pillory in full view of the public a lot of people who may be either innocent or foolish?"

"Since I was a boy up in Vermont I've been taught the innocent have nothing to fear. It's written . . . 'Remember, I pray thee, who ever perished being innocent? Or where were the righteous cut off?' *Job.* Chapter four."

By that time their tomato juice was served, since the chairman never drank anything alcoholic in public. "Actually I never had any hope of trying to influence your decision about TV," Kilzer remarked. "But the men in the industry insisted I ask. And I have. Just so I could report that you said no. Now we can go on and enjoy our dinner."

For the rest of the meal they talked of mutual acquaintances in Washington or the stars who sat at tables immediately surrounding them. And, good as his word, never once did Kilzer allude to televising the hearings.

Kilzer listened to Colby, agreed, nodded, smiled, and toyed with his food, all the while eyeing the room for someone he was expecting. Not spying him, Kilzer poured the Congressman yet another cup of coffee, offered him a second helping of Strawberries Romanoff.

By the time Colby refused, Kilzer's patience was rewarded. Crossing the room to their table came Carl Hunter, producer, and his female star, Monica Dorn. Hunter produced what were called exploitation films. Films which did not fall into the accepted formula of straight family fare, but which depended on some tie-in with the news, some scandalous murder, some highly publicized sex event, so his pictures usually experienced difficulty clearing the Kilzer office. In almost every case in which Kilzer exercised censorship on a Hunter picture, Monica Dorn was directly involved. Usually the problem was some startling exposure of what was euphemistically called her "cleavage." In truth it was not her cleavage that was the problem, but her two full high breasts which together, but carefully separated, created that cleavage. There was even a rumor current that Monica had had artificial materials surgically inserted into her breasts to make them fuller and higher than even a bountiful nature intended.

Whether this was true or not, tonight she was attired in a black satin gown whose steeply plunging neckline revealed more of her magnificent bosom than she had ever been allowed to show on the screen.

Hunter came forward, with Monica lagging shyly behind. "Forgive me for intruding," he apologized to Colby. "But it can save endless amounts of money and lots of bloodshed if I can get Mr. Kilzer's opinion tonight."

Though Colby nodded and muttered something about the intrusion being quite forgivable, he was totally confused. Then Hunter turned to Kilzer. "We might as well settle this now." He reached out, took Monica by the hand, drew her close to the table, and displaying her, invited, "Go on! Take a look! This is the gown I've had designed for Monica in *The Wolf Maiden.* If there's anything objectionable I want to know it *now.* Not after I've spent half my budget and shot all her scenes. So, take a look!"

Kilzer appeared to be both embarrassed and outraged. He half rose out of his seat and started to say, "See here, Hunter . . ."

But Hunter had moved behind Monica, taken her firmly by the shoulders and bent her forward over the table. "There! You're in the same angle as the camera will be when we shoot. Now I ask you, is that objectionable? Is it?" Turning to Colby, he asked, "What do you think? Is there anything vulgar or indecent about something as beautiful and natural as that?" He really meant "as those."

Monica looked into Kilzer's eyes as innocently as she could, tremulously fluttering her lashes as she had in four different films where she played the prostitute with the heart of gold who later reformed and married the hero.

It seemed in that moment that she was about to cry, so hurt was she at being singled out for constant censure and abuse. As the tears welled she turned her gaze on the Chairman, inviting his protection.

Kilzer rose in his place, saying in hushed but urgent tones, "Hunter, please! This is extremely embarrassing! Come to my office with Miss Dorn first thing in the morning and we'll discuss this. Or send me stills of what you intend to use and I'll render a judgment."

"Tomorrow morning at seven Miss Dorn has to be on the set! We can't make pictures with today's budgets and go visiting people in offices all day!"

"Well, I'm sorry about that . . ." Kilzer started to say, at the same time turning to Colby. "And I'm sorry about this unfortunate intrusion!"

But the chairman was too busy enjoying at close hand what he had admired in secret in dark theaters and barbershop magazines for years.

"I insist on discussing it now!" Hunter said.

"Very well," Kilzer finally agreed in a soft voice, as if trying to play down the entire gross encounter. "But not with Miss Dorn present."

"She has to be up at six anyhow," Hunter conceded. "I'll send her on home. . . ." Then he snapped his fingers as if remembering too late. "Damn! We drove down in my car! I'll have to arrange a taxi. . . ."

Before he could turn away to call the captain, Colby volunteered, "I can drop her off on my way back to the hotel."

"Oh, would you?" Monica said, touched by his solicitude. "It's not far, just across Santa Monica on Maple."

Kilzer thanked the Chairman for being so understanding and helpful. They departed together, leaving Kilzer and Hunter to discuss the matter of censorship. Hunter dropped into the place vacated by the congressman.

"That'll do it," he said. "She never misses."

"I don't want to know anything about it!" Kilzer said, self-righteous.

"Okay. Okay," Hunter said, waving to Prince Mike to send over another brandy.

Monica Dorn knew from experience that the worst hurdle she encountered with men was the very desire she built up in them from her continual, and, to her, monotonous appearances as a sex symbol in films. She had never been granted the exalted sex status of Rita Hayworth or the more recently arrived Marilyn Monroe. She had never appeared in pictures with lavish budgets or in parts written by the best screenwriters. But in her own way, with her own kind of promotion, she had built up a steady slobbering following—mainly because she projected a dirty image. She knew that most men liked their sex mixed with a little dirt, except of course with their own wives. So, when she wanted to, she played the tart off-screen by being the aggressor in a very subtle way.

It accomplished two things. It gave the man a sense of being fatally attractive, even to a woman so pursued as he imagined Monica Dorn to be. And it took considerably less time, since Monica usually considered sex a boring procedure.

Mainly she grew bored with the limited, unimaginative and constantly repetitious kissing and sucking that seemed to afflict all men when confronted by her breasts, which she had to admit were magnificent. She often said to herself that if she saw the top of another man's head all night she would scream. She had not wanted, on this particular evening, to seduce the congressman. But, in the same way that her agent had once convinced her to go down on the studio head to get a screen test, Hunter was able to persuade her that what she did now, she had to do for the good of an industry which made it possible for her to live well and in the constant hope that one day soon she would be given a role that would allow her to prove she was as fine an actress as Marilyn Monroe.

The congressman was easy, discreet and overly cautious, but easy. He opened the subject himself by remarking that no matter how frequently he had seen her in pictures, he never imagined that he would wind up sitting in the back of the same limousine with her. He had always wondered what she was really like, being so beautiful and sexually attractive. Was that enough? Or did she aspire to more?

Monica turned to him, took his arm and held it, almost trembling in gratitude for his understanding. Beauty and sex were fine, but after a while one became surfeited on passion and demanded more from life and from the men one met. Here in Hollywood there were only two kinds of men, those who thought only of sex, and the homos. And between the two, she almost preferred the homos, because for some reason they respected her as a human being and did not regard her as a sexual plaything. With a queer you could do other things than going to bed. They were bright and artistic and understanding. But, of course, as far as she was concerned, they were impotent.

Oh, what a delight it would be to find a man who was mature, sexually powerful and still intelligent and understanding.

It was a speech that her press agent had carefully worked out for an interview in *Life*. Unfortunately the layout never got into the magazine.

It served now because it gave the congressman hope. Monica had discovered long ago that even the most sexually attractive woman could go many nights without being dated and even weeks without being laid simply because her very sexuality overpowered men and made their pursuit seem so hopeless that they never even tried.

Thus the first thing to do if you wanted to seduce a man was to let him know that you were attainable by men of special qualifications and that he possessed those very qualifications.

With her interest and her desire made evident, but not too obvious, Colby could proceed with assurance to lure her into an intimate situation, in which the only question, whispered, was, "Your hotel? Or my place?"

For a congressman, wary by nature, and a hypocrite by profession, this was a question of major importance. Her place was less public but might be a trap. He was constantly fearful of that. In fact, if his desire to fondle and kiss those breasts hadn't been so overwhelming, caution would have made him pass the opportunity by. But he had been deeply stirred. His groin was aching with his unsatisfied erection and he whispered to her, "The hotel?"

She nodded, trying to appear as enraptured as he obviously was. She breathed, "I can park on a side street and come in the back way. No one'll see me."

"Bungalow D," he said, as if imparting a top military secret.

"Bungalow D," she repeated, her voice taking on the

secrecy of disappearing ink. "I won't have to go anywhere near the lobby."

Properly and openly, the chairman's limousine dropped Monica Dorn at her house on Maple Drive at a reasonable hour and departed at once. Twenty minutes later, Monica's pink sports car pulled up on Beverly Drive just up the hill from the back entrance to the Beverly Hills Hotel. Monica parked, turned off the lights, and started into the dimly lit garden where the bungalows stood, separate and secluded from one another.

He was waiting for her and seemed to be dressed only in his robe. He had already ordered champagne and canapés.

Christ, Monica said to herself, he's expecting an all-night screw. And I have to be on the set at seven. But she did not permit the thought to diminish her intention to see the job through. When he offered her champagne, she coyly refused, pretending she did not drink.

That left only one other activity and she emphasized that by saying, "I have to. I can't resist it. Ever since Yul Brynner I can't resist bald men." She reached out to run her fingers lightly over his scalp. The gesture had never had an aphrodisiac effect on him before but it did this night. Her closeness, his long-nurtured hunger for her breasts, his own sudden freedom from his sanctimonious hypocrisy made him embrace her and kiss her feverishly.

When she started to slip the strap of her black gown off her shoulder, his hand stopped her.

"No. Let me," he whispered.

To herself she said, Oh, Christ, this production is going to take all night. But having come this far she couldn't object. She allowed him to strip one strap from her white shoulder and kiss it. Then he slid the other strap off and kissed the second shoulder. When he tried to pull the dress down to reveal her breasts he found it impossible to do, they protruded so, so she helped him by reaching back and opening the hook.

There she was, her breasts exposed, firm and high, the nipples standing out proudly erect and decidedly brown in color from three aborted pregnancies. He stood admiring her, unable to move at the sight of the unattainable now within reach. His lips trembled, his eyes grew wider, per-spiration oozed up through his red scalp until it glistened.

She waited, holding her breath deeply, so as to keep her breasts as fully protruded as possible. Finally she lost both breath and patience, and said to herself, You stupid sonofabitch, stop drooling! I haven't got all night! But she whispered, "I'm waiting . . . waiting for you, lover." There-upon she lifted her right breast like a nursing mother and shoved it into his mouth.

His slobbering did not trouble her too much. She had been drooled on before. But his noises, his sucking noises reminded her of piglets at work on their sow. She placed her hand on his bald damp head intending to thrust him back a bit so he could regain his breath but she restrained herself and allowed her hand to rest there. In a few mo-ments she began drumming, somewhat impatiently. He in-terrupted his kissing and looked up with impatience, so she stopped drumming. In a while he took her by the hand and led her into the bedroom where the lights were even dimmer than they had been in the living room.

Once inside, he placed her at the foot of the bed and proceeded to strip the rest of the clothes from her until she stood fully naked. He stared at her, admiring not only her breasts but her body which was slimmer than her breasts would indicate and yet finely formed. He reached out with both his hands to grasp her by the buttocks and pull her to him. She could feel his erection, hard, aggres-sive, and, she estimated, of formidable size.

Ah, well, she said to herself, now it would happen and she could probably still get home at a reasonable hour. He eased her to the bed as gallantly as he imagined a male star would have done.

With the air of a man quite used to such encounters he pulled open the cord of his robe and whipped it off, tossing it toward the chair.

She caught one glimpse, sat up, asked in both aston-ishment and amusement, "Good God, what the hell is that?"

"What the hell is what?" he demanded, his erection starting to subside rapidly.

"That thing you're wearing!" she said.

"These? These, young lady, are B.V.D.'s," he answered indignantly.

"Oh," she said, comprehending, and barely able to contain the outburst of laughter that threatened to ruin the entire purpose of this adventure. B.V.D.'s, she said to herself, staring at the chubby, bald little man who suddenly had been deflated and would have to be built up all over again. He pouted like a child who'd dropped the ice cream out of his cone, until she invited, "Well, get them off and come here. I'm waiting, lover."

He unbuttoned his B.V.D.'s and let them drop. Then he started for the bed, his passion diminished. Resentful, he hesitated and she reached for him, finding his hand and pulling him down beside her. Then she placed his hand on her breast. When it rested there, she turned to him, urged her other breast into his mouth and he began to suck again but not with the same enthusiasm as before.

She thought to herself, I guess I'll have to go down on him to bring him back. But while she was contemplating that possibility, she felt a stirring at her side. He was coming alive again. Slowly, he had begun to pulsate. Then he was firm again, throbbing, then huge and aggressive. He gave up kissing and sucking at her breast. But instead of mounting her as she expected, he moved kiss by kiss down slowly the length of her thighs. She opened to him and he began to kiss the insides of her legs, now moving up bit by bit until his red scalp rested between them and his tongue was delicately seeking to join its moistness with hers.

If his shiny head between her white thighs hadn't presented such an amusing sight, she might have reacted to him more quickly. But all Monica could think was that obviously the Bible-quoting congressman had not spent all his time running for office and making speeches.

Now he moved up, slipping between her thighs which she obediently spread even wider, opening to him completely. He fumbled a bit, found his way in, all the way in and he rested there as if tired from his labors. Then he began to stroke. She made some labored pretense of joining him in the act. As he continued, however, she began to work more earnestly because she was becoming involved, actually, sexually involved, until she began to wonder if it was really true about bald men? Now in her need to embrace him she placed both hands against his bald head, pressing down on the damp skin, but he interrupted his thrusting to demand, "For Christ's sake, will you cut that out?"

She withdrew her hands, allowing him to finish in a burst of ecstasy, which if it had continued longer might have brought her to an orgasm too, much to her surprise. The second time, and the third time she did not feel anything but duty. She was relieved when he finally drifted off to sleep, exhausted. Now she could ease out of bed, find her clothes, dress, slip unnoticed out of the bungalow, up the back walks, through the gardens of the hotel and out to her car.

It was past three. She was due on the set at seven. But no close-ups today. Not with her eyes. She wouldn't stand for it! A star, even a minor star, had to protect herself from unflattering close-ups!

When the hearing resumed again the next morning the chairman seemed unusually chipper and self-assured, a fact most people ascribed to his victory in having secured the court order that permitted the TV cameras to be installed.

Lee Mandell was late for the first time. When he did arrive the TV equipment had already been installed and he pretended to be surprised and upset at seeing the four cameras and the endless battery of bright lights.

At the outset he made no protest. Instead he waited until the counsel for the committee recalled to the stand Alex Bernstone, the writer whose testimony, or lack of testimony, had been interrupted the day before. The lawyer called his name a second time, but Bernstone did not move. Instead, Mandell finished lighting his pipe, then said slowly and deliberately, "The witness refuses to resume on the advice of counsel."

Colby, confident, bristling and eager for combat, leaned forward to project directly into the microphone, "On what ground?"

"On the ground that all this . . ." and Mandell indicated the four cameras, the twenty-odd technicians, the batteries of powerful lights, "constitutes an invasion of his rights. This witness accepted a subpoena from this committee and came here to testify . . ."

"You call his stalling, his refusal to answer questions testifying?" the chairman interrupted.

"He came here to testify," Mandell continued doggedly, "with a full knowledge of his duties *and* his rights under the Constitution. Not this committee, in fact no committee of any branch of any legislature, federal or state, has the right to force this witness to divest himself of his legal guarantees and protections. So he is here, as required. And ready to testify, within legal limits."

Then, turning to the television equipment, Mandell said, "But he is not here to provide a field day for you or for the television networks. He will not resume the stand!"

"Mr. Mandell, if your client does not resume the stand, as he is obligated to do under the subpoena which is still in effect, then we will have no choice but to hold him in contempt!"

"Not before all these cameras! You want to hold a hearing, hold it. And I will produce the witness. But if you want to conduct a Roman circus, then the answer is no!" Mandell said with an air of finality.

The chairman tapped the table a moment, then straightened his tie, took a sip of water and signaled to the television director. Taking his cue, the TV director whispered instructions into the microphone of his headset. The cameras, already heated up, moved into position, one focused on the chairman. Speaking directly into the close-up lens of the camera, the chairman began:

"For the information of the public at large and the television audience which is tuned in to these highly important hearings concerning our national security, let me explain the reason why that witness chair is empty." He pointed to the empty chair alongside of which sat Lee Mandell and Jeff Jefferson. As Mandell saw the camera focus on him and the empty witness chair, he put aside his pipe, leaned forward, and interrupted the chairman.

"Mr. Chairman, if you are going to explain anything to the television audience I want you to know now that I will demand time to state our reasons as to why this chair is empty."

Putting on his heartiest, friendliest smile, Colby looked directly into the camera. "By all means, Mr. Mandell. I am sure the public would like to know why men who have profited so much from our free enterprise system persistently refuse to answer questions which might be of help to the Congress of these United States. Surely no loyal citizen of this country should have the slightest reluctance to testify here."

"Mr. Chairman! I demand that as long as you have undertaken to instruct the public on this you instruct them fully! That for a witness to answer any question, even the most bland and innocuous question, may totally jeopardize his right to refuse to answer incriminating questions as well." Mandell was half rising out of his chair now.

The chairman smiled slightly. "Is that a concession on your part, Mr. Mandell, that the witness *does* have something of an incriminating nature to hide?"

"Mr. Chairman, I am simply saying that this committee has no right to strip a witness of his legal protections either directly by forcing him to testify, or indirectly by drawing inferences from his refusal. Otherwise the next thing you know, you'll be inquiring about his private life, about whether he sleeps with his wife, and how frequently, or even if . . ."

And here Mandell made a groping gesture as if to find the most inconsequential irrelevancy he could, ". . . or even if he wears B.V.D.'s!"

At which point Mandell turned to glare directly at the chairman. Colby's vindictive smile trembled visibly. He stared back, wondering all the while whether Mandell had mentioned B.V.D.'s by coincidence or whether he was aware of the events of last night.

Mandell's expression made no secret of the fact that he was not dealing in coincidences. He picked up his pipe, started to light it. With the lit match hovering over the pipe bowl, he asked, "Mr. Chairman, I ask the indulgence of the committee in a brief recess."

Colby was relieved to grant the request. He left the committee table and the platform at once.

In a small office on the floor below the hearing room, Mandell was waiting. He had sent word as to where he could be found. Colby entered, looked around cautiously.

"There are no bugs or taps," Mandell said.

"What was the meaning of that . . . that reference to underwear . . . to B.V.D.'s . . ." the chairman finally asked.

Mandell didn't answer directly, but started to light up his pipe, pausing to comment, " 'Remember, I pray thee, who ever perished being innocent? Or where were the righteous cut off?' *Job,* if I remember correctly. Chapter four. Right?"

Colby exploded. "Why, you Jew bastard! So you planned it. And Kilzer was in on it, too! All of you!"

"Uh uh," Mandell cautioned, "I wouldn't accuse an attorney of plotting to circumvent justice. Not unless you want to be the defendant in a million-dollar libel suit."

The chairman's face grew red yet he dared not utter a word.

After a long silence, he said, "Okay. What do you want? No television? Is that it?"

"You'll always find me willing to negotiate. I know you fellows have your hearts set on appearing before the cameras. I know you want to run for the Senate next time around and you could stand the exposure. So let's split the difference. You promise to run through the other writers, who I can tell you now are *not* going to testify, and afterwards I won't object to your opening up those cameras."

"You don't want those writers on TV, is that it?"

"I don't want you to smear a whole industry," Mandell corrected.

"I can tell you now we're going to hold them in contempt," the chairman warned, but not quite as strongly as he had issued his previous threats.

"You do whatever your committee is legally empowered to do. Just don't make a circus out of it," Mandell said doggedly.

The chairman pondered a few moments, mopped his sweating scalp. "Okay," he said. "We get rid of the writers. Then TV."

"A deal," Mandell said, holding out his hand to shake.

But Colby refused to acknowledge it. He simply repeated with great distaste, "A deal," and he started out of the room.

"You're never going to believe it, but I want you to know I did not plan what happened," Mandell said.

Colby obviously did not believe him. He stormed out, slamming the door behind him.

The committee ran perfunctorily through the remaining writers, asking only sufficient questions to lay the groundwork for contempt citations. Ten writers appeared, refused to testify, were heroically dubbed by the left-wing press as the "Hollywood Ten," and were recommended for charges of contempt by the committee to their colleagues in the House of Representatives.

Now, the television networks were finally allowed in the hearing room. Most of the committee members were perfectly content that the cameras had been withheld until this point. For no one in the TV audience either recognized or had any real interest in the writers. But the witnesses who now began to appear were actors, both stars and featured players, all of whom were well known to the public at large and so added greatly to the general interest in the hearings.

From the moment the network coverage began, Mandell insisted that Jeff Jefferson sit immediately beside him. He wanted to make sure that every time the camera turned to pick him up they would pick up as well Jeff's all-American face, sober, concerned, intelligent and above suspicion.

Mandell was aware that damaging testimony might be forthcoming. A number of stars had been examined in private executive sessions by the committee, had admitted Communist associations, contributions and even Party membership. Now they were appearing in public to confess and atone. With such a succession of penitent breast-beaters it would do no harm to have an innocent man like Jeff constantly in view as a reminder to the public that not all actors were or had been Communists.

On the eve of what promised to be the last day of hearings, Mandell was having dinner with Jeff at Romanoff's. An endless stream of people stopped by their table to congratulate Mandell on his handling of the hearings, especially his handling of the TV dispute. A few even joked about how Mandell framed the chairman, but he quickly cut them short.

So they turned to congratulating Jeff for having the guts to sit it out day after day and risk his own future for the benefit of the Guild and its members. The third time that Mandell was given credit for having planned the castrating entrapment of the chairman, he became too angry to continue his dinner and asked to be excused.

Jeff insisted on leaving with him. Together they drove up Rodeo Drive toward Sunset.

"I'm sorry," Jeff began, "I thought with the hearings ending tomorrow you would want a night out. A pleasant dinner. I was going to ask you to come home, but Joanne's shooting right now. She doesn't like dinner company when she's on a picture."

"That's all right," Mandell said, but he was obviously upset.

"We wouldn't have run into these people," Jeff said.

"*You* don't think I planned it, do you?" Mandell asked suddenly.

"No."

"You trust me, don't you?"

"Of course. Why?" Jeff asked.

"Because something has been running through my head for the last three days. At the end, just before they close the hearing I would like to ask you to take the stand."

"What could I testify to?" Jeff asked.

"You could put the whole thing in perspective. You could explain how people who are frightened or disillusioned can be duped into doing things they later regret," Mandell explained.

"I'm no expert on that," Jeff said.

"You *are*, you *are*," Mandell repeated. "All I want you to do is answer the questions that I ask, and that the committee asks, and then finish up by telling them what happened to your father back on the farm. Can you do that? I mean, can you tell the story the way you told me?"

"That time was the first time I ever told anyone," Jeff reminded him.

"Can you do it again?"

"I can try." Then Jeff added, "Yes, I think I can."

"That's all I want."

Jeff dropped Mandell at the front entrance of the Beverly Hills Hotel. Even as he drove away he heard someone greet the lawyer, "Hey, Mandell! What a job you did on Colby!" Jeff didn't wait to hear Mandell's reply. He continued on down the curving driveway to the street, turned left onto Sunset and started home, already working out in his mind the most effective way to tell the story of his father's experience during the Depression. By the time

he arrived home he had decided that he would not prepare, instead he would wing it. A story so deeply his own
would sound better with impromptu hesitations, than if it
had been meticulously rehearsed.

He slept fitfully that night, got up before dawn and
ended up on the studio couch in the den. In the morning he shaved, showered, picked out a proper gray flannel suit, a light blue shirt, a plain dark tie and dressed for
his appearance before the committee and the TV cameras.

Word of his testimony had already leaked out in some
mysterious way, for by the time he reached the hearing
room the front benches were crowded with actors and
actresses, a demonstration of loyalty, support, and gratitude.

When the committee announced that it had run out of
witnesses and that its work in Los Angeles was coming to
a close, Mandell raised his hand. He leaned close to the
microphone and asked the committee's indulgence in allowing Jeff Jefferson to testify on behalf of the Screen Actors Guild.

Suspecting some trick, the chairman hesitated. But
when Mandell pressed the point, with the hint of a threat
lurking behind the suggestion, Colby conferred with his
colleagues and finally acquiesced.

Jeff took the witness chair, placed his hand on the Bible, spoke the oath with such sober conviction that the
entire room became silent. Although Mandell had prepared
a list of questions he intended to ask, the chairman took
over the initial examination. He began probing in an unfriendly and hostile manner. But gradually, as Jeff's in-
genuousness asserted itself, Colby became more friendly.
After a while Mandell could sit back and relax, knowing
that the chairman, willingly or not, would lead Jeff precisely in to what Mandell intended him to say.

And he did, eliciting Jeff's whole background, the hard
life on the farm, the good God-fearing woman his mother
was, the drudgery and sacrifice which the land had imposed on his father, his own aborted college career, the
cold gray day the bank closed, the banker's suicide, and
even his father's possible suicide attempt.

Jeff ended by saying, "Whether he intended to kill himself I never did find out for sure. But it didn't matter. As

far as I was concerned the shock, the fear, that terrible sick feeling in my stomach was as terrible as if he had actually done it. After that if someone had approached me and said there is a way to prevent such scenes, to keep other sons from finding their fathers hurt in that way, will you follow it? No matter what it was, I think I would have said yes."

Then he looked straight into the TV camera, "No. I did not become involved with the Communists, or join the Party. But neither am I going to condemn anybody who did. Not after what I've been through."

A spontaneous cheer went up from the entire audience, even from those who were not involved in the picture business. After that there were no questions from the committee, only a brief speech from the chairman thanking Jeff for his appearance, commending him on his loyalty, his patriotism and his personal sacrifice on behalf of his members in coming to testify without a subpoena. The witness was free to leave the stand. The hearings were over.

The audience crowded around Jeff to shake his hand, clap him on the shoulder; men kissed him on the cheek, and all of it was covered by the TV cameras.

As they left the courtroom, Mandell dismissed his car and chauffeur to accept Jeff's invitation to drive him back to the hotel. On the way Mandell seemed depressed, tired rather than elated.

When Jeff remarked on it, the lawyer said sadly, "I hate them both. The self-righteous on both sides. I had my fill of them when I was in Washington. Theoreticians, political and otherwise, who experiment with other people's lives. And who, if they are wrong, as your Commies out here are wrong, will accomplish more harm than good before they're through. Watch them. Be careful of them. Don't let yourself be used."

Jeff nodded, keeping his eyes on the heavily trafficked street, though he was tempted to steal a glance at Mandell. After a few moments of silence, Mandell asked, "Do you think *I* used you?"

Jeff's first impulse was to deny it, to save the lawyer any further self-recrimination. But before he had a chance to answer, Mandell continued, "Well, I did. But in a good cause, I hope. To save a lot of innocent people from being ruined. Of course we gave a reprieve and a free ride to a lot of guilty ones too. I'm sorry about that. But on the whole I think we did the best we could."

"What about the Ten?" Jeff asked, referring to the writers who had adamantly refused to testify.

"They'll be tried for contempt. And found guilty. They. know that. The Party picked them to be victims. They agreed to it."

"Why?"

"Either because the discipline is so strong or else because it makes them feel important to be the central figures in a case that will go to the Supreme Court. Fanatics always see themselves in the roles of great heroes. It's what makes martyrs of them. And assassins."

"But you think we did the right thing?" Jeff asked, seeking reassurance.

"We did the right thing. And for the right reason. To protect the innocent." Mandell seemed to be troubled by an afterthought. "Tell me, are any of them really good writers?"

"Two of them, possibly three," Jeff said.

"Well, wait and see what happens now that they are martyrs. The talent they'll be endowed with, the sheer genius. Political heroes have a way of acquiring reputations from left-wing critics that amazes everyone. After two or three years they'll be the best-known writers who ever worked in Hollywood."

They had reached the hotel. Mandell turned around to haul his briefcase off the back seat. As he swung it over he was face to face with Jeff again. He said, "They'll lionize you for a while after today. But watch out. If you don't go along with them every time." Mandell spoke with genuine fear, as if from personal experience and disillusionment.

He held out his hand and they shook. Mandell said, "Whenever you come to New York or Washington look me up. I have offices both places. And again, thanks."

Mandell slipped out of the car surrendering his briefcase to the doorman. As he started up the canopied red concrete walk to the entrance his gait was tired and dispirited. Jeff watched till the lawyer was almost at the great front door, but an impatient horn sounded so Jeff slipped the lever into "drive" and started away.

When he arrived home Martha was on the phone saying to someone, "Yes, yes, I'll tell him minute he gets home . . . oh, there he is now. . . ." She was smiling and holding out the receiver. He felt too tired to take it, but after Martha's greeting he could not readily say no.

"Hello?"

"Jeff! This is Christopher Crown!" There was a slight pause as Crown waited for some gasp of awed recognition. "I watched the whole thing, Jeff. You were great. Magnificent! It was exactly what this whole damned industry needed! Someone who would stand up and speak for us. And that story about your father . . . terrific! Whoever's idea that was, it was great! I could make a whole picture inspired by that one episode. But I didn't call to discuss pictures. Only to tell you that as far as I'm concerned you are Citizen Number One in Hollywood today!"

"Thanks. Thanks very much," Jeff said, remembering that less than four months ago Crown was casting a new film with a role that would have been great for him, but the deal fell apart when Crown refused to meet Jeff's terms, even though they were substantially lower than his previous price had been.

"Oh, by the way," Crown said, "I'm doing a new Western and there's a great part in it for you. A character part, but great! One of those cameo gems that gets Award nominations!"

"Send over the script," Jeff said, feigning enthusiasm, since he never expected to receive it.

"I will! I will!" Crown promised, intending to send it, although he never did.

Jeff hung up, scanned the telephone pad which had more than thirty messages scribbled in Martha's illegible handwriting. He could make out some of the callers. The others were a jumble of misspelled names. One name stood out. The simplest one. Irwin Cone. The Doctor had called. *Three times.*

Taking the list, Jeff went out to the pool area to sit quietly in the fading light of what had been a sunny but cool afternoon.

He was beginning to unwind somewhat from the tension of testifying. It had been more taxing than he had expected. Unlike playing a scene, there were no retakes. And this time he wasn't portraying a character but being himself. It demanded more involvement and took more out of him. It was the difference between ketchup and real blood in a war scene.

He rose, went to the bar, was mixing himself a drink when the phone rang again. His first impulse was, screw it, let Martha take it. But since his drink was made and he was already up he took it.

A long distance operator was asking, "Mr. Jeff Jefferson? Long distance calling."

"Who and from where?"

"Amarillo," she sang out, the Texas slur in her speech making it *Amarillah.*

"Yes, this is Mr. Jefferson," he said.

Her voice came on in a moment, "Jeff . . . Darlin' . . . you were just great. And very noble."

"Thanks Doris . . . did you watch it all?"

"All! And I loved that touch!"

"It wasn't a touch! It actually happened!" he replied, trying not to betray anger.

"My blue shirt! You wore my blue shirt! I sat there smiling, saying to myself, he's on nationwide television, millions of people are watching, but he and I are the only ones who know."

As she talked, he examined the cuffs of his shirt and realized that in his desire to wear a color that would not create haloes on the TV screen he had indeed selected her blue shirt. But she was reading more into it than he had ever intended. Much more. Still, after some of the disappointments he'd had in the weeks since their meeting he didn't try to disillusion her.

"You going to be in Texas again soon, Darlin'?"

"No plans at present."

"New York?"

"No."

"I could come out there," she offered.

"That wouldn't be wise. You know this town."

"That's why I thought, if you could get away . . . New York, London, Paris. . . . I'd send my plane."

"I've got a couple of pictures on the fire. So I have to stay close. My agent insists on it." He was lying, of course. And she knew it.

So she merely said, "We'll keep in touch. And I'll be waiting." Then she paused, said more softly, more dependently, "Love you . . ." And hung up.

He felt sorry for her, but he couldn't dwell on it for the phone rang almost immediately.

"Doctor Cone calling! From New York!" Alise's bright voice lilted. Then more intimately, "You were great today, just great!"

Before he could respond, Cone said, "Jeff-sweetie! What a performance! Fantastic! I sat here in New York and bawled like a baby!" Jeff tried to envision Irwin Cone meticulously taking off his pince-nez glasses, then bawling like a baby. He failed, but since The Doctor was obviously building up to something, Jeff did not interrupt.

"How I wish I could have been there, to see it in person! But I watched. All of it! My God, what impact! I never knew about your father. Strange, I always suspected that you carried around some deep personal sorrow. I guess that's what makes you such a fine, sensitive actor!"

Now Jeff did become restive. The Doctor had never to his face or to anyone else, claimed that he was a fine sensitive actor.

"Remember when I said this would be a great thing for you to do. Well, it's turned out to be more than that! It gave me a whole new insight into you. I saw a Jeff Jefferson on that TV screen today that I've never seen before! And you know I've seen all your pictures, Jeff, all of them!"

That wasn't so difficult, Jeff said to himself, not in the last few years. He made a sound that pretended to be assent, and he waited, for The Doctor was not one to waste enthusiasm. His cobras, Spence Gould, Freddie Feig or Buddy Black, could be as phony and enthusiastic as any Hollywood agent, but The Doctor withheld his superlatives for those moments when they served important purposes.

This must be one of them. Jeff wished he'd get to the point.

"Jeff, sitting here in New York watching you, I said to

myself, how could we have misjudged this man so? Yes, *we!* I blame TCA! I blame myself! We were wrong to let you get typed. You were wrong to let us type you. Well, that's all in the past. Watching you today, I decided, from now on everything's going to be different!"

"Yeah? How?" Jeff asked, unable to stifle his renewed curiosity. It was the hell of being an actor. No amount of battering could stifle that spark of hope that was constantly ready to burst into flame at the first promise of a good part.

"We have to capitalize on this right away! Before it cools. The minute I get back from New York, two days, three days at the most, you and I are going to take a meeting, a long meeting, away from the office. We will devote a whole afternoon to discussing Jeff Jefferson!"

For the first time in months, in more than a year, Jeff felt that the little man was aggressively involved in his career.

"In a few weeks you'll be combing offers out of your hair!" The Doctor enthused. "Call you the minute I get back, kid! Again, great! Fantastic!" The Doctor hung up as was his habit and he was now free to give his entire attention to the threatening disaster which had summoned him to New York. The star in a new dramatic hour TCA had put together for CBN television had just walked off the TV stage in a fit of rage.

The instant The Doctor was off the phone, Spence, who had been waiting with Freddie in the client's booth of the television studio, begged, "Go talk to Clark Ford again? Please?"

"Where is he this time?" The Doctor asked wearily.

"Back in his dressing room. Won't go on with rehearsal! Says he's never going on the air! Never wanted to do TV in the first place!"

"Okay, okay," The Doctor said, starting for the door, "I'll go back and see him. Tell the director to give everybody five."

PART THREE

1

The disaster which had kept The Doctor in New York while Jeff was testifying in California had its beginnings in events which took place long before the UnAmerican Activities Committee descended on Hollywood.

It was a threat far more subtle and one which took longer to mature than the congressional investigation. But, as usual, The Doctor had been first to detect and diagnose it. And first to realize that it was the kind of disaster from which TCA might stand to profit.

It began with a startling and unexpected speech by the new chairman of the Federal Communications Commission.

Until the night of that fateful speech at the annual dinner of the National Association of Broadcasters, the networks had been merely purveyors of time. Time on the air was their stock in trade. And since the three major networks had a monopoly, every entity like TCA first sold their talent to an advertising agency, which in turn sold it to a sponsor. Finally the agencies competed among themselves for the most advantageous time slots on the air.

Of course there was always a bit of behind-the-scenes maneuvering, personal favors and under-the-table payoffs when several large agencies were competing for the same desirable hour.

Under those conditions, The Doctor, his cobras and TCA had prospered through the lushest years of radio and on into the early days of television. With many stars and many varied packages of entertainment for sale it was not unusual for two or three TCA packages to be competing for the same choice time spot. And since TCA's ten percent was virtually the same on every package, it didn't matter which show was sold and which others weren't.

Most times other places were found for the unsuccessful contenders so that TCA emerged far ahead of all
competition at the end of the selling season.

But the very success of TCA and the huge fees and
profits which TCA clients were now beginning to realize
stirred great envy among the networks and their executives. It was extremely tempting, yet extremely frustrating. They owned the studio facilities, controlled the stations, sold the time, but had to stand by and watch the
major agencies realize the profits. If only they could find
some way to legally pursue both ends of the business, selling programs as well as time.

But always they hesitated, remembering the recent disastrous experience of the picture companies, when the
government forced them to sell their theaters if they
wished to continue making movies. Greedy as they
might be, the networks were not seeking to invite that
kind of retribution upon themselves. Yet as the television
packages became fatter and the profits ran into the millions it became less and less possible for the networks to
resist.

The Doctor had always been aware of this restiveness,
but behind the sheltering wall of anti-trust legislation he
and his cobras believed that they could conduct their
business with complete immunity.

The Doctor was stunned to discover otherwise, at the
elaborate black-tie dinner that traditionally ended the annual convention of the National Association of Broadcasters. The large, well attended affair began routinely enough
in one of the hotel ballrooms, where the executives displayed their success through their ladies' gowns and
jewelry.

TCA had bought its usual table and The Doctor had insisted that Spence, Buddy, Freddie and a few of the other
younger men in his organization put in an appearance.

The usual speeches began right after dinner. Men in the
broadcasting industry lauded men in the broadcasting industry for their great public service. The main speaker, as
always, the chairman of the Federal Communications
Commission, was Gordon Willis, newly appointed to that
powerful office.

His introduction ran true to form. He was proclaimed a
brilliant young man, a man who had put aside personal

profit as a lawyer to dedicate himself to public service, a man who would help to keep the broadcasting industry devoted to its high level of public service. . . .

The Doctor stopped listening. It sounded too much like a political convention. Even when Willis stood up to speak, The Doctor allowed his mind to drift. But after Willis proffered his obligatory quota of praise to broadcasting, his attitude suddenly seemed to become startlingly hostile. True, all the praise he had handed out was justified, but, he added, there was blame and onus to be shared as well.

The Doctor sat up alertly in his uncomfortable armless chair. These men, accused Willis, charged with great public responsibility, had been derelict in their duty. They had allowed the level of performance, taste, and creativity to sink to such depths that they had turned television's enormous potential into a cultural wasteland.

As unexpected as this charge was to The Doctor, it stirred open consternation on the dais. Faces grew red. Or paled. Top programming executives could feel their highly paid jobs suddenly thrust into jeopardy.

Even at the TCA table there was a sudden uncomfortable stiffness. But in a few moments The Doctor himself began to relax again. His diagnostic eye had detected a phenomenon that seemed to have escaped everyone else. Up on the dais, where the turmoil and terror was most noticeable sat three men who had difficulty making themselves appear even suitably disturbed.

Those three seemed neither surprised by the FCC chairman's remarks, nor threatened. They listened placidly. One of the three, an elder statesman of network broadcasting, even nodded his head gravely, as though actually agreeing with the severe charges being leveled against his industry. The other two network presidents were more contained in their reactions, but, significantly, evinced no surprise or panic. They were three very calm men.

To The Doctor, that seemed to be a symptom of remarkable importance. Gordon Willis had, meantime, gone on to say that since he had made it a public issue he expected that the networks would assume a far greater degree of responsibility in the selection and preparation of every program they permitted on their stations.

The evening ended with applause as limp as the salad

had been earlier. The program chairman who felt called upon to offer some response, promised that the networks would certainly take Willis's remarks to heart in their future program planning.

The Doctor and Spence Gould were walking back to The Doctor's hotel. The night air was cool and it seemed far cleaner than it actually was after the huge smoke-filled dining room they had just left. The Doctor was quiet and thoughtful. But Spence, out of his own personal insecurity, spoke animatedly.

"Jesus! What a kick in the balls! With the whole industry there! And all the papers. It'll be front page in the *Times* tomorrow morning!"

The Doctor did not respond.

"Why the hell would he do such a thing! He threw the whole industry into a shit hemorrhage with one lousy speech!"

The Doctor remained silent, still mulling over that significant symptom.

"Does he think he's going to change anything, making speeches that run down the whole industry? He'll stir up a lot of ulcers but in the end he won't change one goddamn thing!"

For the first time The Doctor spoke, "If nothing's going to change, what are you getting so excited about, Spence?"

"We've got enough aggravation without speeches like that! Think what this is going to do to the agencies and sponsors. I've got three deals cooking right now, and when the sponsors read that speech you know what they'll say, 'Is this the right kind of program to buy?' With production costs going up by the minute, it's tough enough to get a decision these days!"

"I don't think so," The Doctor said thoughtfully.

"You don't think it's tough?" Spence asked, appalled.

"I don't think that's what got you upset," The Doctor corrected. "Whether you know it or not, things *are* going to change. Starting tonight. In fact, I suspect things started to change *before* tonight."

"What do you mean?" Spence asked, bewildered.

"Spence, I have a theory. In about a year, our bright young commissioner will retire from his job as a great public servant. He will decide that there is something to be said for personal profit after all. He will return to the

law. And when he does, I am willing to give you ten to
one right now that he will get a big fat retainer from one
or two or all three networks!"

"For knifing them tonight?" Spence was incredulous.

"A year from now you'll know that I'm right."

"But why? Why?" Spence demanded.

"Because, my dear young man from Harvard where
they taught you how to speak so nicely but not how to
use your *seichal,* because what he did tonight in one single
speech was to hand the networks a complete monopoly
over all programming!" The Doctor declared, becoming
emotional for the first time.

"Monopoly. . . ."

"Of course! What better strangle-hold do they need
than to be able to say, '*We* are responsible for everything
that goes on our network. The FCC Chairman himself
said we have to control all programs. In fact, *we* will buy
all the programs or create them or produce them and
then *we* will sell them to the sponsors.' "

"You think they'd dare. . . ."

"I know it! Six months from now they're going to be
our partners. It'll be the only way anyone will be able to
get a show on the air!"

"That'll mean payoffs! Big payoffs!" Spence moaned.

"Payoffs? It's the biggest steal since Teapot Dome! No
more little under-the-table personal handouts. These will
be corporate payoffs! The networks will want a piece of
everything! A big piece!" The Doctor declared. "No wonder those three didn't seem surprised . . . or upset. . . ."

"Who?"

"Never mind, Spence. Of course, on the other hand, the
bigger things become, the fewer buttons there are to push.
The more results you can get from putting your muscle
against a few weak points. . . ."

"If they own the store and they own the merchandise
. . . what weak points can they have?" Spence asked.

"Haven't I told you often enough? Where there is no
weakness, *create* one. Good night, Spence!" The Doctor
abruptly turned to enter his hotel.

Things worked precisely as The Doctor had predicted.
His timing was a little off. Gordon Willis did not resign
as FCC Chairman at the end of a year. That took thirteen

months. But when he did, he returned to his old law firm with a fat retainer from CBN in his pocket.

The Doctor's other prediction came true even faster than he had feared. In less than six months all three networks had moved into production in a major way, justifying every monopolistic step by quoting their "duty of ultimate responsibility." They no longer sold time. They made up "balanced" schedules for entire nights. Yet the programs in those schedules were of no better quality than before. The same number of cowboys, detectives, thieves, murderers, lawyers, doctors, comedians continued to appear. Only one thing had changed. The networks now either owned each show entirely or else had a half interest in it.

Even TCA had to knuckle under and make payoffs on a grand scale, no longer to agency account executives, but to the networks themselves.

The fact that The Doctor bowed to the policy did not mean he liked it. He had not yet discovered the weakness against which to put his muscle, but neither had he given up trying. His opportunity came one evening when Spence Gould made his regular nightly call to the Coast to report the day's activities in New York.

The most significant bit of information that Spence passed along was that at Continental Broadcasting the whole Tuesday night schedule seemed to have fallen apart. A comic around whom CBN was building its Tuesday prime-time programming had taken ill. The word was up and down Madison Avenue that it was cancer and he wouldn't be back. That meant the whole night's lineup was in jeopardy. TCA had two packages in contention in that original lineup, a half hour family series and an hour-long drama. With this sudden emergency both shows might now be thrown out depending on what replacement was chosen for the ailing comic. Of course William Morris had one package in contention, too. The rest were network-owned shows. The independent packagers had virtually been squeezed out of the business since the famous "wasteland" speech.

The sum of Spence's report was that if TCA's Coast office had developed any new program ideas, this might be the time to spring them instead of holding back for the following season. In fact, Spence informed The Doctor,

Anson Taft, president of CBN-TV had practically told him late this afternoon that they were now wide open for any ideas for all of Tuesday night.

The Doctor listened, listened very thoughtfully. For the first time since the night of the industry dinner, he found a glimmer of hope. Anson Taft . . . the entire Tuesday night lineup . . . Spence had said it was wide open . . . Anson Taft. . . .

But to Spence The Doctor only said, "I'll be back to you tomorrow morning." And he hung up at once.

Less than half an hour later Spence's private phone rang.

"Spence?" said The Doctor. "Taft, Anson Taft, isn't he in a bit of a bind?"

"How can you ask when a whole Tuesday lineup falls apart!"

"No, I mean personal trouble. . . ."

"With his divorce?" Spence asked, almost annoyed at such irrelevancies.

"Exactly," The Doctor said. "How does it stand?"

"They're haggling over the property settlement, far as I know."

"That's what I figured," The Doctor said thoughtfully.

"Why? What difference does it make?"

"I'll tell you, Spence. These executives in big jobs, with lots of power and leverage, whatever the hell they make, even with expense accounts and all, they're still just hired hands. Always broke. Now when a guy like that has to make a property settlement, the judge bases it on how much he makes gross. But the poor *shmuck* has only his after-taxes income to depend on. It's a squeeze. . . ."

Spence lowered his voice a bit, "You mean, make him an offer under the table. . . ."

"Of course not!" The Doctor said indignantly, not because he was against such practices but because he felt that bribery was a risky weapon in this instance. "We do him a favor, a nice timely favor to help him settle this matrimonial mess he's in."

"Such as?"

"Without taking a bribe, where can a jerk like Taft net the money to buy his way out of his marriage? Legitimately, I mean?"

"I don't know."

"Call you back." The Doctor hung up, leaving Spence more puzzled than ever.

At ten o'clock, as Spence was leaving the theater after previewing a play in which one TCA client starred, another directed and yet another had written, he found Freddie Feig waiting in the lobby.

"The Doctor's been trying to reach you all night. Get on the phone right away." They crossed Forty-fifth Street, raced through Shubert Alley, into Sardi's, where Spence asked for a phone to be plugged in upstairs. There, in a corner of the large, empty room, Spence Gould contacted The Doctor who was dining at Chasen's in Beverly Hills.

Using his unprivate surroundings to excuse his cryptic phraseology, The Doctor said, "Spence, I got word from my broker today. There's a new issue coming out here— Federated Electronics. Issue price is five. The asking price is already seven. It's got to go to twenty or more in a matter of a week. Now, I'm due to get ten thousand shares. I'm willing to let Anson Taft have any part of my ten thousand if he wants it."

"Any part?" Spence asked.

"Or all of it," The Doctor declared nobly. "That way he can make a killing, a legitimate killing. No chicanery. No bribery. A straight, clean deal. Try it out on him tomorrow."

"Okay, okay," Spence said. Then he remembered to ask, "What if he doesn't have the money to swing it?"

"Let me know. I'll even be able to arrange that."

At nine-thirty the next morning Spence was in Anson Taft's office at CBN. He explained the stock opportunity and sat waiting Taft's reaction. When Taft remained silent Spence said, "If you need the cash to swing it, The Doctor said he can get it for you."

That changed Taft's expression considerably. He smiled but cautioned, "It's got to be a loan. Not a gift. No screwing around. I don't want anything that can be investigated by the FCC."

"It will be a loan, I promise you," Spence said.

"Okay, then." Taft nodded.

Within three hours Anson Taft received a visit from a Mr. Barton who was recommended by Dr. Irwin Cone.

Barton, a young man, dark-skinned, short and somewhat fleshy, spoke softly, with diction that strove too deliberately to be precise and correct. But he made his point.
A fifty thousand dollar loan for a short term on a highly
speculative situation like a new issue could be had. But,
because of the aforementioned facts, it would come at a
rate of 5 percent a week, in cash.

Taft listened, his mind performing mental gymnastics,
ten thousand shares, at a fifteen-point rise within a week,
meant a hundred and fifty thousand dollar profit. Five percent of fifty thousand dollars for that same period was
twenty-five hundred dollars. He could be in and out, pay
a Shylock's rate of interest and still be ahead over a
hundred and forty-five thousand dollars. Even after taxes,
it left him enough to make a settlement with his wife.

Figure the worst, if he had to hold on for two weeks,
the interest only amounted to five thousand dollars, a
mere trifle compared to the overall gain. Or even if the
gain was a mere ten points rather than the optimistic fifteen he was still ahead ninety thousand dollars. Taft
agreed to Mr. Barton's offer. They shook hands, Barton
promising that the money would be in Taft's hands in time
to settle up for his stock.

Later that afternoon in his office at TCA The Doctor
took a call from an old friend, Cat's Eye Bastione.

"Doc? My kid was in there this morning. We made him
a nice deal. As a favor to you. Five percent a week. The
whole fifty big ones."

"Thanks, Cat's Eye. But don't forget, when he gets into
a jam, call me first. Before you do anything."

"You know me, Doc." Bastione paused then said a bit
self-consciously, "Doc . . . Maybe you do something for
me. . . ."

"Sure, Cat's Eye! Anything!"

"I got this here little girl. Nice Italian kid. I mean,
good banging and she don't talk. Won't embarrass a man
with a big mouth. After all, I got a wife and kids, you
know how it is," Bastione said, sounding like a high school
junior.

"Of course, Cat's Eye. So?"

"She ain't satisfied singing in the Chez Paree. She wants
on the TV. She says with her voice and her tits she could

be a big star in TV and pictures. Now I got no muscle in the TV."

"*You* think she could be a star, Cat's Eye?"

"The tits she got. But the voice, *mezza, mezza*," Cat's Eye said quite frankly. "Anyhow spot her on some show, huh? Otherwise with every fuck all I get is talk and tears. I'm ruining her life she says, destroying her career. What's botherin' me, now she is starting to talk *before* we get in the hay. I don't mind *after*. I can fall asleep. But before, it takes all the fun out of the fucking. You know?"

"Cat's Eye," The Doctor said, "if this deal with Taft works, I'll spot her. Even if it doesn't, I think I can find a way."

"Thanks, Doc," Bastione said gratefully. "I knew you'd understand."

Federated Electronics was issued as planned at the price of five dollars a share, but it opened on the Pacific Coast at nine. Anson Taft received the news in the middle of a staff meeting at CBN, in the form of a note slipped to him by his secretary, Buffy, a tall blond young woman who appeared aloof and business-like during office hours, but who, after work, was Taft's mistress. She could, by refusing his sexual advances, throw him into a fury of frustration that would reflect itself throughout the network. Careers, entire shows, were jeopardized by Taft's furies. After Buffy had slipped him the note, she went to the door, waited an instant while he read it and looked up at her. Their eyes met. They were both delighted but masked it well. Another week or two and they could be free to marry.

On the third day after the issuance of Federated Electronics Cone placed a call to Anson Taft, who had three other calls held while he took The Doctor's.

"Anson. Irwin Cone."

"Yeah, Doctor, how's it going?"

"Opened here at twelve bid, thirteen and a half asked."

"Great!" Taft responded heartily, computing swiftly, ten thousand, times thirteen and a half, a profit of eighty-five thousand already and the week only half over.

"You could get out now with a good profit," Cone suggested cautiously.

"I'll ride with it," Taft said. "All the way up to twenty!"

"Okay," The Doctor said, having anticipated the reply. Then he added, in a light, joking way, "Don't forget, they say there are three kinds of animals in Wall Street, bulls, bears, and hogs."

They both laughed. The Doctor hung up. He immediately placed a call to his own broker over on Beverly Drive.

"Dave, Federated Electronics, how does it look?"

"Jesus! You're not still holding any of that, are you?"

"Just asking. For a friend."

"Oh," the broker said, relieved. "We've got most of our people out. We figure it's topped and ready to slide. And when it does, watch out! Call your friend, tell him to sell."

"I will, I will," Irwin Cone said hastily as though he couldn't get off the phone fast enough to perform that friendly service. But when he hung up he called not Anson Taft but Spence Gould. To all of Spence's questions The Doctor had only one reply, "Call me the minute Taft calls you."

On Monday when the market opened on the Coast, Federated Electronics was down to five bid and six asked. At eleven o'clock Anson Taft received a phone call from Mr. Barton, who was calling, so he said, to remind Mr. Taft that the first weekly interest payment of twenty-five hundred dollars was due. In cash.

"Don't worry!" Taft answered a bit frantically, "I'll have it for you."

"When?"

"Tomorrow!"

"Good. Else I will have to turn it over to our collection department. And I hate to do that to any man with a wife and kids," Barton said, making it sound exactly as ominous as he intended.

Taft hung up, determined to wait out the day. By six o'clock New York time, when Pacific Coast trading closed, Federated was down to three and a half bid, four asked, and not much stock was changing hands.

At CBN, the rest of the staff had gone. Only Taft remained in his darkened office high over Rockefeller Plaza. He looked out over the city, glanced down at Fifth Avenue which was lit up by store windows and the headlights of cabs, cars, buses. Below in the plaza people were ice skating to music that did not penetrate Taft's well-insulated office.

Buffy came in quietly. When the reflection of her pretty face, her blond hair appeared in the window beside him he reached around to embrace her, his hand going for her breast. She pulled away just a little. When he looked at her, her face was composed, but very firm.

"Buffy?"

"What are you going to do?" she asked, quite practically.

"Let's go over to Twenty-One. A martini and some dinner and I'll think more clearly."

"Uh uh," she said, rejecting his invitation.

"Buff?" he asked, taken aback.

"I made up my mind today. I am never again going into Twenty-One with you unless I go as Mrs. Anson Taft. And that doesn't look very likely now, does it?"

He turned to press against her, feeling the outlines of her body. "I'll work it out! Somehow I'll get the money to pay off Celia, to provide for the kids."

"Ans, I have been eating around, drinking around and sleeping around with you for three whole years now on that promise. And nothing has happened," she said with a coldness that took him by surprise. "You better realize that I am not something to wear on your arm into Twenty-One. I am not a stopover on your way back to Greenwich every night. And I am not getting any younger. With what I have, I can do damn well for myself now. And that's what I mean to do."

Some harsh truths are spoken in the offices surrounding Rockefeller Plaza after day is done.

"Buffy . . ." he said, surprised and hurt.

"I love you, Ans. But not quite as much as I love the kind of life I have planned for myself."

She started to remove his hand when his private line rang. Answering it, he heard a voice that was all too familiar by now.

"Mr. Taft, what time tomorrow do I make my pick-up?"

"How did you get this number?"

"Why? Is it the wrong number?" Barton asked. "Look,

Taft, we have rules here. Once we hand over an account for collection, we have no control over the methods used to collect it. Make myself clear?"

"Yeah, yeah. It's clear."

"So?"

"Call me in the morning," Taft said, trying to end the conversation.

"What time?" Barton persisted.

"The morning."

"What time in the morning?"

"Eleven. Eleven o'clock."

"Okay. Eleven," Barton said.

In the fifteen minutes that ensued Buffy and Anson Taft were finally able to locate Spencer Gould in the steam room of the City Athletic Club. Spence called The Doctor in Beverly Hills at once. Before a half hour passed the private line in Anson Taft's office rang again.

"Anson, Irwin Cone! Sorry to hear about your trouble. Remember, I tried to get you out of Federated, but you said no. Well, that's past history. First, I don't want you to worry about Bastione."

"Bastione?" Taft echoed, fearfully.

"Yeah. His son uses the name Barton. For business purposes. But it's Bastione. Now I don't want you to worry about him," The Doctor continued, able to detect from the dead silence on the other end that the name Bastione had accomplished its purpose. "I'll take care of him."

"How?"

"The only way anyone *ever* takes care of a man like Cat's Eye Bastione. Pay him off. Principal and interest."

"You do that and I'll make it up to you! I'll pay you back! Every month! It'll take some time, but I'll pay it off. Every nickel!"

"We can worry about that later. First thing is to take care of Bastione. Call you back."

Within half an hour Taft's phone rang again. It was The Doctor.

"Just talked to Bastione. The money will be in his hands by morning. No one will bother you anymore. You can forget it!"

"I don't know how to thank you. We'll get together. We'll work out a deal to repay you. . . ."

"Anson, Anson," said The Doctor. "I feel this is all my fault. I was the one who suggested Federated. True, I thought it was a chance to make a killing. I thought I was doing you a big favor. But it didn't turn out that way. I think I should bear the brunt of this."

"Bear the brunt?" Taft asked, groping for The Doctor's meaning.

"Forget it! The whole thing! We'll write it off. Somehow," Cone said, vaguely hinting that he himself would take the loss.

"There has to be something I can do." Taft kept insisting.

"I told you. Forget it. That's all you have to do. And don't worry about a thing," The Doctor said reassuringly. Then he hung up.

Anson Taft, his shirt damp and clinging to his back, dropped the phone back into its cradle. Without looking at Buffy, he said, "Tonight, tonight let's go somewhere. Not Twenty-One. Some nice, quiet, out-of-the-way place. I need a drink. I need two drinks. Tonight I need someone to love me."

He reached out to her. She hesitated, then because she did love him, she took his hand. It not only forgave him, it let him draw her close. He embraced her and she could feel his tenseness.

Gently she wiped the perspiration. At the same time his hand started moving up her firm nylon-clad legs, then gently and without her objection it ventured up under her dress and along the soft skin of her thighs, until he was gently fingering the silken hair between. In a while she began to respond. Thus encouraged he rose to confront her, pressing against her fiercely, his erection throbbing violently.

She allowed him to undress her, a process with which he was so familiar by now that he needed no help. He drew down the long zipper at the back of her dress, slid his hand in, turning her so that now he had both hands on her naked breasts which were so young and high that she rarely wore a bra. She leaned back undulating against him, for she liked to feel him against her that way, hard and stiff.

Now he had freed himself from his trousers and opened

her thighs, his hands even tighter against her breasts.

Suddenly she found herself wondering if the skaters she saw below making their monotonous rounds of the rink had any idea of who was watching them or what they were doing. But she was too aroused to wonder for very long. She turned to face him, reaching down to take hold of him. So he had her, half-clad, on the twenty-four-dollar-a-yard executive-quality wool pile of his office floor.

As she lay there, wide open and welcoming him, feeling him thrusting with an intensity that he had never quite revealed before, she decided that he was even better tense than relaxed. His thrusts were stronger, reaching into her deeper and deeper till when he flooded her she could feel it throughout her whole being. They climaxed together and she felt good about that. Because this time he had needed to restore his confidence and wipe out the terror of the past few hours.

2

Two days later, without reference to the events of that particular evening, Spence Gould presented Anson Taft with "a new concept in network program planning." It consisted of allowing one talent agency to fill an entire block of consecutive hours of network time with a balanced group of programs, hours and half hours. In other words, TCA offered to take care of CBN's entire prime time problem for Tuesday night.

Acting with unusual dispatch for such an innovative policy, Anson Taft approved the idea and it became the lead headline and story in *Variety* that week. A solid block of CBN programming from seven-thirty to eleven was being booked through TCA. Once more The Doctor had turned disaster into profit.

One of those shows, a variety hour, introduced to network television Della D'Angelo, a young Italian singer from Chicago. Her voice was adequate. Her gown was magnificent and her breasts sufficiently exposed to create such a flurry in the control room that just before air time the network censor insisted on having a bit of chiffon tucked into her cleavage.

But as Della walked on stage, Spence Gould plucked the chiffon out of her bodice so she went on in a way that warmed the heart of one old man in Chicago.

However, in the long-range plans of Doctor Irwin Cone and TCA only one show in that Tuesday night lineup figured prominently. And that one was to affect the entire life of Jeff Jefferson.

It was called "Broadway Star Theatre," a name conjured up by Freddie Feig, at a spur-of-the-moment meeting. Third of TCA's three-man cobra squad, Freddie's most distinguishing characteristics were a lean, menacing face with

186

a hairline mustache and a slight limp which he referred to as a service-connected injury, but which was actually self-inflicted. During World War II, when shipment overseas became imminent, Freddie had deliberately dropped a cartridge case on his right foot, breaking several small bones. He was mustered out after his recovery, granted a small lifetime pension and thereafter he referred to his wartime wound in a modest, but martyr-like manner.

It was this same limp and the sympathy it evoked that caused The Doctor to relax his standards for promising assistants and to hire Feig despite the fact that he had not attended an Ivy League college and that his grades were not of the highest. But Freddie had proved himself to be as worthy as either Spence or Buddy.

Freddie Feig's contribution to the Tuesday night line-up, "Broadway Star Theatre," was an hour of dramatic entertainment done live from New York under the direction of an eccentric young homosexual producer who was a TCA client. The show would ostensibly feature adaptations of great Broadway plays and American novels performed by the finest American stage stars of the time.

When presented to Carl Brewster, Vice President in charge of Radio and Television at S.S.D. & O., "Broadway Star Theatre" was the most costly, ambitious, and promising package of live television entertainment yet assembled. It was designed for some large sponsor seeking a vehicle of great prestige to mark its entrance into television.

As he sat in his office, his feet up on a corner of his huge desk, Carl Brewster did not make any effort to conceal his interest. To himself, he figured, the time spot was right, Tuesday night from nine to ten on the CBN network. And, even if TCA delivered only half the talent that Freddie Feig promised, it had sufficient prestige to make S.S.D. & O. look good with any sponsor for a long time to come. It did no harm for Brewster to betray his interest. He would contact his sponsor in Pittsburgh and get back to Freddie Feig within a week.

Freddie smiled, saying, "Of course, I'll hold it open as long as I can, but I have a strong interest at two other agencies."

Recognizing that as routine pressure, Brewster nodded,

saying to himself, "Fuck you, Freddie boy! We don't jeopardize our account because one of you cobras is anxious to make a quick sale." To Freddie, he just said, "For the opening show we'd need something really strong, to let the critics know exactly the kind of series we intend to do. What would you suggest for the premiere?"

Freddie Feig was at the door, had already turned the knob when he heard that question. It aroused in him exactly the kind of greedy hope which Brewster had intended.

"Why for the opening show," Freddie spitballed, "we could deliver, well, say . . . Clark Ford . . ." seizing on the name of TCA's most prestigious Broadway star.

"In?" Brewster seduced.

"Why . . . in . . . in . . . *Dodsworth!*" Freddie exuberated, it being the most important literary property that came to his mind at the moment.

"Clark Ford in *Dodsworth!*" Brewster tasted that, letting it roll luxuriantly over his tongue. Then, using his expressive right hand, he billboarded it, "Broadway Star Theatre . . . Clark Ford in Sinclair Lewis's *Dodsworth!*" He smiled. "Sounds pretty good. I'll fly out to Pittsburgh tomorrow."

Elated, Freddie Feig limped nobly out of Brewster's office, then raced swiftly to the elevator, waited impatiently till the down car arrived, stepped in, hurried back to the TCA office up on Madison without even waiting for a cab.

When he reported to Spence, instead of the enthusiasm Freddie expected, Spence observed dryly, "Look, Freddie, next time, don't promise! Make it tentative, like say, 'We're considering putting Clark Ford into television.' Or 'I'm not promising, *but* it might be possible to deliver Clark Ford, at a price! But for Christ's sake don't ever get pinned down to deliver someone like Clark Ford."

"Okay, okay," Freddie promised. "Meantime if it comes to that we'll find a way around."

"Right," Spence conceded.

Two mornings later, Carl Brewster called Freddie Feig to report that he had been to Pittsburgh, had conferred with his sponsor, had received a highly enthusiastic response. In fact, if TCA could guarantee that the opening

show of the series would actually be Clark Ford's television debut in Sinclair Lewis's *Dodsworth*, Brewster
thought a deal could be made. And quickly. He did not
disclose to Freddie that the sponsor had agreed to "Broadway Star Theatre" without any reservations about the
opening show. The condition on Clark Ford was Brewster's.
He said no more. He knew what would ensue at TCA as
soon as he hung up.

And it did.

Freddie Feig raced out of his English-antique office,
courtesy of Mrs. Irwin Cone, and into Spence's, which
was equally well furnished. Excitedly, Freddie reported his
conversation with Brewster. Spence took the news more
calmly but with much more concern than the younger,
less experienced Freddie.

Yes, of course there was the chance to pick up a series
that would throw off a TCA commission of over six thousand dollars a week, over three hundred thousand a year.
Spence was not demeaning that possibility.

But Clark Ford. Delivering Clark Ford for a television
show, a medium he'd never agreed to try before. . . .
There must be another way.

"Another star?" Freddie Feig ventured.

"Of course. But first we have to get off the hook on
Ford," Spence said. He lifted his intercom phone, pressed
down the button that put him into immediate contact with
Janet Flynn, TCA's woman in charge of legitimate theater,
and Clark Ford's own personal contact at TCA.

"Jannie," Spence crooned, "what's on Clark Ford's schedule, say the next six months?"

"He's reading," Janet responded with the usual cliché
politely explaining that a theater star was actually unemployed for one reason or another.

"Found anything he's interested in?" Spence probed.

"He's not going to do TV!" Janet said, always practical,
always honest, always cutting to the heart of the matter.
"He hates the rush, the short rehearsal time, the sloppy
production. The answer is no! Now what else?"

"Of course the answer is 'no.' That's why I'm calling. To
find some graceful way of putting off a sponsor who's desperate to get him."

"Then say he's weighing two plays, one from the Guild,

one from," she had to improvise, "one from Leland Hayward."

"Okay!" Spence said. He pressed another button, summoned his secretary, instructed her to place a call to Carl Brewster at S.S.D. & O. Since Brewster was expecting the call he answered immediately.

"Carl!" Spence elated, as though greeting a dear friend. "Howareyuh? What's new? How's Ellie? And the kids?" He asked his questions in bunches, not giving Brewster time to answer until he was finished.

Brewster, meantime, made his own assessment. Freddie had not called back, but Spence had. That meant TCA could not deliver Clark Ford. Spence was too warm, too cozy, too personal, too hearty. Spence was going to try to sell him off Ford and onto some other star. But Brewster had made up his own mind. He knew that a year from now, or when the time came for the big power struggle at S.S.D. & O. his only weapon would be those few sponsors he had carefully cultivated. Those clients who, out of loyalty to him for work well done, would switch their business if he left the agency. The sponsor in Pittsburgh, the largest producer of aluminum in the world, was one of those clients whom Carl Brewster was determined to make his own.

He was not about to be jollied out of the idea of Clark Ford. It would be a headline event on the TV page of every newspaper and magazine in the country. It would be the biggest, best publicity coverage his sponsor could possibly get. Brewster was not going to give up that advantage.

So he sat calmly at his desk, listening to Spence while thinking to himself, "You just keep talking you shrewd Jew bastard, because as soon as you stop to draw one sinusy breath I am going to say no!"

Gould stopped, Brewster said, "Spence, let's get to the point! No Clark Ford, no deal. Period!" He said it as softly as he could, for he knew that would upset Spence Gould more than an argument. Arguments are invitations to negotiation. Flat statements, softly delivered, leave the opponent with little traction. He could literally hear Spence change gears, as he used yet another piece of Kleenex. Brewster had done business with Spence Gould often enough to know that his emotions controlled the flow of his nasal excretions.

To himself, Spence Gould said, you cold-assed Protestant sonofabitch! So you own the companies, you own the agencies! And you're going to make every Jew dance to your tune. Not for long, *shmuck!* I'll cut your balls off one day!

To Brewster, Spence gave it a Harvard reading: "Look, Carl, why don't we discuss this over lunch? You, Freddie and I. Twenty-One. Can you make it today?"

"I don't know what we'd have to talk about," Brewster said.

Spence laughed as heartily as he could, considering the agitated state of his sinuses. "We'll find something. Even if it's only broads."

Brewster considered it a moment, then said, "Okay. Twenty-One, twelve-thirty."

Through three martinis apiece, through a lunch of tasty thin Scotch salmon with fresh black pepper, Steak Diane and coffee, no one mentioned Clark Ford. Over the second cup of coffee, Spence Gould finally said, as though summarizing everything all three of them had been thinking, "Look, Carl-baby, we're all in the same boat. Clark Ford is going to do a play for the Theatre Guild. He is absolutely unavailable. Now, that means that your agency is going to lose TV billing with commissions of twenty thousand dollars a week. Twenty grand a week!" Spence reiterated.

"Don't I know it!" Brewster pretended to commiserate.

"What I suggest is this. The three of us go out to Pittsburgh. I take with me the most impressive list of available stars in the entire industry and together we sell your client off Clark Ford and onto someone else, just as good. Better! Yes, better."

Brewster reacted skeptically.

"What makes you think that Clark Ford is so hot?" Spence asked. "I mean after all, he is a star *where?* In the theater! Which is what? A lot of pretentious shit! How many theater-goers are there in this country? Less than a million. How many moviegoers? A hundred million. Has Clark Ford ever really made it in pictures? Never. And he's had chances! Outside of New York he's no star at all!

Even though he's our own client I have to be honest with you, Carl. He isn't worth a nickel outside of a legitimate theater! That's the truth!"

Brewster had not expected Spence's onslaught against Ford to become that furious that fast. It was a sign of TCA's desperation. And if they were that desperate, they might yet produce Ford. Brewster said simply, "Look, Spence, I'm an instructed delegate. My client said to say no to everyone but Clark Ford."

"That's why I'm saying," Spence interrupted, "let's *all* go to Pittsburgh! Maybe *we* can change his mind!"

"I don't think it would work. My client does not like to talk to . . . to . . . well, he doesn't like agents."

Spence Gould and Freddie Feig both reacted with thin smiles that tried but died. Both of them had silently transposed "agents" to "Jews." They were right. All three of them knew it.

At seven o'clock New York time, four o'clock Los Angeles time, Spencer Gould placed the one phone call he always hated to make—a call for help to The Doctor. With Freddie on the extension, they patiently explained the situation. Reduced to its essentials it was: produce Clark Ford or TCA would lose out on a six thousand dollar a week commission. The Doctor listened, asked for a few days to think it over and hung up.

To both Spence and Freddie it seemed an abrupt answer, disheartening. Their plea for help had done them more harm than an outright failure. It had been a mistake to call. A bigger mistake than they knew.

For The Doctor had been in the process of seducing a particularly stupid but highly attractive young blond actress to whom he had offered the bait of promised stardom. He disliked doing such things. But occasionally he did them. He was not strongly sexed. His weakness was usually for girls who were obviously stupid, obviously used, obviously easy. He could be almost as relentless in pursuing such a girl as he was in the pursuit of lucrative business. This had been one of those days and one of those girls. And his two young idiots in the New York office had just spoiled it for him.

When he finished his conversation with them, Irwin

THE KINGMAKE

Cone turned back to the girl who stood be
dress down over one shoulder, her high, perfe
breast confidently exposed. He tried to go back to
his lips over the nipple as he had been doing a mo
before, but he had no interest in it. His erection had subsided and would not return.

They had pricked him in his most vulnerable spot, with
the challenge of a huge deal that needed intricate maneuvering in order to become a reality. He started stuffing the
girl's breast back into her dress.

Meantime the pathetic girl, who had never been refused
before, even by directors and producers, suffered the hu-
miliation of being unlaid and turned out by an agent. The
Doctor, true. But still an agent.

"Did I do something wrong?" she pleaded, seeing her
whole promising career destroyed by some unintentional
blunder.

"Some other time," The Doctor said. He hustled her
out, reminding himself, as he did each time this happened,
that he must get over his weakness for cheap screwing. It
was like his intern days with linen-closet lays on the dull
early shifts.

It didn't take The Doctor long to determine his strategy.
By midnight New York time, he had put in a call to Janet
Flynn at her apartment. She was still up, just back from
the run-through of a new play by one of her clients. After
the few niceties which The Doctor always made it a point
to proffer his hired hands, he asked her an abrupt question, the directness of which silenced her for a moment.

"Jannie, what's the one thing in this world that Clark
Ford wants to do most?"

Being a strong-minded girl and a protective agent she
said straightforwardly, *"Not television!"*

Although furious, The Doctor laughed. "Jannie, Jannie,
that I know. I said tell me what he *does* want to do. In
the theater. Some play. Or perhaps he's always wanted
to direct. Something. Some secret desire. He must have
one. What is it?"

"I don't know," she equivocated.

"You're the only one who is close to that moody man.
If he talks to anyone, he talks to you," The Doctor persisted.

All of which was true. All of which imposed on Janet Flynn the same kind of silence which governs priests, doctors and lawyers. Though she worked with men like The Doctor, Spence Gould, Freddie and Buddy, she did not trust them. She knew that right now she might hurt Clark Ford if she made any admission. Still there was something "the moody man" did want to do. There was a play he loved and in which he saw values that no producer would admit, even those producers who were always saying, "Clark, you find a play you want to do and, sight unseen, I'll produce it!" They had all balked at this one. It didn't read well. It was ahead of its time, formless, vague, its message turgid, unclear. Janet Flynn had to admit that she did not appreciate the play herself.

Perhaps that made her decide to answer. She felt that Clark had brooded too long on a bad play. She said to The Doctor, "Well, there is one play that he loves, but nobody wants to produce it. After all, who's going to blow fifty thousand dollars, just in the hope that, out of gratitude, Clark Ford will agree to do his *next* play?"

"Of course, I understand. A producer has to go with his own gut reaction," The Doctor clichéd. But just before he hung up he asked, "If I get to New York tomorrow night can I see Ford for supper?"

"I'll try to arrange it," Janet said.

"Arrange it!" The Doctor commanded and added, "By the way, what's the title of that thing? That play he likes?"

"*King, Queen, Check,*" Janet said.

"What's it about?"

"That's the trouble. No one knows. Not even the playwright."

"Have a copy waiting at my hotel tomorrow evening," The Doctor said. He hung up, absent-mindedly scratching his crotch and vaguely remembering the cheap blonde of the afternoon. Then he went from the library into his bedroom, got into bed with his wife and the feeling died a natural death.

Clark Ford was a lean, morose man. A fugitive from himself, he found release only in living his life pretending to be someone else. Hence to him acting was not only a profession but a means of emotional therapy. Things he dared onstage he could never do in his own tangled life. In his off hours he was constantly in search of love, acceptance, warmth, human contact.

When he found them, or their counterparts, he could not recognize them, or recognizing them, could not justify them and always turned in the end to doubting all others so that he did not have to doubt himself. He had been married four times, each marriage having terminated unsuccessfully, two by divorce, one by annulment, one by suicide.

The children he had were strangers to him. He had no time for them in his frenetic pursuit of his own unrequitable passions and fears. He was constantly eligible and considered himself so, seeking out younger and younger potential wives. His lean hard body allowed him to keep the illusion of youth, helping him to justify his sexual proclivities and choices.

All these problems, complex and obvious as they were, reflected themselves in his work. Because of them he devoted himself to his art with greater concentration than most other actors. Each venture onto the stage before an audience was an act of self-justification. If the audience accepted him, they forgave him all his shortcomings. So, for that one night at least, he had absolution.

Only when a play had opened, and to reviews that lauded Ford for his delivery of yet another controlled, underplayed, superb performance, did his mood improve. Once he had had his nightly reassurance onstage, he was able to relax.

During those times Clark Ford was, for a month or two, a relatively happy man. He could make love unselfishly. He could entertain thoughts of getting married. He could do almost anything that any average man could do.

It was for this same reason that he had never quite made it in pictures. Pictures did not offer that same regular reassurance. Pictures one made, walked away from, and never did discover the outcome till months later. Not much consolation there.

So he had become the ultimate American stage actor mainly because he had no other place to go. If he failed on Broadway, he knew he would die.

Of course, he had failed there on occasion. The most recent, just five months before. Ford himself had gotten his usual fine reviews, but the play had been found wanting, and since it was a serious play and not a comedy it died in three weeks. Comedies survive vast ineptnesses. Dramas rarely surmount slight ones.

Deprived of his solace, Ford had turned on the world by turning inside himself. He hated the producer, hated the author, hated everyone who had assured him that it was a play worthy of his talents. He had even, in some darkest moments, hated Janet Flynn, though he knew, lucid or not, that he could depend on Janet if on no other human being in the world. He had even once had a brief affair with her. She had cut it off, because, as she said, she would rather represent him than marry him or be his lover. And to represent him properly and honestly she had to be emotionally free.

When Janet called the morning after her midnight phone call from The Doctor, Ford came to the phone grudgingly. A petulant boy, she had to coax him, knowing all the while it was just this coaxing he desired. She said the expected things. He responded in the usual way by belittling her reassurances and her flatteries.

Finally, when she seemed genuinely hurt and he had achieved his goal, he offered his usual line of reconciliation. "I don't know why I treat you this way, Jannie. You're the only one who understands me. Who loves me." He had used that line every time he had made love to her. It was the signal he emitted when he was ready to put himself into her hands and be guided by her judgment.

"Clark," Janet began, "I got a call from the Coast last night. . . ."

He interrupted, "I don't want to do pictures! Every time I have a flop on Broadway they think I'm ready to go back into pictures again. No, no, no!"

Without mentioning the fact there had not been a single inquiry from any studio, Janet said, "If that's what it was, I wouldn't bother you, darling. You know that."

Mollified, he made an indistinct sound signifying acknowledgment and she felt free to continue.

"Clark, the man who called me last night was Irwin Cone."

"The Doctor?" Ford was instantly suspicious, hostile. "What does he want?"

"He wants to come all the way to New York to meet you," Janet said.

"About what?"

"It's about a play."

"Another piece of shit like the last one? By another lousy TCA writer?"

"*King, Queen, Check*," Janet said softly, deliberately playing under the level of his outrage.

She could feel him smile. Then he said more warmly, "*King, Queen, Check?* He likes it?"

"He didn't say anything except that he wanted to talk to you about it. Tonight. Supper, if you can make it. He wants to meet you any place you say."

That degree of deference from Irwin Cone was flattering even to a star of Clark Ford's eminence.

"Well," Ford tried to conceal his interest. "Well, tonight I was kind of busy, but if the man's flying all the way in . . . Look, I'll cancel my other date. I'll meet him." He paused to consider a place which would have the desired effect on The Doctor. "Say, Pavillon. How about that?"

"Fine! I'll make the reservation. Pavillon. About nine."

"Good!" said Ford exhibiting a degree of enthusiasm. Then he lowered his voice. "Jannie, if you were here right now you know what I'd be doing."

"Please, Clark . . ."

"I *did* make you happy in bed, didn't I?" he demanded, begging again for reassurance.

"Yes. And I told you why it had to stop."

"Once more before I die, Jannie, once more. Your breasts are like coming home."

"Please, Clark."

"Once more before I die," he said and he hung up.

When she put down the phone there were tears in her eyes. If he weren't so destructive, so despicable in so many ways, he could be the ideal lover, because beyond loving her he needed her, depended on her. Yet being a rather simple young woman, with a plain face but a startlingly good figure, she knew that to become seriously involved with him would lead, as all other of his relationships with women led, to disaster of one kind or another.

He would blame her for his failures. He would chase af-

ter other women. He would be sullen and morose except
when he was in the act of making love. All of it must result in her destruction. What made her weep was being
deprived of all that by virtue of her own good sense. She
was strongly tempted to endure such agony for the simple
reason that she loved Clark Ford. And suspecting, but not
knowing for sure what The Doctor had in mind, she felt
that she was delivering Clark into his hands.

The late dinner was the same for both men. A cup of
lobster bisque, cold chicken en gelee, a distinctive white
burgundy. During the meal, of which The Doctor ate little, he lamented the state of Broadway, consoled Clark
Ford over how little of worth the theater offered a star in
these days, casually mentioned that the theater of tomorrow was television.

To all of this Clark Ford responded with an occasional
nod or sound of assent. Feeling he was meeting with, if
not success, then little opposition, The Doctor decided
to press his plan a bit more strongly.

"Of course, the reason for any medium slipping, or failing altogether, is the producer, the one person whose
function it is to bring all the talent together, and provide
them with the tools, sets, costumes, and a theater. But
above all he must have the script!"

Clark Ford looked up, presenting a frankly interested
face for the very first time.

"Without the right script, where are we? No place! Yet
this is where producers fail worst. Either they can't appreciate a script. Or, having read one and liked it, most
times they haven't got the guts to back their judgment and
risk possible failure."

When Clark Ford nodded this time it was a strong, resentful nod. He put aside his fork and was prepared to
listen without the early reservations that he, and every
actor, had about a notorious schemer like The Doctor.

"I know what it's like," The Doctor said sadly. "I
wasn't always an agent. And I don't mean being a doctor.
I was, from the age of ten, a violinist! Yes! From ten until sixteen I worked at my violin four hours a day, every
day. And if I didn't have the best of instruction, it was
good. And I was even better."

He paused an instant as if to excuse his pride and then added, "If not for financial pressures I might well have become a concert violinist!"

"Really?" Ford sympathized.

"I'd be on your side of the lights instead of mine. But my father ran a little grocery store, in a poor neighborhood. And his worst habit was his belief in human nature. The A & P had a much bigger store, but my father a lot longer list of accounts receivable."

The Doctor smiled in tribute to the old days. "He used to write his accounts on brown paper bags. And then lose the bags. On purpose, most times. By the time I was fifteen I had to give up all thoughts of serious music and start playing in tinny bands to make a living until I grew to hate music."

It was a speech The Doctor had made before, whenever he wanted to establish personal rapport with a writer, director or actor. It worked. Every time. It was working now, he felt.

"Clark, I don't want the same thing to happen to you. I don't want you to go on doing those 'Clark Ford parts' 'til you get so sick of the sameness that you give up. So . . ."

He let it hang there, as though debating with himself whether to present what he had in mind. Ford waited, his sad eyes hoping, then finally pleading for The Doctor to go on.

"*I* have come across a script. A play with new dimensions. A new approach to theater writing. Free. Uninhibited. Challenging! I'm sure you'll love it."

"I do!" Ford said as angry as he was enthusiastic. "But nobody will do it!"

The Doctor pretended to be completely silenced by the fact that Ford knew of the play. Then he deliberately fumbled, "You mean you know the play I'm talking about?"

"Of course! *King, Queen, Check*."

"Yes, yes! Strange, Jannie never told me," The Doctor lied. "When I mentioned that title to her, and told her not to tell you, she never said you knew the play."

"I've had that damn thing for a year now! I've taken it to every producer in New York! They won't touch it!"

"Producers! These days producers either have no taste, or they have no guts!"

"You can say that again!" Ford seconded.

"Well." The Doctor smiled. "Now that you already know the play and love it, as I do, the rest is easy. For me. But not so easy for you."

He made it sound like a challenge, to which Ford was angry enough to rise.

"I want you to produce the play. No, no, no," The Doctor anticipated quickly, "not to say 'Clark Ford presents Clark Ford in *King, Queen, Check*.' We'll get some new young producer, or else some general manager to front the production. But together you and I will do this play! *You* will star in it. *I* will put up the money."

"All the money?" Ford asked, surprised. "It'll take fifty thousand, maybe even sixty."

"All the money," The Doctor affirmed.

Ford was impressed, deeply moved to find a patron so devoted to good theater.

"Now, what I would like to do is make a gentlemen's agreement before I leave New York tomorrow," The Doctor said.

"I'll give you my hand on it now!" Clark volunteered.

"No. Don't react emotionally. Imagine that instead of your agent, I'm your enemy. Suspect me. Diminish what I offer you. Figure out tough terms. Do as you would do with any ordinary producer, then give me your answer."

"Okay. Tomorrow," Ford said, now secretly admiring this man who so openly invited suspicion.

"Oh, there is one more thing," The Doctor said. "Due to my schedule I would like to go into production about mid-November to open on Broadway right after the New Year. How does that fit in with your plans?"

"I think that would be fine."

"Then call me in the morning!"

They both rose, The Doctor small, almost tiny alongside Ford's lean six feet three. In accordance with his habit, Ford left the table first. The Doctor gracefully permitted it, knowing that it was Ford's desire never to be left alone at a table, never to be left alone anywhere.

As The Doctor watched him go, his mind quickly toted up the score. He had won Ford's friendship and admiration. More important, he had made absolutely sure that Clark Ford was professionally free from now through October but firmly committed from November on. That precluded his taking any other stage assignment in the meantime. And with no film offer on the horizon, there was no doubt in The Doctor's mind that Clark Ford would thus be free for the big, important TV premiere of "Broadway Star Theatre."

At eleven-o-five the next morning Clark Ford called the TCA office in New York. He said yes to *King, Queen, Check* and to The Doctor.

"And about the dates, Clark?" The Doctor persisted, to be absolutely sure.

"November fifteenth rehearsal is fine with me!"

"Great!" The Doctor said, nodding at the same time to Spencer Gould and Freddie Feig who hungrily awaited the outcome of the conversation. "One thing more, Clark, not a word about this until we're all set to go. I want to break it myself."

"Depend on me, Doctor!" Ford said, as eager for the proper handling and success of the venture as The Doctor seemed to be.

When Cone hung up, Freddie exploded eagerly, "He'll do it!"

The Doctor, with the special disdain that he employed to punish young men who had failed, said only, "Get me Carl Brewster!" He handed the phone to Freddie. The Doctor remained silent till Freddie handed the phone back to him, saying, "Brewster. . . ."

"Carl? Irwin Cone. In New York. I flew in on business, *your* business." He allowed the enormity of his sacrifice to sink in. "After all S.S.D. & O. is an important client to us. So, for you, I did it. Now, if you can keep this absolutely confidential, I will deliver Clark Ford for the opening telecast of 'Broadway Star Theatre.' "

"You will?!" Brewster was too surprised to conceal his delight.

"Yes, I will. But the terms may be a bit stiff."

"Stiff?" Brewster's ulcer started its acidy scratching.

"I am going to lay out sixty thousand dollars of my own money to insure this deal. Now, what I would like is to tack onto the budget we sent you an extra three thousand a week. Call it, call it, an artistic supervisory fee. . . ."

"Three thousand a week." Brewster hesitated, since he felt the budget was dangerously fat as it was. "Three thousand a week over thirty-nine weeks, that's . . ."

"One hundred and seventeen thousand dollars!" The Doctor snapped.

"You said your expense is only sixty thousand," Brewster protested.

"Right! That leaves fifty-seven thousand," The Doctor said simply. "We can put it into a corporation and turn the stock over to you later. Or we can put it in an educational fund for your kids. Any way you want, because we appreciate the way you handled this whole thing with your sponsor. Well?"

"Let's, let's discuss it away from the office. Lunch tomorrow?"

"Okay! Lunch tomorrow," The Doctor said. "I'll stay over."

He hung up. Spence and Freddie were smiling. But The Doctor was quite grave when he said, "They can say what they want about Jews. But you can always buy a *goy* cheaper in the long run."

Within days and with an absolute blackout on all publicity, the deal was signed for ALUMCO of Pittsburgh to sponsor "Broadway Star Theatre," through S.S.D. & O. It was contingent, of course, on TCA's promise to deliver Clark Ford in *Dodsworth* for the opening show.

One other bit of unpublicized business was involved. It had been arranged in a meeting between The Doctor and Carl Brewster in the secluded confines of the Plaza's Oak Room.

Their arrangement was to be straight, clean aboveboard. They would report the income. And pay the taxes, so that there could be no foul-ups later.

"Consultants, Ltd.," a firm of "Creative Television Advisers" would be established. The stockholders would consist of Spencer Gould, Betsy Brewster and Robert Brewster, aged thirty-one, eight and six respectively. "Consultants, Ltd." was signed at once to act as "creative consultants" to "Broadway Star Theatre." The fee was to be three thousand dollars each week for as long as the series remained on the air.

With all that arranged, and with a tentative opening date of October 14th, The Doctor turned his attention to securing Clark Ford's agreement to appear on television. Immediately, he ordered a first-rate TV adaptation of *Dodsworth*.

At the same time, he involved Clark Ford in a series of phone calls between Beverly Hills and New York. They were always, of course, about *King, Queen, Check*, always about such important decisions as the selection of a director in whom Clark had confidence, or the selection of the manager to front the production. And, of course, work must be done on the script, which even Clark agreed was not quite perfect. Daily they conferred by phone till The Doctor had Clark Ford totally involved in the project.

When The Doctor judged the time to be right, he gave Spence and Freddie their cue. They made a firm offer to Janet Flynn for Clark Ford to make his debut in television in an outstanding American work, and at the highest fee ever paid to any star for a single performance in that medium.

As they had been instructed, they told Janet that they expected Ford to say no, but felt compelled at least to speak to her because they had promised S.S.D. & O.

Their lack of pressure was so noticeable that Janet was instantly suspicious. Still she was so confident that Clark would say no that she called at noon that same day. She was not surprised when he said he did not wish to do television. He was so immersed in preparing *King, Queen, Check* that he had no time for anything else. Thanks, but no thanks. Even for that money, the highest fee ever paid? Even for that money, no thanks.

The message was relayed to Spencer Gould who in turn phoned The Doctor. That afternoon, Coast time, when the Doctor knew that Ford would be getting ready to go out to dinner, he called. Apologizing for his interruption he said a sudden thought had struck him so forcefully on *King, Queen, Check* that he had to pass it on.

"You know what I think, Clark. I think I'm getting a little stale on it. I find myself going over the same scenes again and again. That's bad."

Clark Ford hesitated a moment, then admitted, "Me, too."

"Really?" The Doctor manifested great concern. "That

is bad. Very bad. I don't want you to go stale before rehearsals even begin. It's not healthy. Maybe you and I
should knock off on it and turn the script over to one of
the pros. Say Sam Behrman. Or Max Anderson. Or maybe
we can even get Bob Sherwood. Give them a few weeks
at it and see what they come up with. All we can lose is
money." The Doctor laughed. "And that's all mine." Then
he asked, "What do you think?"

"Gosh, I don't know," said Ford. "Oh, by the way, talking about a change of pace, I just got an offer to make my
TV debut. Fat price, too."

"TV? You? Who the hell asked Clark Ford to go on
television?" The Doctor said, pretending outrage.

"Jannie. Through Spencer Gould."

"I will call that nervy sonofabitch and eat his ass out!
How dare he!" The Doctor fumed. "Television! I wouldn't
let you do television!" He paused, then continued, only
slightly less angry. "Why, I wouldn't let you go on TV
without reading the script and approving it myself! And
unless we were guaranteed that you'd get not ten days'
rehearsal but three weeks! I don't want you caught in the
kind of rush job that passes for quality production on television. If they want Broadway's best star, let them pay for
Broadway rehearsals! Three weeks!"

"I wouldn't consider anything less than three weeks!"
Ford agreed.

Having established his beachhead, the Doctor said,
"What did they offer? Fifteen thousand?"

"Twenty," Ford said, unable to conceal the flattery involved in the highest price yet reported for a star appearance.

"Not enough! Not anywhere near enough!" The Doctor said, sufficiently angry to give Ford the impression that
he wanted to kill the whole deal. "Listen, I'll save you the
trouble. I myself will call Spence and tell him to go to
hell!" The Doctor then pretended to be seized by a second thought, "You know, that's one problem about getting
emotionally involved with a client, liking him too much. I
don't think straight. But given a moment to reflect, you
know what I was saying about going stale on *King,
Queen, Check?* It occurs to me, what are you going to
be doing all the while Behrman or Anderson is working
on the script?" He paused, "Did Spence say what property

they wanted you to do in this TV thing?"

"*Dodsworth*," Ford said, a bit impressed by that vehicle himself.

"*Dodsworth?*" The Doctor mused. "Excellent property! You never played *Dodsworth* on the stage, did you?"

"I was too young," Ford said, vainly.

"A Sinclair Lewis piece, a great book, a hit play, and a hit picture, too! Let me think about it. Overnight!"

The next day at noon New York time Ford's phone rang.

"Clark, I thought it over. You in *Dodsworth* would be the biggest thing that's ever hit TV! If the money is right, if the terms and conditions are right, if you have script and director approval, I think you should at least consider it."

"You do?" Ford asked, not in surprise, but in a sober tone that indicated he would now seriously consider the project.

"But only if the terms are right!" The Doctor insisted.

"Of course!" Ford agreed.

The Doctor chuckled a bit then said, "Clark, I am now going to show you how I can screw shrewd young bastards like Spencer Gould. I'll teach him to go to you behind my back! Let me negotiate this against him and we'll have more fun than you ever thought possible. First," The Doctor made an obvious ploy of planning his strategy with Clark, "first, we'll ask for a script. Then after we get it, no matter how good it is, you won't like it."

"How do you know?" Ford asked.

"I don't care if it's Shakespeare, you won't like it," The Doctor declared. "That'll throw them into a panic and they'll give us the script approval I promised you."

"I see," Ford said, smiling himself a little now.

"Then, while the script is being fixed, I'll bring up the business about rehearsal time and the director. When we get that settled, you'll agree to do the part. *But* two days later you'll call me back and say you're unhappy about the whole thing. And that's when I say, unless they up the price, we're walking out."

"Uh uh," Ford agreed eagerly.

"More deals are made by walking out than by saying yes!" The Doctor declared. "Okay? Got the strategy?"

"Got it!" Ford agreed.

"Then don't say a goddamn word to anybody. Let me handle it!"

For the next six days The Doctor called Ford every day and, on one day, twice. He reported in detail with great glee how he was putting the pressure on Spencer Gould and S.S.D. & O. How they were resisting point by point, yet eventually yielding point by point.

"And wait till I give them the crusher about the money!" The Doctor gloated.

At the end of six days, Ford was so involved in the negotiations that winning was more important than his feeling about not doing television. By the afternoon of the seventh day, when The Doctor called to say, "They gave in! Every single point. Including the money. Twenty-five grand!," Ford had forgotten all his reservations about television and looked upon the deal itself as an enormous victory.

But The Doctor did not let it rest there. "Clark," he added, "I slipped in a little bonus for us."

"Bonus?"

"I felt, after all we've been through negotiating this, we're entitled to a bonus."

"Oh?" said Ford, not knowing what to expect.

"Right after the telecast, the sponsor has promised to give a big party at Twenty-One, in honor of your TV debut. At that party we announce your next Broadway project, *King, Queen, Check!* Those bastards! Let them foot the bill for our big announcement!"

"Good idea!" Ford agreed, laughing as he hung up the phone.

The Doctor called Spencer Gould at the New York office at once.

"Spence, the deal is made. Ford will do it!"

"He will? What about the party and Ford meeting the sponsor? The old bastard's star struck."

"I told you I would deliver Ford at the party at Twenty-One. Well, I will! Don't worry about it, kid!"

"Oh, great, great, Doctor!" Spencer cheered.

"Spence, do me a favor. . . ."

"Of course."

"Warn that young prick Freddie Feig not to make any more rash promises. Else I'll throw him out on his ass!"

3

Rehearsals anywhere in the world are always the same. Finally it comes down to shredded cigarette butts floating in soggy coffee containers. The rehearsals for the TV version of *Dodsworth* were no different. They began and proceeded as did those of any Clark Ford production. He was grave, professional, moody, uncommunicative. During breaks, instead of exchanging smokes and pleasantries with the rest of the cast, he sat off by himself, ostensibly studying his lines. But actually, as the actress playing Fran, Dodsworth's wife, observed, he had known his part perfectly the day he arrived for the first reading, so what was he studying?

Occasionally the young director—in those days all TV directors were young—went over to Ford to make conversation, usually on some pretext relating to a scene they'd just run. He would remind Ford where Camera One would be at a certain moment. Or when Ford was required to hold for one beat, so that Camera Three could catch him in closeup.

Ford listened, always looking past the young man, then rewarding him only with a single curt nod. After five days of being ignored, the young director's work began to suffer. He became uncertain in his judgments, irritated by the slightest infraction by any other cast member. At the end of the sixth day he called Spencer Gould to resign from the show.

At that point, and as she did during the second week of every Broadway production Clark Ford had done in the last eight years, Jannie Flynn had to step in. Over cocktails, she explained to the young director that there was nothing personal in Ford's behavior. He had been the same with Josh Logan, Guthrie McClintic and even Kazan, that tyrant among tyrants. And she promised to appear at every rehearsal at least once, which she did from then on, arriving just before the noon break.

Each day the cast went down to Ratner's, the Jewish dairy below the old rehearsal ballroom, and famed for its bagels, lox, cream cheese, and rich Danish pastry. Jannie and Ford always sat at a table by themselves. Ford ate as morosely as he rehearsed, but Jannie was used to that.

Only when he asked questions about the progress of *King, Queen, Check* did he seem to brighten. Had The Doctor been able to get Sherwood to work on the script? No. Then Anderson? Max was considering it. He didn't like to rewrite the work of other authors as a general rule, but out of deference to Clark Ford he was "considering." What about S. J. Perelman? Busy on a book. And Behrman, The Doctor's first idea? Behrman was out on the Coast toying with the idea of doing a picture.

Jannie stayed clear of any discussion about the TV show, except to remark, dutifully, that from what she'd seen this young director was very good.

"He stinks!" Ford interrupted.

"He's really very good, Clark." Then, because she didn't really feel as enthusiastic as she had pretended, she appended somewhat casually, "For TV, that is."

"For TV!" Ford seized on it. "TV! Shit! That's what it is! The goddamn script is cut down to one third its size! The audience won't even be able to follow the story. And as for a performance, you've got no time! Hit this mark! Face that camera! Hold that reaction! They call that acting?"

Poor Jannie kept saying, low and pleading, "Clark . . . darling . . . no, please . . . the cast is listening."

"Fuck 'em!" he said, louder now than before.

Though Jannie was embarrassed she was not surprised. He went through this phase in every production. If he followed his usual pattern, tomorrow he would ask to have the director fired.

He did. It took frantic calls to Jannie and Spencer Gould, plus hasty taxi rides downtown to the Second Avenue rehearsal hall to mollify him. In the end, before Ford would agree to continue, The Doctor himself had to call. Only after that did Clark Ford go back to work.

So it went through three torturous weeks.

New traumas, fresh rebellions set in when for the first time Ford was faced with the actual studio. The sets didn't suit him. The lights were too strong, too hot. The multiplicity of cameras and crews made it far worse than any movie he'd done, where there was only one camera, one crew.

Most of all, he objected to the director's voice from inside the control room coming at him over a loudspeaker like the voice of God. Jannie lurked nervously in the dark control room. So did Spence. Freddie Feig limped back and forth, his limp becoming more pronounced as Ford's complaints became more vitriolic. Carl Brewster was deliberately kept out of the studio until dress rehearsal.

Between breaks Jannie would talk to Ford and try to explain away his every irritation. The lights had to be strong for the cameras to effectively photograph the production. The multiplicity of cameras was considered a costly concession to his stature in the theater. His close-ups were very telling, he had no idea how his smallest gesture projected on the screen. There was no need to cut loose in what he called "real acting." And the sets were fine. The work of a Broadway designer, they would look much larger and much more lavish on the television screen. Any larger they might dwarf the drama.

But by now Clark no longer even nodded when Jannie spoke. She knew from experience that was the worst sign. She was right.

Near the end of the second day in the studio, Clark turned suddenly crossing up the camera blocking, and the director had to press down the talk-back button still another time.

"Mr. Ford, at that point you're supposed to look stage left, to favor Camera Four for your close-up. Please?"

Clark Ford turned toward the black window of the control room and shouted, "Listen, you snotty young bastard! You move your fucking cameras to suit *me!* I am through lousing up *my* performance to suit *you!*"

With that Clark Ford stalked off the set, across the large studio, snatched his coat out of his dressing room and slammed out of the building. It was then they put in the red alert call to The Doctor.

Once The Doctor appeared in New York and talked to Ford, he agreed to come back. From then on, all the while Clark worked, The Doctor sat in the rear of the dark control room. Jannie sat on one side of him, Spence and Freddie on the other. Clark was cooperative, but he was not delivering a performance. During one crucial scene, Dodsworth's renunciation of his wife Fran, it went very badly.

The director lamented loud enough for everyone in the control room to hear, "If he screws up that scene you can forget the whole fucking show! I should have quit when I wanted to!"

The Doctor tapped Jannie on the arm, then rose and exited. She followed. He found an empty dressing room. Allowing Jannie to enter first, he carefully closed the door.

"Jannie," he began, "what I'm asking is not for me. Not for TCA. He'll get through Saturday night. He'll do the show. Because he wants to do *King, Queen, Check*. But," The Doctor hesitated. "But he might be so bad he hurts *himself*. *We* can't lose. We've got a firm one-year deal with options. But this is his nationwide debut in television. I don't want him to louse himself up like he has in pictures."

"So?" Jannie asked.

"I've never asked anyone to do this before. And I've asked a great deal from people in my time. Tonight, after rehearsal, go out to dinner with him. Get him drunk." The Doctor paused, then said softly, "And then take him to bed."

Her face flushed, with anger and embarrassment.

"Look, darling, it's no secret about your affair."

"That's over with!" she snapped angrily and turned to go.

The Doctor took her arm firmly and turned her back.

"Jannie, I want to make one thing clear. However you decide, your job is safe. I'll send over a long-term contract in the morning if you don't believe me."

"Why would anybody not believe you?" she said sarcastically.

"All right, I'm a shit. I lie. I steal. I cheat. Even cheat my own clients sometimes. But," he said, "show me one agency that does better for its clients! One! We get them the highest money, the best terms, the most opportunities!"

The Doctor relaxed his grip but she did not move.

"It's for his good. And I mean it!" He pleaded, "Take him out. Get him drunk. Let him make love to you. Tomorrow you'll see a new man. All he needs is confidence. A victory someplace. Bed is best."

After the dinner hour in the back room at Twenty-One, you usually find only those advertising executives who are stuck with entertaining out-of-town clients who don't wish to return to their hotel suites alone. So the room itself was sparsely occupied. With so few customers, the place reverted finally to the clublike atmosphere to which the paneled walls and checked tablecloths pretended.

The table in the far corner was set and reserved for two. When Jannie and Ford arrived they were led to it at once, the captain lavishing an expansive greeting on Ford. Ford returned the courtesy with a grunt and followed Jannie to the table, his battered script book under his arm.

They said little before each ordered two double scotches. The first drink went down fast, and Jannie knew that getting Ford loaded was going to take no special effort on her part. After they had been served their third set of doubles, Jannie suggested they order some food.

Whenever he was in rehearsal, Clark Ford ate like a boxer in training. He believed that overindulgence softened him; that a soft actor was no actor. Whether this was a hangover from the days when he actually had been a hungry young man, or whether it was penance for his success, Jannie never knew. But they both ordered steak tartare with capers, dry toast, and coffee, black.

Once they were free of the overbearing service of the captain, Ford said grimly, "Like a bull in the ring!"

Jannie interrupted her drinking, but said nothing.

"Like a fucking bull brought out to be teased, toyed with, stabbed with banderillas, 'til I'm bloody and worn down and ready for the kill Saturday night!"

"Aside from that one camera mistake, it went very well today," Jannie said softly, not wishing to intensify his wrath. In the throes of production Clark Ford could be nasty and abusive, especially toward women, most especially toward women he loved. The wife who had committed suicide had done so right after the opening of one of his unsuccessful plays.

"What if a mistake like that happens on the air and I'm out there naked and foolish grimacing like a goddamn ape with millions of people watching me! It's *my* reputation. It's *my* career! It's *me,* out there! Not that goddamn prick of a kid director!"

Jannie was conscious that other people were listening. She was thankful when the food arrived and the waiter made such a production of preparing, mixing, spicing the raw steak. It kept Clark quiet, made it possible for Jannie to order him another double. They ate silently, without much enjoyment.

As they left Twenty-One there was a limousine waiting. Courtesy of The Doctor. The little man left nothing to chance. The driver held the door for them, saluted with a quick hand to his cap, and got into the front seat.

"Where to, sir?"

"Seventeen East Sixty-second," Ford sullenly gave Jannie's address.

"No," Jannie said. "Let's ride around a bit. Through the park. I don't want to go home so soon after supper."

"Okay," Ford answered; then to the driver, "Once around the park first."

The driver turned the limousine left up Fifth Avenue and north to Sixtieth. There he swung left into Central Park, easing along the deserted winding roadway that went north between fields, trees and malls. It was long after midnight.

At first Clark sat sullen, silent, a bit under the weather from all the whiskey. But soon, as she anticipated, his hand reached out, taking hers, then venturing slowly toward her breasts. Normally she would have put him off and eventually he would drop her at her place and go on home alone. Now, although she pretended to avoid him, it was only with that degree of restraint which she knew would not discourage him. Then, finally, she permitted his hand to slip into her blouse. When he leaned over and kissed her full on the lips, she opened her mouth and it seduced him completely. His tongue invaded her and she kissed him back.

When he whispered, "Let's go to my place, please, Jannie, darling, please?" she assented with a soft yes.

His apartment presented no challenge to her, no secrets.

She had spent too many nights there before. The only thing that did distress her was the look on the face of the night elevator man who recognized her, bid her good evening by name, and could not completely suppress his surprise that she was back and staying the night again. When they reached the apartment, Ford started to throw the light switch, but she begged, "No, don't. I like the view in the dark."

They went into the living room. She walked straight to the wide expanse of drapery that Clark's house man had drawn shut before leaving. She pulled it back.

Across the river, Long Island was dark except for the signs advertising Chiclets, Pepsi Cola and other less well-known products. The river was black, oily, and occasionally afire from the reflection of red neon. She waited. But not for long. He had gone into his bedroom, taken off his rehearsal clothes and put on a robe. She saw his reflection in the glass, felt his hands reach around her. He rested his face against her neck, causing a chill that trembled her entire body. It made him start to pull back.

But she pressed his hands tightly against her breasts. Now she could feel him hard under his robe. Then he turned her about, kissed her and while still kissing began to undress her. When he fumbled she helped him unobtrusively, knowing that it gave him a sense of dominance to undress his woman.

He had removed her dress, which slipped easily to the floor for she had worn it exactly for this purpose. Now his hand reached behind her, unhooking her bra. He took it off and flung it backward across the room to land against a lamp as though it were the one article of female clothing that offended him. Her breasts free, he kissed and teased her nipples with his tongue. Watching his reflection in the window she suddenly felt like a voyeur at her own seduction.

Then he took her by the hand, led her into the bedroom. The sheets were so fresh and cool they made her tremble but soon he was beside her, warming her, kissing her, rising up to look down at her, then burying his face between her breasts while his hands never stopped caressing her.

She held him tightly as she felt him become rigid

with desire. Straining upward to meet him, she welcomed him in her, firm and large. She enveloped him with her arms and her legs and lost all sense of guilt about her deception. She loved him. And everything she did was for his benefit, his security. She kept telling herself that, even as she writhed under him in great desire until they were both spent, and he had slumped forward over her, empty but victorious. He was still in her enjoying her continued pulsations. It made him feel strong, justified, and good for the first time since those hated rehearsals had started.

He slipped out of her, eased over on his back. He lay there naked and damp, breathing more easily. Suddenly he got up and left the room, his lean body like a Greek statue of a young boy.

Moments like this, Jannie could love him. He came back, a frosty drink in each hand, scotch over the rocks. He gave her one, sipped the other himself, let his free icy hand spider across her belly, causing her to contort convulsively, to laugh and say, "Don't."

So he didn't. The fact that he stopped playing with her when she asked was a bad sign. The depression was on him again.

"It'll go well," she consoled him. "The publicity's been great so far. The best in the history of TV."

"One mistake, one fucking mistake on the air and the whole thing can blow! I'll go up in my lines, in front of twenty million people. *I'll* be the one standing there like a dumb *shmuck* while the rest of you are hiding in the control room!"

"Nothing will go wrong," she soothed. "Trust me, darling. I've never been dishonest with you before, have I?"

"It's never been like this before," he exploded, making her tense. Did he suspect? He went on, "Used me! That's what The Doctor did. Used me. I don't think he ever means to do *King, Queen, Check.* Do *you?* Tell me honestly, *do* you, Jannie?"

"Of course he means to do it," she lied and, terrified that he would discover the truth, she reached out for him. Her fingers found his thigh, slowly moved upward. But he did not respond, which meant trouble. Because she knew, as did any of his women, that having sex less than twice in one night deprived him of proving himself and served to upset him the more.

She sat up in the dark, still caressing him. Leaning closer she took his free hand and pressed it against her breast. Now she could feel him rising. When he put aside his glass and began kissing her she knew it would be all right. Finally he was on her again. She opened to him, receiving him more easily this time than she had before. More relaxed he moved with long slow strokes so that she climaxed twice before him.

When it was over, he rolled onto his back, content. She turned to him, crooning into his ear like a mother putting a child to sleep, "It'll be a great show. They made all their mistakes today. On air, they'll be perfect. And so will you. You'll see, darling. You'll see," she promised.

He fell asleep that way with her breast pressed against him, her mouth against his ear. When she was sure that he was sleeping soundly she slipped out of his embrace and out of his bed. She moved naked and barefoot across the room, stopping only to glance at herself in the mirror. Damn it, she did have great breasts! Good sexy thighs too! Only her face was plain. But she could love the man with the best of them, and offer him more. Much more. Only she would not accept melancholy and madness in return.

She found her clothes out on the living room floor. When she was dressed she opened the door, stood there an instant before she closed it. For the first time in her life she felt like a whore. She hesitated, then pressed the buzzer, ready to face the proper, uniformed elevator man.

Until he arrived she kept saying to herself, Jannie, Jannie, Jannie, the things you do for TCA.

She stayed with Ford constantly. During the dress rehearsals she sat in the dark control room, not talking to anyone, especially The Doctor. Several times he tried to speak to her but she avoided him. When he invited her into the client's booth to watch Jeff Jefferson testify on TV before the UnAmerican Activities committee she refused.

The director was forbidden to give any notes directly to Ford. They were transmitted to Jannie who relayed them as if they were her own suggestions. That made them acceptable. Ford was working well now, depending on her companionship and help during the days, on her warmth and her love during the nights. His performance was finally beginning to emerge.

During the last run-through before the show, the entire production came together. For the first time every camera cue worked perfectly. Every shot appeared on the monitor in perfectly smooth sequence.

Best of all, Clark Ford gave his first real sustained performance. He came back to his dressing room and this time not only Jannie but The Doctor himself was there. The Doctor embraced Ford, beaming, "That performance was good enough for an opening night on Broadway!"

But Ford interrupted, "The script! Did you get Max Anderson?"

"His agent promised I'd hear from him on Monday," The Doctor answered quickly.

"Sam Behrman, is he back?"

"Still on the Coast, talking a picture deal."

"No, he isn't!" Ford snapped. "My lawyer saw him in Sardi's last night!"

"Oh, well, in that case I'll track him down before the night is out."

"Do that!" Ford said, but there was an ominous tone to his voice.

The Doctor glanced at Jannie seeking some clue but she had none to give, or, having one, refused to give it. He left the room. As soon as the door was shut, Ford slumped, rubbing his eyes, giving way to exhaustion. Jannie spoke softly, her fingers rubbing gently at his tense neck and shoulders, "I'll go out and get you some coffee."

"Send my dresser!" Ford interdicted. "I don't want to be alone now!"

Jannie dispatched the waiting dresser for coffee, hot and black, and sandwiches. Then she closed the door again and locked it, because she knew Ford liked privacy before an opening.

Alone for a few moments, Ford reached out for her, pulled her close. She tried to hold herself stiffly aloof but soon responded to him. Encouraged, his hand started moving slowly and seductively up to that softest part of her. In moments he was no longer tired. She was no longer able to disguise her own hunger. He rose up from his chair to embrace her violently in a way that demanded satisfaction. Swiftly, he stripped her of her clothes, though she kept protesting in small breathy whispers, "Clark

". . . darling . . . people . . . there are people right outside."

But that did not deter him. He urged her down onto the cot that had been set up so he could rest between scenes. He stripped off his costume and lay down beside her. But when he tried to slip into her, the cot began to sway precariously. He rolled off it, dropping to the bare floor, pulling her down on top of him. His hands reached out to enfold her buttocks. The rigid pulsing part of him found its way into her, brusquely and painfully at first, but even the pain was welcome to her now. The moist inner part of her embraced him, held him tightly. Then she began moving slowly, feeling him thrust upward to her.

She drew him into her more and more intensely. And he responded until there was a knock on the door. Angrily he called out, "Put the goddamn coffee down and get out of here!"

She could feel him threaten to go limp and she knew that it was the kind of failure that could destroy him for the rest of the night. So she tensed her muscles, keeping him within her, and she continued moving up and down until she felt him grow hard again. Finally he was pressing her to him with a ferocity that frightened her. Then with one last desperate effort she felt him pour himself out inside her. She had not come, but she pretended that she had. She was glad that it was over, that he had succeeded, and that she was able to slide off him and lie alongside, watching his naked chest heaving.

After a few minutes she rose, washed up as best she could at the little rust-stained sink which had only cold water to offer. The icy water shocked her thighs and between, but she managed.

While she dressed he put on the tattered old robe that he kept for a good luck charm and lay down on the cot and closed his eyes. He seemed to doze off. Suddenly he sat up, saying, "The Doctor, that sonofabitch! He won't do *King, Queen, Check!* He'll find some way out soon as tonight is over! Bastard! Prick! Double-crossing prick!"

Jannie begged, "Please, darling. Don't upset yourself before the show. You'll destroy your performance."

"Who cares! Nobody! Nobody but you, Jannie! Darling marry me?"

"Please, Clark, not now. We'll discuss it later."

"You're the only one I can trust. The only one who hasn't lied to me in this whole fucking charade!"

She went to him, touched his face, kissed him tenderly on the cheek. And wondered. Who had betrayed him most? The Doctor? Or she herself? "We'll get married," he kept insisting. In order to make him get back into costume, she had to promise she would marry him. She would think of some way to beg off later if he still insisted.

The stage manager was announcing, "Five minutes to air, Mr. Ford. Five minutes!"

She sent him out with a kiss and remained behind to tidy up the room. She wiped the floor where they had stained it, bundled up the towel, and tossed it into the wastebasket in the corner hoping no one would find it, or if they did that they would not suspect.

She could barely stand to look at herself in the mirror even to redo her hair. Quickly she patted on some powder and started out of his dressing room, just as the director's voice was booming over the studio speakers.

"All right everybody stand by. Ready for air in sixty seconds. And I mean ready. You'll be great! Love you all!"

The loudspeaker was cut. Jannie entered the control room just as the director was saying to his technical director, "Okay! Air! Up on one!" Camera One flashed its picture on the monitor, blazoning "ALUMCO presents BROADWAY STAR THEATRE!" The voice of the announcer echoed the words and went on to say, "Each Saturday night ALUMCO is proud and privileged to bring into your home the finest in Broadway entertainment, the greatest stars, the greatest stories in American theatrical history. Tonight . . ."

And he began to laud Clark Ford for his historic television debut in the American masterpiece *Dodsworth*. Once Jannie saw Ford go through the opening scene, smiling, joking, hearty, and bright, she knew he had become Dodsworth and that Clark Ford would not be a problem for the rest of the show. He moved well, seeming to welcome the precision he had objected to during rehearsals.

He was so good that she did not go out to encourage

him during the act breaks for fear of upsetting him.

It was not until the third and final act that the accident took place. Ford was making his way down the fake steps of the fake Italian street to find Edith Courtwright, the widow to whom he was so strongly attracted, now that he had rid himself of selfish Fran, his wife. On the next to top step of the multilevel set his shoe caught against a nail that had not been properly hammered into place. It was something he had warned the director about, who had warned the assistant director, who had warned the set designer, who had passed the message on to one of the carpenters who said he'd fix it after his union coffee break. But he never had.

So now, Clark Ford, in the midst of his most exuberant scene suddenly tripped and was forced to brace himself against the wall of the set. The flat sagged, only slightly, but enough to show on the television screen.

In the control room everyone rose in alarm—The Doctor, Spencer Gould, Freddie Feig, the director, all the technicians.

In the back booth Carl Brewster and his sponsor sat stiff and tense, Brewster afraid even to glance at his sponsor.

But Jannie, most of all Jannie felt a sense of panic. She knew that what Ford feared most had just happened. He had been made to appear inept before millions of people.

Yet the miracle of it was that Ford did not fall. Using that brief instant to brace himself, he summoned up the experience, grace, and sheer sense of survival that sustains all good actors. He righted himself, continued down the steps to where the actress playing Edith Courtright was arranging flowers, supposedly unaware that Dodsworth was returning.

"Edith!" he called out. She turned. They rushed into each other's arms. She was half laughing, half crying to realize that he would spend the rest of his life with her. In the original script Ford had no lines, but now he smiled and ad libbed smoothly, "Of course, if I'm going to spend the rest of my life here, I'll have to master those old Italian steps."

His quick thinking saved the scene. In the control room everyone laughed loudly from sheer nervous relief. The young director exclaimed with great admiration, "That sonofabitch! That magnificent fucking sonofabitch! Leave it to an old pro!"

Back in the clients' booth the president of ALUMCO, his thin lips wearing as much smile as they were capable of, said, "Brilliant! What a brilliant recovery. Carl, you were absolutely right to have insisted on him!"

Carl Brewster could feel that the ALUMCO account was safe for another three years at least. The Doctor, however, who heard the president's remark realized for the first time that it had been Carl Brewster, not the sponsor, who had put him to all that trouble to get Clark Ford. The Doctor would not forget.

But now was a time for celebration. Everyone crowded toward Clark Ford's dressing room to congratulate him on his magnificent performance. His door was closed and locked and it was not until Jannie pushed her way through to call softly, "Darling it's me," that they heard the key being turned. The door opened only wide enough to admit her.

The Doctor explained to the sponsor, "You understand, of course, a man can't be that great without being enormously tense."

Inside the dressing room, Clark Ford sat in his chair, dripping wet. Jannie said nothing, knowing that in moments like this he suspected all praise.

Instead, she applied toilet water to his body, massaging it gently as she did so. Soon the tenseness went out of him. She turned to the door to take down the dinner jacket that he was going to wear to the party at Twenty-One.

"I'm not wearing that!" He reached for his old baggy rehearsal slacks.

"You're not going to the party in those, darling."

"I'm not going to the party! Period!" Ford said.

"Darling, all those people, they'll be so disappointed. It won't be a party without you."

"Who gives a fuck!" he said, defiantly putting on his old slacks, and a work shirt which smelled of perspiration. As he did up the buttons, she continued to plead with him.

"Whose side are you on?" he demanded suddenly.

"Mine? Or The Doctor's? Do you go to bed with *him*, too?"

"Clark, darling, people are outside. And you know damn well I don't go to bed with him. Now, please, I'm only going to ask you once more. For my sake, go to the party." Her eyes filled with tears.

"I am not going to any party! Tonight I am going to get drunk! And laid. And stayed with! I'll do all the things that *I* want to do, for a change!" He said it in such a way that she knew she would not change his mind.

She unlocked the door, which only served to increase the clamor outside. The Doctor, Spence, Carl Brewster and the sponsor all tried to crowd in. But Clark Ford, Jannie's hand tightly in his, pushed through them, rudely, angrily. When he had reached the outer door he turned and called back, "Fuck you! Fuck all of you! You used me! You got what you wanted! Now leave me alone!"

He trudged angrily down the hallway dragging Jannie behind him, leaving an embarrassed Doctor and a red-faced Carl Brewster. The sponsor stood there staring, not knowing quite what to make of such ungentlemanly conduct.

The Doctor tried to gloss over it, "Let's go! After all, this is a party to celebrate a new series on television, not the acting debut of Clark Ford."

They got into the limousines, Carl Brewster and the sponsor into the first, The Doctor, Spence and Freddie into the second. Spence and Freddie said nothing. Freddie feared The Doctor's wrath most, for the whole night had all started with his original reckless promise to deliver Ford.

But The Doctor, who had been insulted and abused by temperamental singers, comics, and actors for a generation now, was less troubled by that than he was by one other persistent thought.

"You go to all that trouble! Lying, scheming, cheating, screwing your own clients! And what does it all add up to?" The Doctor asked suddenly.

To Spence and Freddie it sounded like an observation of the moment brought on by Ford's bitterness. Then The Doctor said, "If you *do* go to all that trouble, you should at least wind up with something that makes it worth while." He repeated, "Yes, all that effort shouldn't be squandered on one night. It isn't fair!" Which in his vocabulary meant it was not particularly profitable to himself or TCA.

The party at Twenty-One went well. Whatever hurt feelings there were were more than assuaged by the reviews which they received by phone. *The New York Times* called it "a high water mark in Television." *The Daily News* lauded the entire production, especially Clark Ford and his highly inventive ad lib, and it thanked ALUMCO for bringing such a fine series to television.

For Carl Brewster, for ALUMCO, for Spence and Freddie the night was an outstanding success. Only The Doctor remained dissatisfied. Only he brooded over the outcome. "There must be a way . . ." he kept saying as Spence and Freddie walked him back to his hotel from Twenty-One in the early morning hours.

Just as they reached the hotel, The Doctor announced suddenly, "Film!"

"Film?" echoed Spence.

"Film is the answer! Those goddamn old cowboys know the answer better than we do! William Boyd with all that twenty-year-old Hopalong Cassidy crap of his is cleaning up a fortune on TV. We got to go to film."

"Sure. That's okay with small shows like Jack Benny or Burns and Allen. But with a big dramatic spectacle, film would cost a fortune," Spence said.

"And be worth it!" The Doctor exclaimed. "Film is a tangible asset. Just imagine if we had Clark Ford's performance tonight in *Dodsworth* on film! We could show it over and over again! Then it would be worth all the trouble!"

"Sure. But think what it would have cost!" Spence said.

"Spence," The Doctor said, in an indulgent patronizing tone, "Spence, whatever it costs it costs the sponsor. What if we wind up with a piece of film that *we* own?"

"Own?" Spence echoed with dismay. "Studios can own. Producers can own. Clients can own. But not agents. Conflict of interest!" he warned, remembering his year of Basic Commercial Law at Harvard Business School.

"I don't know," The Doctor said reflectively.

"We can't represent actors, directors and writers and

hire them too. *That's* a clear conflict of interest."

But The Doctor said, "I'm staying over in New York for a few more days. Let's get with the lawyers and discuss it!"

"Sure!" Spence agreed, but was as puzzled after they left The Doctor as he had been before.

4

Several afternoons later The Doctor, Spencer Gould and
Freddie Feig were gathered in the office of Philip Rose,
senior partner of Rose, Rosenbloom, Scott, and Levin, attorneys at law, specializing in matters involving show
business. Rose, a short, stocky man, with the black, tight
curly hair of a Levantine Jew, listened quietly, making no
notes, revealing no reactions. Though in a courtroom he
was quick as a cat, Rose was not one to reach swift conclusions elsewhere, because the longer his period of deliberation, the larger his fee. So in his office he seemed to
have an endless supply of time and patience.

Spencer Gould had been assigned the task of making
the primary presentation. The Doctor held himself in re-
serve for what he called the short strokes.

Relying on his Harvard accent and what legalisms he
could remember, Spence explained the problem to Rose.
How could TCA continue to represent talent, of which
they had the most impressive roster in the world, and at
the same time produce and own films for television without
running into a conflict of interest suit.

Spence ended by saying, "You know Dr. Cone. When
he consults an attorney he doesn't want to find out what
he can't do, but what he can do."

Rose smiled. He was used to hearing that bromide from
every client who came seeking permission to do something
either illegal or at best highly unethical. He sat quietly
a long time, polishing his thick, heavy-framed reading
glasses. Finally he said, "Dr. Cone . . . everything I say today is, naturally, a curbstone reaction. But for the moment let's break the problem down and study both its
aspects."

The word "both" made The Doctor glance at Spence.

What second problem could there be?

"There is, of course, the conflict of interest to consider. *But,*" and Rose laid strong emphasis on that single syllable, "but there is also a federal matter to be considered, a possible anti-trust action. After all, television or film, that crosses state lines is clearly under federal jurisdiction.

"The first thing I would advise is that whatever you do, don't do it in secret. Act forthrightly and with the full conviction that everything is aboveboard and completely legal. That way we can always plead later that you thought you were doing the right thing. That always works well with any government agency or jury."

Spence spoke up at once. "We never intended to do anything secretly. That's why we came here." He glanced at The Doctor, who nodded approval.

Rose was ready to continue. "Now as to the conflict of interest, unfortunately the best way to proceed may be impossible."

"And that is?" The Doctor asked, leaning in a little, intrigued for the first time.

"We could proceed on what we call the Doctrine of Informed Consent," Rose pronounced as gravely as a judge.

"Doctrine of Informed Consent," The Doctor echoed. He liked the sound of it. It had a familiar, comforting ring. *The Doctrine of Informed Consent.*

"That means you make a complete disclosure to the party who might have a right to complain. And after they know all the facts, they give you their consent in advance. It's a term more usually applied to legal questions involving medicine and malpractice."

Now The Doctor remembered where he had heard the term, long ago as an intern. The older doctors had told him that the safest way to treat a touchy case and remain immune to a malpractice suit, was to make a complete disclosure to the patient as to the means, purposes, and risks of the treatment and have the patient give his consent. Then you were safe.

He looked at Rose and asked, "You mean that would work here?"

"I see no reason why any court would object to applying the same doctrine. Of course, as I said, it may not be possible as a practical matter. It would involve wrangles with clients each time a deal came up. And some clients wouldn't consent after being fully informed. They could make trouble."

The Doctor leaned still a little closer to Rose. "Is there a form, a contract that you could draw up that would protect us?"

"I'm afraid not," Rose said. "Of course we're going to do extensive research."

"Yes, yes, I know," The Doctor said impatiently.

"Give us about a week or ten days. We'll get back to you."

"Fine, fine," said The Doctor, though it was the last thing in the world he meant, but he was in a hurry to leave Rose's office.

In the limousine on the way back to TCA's office on Madison Avenue the three men were silent. Just before the car pulled up at the front door, The Doctor said, "Stripping away all the legal crap, he said we can't do it. Not without great risk. *Unless . . . The Doctrine of Informed Consent. . . .*"

The Doctor did not complete his thought. He spent the next few days in routine business matters concerning the New York phase of TCA's operation. By the end of the week he seemed glad to depart on the late plane to California.

That night, though he had a berth on the plane, he could not sleep. He kept trying to figure out where to put his muscle. Get consent, Rose had advised. Get consent in advance. But he had also said it would be impossible as a practical matter to get consent from all TCA clients. And the ones who refused were precisely the ones to fear, the troublemakers.

Still, there had to be one button that he could push, one pressure point against which his muscle, properly applied, would produce the right result.

If one couldn't approach each individual client, why not get group consent? And if one wanted talent en masse, where did one go? Why to the Guilds, of course! The right man in the right Guild could deliver that group consent to him! And once he had approval from one Guild the others would follow. It would take the most skillful handling to convince a Guild of working people to give up their main guarantee of fair representation, but it could be done. It had to be done.

As his mind raced through the Guild presidents who were involved, he suddenly remembered Jeff Jefferson's brilliant performance at the hearings the previous week. And he recalled Jefferson's personal story which had endeared him not only to the nation at large, but to every actor, writer, and producer whose Communist connections he had helped gloss over with his touching story.

Jeff Jefferson! President of the Screen Actors Guild! He could be, must be, The Doctor's pressure point.

Of course Jeff's newly won prestige cut two ways. It made him a more powerful ally but it also gave him more leverage. He might be saleable again. Desirable again. That meant he could not be manipulated as easily as before. The challenge was how to take advantage of Jeff's prestige without letting Jeff capitalize on it enough to become immune to The Doctor's pressure.

It would take handling, very skillful handling, but it was the kind of challenge that the little man loved.

Jeff Jefferson, and all the problems the new Jeff Jefferson posed, was the target.

Having reached that conclusion, and comforted by the possibility of informed consent on an industry-wide scale, The Doctor relaxed. Somewhere over Nebraska he dozed off and slept until touchdown at Los Angeles International.

PART FOUR

1

In the days since his appearance before the congressional committee, Jeff Jefferson's life had changed considerably. Writers who had never been his especial admirers now sought him out. And no Hollywood social function or event of industry concern took place without Jeff's presence.

His time was not only occupied, it was oversubscribed. His need to be needed was more than fulfilled. Most important, scripts had finally begun to arrive, not all of them for "A" pictures. The leading parts in the major scripts were not being offered to him. But they were good scripts, containing solid, second leads, or excellent character parts.

Still his life was not all as affirmative as it appeared. There was Joanne. With the Academy Awards coming up in the next few weeks, she was growing increasingly tense. She drank more, ate less. Her face, with magnificent marble cheekbones that photographed with such exquisite beauty, had grown too thin, betraying her inner tension.

He was forced to speculate: What if Joanne didn't win? True, she was the sentimental favorite. Unlike the Broadway stars who were given preferential treatment, she'd had the kind of career most applauded by real Hollywood veterans, who all started at lowly jobs and worked their way to the top. They would naturally vote for one of their own.

Besides, Joanne had succeeded in a part that most people had thought would exceed her talents. She had put aside her beauty to play a plain, ignorant girl in a story of great sensitivity, a role far removed from the comedy parts she had played before. Hollywood was proud of her and seemed determined to reward her with the highest honor it could offer.

Jeff wished she would win simply to spare himself the agony of finding out how she would behave if she lost. Yet he had to admit he deeply resented the fact that she might be given an honor for which he'd never been even nominated. So he began reading the scripts submitted to him seeking not only for a good story but for a showy part for which he might possibly be considered, if not for Best Actor, then at least for Best Actor in a Supporting Role.

When he was almost ready to despair, he found it—a part which impressed him enormously. It was not the lead, but a strong second-lead character role, which might just have Award possibilities. Still, he didn't want to make a mistake. The next morning he re-read the script a third time before he called The Doctor to tell him that he'd finally found the ideal part. He was crushed when Alise told him that Cone was still in New York, and all she could do was leave a message asking him to call as soon as he came back.

But The Doctor did not call Jeff the day he returned. Nor the next day. It was late in the afternoon of the third day before he finally put through the call. It was not an oversight, nor the result of accumulated business pressures. It was a cold, deliberate decision to let Jeff wait—part of the larger plan which had germinated in the little man's mind during his cross-country flight. When The Doctor did call, he apologized profusely for the delay and then, after relating to Jeff how people in New York were still talking about his wonderful job on TV during the hearings, The Doctor seemed ready to listen. Jeff described the story, the role, and what he was sure it would achieve for him.

The Doctor's first question was, "Who's going to direct?"

"Hathaway," Jeff reported.

"Hathaway would be great for a story like that! I'll check it out to make sure!" The Doctor said. Then he added, "Let me send for the script. I'll read it myself over the weekend."

Jeff felt secure for the first time in months. When The Doctor took the time to read a script that meant he was going to handle the deal himself—if he liked it. And if The Doctor liked a screenplay, things began to happen.

The right director somehow was free. Excellent casting for the other parts appeared miraculously. And the budget was always ample.

The weekend seemed interminable. Jeff hadn't told Joanne about the script. Now that the Oscars were only weeks away she had problems enough of her own, despite the fact that her studio was spending thousands of dollars in trade paper advertising to assure her enough votes to win. Still, until the Oscar was hers, she could not relax. She waited, sipping imported Dutch gin, from a graceful Delft-blue mug.

Without the aid of alcohol, time passed even more slowly for Jeff. By Sunday he could stand it no longer and he called Sam Houseman, a writer he knew only casually, but who had been most warm and friendly since the day Jeff testified. Sam was an excellent tennis player. If there was a good match going on anywhere in or around Beverly Hills, Sam would know. It turned out that Jack Warner was having a tennis Sunday at his place. Naturally, Sam had been invited and surely they'd love to have Jeff. So he drove to the Warner estate.

Jeff didn't particularly like Warner, but it was a means of passing the day. In the evening he considered asking Joanne out to dinner. It would do no harm for her to show up at Chasen's or Romanoff's at the peak of the Oscar campaign.

But when he went to her room she was asleep—too much gin. He'd have to get through the evening alone.

It was almost eleven the next day before the phone finally rang.

"Hi, Jeff-baby!" Instantly Jeff realized that this was The Doctor's way of easing into a negative response. He didn't like the script. "Let me give you my reaction straight," said The Doctor. "This is a picture could make money. This is a part might do you a lot of good. *Provided* that you don't get overshadowed by the lead. This is one case where the deal is as important as the role. We want equal star billing! And the money we got on your last picture!"

"But you yourself said it's time to cut the price."

"That was before your great job at the hearings! You're not only a star now. You're a big man in the industry. A spokesman for the entire picture business!" The Doctor pontificated.

"I know. But I want that part! I know what I can do with it. And what it can do for me!" Jeff said, almost pleading.

"Of course! Exactly why I say you'll be able to do it better if you get the right money, the right treatment, the right everything! Leave that to *me!* First thing, I'll call and say you are interested enough in the part to consider it. That I would like further details. Okay?"

"Okay," Jeff agreed, then added "Look, Doctor, I want that part! Understand?"

"Jeff, sweetie, who understands better?" Cone hung up.

Near the end of the day, Alise reminded The Doctor that he had meant to call the studio about Jeff. When she had the studio head on the phone, Cone said, "Benny? Irwin. On my desk I've got the script you sent Jeff Jefferson. Interesting piece. Now we'd like to talk numbers. What is the deal?"

Benny Ganz, an expert at business affairs, having run that department of his company before becoming studio head, was as cozy as The Doctor. "Irwin, you know our policy. We don't like to haggle. Whatever he was paid in the last six months, we'll meet his price."

Benny knew as well as The Doctor that Jeff Jefferson had not worked in almost a year. He was simply employing a diplomatic means of pointing up that damaging fact.

"You mean his last price?" The Doctor pursued.

"In the last six months," Benny reiterated.

The issue was clear. "Let's leave aside dollars for the moment," said The Doctor. "Billing is the important thing. It's equal star billing or no deal."

"Irwin, Irwin," Benny began to plead, "you know I can't agree on billing without setting the lead first. I'll give you a best efforts clause. We will do our absolute best to get him equal star billing with the lead. Okay?"

"Benny, you can take your 'best efforts clause' and shove it!"

"Irwin, you talk that way to me? Me? When I say 'best efforts,' I mean 'best efforts,'" Benny answered indignantly, though they both knew he was lying.

"Look, Benny, if this was the old Jeff Jefferson, I wouldn't be calling myself. You know that. But at TCA we look on him as a whole new personality. Since the hearings he has stature!"

"Of course!" Benny agreed. "But is that going to pay off at the box office?"

"*We* think it will," The Doctor said.

"And *I'm* from Missouri. Me, you got to show." Actually Benny was from Bensonhurst in Brooklyn.

"Look, Benny! Equal billing and the same salary as on his last picture or the answer is no!" Cone said firmly.

"His last salary," Benny Ganz echoed in pain. "He hasn't been able to get *any* salary for the last year!"

"Benny, I am going to pretend that you didn't say that. Because if you did and if it ever got out, then there'd be no deal at all! You are not going to treat any TCA star like that! *Fahshtest?*"

"Irwin, this studio doesn't rise or fall on whether or not we get Jeff Jefferson. We'll pay him the last price you offered him at, one hundred and fifty thousand for the picture, plus a 'best efforts' clause on the billing."

"I will report that to my client," The Doctor said, indicating he was hurt.

"Irwin, you want some advice from an old friend?"

"Yeah?" The Doctor responded guardedly.

"Don't play that testifying bit too long or too strong. People in this industry have short memories, especially when it comes to paying back favors. Strike while the iron is hot. A couple of weeks from now may be too late."

Suddenly The Doctor wondered if Benny Ganz had guessed what he was doing. Cone had every intention of letting the effect of Jeff's testimony dissipate. The Doctor knew the tide would turn; he had only to keep Jeff out of work long enough. No, since Benny had no idea of The Doctor's big plan he could never suspect this strategy.

So The Doctor contented himself with, "Benny, I will report to my client and let you know!"

He hung up the phone and decided not to report right back to Jeff. It would help to make him as anxious as possible. Waiting was the worst torture for unemployed actors. It hardened their arteries, shortened their wind, sapped their will, and finally made them completely pliable. Tomorrow, The Doctor decided, tomorrow would be a more advantageous time to call.

By Tuesday, Jeff was in no mood for pretense. He was plainly anxious.

"Kid," The Doctor began, "I have just been talking with Benny Ganz."

"And?" Jeff asked, a bit too quickly.

"The way I figure it, Jeff-baby, this is a time to be strong. For two reasons. First, the testifying has put you in demand. Second, and to my mind more important, we cannot, repeat, *cannot* let ourselves appear to be hungry for the part."

"Of course," Jeff agreed, suppressing his desire to shout, "Get me that part, and to hell with the money!"

"So . . ." The Doctor strung it out till it became a three-syllable word, "I told him we are not greedy. We only want the same price as you got on your last picture."

"The same price?" Jeff asked, unable to conceal his surprise. "And what did Benny say?"

"What does Benny always say? We are asking for the moon. We are looking to bankrupt the studio. Par for the course."

"Well, how did you leave it?"

"He's going to talk to his New York office. And I'm going to talk to you. So I'm talking," The Doctor said and Jeff could visualize the confident smile on the little man's face.

"Play it as strong as you can, Doctor," said Jeff. "Only, only don't lose the deal. *I want that part!*"

"Kid, I am not going to let you jeopardize your bargaining position for the next five years just to get one part. Let me do this my way."

"Okay. Your way. Only don't lose that part!"

Just before five o'clock, The Doctor placed a call to Benny Ganz. After the usual pleasantries The Doctor eased into the business at hand. "What did they say in the front office?"

"No."

"Just 'no'?" The Doctor asked, seeming disappointed.

"Just 'no,' " Benny said, holding fast.

"No arguments? No yelling and screaming?" The Doctor asked.

"Not even one fuck, shit or damn. In fact, New York didn't even threaten to run him out of the picture business. They weren't that excited. They just said no, and we went on to talk about other casting."

Benny was cool. Too cool, The Doctor felt, more must be coming. Benny Ganz without a threat was not Benny.

"Irwin, you know what I think, off the record? I think if I went back to them and said we could get Jefferson for his last offering price, a hundred and a half, we could make the deal. Then I'll use my weight to get him a break on the credits and we'll both have done a good day's work."

When The Doctor did not answer at once, Benny asked, "Irwin, you there?"

"I'm here, I'm here," The Doctor said sadly. "I was just thinking. If I have to go back to that man who fronted for the entire industry in its time of trouble and tell him that you won't pay him more than a hundred and a half, it'll break his heart."

"With a hundred and a half to recuperate on, he'll get over it, Irwin."

"An actor *never* gets over something like that!"

"I know, I know," Benny agreed expecting this was just a preamble to The Doctor's coming down on his price.

"Benny, you go back to your front office and say that *I*, yes, Irwin Cone, will not allow you to break that man's heart with such a cheap, lousy offer!"

There was such finality in The Doctor's voice, that Benny Ganz felt called up to warn, "Irwin, off the record I am not blowing smoke up your ass. They won't budge. A hundred and a half is it."

"Then let me tell you something," The Doctor shouted back. "I won't budge either! His last price or no price! Got it? Call me back, I'll wait right here!" And he hung up.

Within twenty minutes, Benny Ganz was back on the phone.

"Irwin, a hundred and a half. And they want an answer by the opening of business tomorrow." Benny Ganz said it without emotion, in such a tone that The Doctor knew that was the last, the final word.

At nine-fifteen the next morning The Doctor called and told Benny Ganz there was no deal. Late that afternoon, after the other cares of the day had been attended to, he asked Alise to put through a call to Jeff Jefferson. Jeff responded instantly.

"Well? What did they say?"

"I don't like their attitude," The Doctor began.

"Screw their attitude! What did they *say?*"

"I'm not going to let any client of mine be pushed around!" The Doctor said indignantly.

"What did they say?" Jeff persisted.

"I don't even want to repeat their offer!" Cone fumed.

"That bad?" Jeff asked.

"No guarantee on credits. And only, Jeff, I'd rather not tell you."

"Tell me."

"Only a lousy seventy-five thousand dollars." The Doctor sounded like a broken man.

"That's all?" Jeff asked, startled.

"All? I had to fight to get them up from their original offer!"

"Christ!"

"Jeff, Jeff, look, kid, I know how you feel. I'm as hurt as you are. Jeff, are you listening?"

"Doc, I was thinking, the part's such a good one and it comes at just the right time for me. . . ."

When The Doctor realized what Jeff was about to say, he interrupted at once, "Jeff, you listen to me! Now is the time to have guts! To hold out! You'll ruin your career taking a role for that kind of money. Sometimes the smartest thing an actor ever does is say no!"

"It's a hell of a part, Doc!"

"I've seen better."

"But it's been a year now," Jeff said.

"That's the way *they* think. It's been a year since Jefferson's had a real part offered to him. He'll work for any price. Well, don't prove it by accepting their lousy offer. I'd rather pay you out of my own pocket than let your price be cut so ruthlessly."

"Look, Doctor, I understand . . ."

"Kid, you need the money? TCA will advance it to you. Just say the word."

After a question like that, even if he needed money desperately, Jeff would have said the same thing, "No, of course not!"

"Then sit tight. Someone'll come to us with the right part and the right deal," The Doctor declared.

"You're sure they won't budge?"

"I wouldn't even dignify their offer by going back to them! Screw 'em!" The Doctor declared vehemently. Then he hung up.

Cone leaned back in his chair estimating the possibilities that Jeff might discover what Benny's real offer had been. Benny was not much for dining out except when the brass came in from New York. Jeff was not a member of Hillcrest, so where would the two meet before The Doctor could put the second phase of his plan into operation? It was a very slim chance, a very good gamble. And if it did happen, The Doctor could handle it.

A week had gone by. Jeff had had little word from TCA. One call from The Doctor. A vague tantalizing call which hinted at possibilities, at interesting situations developing, at a new script which was being awaited with excitement from one of TCA's top writer-clients. There was a call from Buddy Black, too. Also vague. Finally he did send over two scripts, both routine Westerns. In one, Jeff was offered the lead, but it was a dull part, too typecast to intrigue him. When he finished reading the second script, Jeff knew they both had the smell of cheapies—quick production, mediocre direction, more dangerous than promising. He suspected, and rightly, that Buddy had sent them over merely to simulate activity.

All the anxieties of the past year began to return. For some reason The Doctor had touted him off the only part he had liked in ages, had seduced him with the promise of better roles, better deals, yet there was not a single offer in sight.

Still, Jeff reassured himself, The Doctor was the shrewdest man in the business. If he had insisted that Jeff say no, there must have been a good reason. Finally, he was driven to the ultimate consolation that every out-of-work star resorted to: "The Doctor can't make a dime on me unless I make money up front. So why would he deny TCA a commission at my expense?"

As the days passed without new scripts and with the Academy Awards coming closer, Jeff found himself growing more and more tense. His fears seemed to be converging. This might be the end of his career, his marriage, of everything. The respite he had won by testifying had been dissipated. He might well wind up with an alcoholic wife, who, to make matters worse, had just walked off with an Oscar at a time when he couldn't even get a job.

The speech he had been invited to make at the Awards ceremonies, a courtesy to him as president of the Screen Actors Guild, could easily be his farewell speech. He even considered not making it. But Abe Heller had already written it, and it was a good speech, so he decided, finally, to deliver it.

All the while though he kept hoping for a call from The Doctor, or from Buddy Black, or from anyone at TCA.

2

On the night of the Awards, intensely bright arc lights crisscrossed the dark Hollywood sky. The motion picture industry, as though challenging nature itself, was seeking to make room in the heavens for its own stars. From a distance, Jeff could see the spots moving across the sky like probing fingers, which then crossed with other lights forming sudden sharp geometric shapes and angles.

He stared ahead through the windshield of the limousine, bending forward slightly to see from his place in the front seat. Normally he would have driven the Cadillac convertible, but on Oscar night it was mandatory that there be a chauffeur so that Joanne and he could step from the back of the car, untroubled by details like parking. They would immediately face the photographers' flashlights, the shouts and gasps of the thousands of fans gathered to cheer.

Of course tonight the screams would be for Joanne. Columnists, gossip writers and odds makers had already made her the favorite, sentimentally and mathematically.

So Jeff knew that his job would be to stand beside her, smiling. The prince consort, pleasant, but without power or personality of his own. His smile must thank the people for their ovation, while at the same time endowing Joanne with his own admiration. It would help her image. It would certainly help his. The ideal American couple, as they had been called in almost every movie magazine in the world. Two fine-looking human beings, not only in love with each other, but selflessly so—the husband glorying in the wife's achievements, the wife, seeming timid and humble in the face of the huge honor which was about to be thrust upon her. Joanne gave her best performances when she was acting the sweet, simple, helpless girl who

241

needed the protection of a man. She would do that damned well tonight.

And Jeff would play straight for her. He would be just-ly proud, overly concerned, would stand aside a bit as she accepted the wave of adulation that would envelop her. Then when the applause and the shouting seemed about to ebb, he would warmly and graciously take her arm and protectively lead her into the Pantages Theater, past yet another battery of flashlights.

From the beginning of the evening Jeff had made his adjustment. There was his own speech, of course, but he knew it practically by heart. Still he felt uneasy, as though he were going not to a celebration but to a funeral. He was riding now on the front seat alongside the driver, as he had done on the day of his father's funeral. His mother, two aunts and an elderly uncle had sat in the back. Rather than crowd them by putting up the second jump seat, he had insisted on riding with the driver. In truth, it was to avoid being so close to his mother. When she had called him in Hollywood to tell him about his father's death she sounded dry and relieved, but by the time he had flown back to Iowa, he found her playing the widow, weeping, inconsolable. So much so that his Aunt Maytha was moved to say, with compassion, that she was in danger of grieving herself into an early grave.

In the day and a half after he had come home his mother wept more tears than Jeff had seen her shed in a lifetime of adversity and tragedy. Perhaps she did miss his father, perhaps the feelings that she had kept pent up behind that wall of cold, religious morality were finally bursting forth. Perhaps, but he had not believed it. At the cemetery he had stood apart from her, until the minister glanced up from his worn missal and gestured Jeff to move closer.

Somehow it was the same tonight. Here he was riding in front with the driver again.

Though this time the choice had not been his. His exile had begun when the studio hairdresser was just finishing Joanne's coiffure, one created to set off the gown which had been especially designed for her. As a matter of pride, the studio would not allow its most eminent candidate to appear in public on this night of all nights in any but the most flattering dress or hairstyle.

Gown, dresser, and hairstylist, had all been dispatched by the studio to the Jefferson's. The studio had even written the speech Joanne was to make, if she won, listing the persons she should thank, and most particularly the moment when it would be appropriate and touching for her to cry.

By the time she had been readied to leave the house, the designer of the gown, a finicky fretful fag, insisted on installing her in the car with her skirt carefully laid out in all its pleats. He became so upset at the thought of re-arranging them that Jeff had little choice but to volunteer to sit in front so as not to destroy the lamé creation.

When the limousine stopped a block from the theater to take its place in the line of cars moving toward the theater marquee, Jeff got out of the front seat and opened the back door. The crowd would expect the happy couple to be together when they arrived. Joanne did not move. With the self-righteous innocence of a vestal virgin she remained stiffly immobile, as though not just her hair but all of her had been lacquered into place. Jeff lean-hipped his way into the back, huddling to one corner so as not to make contact with the precious lamé. He kept his uncomfortable pose while the car moved the last block to the entrance of the Pantages.

Uniformed police accompanied the limousine the last fifty yards, running alongside like the President's Secret Servicemen. Already Jeff could see the faces peering in through the windows, trying to identify the occupants. When they did, the ovation began. No conquering emperor had ever won greater acclaim. Feeling a foolish supernumerary, Jeff nevertheless smiled and waved. Even Joanne made a feeble attempt to acknowledge the huzzahs.

The cheers grew. Those spectators fortunate enough to have seats in the temporary grandstands stood up and screamed. Thousands on foot surged closer, slowing the limousine almost to a halt. But the chauffeur managed, finally, to reach the brightly spotlighted marquee. Crimson ropes of velvet made a polite pretense at holding back the crowd, while Hollywood police in dark blue actually did so. The car door was opened by a dinner-jacketed functionary whose purpose was to lead the royal couple from the car to the microphone where they would graciously pause for an interview.

Jeff stepped out first. Then, smiling, his warm final-take smile, he turned back to assist his wife. She placed her hand on his and moved for the first time since she had been installed in the limousine. She moved well, he had always noted that, whether she was leaving their bed to go to the bathroom to attend herself after sex or emerging from a limousine to accept the plaudits of the crowd, she moved with ease, never in a hurry. Maybe that was one of the few things he still liked about her. Whatever she did, up to and including adultery, she did with grace.

Now the shouts and cries overwhelmed them, the crowd threatened to break through the cordon of sturdy police. Just in time, the official took her by the arm and moved her swiftly toward the microphone where the host-announcer, a star of another day, introduced her with the proper degree of awe and respect.

"And now, the first young actress since Mary Pickford to deserve the title of America's Sweetheart, a great beauty, a fine human being, and above all a great actress, Joanne West!" More clapping, shouts and cheers. When the applause died down, the host continued, "And her husband the ever-popular Jeff Jefferson!" This was spoken with somewhat less admiration and was greeted with considerably less applause.

Why was it, Jeff asked himself, that in Hollywood when one ceased to be popular he was always dubbed "the ever-popular"?

The host made no attempt to position Jeff at the microphone but devoted himself entirely to Joanne.

"Joanne, darling," he said although he had never met her before, "how does it feel on this magical night when every sign seems to point to your winning that most coveted of all trophies? How does it feel, honey?"

"I can tell you this, Neil," Joanne answered hastily remembering the ex-Star's first name, "just to be nominated is more of an honor than I ever thought possible in my wildest dreams. It was such a surprise that even if I don't win, this will be enough to last me a lifetime," she breathed, with the look of a sincere novice taking her final vows at the altar.

"Oh, shit!" Jeff said. To himself, of course.

A few more inane questions, a few more dishonest replies, and the princess had done her duty. Now Jeff took her elbow and, careful not to crease the lamé, guided her toward the entrance of the auditorium. There it was even worse. As they started down the aisle, the crowd rose to cheer. Joanne accepted their acclaim with her sweet smile as Jeff escorted her to a pair of aisle seats that were usually accorded the favored nominees.

Since Joanne and Jeff were among the last to arrive they had only a brief wait till the ceremonies began. The president of the Academy, a writer, himself an award winner, read a carefully written statement of greeting. And "the night that Hollywood honors its own craftsmen, creative artists and brilliant stars" was under way.

All that went before the final three awards for Best Actor, Best Actress and Best Picture were torturous moments to be lived through by Joanne as best she could. Even when Jeff was introduced as that "courageous warrior for freedom *of* the Arts and *in* the Arts, president of the Screen Actors Guild, a great star in his own right" and started down the aisle, Joanne did not applaud any longer than absolutely necessary, so as to avoid jeopardizing her hairdo and her gown. She was already beginning to feel lines of perspiration starting under her arms. She hoped desperately that the stains wouldn't show by the time she had to go up and receive her award. She had even begun to sniff at herself, subtly of course, to determine if she had started to give off any noticeable odor. She knew, as did some male stars she had worked with, that for all her angelic looks, when she was put under great tension she could smell like a men's locker room after a basketball game. During shooting, she would be at her armpits a dozen times a day with deodorants and perfumes. When she was expecting to go to bed with anyone, including Jeff, she was even more meticulous. Now she could feel the deadly stuff oozing like acid into her gown.

She did not listen to Jeff's speech, only hoped that it would be over quickly so that they could get on with the main awards before the stains advanced so far that her brief, sequined jacket would not cover them. The longer his speech went on the more she hated him. Finally she cursed him for deliberately slowing his pace to make her disgrace herself.

When he returned to his seat, she whispered viciously, "Did you have to take all fucking night?" though she smiled as she said it.

Somehow the knowledge that he had served to irritate her pleased him. Furtively, Joanne began swabbing inside her jacket with her handkerchief.

They had arrived now at the golden moment. The Oscar for the Best Actor in a Leading Role had just been presented. Two awards remained, Best Actress and Best Picture. The winner of Best Actor for the previous year was given the honor of announcing the list of nominees, which also included the perennial Bette Davis, Olivia de Haviland, Madeleine Carroll, and a little-known French actress. When the names and the pictures had been announced, the "man from Price-Waterhouse," whose presence lent the rectitude of a church service to the occasion, handed over the precious envelope. The Donor pretended nervousness as he struggled to open it. Finally achieving his goal, he smiled and announced with great enthusiasm, "And the winner is . . . Joanne West!"

The entire theater rose in a tumult of applause to endorse their own decision. Jeff stood up graciously, held out a helpful hand to assist Joanne from her seat and with a hasty kiss on the cheek sent her down the aisle to glory. To himself, he said, "Christ! Does she smell!"

She made it to the stage, allowed herself to be kissed, then stood to receive the little statue. At the appropriate moment, tears rolled down her cheeks evoking even greater applause. Then as the second wave of the ovation receded, she moved to the microphone and delivered her speech, thanking her director, the writer, the producer, and those "hundreds of people who are the lifeblood of every picture, and without whom none of us could perform, or even exist."

Once her speech was made, still clutching the golden statuette, she was hustled backstage to pose for the endless press and magazine photographs that would guarantee that the reissuance of her picture would make more millions for the studio. Especially, in this case, since immediately thereafter Joanne's picture was also chosen Best Picture of the Year.

The last Oscar having been bestowed, Jeff rose, as did the rest of the audience, to adjourn to the hotel where a late supper dance would wind up the evening. He lingered in the aisle to receive congratulations on Joanne's victory and by the time he found his way backstage the flurry of excitement over Joanne had begun to abate. She was posing for the foreign press, with the same gracious smile, though tired now, and Jeff could see that the dark stain was beginning to betray itself just below the line of her jacket. Even before she said anything, he knew that she would want to go home, shower, and change into a fresh dress before going on to the dinner.

She had a look about her, which she only wore when she really needed him. He pushed through the photographers to her side and announced, "Miss West is expected at the dinner, so, please?" He guided her past the persistent photographers and toward the stage door.

He had located their limousine and they were speeding back toward Beverly Hills. She sat there fingering the uninscribed statuette which served as a symbol until the real one was sent to her properly engraved with her name. Jeff noticed that she fondled it like a little girl reassuring herself with a new and highly favored doll.

She had won it. Now she didn't care that the costly lamé creation was wrinkled beyond saving, that her hair was askew or that she smelled like a longshoreman after working all afternoon in the summer sun. The Oscar was hers, no matter what she would ever do again in her entire lifetime.

They reached home. Joanne raced from the limousine as Jeff asked the chauffeur to wait. Inside he noticed more than a dozen telegrams on the hall table. Joanne did not bother to stop but hurried for the shower, and relief from the smell of herself that she hated so. She was already stripping off her sequined jacket as she started up the stairs.

He began opening the yellow envelopes hearing her opening doors, slamming them. He smiled until he opened a telegram and read, "How I wish I could have been with you tonight. But soon. Soon. Love, Mel." Every wire had ended "Love," followed by some name or other, but this one irritated him. It was from Mel LeVine, who had directed Joanne's award-winning performance, and who was now on location in Connecticut.

Her affair with LeVine had not been a mere jealous suspicion in Jeff's mind but open gossip all over Hollywood. On the night that the picture was previewed in Tarzana, Joanne never did get home. It was the first time, the only time in their marriage, that that had ever happened except when one or the other of them had been on location. The story that she had been marooned by one of those week-long January rains that periodically afflict Southern California, while possible, was not really believable. Though Jeff had pretended to believe it, as much for his own sake as for hers. His long lay-off had already begun to affect his ability to make firm judgments and especially to give vent to his anger. He had been as much cuckolded by the hazards of his profession as by his wife and her Jewish director.

As far as Jeff knew, he was not anti-Semitic, but somehow LeVine, with the phony spelling of his obviously Jewish name, annoyed him more than all the other men with whom he suspected that Joanne had had affairs. Was it that LeVine was Jewish or was it that he had been the director who had won that damned Oscar for her? Jeff hadn't thought of it that way. But now, standing in the foyer of his huge Beverly Hills home, with a handful of telegrams in his hand, with the limousine waiting outside to take them back to the dinner which would mean endless kisses and congratulations for her and endless waiting and empty smiling for him, Jeff suddenly realized that this night was really the end for them. That was why he hated LeVine. With one picture, one performance, the director had not only lifted Joanne to the top of the business, he had removed her for all time from Jeff. And much as he hated her, he loved her more. Or needed her more. Or perhaps needed the sense of security that this house, this faulty marriage had given him during the last fifteen months.

He had finished the wires, tossed them back on the table, walked to the bar. The trim hard heels of his patent leather dress pumps made sharp sounds on the marble floor of the foyer. He was passing the den when he noticed a dim light. In the center of the room stood the wine cooler they had bought in London on a visit to the silver vaults some four or five years ago. A green bottle was buried in it, its protruding gold foil proclaiming its contents. He went in, looked at the card that rested, a bit damply now, against the bottle which floated in the icy water.

He assumed it was from Martha. A nice touch. But when he picked up the card, he discovered it was from Henry Waterman, the writer who had written two of Joanne's pictures. Jeff glanced at the message.

"To my Princess, on her great night! All my love, Hendry."

The anger that had been triggered by LeVine's wire grew stronger. He crumpled the card, shoved it deep into the icy water. Then on a sudden impulse he seized the bottle and hurled it through the glass lanai door. From above he heard Joanne call out in great apprehension.

"Jeff, what happened? Jeff?" She paused, then called out again, "Jeff! Are you there? What happened?"

Instead of answering, he started for the foyer. There at the top of the stairs he saw her, naked and still drying herself with a thick emerald-green bath towel. He started up the steps, slowly, but with a determination which made her ask, "Jeff, what happened? What was that noise?"

"Nothing," Jeff said.

"That was glass crashing," she said, quite tense now as she saw his set expression. "Jeff? What was that noise?"

"Just someone throwing a champagne bottle through the lanai door," he announced, making it sound as casual as he could.

"Champagne bottle? Who would do a crazy thing like that?"

"I would," he said. He was just two steps below her, able to reach out and tear the towel from her hands.

"Jeff," she half pleaded, half protested.

He tossed the towel aside furiously and reached out to take both her arms and kiss her fiercely on the lips. He could feel her soft skin against his face even though she tried to elude him. When her struggles increased, he slapped her face and lifted her up, his large hands so tight around her slim waist that she gasped for breath. He kissed her angrily first on one breast then on the other. Then he bit into her lower lip till she gasped in pain and began to cry.

Holding her so she couldn't move, he carried her into their bedroom and hurled her onto the bed. She gasped, tried to catch her breath. Quickly, he stripped off his dinner jacket, ripped off his tie, tore open his shirt without even troubling to undo the gold and sapphire Cartier studs she had given him one happy Christmas long ago.

When she tried to skitter across the bed, toward the door, he reached out and seized her arm so tightly that the bruises remained for days. He drew her to him, using his other hand to rip free from his shorts. Then he pushed her down onto the bed, threw himself across her, his erection hard against her.

"All right, Jeff, darling," she said softly, almost prayerfully. "All right, just don't hurt me." Ready now to let him make love to her, she struggled to turn onto her back and open herself to him, expecting that he would follow their usual pattern of foreplay and love. Instead he ripped into her angrily with no preparation. The pain was so great she could not even cry out. Her vagina contracted in a tight spasm that made him wince. But it did not stop him.

He began to work at her, pressing a bit forward, withdrawing a bit, her vagina dry and unyielding moved with him. The more it pained him the more he knew it must pain her so he persisted. Then slowly, very slowly the wetness began. She seemed to relent and when it stopped hurting his need vanished.

Without achieving an orgasm he pulled out of her, glad in his way to be rid of her. They lay there in the dark. He could smell the pungent odor of terror that he had evoked.

When she was sure that his rage had passed, she became less tense, but she was still uncertain. Her impulse was to race to the bathroom, shower again, dress and join the others at the celebration dinner. But, fearful that she might antagonize him since she had never seen him act this way before, she reached out to him, playing with him, and saying, "We'll try again."

Before he could come erect he shoved aside her practiced fingers. She took it as permission to safely leave their bed. He heard her move across the thick soft carpeting, watched her silhouette as she disappeared into the lit bathroom-dressing room. He could see the fringes of her pubic hair between her graceful thighs as she moved, not hurrying, even now. She was making her usual graceful exit, even after an unsuccessful rape.

She had been gone only a moment when he heard her cry of dismay, followed by "Goddamned sonofabitch! Look what you did to me! I can't go back! I can't! I can't! I can't!" She dissolved into uncontrolled tears.

He reached the doorway to find her, still naked, leaning over the marble and gilt-fauceted wash basin, dabbing at her lips with a piece of damp, bloody Kleenex.

She turned on him. "You dirty bastard, look what you did!" She pulled the Kleenex from her mouth to reveal a bleeding cut.

"You did it intentionally! You didn't want me to go back. You couldn't stand it. You were too jealous. Because I've got it! Something you'll never have if you act in pictures for the next hundred years! And you couldn't stand it. So you did this! Admit it, you no-talent bastard! Admit it!"

She began to cry again. More from fury now than frustration. Somehow it amused him.

He said softly, but with a small smile on his lips, "I always wanted to know how it felt to fuck an Academy Award Winner. Now I know. Overrated. Highly overrated."

She dropped onto the cushioned lid of the toilet seat, crying like a disappointed child. He turned and started out of the room, intending to go downstairs, when he heard the phone ring. He answered it. Standing naked except for his English dress pumps, and his black silk hose held up by fourteen carat gold garters from Tiffany's.

It was Irwin Cone.

"Jeff?"

"Yeah, Doctor, what is it?"

"What *is* it? The whole place is in an uproar! Where is she?" Jeff could picture Cone's trim pince-nez glasses trembling on his nose.

"Home. Having a little private celebration."

"Private celebration?" the little man screeched, losing his composure for the first time in all the years Jeff had known him. "She has a duty to be here!"

"Well, Doctor, I'll tell you what really happened. Winning stimulated her so that she just had to get laid. You know how she is when she gets the yen to get laid. It has to be *now*. And it can be *anyone*. Even her own *husband*. . . ."

By that time Joanne was seizing the phone from his hand.

"He's lying!" she said. "He beat me up. That's why I can't go! I'm bleeding. I'm bruised. I don't dare show my face! That's why!" She was crying again.

Jeff retrieved the phone from her trembling hand. He did not speak, only listened to the little man saying, in disbelief and anger as well, "How could he do such a thing! Is he out of his mind? He must be crazy! Joanne, Joanne, honey, listen to me. You wait right there and I'll send a doctor over. No, I'll come myself."

Instead of answering, Jeff hung up the phone, cutting off Irwin Cone, possibly for the first time in his professional life. Then Jeff slipped on a silk robe, went down the stairs into the bar and mixed himself a drink, not too strong, not too weak, a good scotch and soda. He carried it out to the pool and sat there listening to the breezes stir the dry palm leaves, listening too, to Joanne weeping and cursing him from above.

It wasn't fifteen minutes before The Doctor's limousine pulled into the Jefferson driveway. The car drove almost to the garage so that The Doctor could make his entrance unobserved through the pool door. Jeff did not move, except to raise his glass. He heard the car door open, heard the fence door squeak, heard the little man approach.

"For Christ's sake, Jeff! What happened? What did you do to her?"

"I don't know," Jeff said. "But whatever it was, I'm glad I did it."

The Doctor stared at him, seemed to consider arguing but instead turned and entered the house. In moments Jeff could hear them talking. Although he couldn't make out the words, it was obvious that Joanne was crying and accusing, while The Doctor was trying to quiet her.

It seemed like a long time. The Doctor finally came down to find Jeff out at the pool with a fresh drink.

"She could never go now. Not the way she looks." Suddenly The Doctor demanded, "Why the hell did you do it? You ruined everything! Everything! Mostly for yourself!"

Jeff didn't answer, didn't defend himself or try to explain. In the hour that he had been sitting in the dark alone he had been asking himself the same question. And had found no answers. Times past he had done things, foolish things which he had regretted, but at least he knew, or thought he knew, the reasons for those mistakes.

This time he could find no explanation that satisfied him. Perhaps, as she said, he was jealous of her because she had achieved an honor that he knew he would never attain. Or because her sudden ascendancy had come at that moment when his career was at its lowest. Or, it could have been sexual jealousy of other men. It had started with the wire from that Jew director. Maybe there *was* a streak of latent anti-Semitism in him. And if there was, the little man facing him now was partly responsible. Ever since The Doctor had advised him to hold out for "his price" and thus lose the one part he really wanted, Jeff had begun to think of him as "that arrogant little Jew." He felt a strong urge to smash Cone's glasses, then seize him by the satin lapels of his custom-tailored dinner jacket and shove him back into his limousine. Instead Jeff sat there, silent.

"You know," The Doctor said, "this couldn't have come at a worse time. Not for Joanne, for you." He expected to evoke some response, but Jeff only stared.

"So she won't show up tonight. That could even be turned to advantage," The Doctor continued. "When I left the dinner, the head of the studio was already working on a release explaining how Joanne was so emotionally overcome by winning that she couldn't go on to the party. That's never happened before. There's lots of space in such a story. Sympathetic space. She can have the cover of every fan magazine in the world for the next six months just by explaining how it felt to be so overcome.

"But if the real story gets out." For the first time Jeff interrupted The Doctor's flow by shifting to look into his face. "Of course it's going to get out," The Doctor said, this time with a little more bite. "She'll have to go to a doctor. They'll be wanting to photograph her tomorrow. And she's got a picture scheduled to start shooting next week. She can't do anything with that face. Why, Jeff?"

Jeff turned away to avoid answering.

"The rumors will start. First they'll say it was her drinking, but her doctor will see that she didn't fall. And there isn't a doctor in Beverly Hills who doesn't consider himself Louella Parsons and Hedda Hopper rolled into one. An hour after he leaves her it'll be all over town. The only way Jeff Jefferson could take his wife to bed was to rape her. That's what it was, rape. Not actionable, but rape, nevertheless.

"I haven't done a vaginal since I was an intern over twenty-five years ago, and even I could see the unmistakable evidence. And I keep asking myself, why? Why?"

Jeff did not oblige him with an answer.

"Jealousy? I mean *professional* jealousy?"

Jeff shook his head.

"All right, then, another kind of jealousy! So there have been other men." The anger on Jeff's face did not prevent The Doctor from continuing.

"Let's face it, *boychick,* your record isn't spotless. A few starlets. Two airline stewardesses. Even the hostess at the Tail of the Cock over in Santa Monica. Yes, it's my business to know all about all my clients. And, of course, that little matter down in Texas. . . ."

"What the hell do you know about that?"

"Enough."

"A one-night stand. I've never seen her since."

"Or spoken to her?" The Doctor asked.

Jeff didn't answer, which was admission enough.

"So you see, your jealousy really is not justified. No man likes to have it happen. No matter what he's done. But it does happen. Sometimes. . . ."

The Doctor hesitated, pretending to consider whether a personal revelation of his own would further his purpose. Finally he said, "How do you think *I* felt? My own wife! With an AC-DC decorator who was helping her pick out antiques for the TCA office. It happens to all of us. How we handle it is what makes the difference."

The phone was ringing again.

"It's for me," The Doctor said. He stepped inside the lanai to pick up the extension.

"Yes, yes, it's me. No, I'm sorry, Sol. You can tell the press that she is emotionally overcome by winning and cannot appear in public tonight. Tomorrow? Tomorrow, we'll see." The Doctor had barely paused for breath when a question enraged him enough to make him shout, "That is precisely the reason, emotional exhaustion!" He drew breath, then more slowly, "No, there's no trouble. Nothing that can't be cured by a few sedatives and a couple of days away from photographers, studios, and nosey executives like *you!* Okay, *call* me a prick! Call me anything you want, the fact is she is not going to be there tonight!"

He hung up abruptly, as was his custom even when not provoked. He mixed himself a light drink, took one gulp, and said, "The important thing now is to retain an appearance of harmony. The first few times she appears in public, you will be there. Together. The all-American couple. For your sake. Not hers. She doesn't need it. *You do!*"

"I can live without it!" Jeff said angrily.

"You *think* you can live without it. You think maybe there are greener pastures down in Texas. She's loaded that girl, no doubt. More than a billion, I understand. But that's not where you belong. Jeff, you listen to The Doctor. Your future is only beginning."

"I'll bet!" Jeff said bitterly, almost viciously.

"I say it's only just beginning. I can't explain tonight. But I will. Soon. The important thing now is to keep everything peaceful. As far as the world is concerned you're still the adoring couple. No hint of what happened here tonight. I won't even let her see your doctor. Do you realize what rape would mean to your sexual image?

"Until everything calms down, you live here, appear in public with her, everything is fine. Then in about three or four months you can quietly drift apart. Let the world put whatever interpretation they want on it. By that time the sympathy will have swung over to you. It'll be the old show business cliché. One spouse becomes more successful than the other and selfishly decides to go it alone. That'll make you the loyal, devoted husband, who married his wife when she was only a starlet, helped her become famous, then was cast aside."

That appealed to Jeff, and because it did the tougher side of him began to question. Why now? Why tonight, when his client had just won the most coveted honor the industry had to offer, was The Doctor evolving a strategy that would work against her?

The Doctor read him, clearly and unequivocally. "Why am I so worried about you? I told you that a moment ago, but you didn't believe me. Because, my boy," and here The Doctor put aside his glass to seek Jeff's eyes in the darkness, "because your future is only beginning. The fact that I'm willing to risk her career for your protection should be proof enough."

Jeff stared at Cone, wondering whether to believe him. The only thing that argued in favor of it was that the man had disclosed two secrets to him, damaging secrets. He had said that Joanne was not the most preferred client at TCA. And he had admitted that his own wife had committed adultery with a British fag. If he were less than serious, a man like The Doctor would never have revealed either.

In fatherly fashion The Doctor reassured Jeff with a gentle pat on the arm. "You just do what I say. The next few weeks everything nice and calm and usual. Maybe you even take her away."

"But her new picture," Jeff began.

"I'll get a delay. Don't worry. The main thing, no public arguments, no moving out, no sudden trips alone. Usual is the word. You go to your usual Guild meetings. You read scripts. And you turn them down."

"All of them?" Jeff asked, puzzled.

"All of them," The Doctor said firmly.

"Even good ones?"

"There aren't any good ones, Jeff. Not for you. But that can be the best thing!"

"How?" Jeff demanded bluntly.

"I told you. Trust me." He patted Jeff on the shoulder and started back toward his waiting limousine.

Once the car had backed out of the driveway Jeff rose, still puzzled. He climbed the stairs slowly, could hear the water running in the bathroom, another shower. She would spend the rest of her life trying to rid herself of her own smell.

He went into his own dressing room and took out a pair of silk pajamas, noticing at the same time that Doris Martinson's blue shirt still rested on the bottom of one of his shelves. He wondered, how did The Doctor know about her?

The water had stopped running in Joanne's bathroom. He put on his robe, went in. She was drying herself with a fresh emerald towel.

"You lay a hand on me and I'll kill you!" she said, and meant it. Though there was little she could have done to defend herself if he had wanted to attack her again.

"I only wanted to say I'm sorry."

"You should be. Look, look at that." She thrust her face upward for him to see. He had left quite a cut on her lip. Her cheek where he'd slapped her was still red.

"I'm sorry."

" 'Sorry.' Fuck you!" she said and went back to drying under her armpits. Then she applied a deodorant, followed it with powder and finally with cologne.

"The Doctor said we have to play it cool. *Usual.* That was the word he used."

"He said the same thing to me," she answered impatiently. "But I'd like to let this whole town know the kind of sonofabitch you are! And if you ever lay a hand on me again I *will* let them know! You're an animal, that's what you are!"

"There are a couple of wires down there for you. One from Mel LeVine."

"So?" She stared back defiantly.

"And that bottle of champagne. That was from *Hendry.*"

"What about it?" she demanded fiercely.

"I'm just trying to explain," he said.

"You're just trying to pick a fight, so the whole thing *will* come out. You want to destroy my career. That's what you want to do. On my biggest night. . . ." And it seemed her anger would turn to tears again.

"The Doctor is right," he said. "Let's just keep it usual. At home too. Let's not talk at all."

He turned and started down the steps, to sleep in the

guest bedroom on the ground floor. It was the end of
the marriage. Final. Complete. Except for the formality
of the property settlement.

Sitting in the back of his limousine, Irwin Cone rested
his nervous fingers on the telephone, itching to call someone. It was too late on the Coast and too early in New
York. And the boys from his Beverly Hills office were still
at the Academy dinner. So he let his fingers dance nervously over the instrument while he evaluated the events
of the evening.

Two careers were involved.

Joanne's, which at the moment seemed the most promising, was the one most subject to erosion. One didn't have
to be a practicing physician to recognize the symptoms of
incipient alcoholism. It was written all over the delicate,
lovely face.

As to her acting, Academy Award or not, her performance would always depend on her director. She never
really played any part. The part played her. Sheer perse-
verance by LeVine, on the set and in bed, had brought
forth the Academy Award performance.

How it had been won didn't matter. That it *had* been
won was everything. The usual technique in handling an
Award winner would be to make a one-picture deal, at
the highest possible price, thus establishing a level for all
her future pictures. If Joanne were more stable that is exactly what The Doctor would have done.

But given her long-range physical and mental prognosis,
he decided that he would move for a five-picture deal instead, giving her script and director approval, plus holding
money during any year in which the studio did not come
up with a satisfactory vehicle. That way, Joanne and
TCA would be protected for at least five years. After that,
if she lasted that long, he would worry about her future.

That was the main reason he had decided not to let her
go see her doctor now, to keep anyone else from detecting
the incipient alcoholism that he suspected.

The risk of gossip about which he warned Jeff was his
own convenient invention. As was the story about his wife
and the fag decorator. A lie. Complete and total. Made up
to buy Jeff's confidence and cooperation, which at this
critical juncture in his entire plan was necessary to have.

Maybe, The Doctor admitted to himself, the story was going a little far. But it didn't matter, actually. In this town where gossip was far more interesting than the actual facts of life, Melba had been subjected to infinitely more slanderous stories than that. Several times it had reached him that she was having a lesbian affair with the wife of a studio head. Sometimes, in moments of special pique and irritation, he believed it himself. So one more lie, even from his own lips, could do no harm.

And it was necessary. Especially with Jeff. The Doctor needed that man, needed him desperately.

The irony of the entire evening was that the only bit of truth The Doctor had revealed was the part that Jeff doubted most—that Jeff's career was only just beginning.

But the time had not come for The Doctor to discuss his plan. The events of this evening were a highly fortuitous bonus. The Doctor couldn't have planned it better himself. It provided the perfect way to keep Jeff out of work, isolating him, subtly forcing him to lose confidence in his career, and in himself. When the doctor was ready to make his move, Jeff would have no choice but to agree.

The next morning at about ten, when he was sure that Jeff had finished his calisthenics, had his swim and his morning coffee, The Doctor had Alise put through a call. Both lines were busy the first six times, congratulations for Joanne, of course. But, toward noon, Alise managed to get him on the phone. She buzzed The Doctor.

"Jeff-baby? How is it today?"

"Okay. Quiet. Except for phone calls. From all over. London. Rome, Madrid. Paris."

"Good, good. And Joanne?"

"Okay."

"How does she look?"

"Well, she's . . . she's got that lip."

Cone sighed, "I thought so. Remember, keep her away from your doctor!"

"Okay."

"If anything changes, call me at once. Especially if she gets restless. In fact, maybe you two should drive down to the Springs for a week or two. Use my house. It's absolutely isolated. A quiet week or so in the sun wouldn't do either of you any harm."

"I'll mention it," Jeff promised, in such a way as to indicate the conversation was at an end.

Which was the cue for The Doctor to come to the real purpose of his call. "Oh, Jeff, before I forget . . . what I said last night."

"What?"

"About *your* career."

"Yeah?" Jeff asked, suspiciously.

"Devote your time to her 'til the day she goes back to work. Then you and I will sit down and have a nice long quiet talk. Away from Romanoff's or Chasen's or the Beverly Hills. Maybe we'll drive down to La Jolla. But we'll have a nice long quiet talk."

"About what?" Jeff asked.

"The day she goes back to work," The Doctor said. He hung up at once.

3

That The Doctor was able to delay the starting date of Joanne's picture was no surprise. And since a vacation seemed the only graceful way to avoid photographers, Jeff and Joanne left for the Cone house in Palm Springs.

Jeff had stowed the bags in the trunk. Though it was a hot summer morning, Joanne insisted that the windows of the convertible be up and the top in place before she would make her brief sortie from the pool area into the car. For the swelling in her lip had now begun to discolor, a mottle of blue and yellow. Holding a handkerchief to her face, as though tending a bad cold, she succeeded in slipping into the car unseen. Jeff backed out of the driveway and down the slight incline onto the street.

Even going against the inbound traffic the trip took more than two hours. Once they left the freeway, cross traffic from feeder roads made fast driving dangerous, and Jeff realized that Joanne was tense enough without adding to it with his usual high speed.

She said not a word, seeking to punish him with her silence. She held the handkerchief to her face as if she feared that other motorists might overtake them and peer in at her, even though she wore sunglasses and a scarf that helped conceal her face.

Some distance out of Palm Springs, approaching Redlands, Jeff spoke to her for the first time in more than an hour to ask if she would like to stop and have some coffee.

"And let everyone see what you did to me?" she demanded fiercely.

He didn't answer, just drove on, wondering how a man could ever let everyone see what some woman had done to him.

Traffic passing through Redlands was slow. It looked like every other town in Southern California, same gas station signs, same supermarkets, same branch banks, seemingly arranged in the same way. No place in the entire southern part of the state seemed to have a personality of its own.

They were in desert country now, off the main road and onto the spur that veered to the right and down into the valley that was actually Palm Springs. The earth was dry, dusty sand. The mountains were rocks of changing colors depending on the position of the sun. Here and there sprouted tufts of tough, hardy vegetation, lending green color to the otherwise dusty landscape. Through the cut in the mountains and down into the valley Jeff drove, until finally before him there lay the flat town which was the seasonal capital of the motion picture industry.

He knew the way to The Doctor's house—a left off Palm Canyon, a right onto Avenida Las Palmas and there between Jack Benny's house on the one side and Cary Grant's on the other, was the tree-lined estate of Irwin Cone. The words on the mailbox said, *Casa del Ysidro,* which was The Doctor's private joke, meaning House of Isidore.

The driveway was so overhung with tropical trees and vegetation that every time Jeff drove into it he felt that he might be disappearing for all time. From the outside the place never seemed inhabited, as nunneries never seem to be inhabited. Servants were there, they moved about, dusted, ordered food, prepared and served it. Guests lived there frequently but somehow one never saw them. Only on those afternoons or early evenings when The Doctor and his wife were in residence and having a cocktail party did one see any outward signs of life or activity.

So Jeff always had the eerie feeling that one time, perhaps today, he would disappear into the driveway, be swallowed up by some giant carnivorous plant, and never be heard of again.

Aside from two Cadillacs which, because they were two years old, Jeff knew belonged to the servants, there were no other cars, either in the garage or in the parking area which was quite extensive, looking like a concrete landing area in all that vast tropical jungle.

Before Jeff had even turned off the ignition, Calvin, the houseman, was ready to assist him with the bags. Joanne waited till Calvin was out of sight before she opened her door and swiftly moved into the house and down the hall of the wing that accommodated the several guest suites. She waited while the houseman entered one suite and set down the bags. Then, careful to avoid his stare, she entered, closing and locking the door behind her.

Jeff had to jiggle the knob before she would let him in. He started to draw the draperies to look out at the pool.

"Don't touch those! You want the whole world to see me?"

"Are you going to keep yourself penned up in here in the dark for the next ten days?"

"Until I dare show myself," she declared. She would have gone on but there was a discreet knock at the door. "Yes?"

"It's me, Miss Joanne. Mima." Mima being a contraction of Jemima which was not her real name. But it pleased Melba Cone to call her that because it sounded chic. "Shall I help you unpack?"

"No thanks. Not yet. I . . ." she improvised, "I have to rest a bit first."

"I understand," Mima said gently. "You just tell me when you ready."

Then Joanne actually made a pretense at resting. Kicking off her shoes, she lay down on the twin bed, at the foot of which Calvin had placed her luggage, and pretended to drift off to sleep. Jeff watched the entire procedure, more amused than irritated, wondering how long she was going to carry on the charade. He started to unpack. Without stirring, she demanded, "You're not going to stay in *here*, are you?"

"The Doctor said, 'usual,' " he reminded her.

She considered it, relented and said, "Okay. But you lay one fucking finger on me and I'll kill you! Do you understand?"

He wandered out to the pool, where Calvin was setting the umbrella-shielded table for luncheon for two.

"Mrs. Jefferson won't be having lunch out," Jeff told him.

"Shall Mima send something in to her?" Calvin asked,

giving no sign of curiosity or personal interest.

"No, I'll take something in to her later," Jeff said.

"Would you care for a swim before lunch?"

"Good idea."

"You'll find everything you need in the poolhouse," Calvin suggested, suspecting that Jeff would find it awkward to go back into the suite for his swim trunks.

He ate his lunch, ending with iced coffee and only a bit of the excellent strawberry pie which Mima had baked. Then he decided to go over to the Racquet Club to see who was free for a few sets of singles. As he was about to leave the house, he remembered Joanne, went to the bar and took an unopened bottle of gin. He knocked on her door, did not wait for an answer, opened it and said softly, "I brought your lunch."

She didn't stir until she heard the sound of glass on glass. She took one look at the bottle and said, "Screw you!" He withdrew.

On his way out he stopped to ask Calvin for tennis gear and a racket. Jeff pulled out of the driveway and started for the Racquet Club.

It was off season in Palm Springs so there was not much activity at the club when he arrived. Only two of the front five courts were in play. He went through the narrow passage to the pool and outdoor dining area. There were a few familiar faces—a junior executive from Fox whom he'd met once during some Guild negotiations, a youngish actor having lunch at a small table with a girl who looked as if she might be an actress. On spying Jeff, the young man leaped up and came forward, his hand extended, calling, "Hi, Jeff!"

Worse than fans who presumed familiarity, Jeff resented those in the business whom he did not really know. Quite obviously the young man was doing it to impress his girl friend.

"Scott Burgess," the actor said, "I was on *Snake River* with you." It was a picture that Jeff had made four, or was it five, years ago.

That tactic of immediately announcing his name was the surest sign of insecurity in an actor, the assumption that the person you were greeting didn't know you.

Nevertheless Jeff smiled, held out his hand. If the kid

wanted to impress his girl or his wife or his broad, Jeff thought, okay, what the hell.

"Join us for a bite?"

"Thanks, but I've had lunch."

"Coffee, then?" Burgess asked eagerly.

Jeff decided to reward his persistence. "Coffee will be fine."

"Great!"

The young man led the way to the table. "Honey, Jeff Jefferson!" Then he added, as though apologetically, "This is Charlene."

Charlene, it turned out, was not the young man's wife, or even his girl friend. They had not come down to the Springs together but had met at the club only yesterday. She was not an actress but the daughter of a wealthy Jewish family in Chicago.

She spoke well and her knowledge of pictures surprised Jeff until he learned that her family owned one of the larger theater chains in the Midwest and she had been brought up on films. Her earliest memories were of screenings in her own home. She knew all of Jeff's films and could remember seeing them from the time she was seven, a fact that did not please him greatly. But she made the statement to underline her admiration, not to emphasize the difference in the ages.

When she got up from the table, Jeff discovered she was almost as tall as he was. Her figure was full and lush, but it was not her height or her long black hair which impressed him. It was her frank expression. Her eyes were violet, wide, direct and penetrating, as though announcing that she had no secrets or defenses. And when she spoke to him, far from avoiding his face or staring, as people tend to do with stars, she looked directly into his eyes and he found after a while that he was becoming conscious of his genitals in a strange way. There was a tingling there and an awareness, a sense that she was equally aware and it only increased his interest in her. In truth, what disturbed him was that he had not expected to react that way to a girl of twenty-two or -three.

Now, Scott Burgess was suggesting, "Would you mind playing mixed doubles, Jeff?"

If the girl hadn't made such an impression on him he

would have begged off, saying he had a prearranged match. Instead, he said, "I'm meeting someone, but until he shows up, let's hit a few." Thus he left himself an escape, in case the game turned out to be too dismal.

Charlene wore tennis clothes well. Her thighs flowed nicely from her brief tennis dress. She had long tanned legs and her buttocks were rounded but not out of proportion. Only her breasts made Jeff think that she could not be an excellent player, for Jeff had noticed that women with full bosoms were rarely top flight players, possibly because voluptuous breasts inhibited a good swing.

So Jeff did not expect much from Charlene as they stepped onto the court. While Scott went to round up another girl, Jeff and Charlene began to warm up. He started out easily, hitting indulgently to her forehand to put her at ease. He was surprised when her return was resentfully sharp and deep to his backhand. He barely managed to return it, a short, unintentionally sliced stroke that made her move up to forecourt, which she did gracefully in a few long easy strides, instead of the many short steps most women resort to under pressure.

It revealed several things about her. She was well coached and grounded in the game. She had poise. And she was determined to let him know at once that she was good, and did not have to be babied like many women players.

Soon they settled down to a steady volley, neither one attempting to out-hit or embarrass the other, but gradually building up in tempo and sharpness. After a dozen shots had crossed the net and been returned, he sent one deep into her backhand corner which she couldn't quite reach. She let it go, calling out, "Good hit!" without frustration or envy.

By the time Burgess showed up with a fourth, Jeff resented the interruption, particularly since the girl was a pretty blond starlet, with a very highly styled tennis dress and a chic hairdo of ribbons and elaborate curls. He knew, even before she stepped onto the court, that she couldn't hit worth a damn, that she would spend most of the afternoon trying to work him into a contact whom she could use to further her career.

Because to do otherwise would make the teams unbalanced. Jeff selected the blond girl as his partner. She seemed flattered, apologizing, "I want you to know I haven't played much this season. I've been too busy."

Jeff smiled. "Don't worry about it. I need the exercise."

They started playing. It became apparent almost at once that the blonde, whose name he had failed to catch, hadn't played much tennis in any season. And it turned out that Charlene hit better than Burgess. By unspoken agreement the game settled down to a personal duel between Jeff and the tall girl from Chicago. The longer the set went on, the more Jeff enjoyed playing against her. Finally he let it go to seven-five, though he could have won it at six-four if he had wanted to. The blond girl was relieved that the game was over. She smiled and apologized profusely until Jeff assured her that she had actually done quite well and that they would have to team up again some time.

When she finally left the court, taking Burgess with her, Jeff turned to Charlene. "Drink?"

"Sure," she said, openly flattered, "but not at the bar." When he seemed surprised, she added, "My bungalow." She started away and he followed her up the steps to the bungalow area and along the red concrete path bordered on both sides by lawns so meticulously trimmed they seemed manufactured. The air was refreshingly pungent with the smell from the orange, grapefruit and jasmine trees set back from the paths.

As they walked along, squinting against the strong sun that was getting ready to plunge behind snow-topped Mount San Jacinto, she said, "I don't like that bar. Every man assumes you're a B-girl or a starlet, which means you're there because you're available. Willing."

He wondered if she were telling him this so that he would not come to her place under any illusions.

Then she added, "When I'm willing, I don't make a public display of it."

They said no more, just kept walking. Charlene's bungalow was the last one in the line. Her patio looked straight out toward the top of San Jacinto. Two chaises faced the sun. She invited Jeff to use one with a gesture of her hand, as she asked, "What do you drink?"

"Scotch?"

"Of course. How?"

"Rocks, soda, and a twist."

She disappeared through the curtained sliding glass door that moved back and into place again without a sound. He dropped onto the chaise, faced the sun, with his eyes closed, feeling the heat so strong that his skin stung. Suddenly she was at his side with two glasses in hand. She gave him the scotch and soda, kept for herself a glass of colorless liquid, probably vodka and tonic.

Strangely, without preamble, she was asking, "Is it true?"

"What?" He turned to look at her.

She avoided his eyes. "The night of the Awards, did you really beat her up?"

"Of course not!"

"I didn't think so." She seemed glad to have confirmation. "There was a lot of talk around here the next day that you got drunk and beat her up out of jealousy. Some silly bastard even said you tried to rape her."

"You didn't believe that, did you?"

"No," she said. "Though I could understand why, if you did."

He sat up, stared across at her. She was still facing the sun, but she heard him move and she added, "I figure she's a cold-assed broad. Any woman who always looks that perfect in public is too concerned about herself to be good for any man."

He didn't answer. It wasn't necessary.

"She plays around a lot, too," Charlene said. "If you didn't know it I wouldn't have said it. And if I didn't like you I wouldn't have mentioned it. But I do like you. You're a very good-looking man, sure. But more than that, you're a nice man. I could tell when you were playing with that poor little idiot with the blond hair and the designer outfit. Most men would have brushed her off fast, unless they wanted to lay her. I don't think you would hurt anyone's feelings, unless you were forced to."

"Thanks," he said, not completely hiding his resentment at being so thoroughly analyzed, even though favorably.

"There's a reason why I'm telling you this," she said. "In a few minutes that sun's going to be completely gone. It'll get to be too cold out here. You'll have to leave. Or else

I'll have to ask you to come inside where it's more comfortable. Before I do, I want to know one thing. Whatever happens in there, will it be because you're angry with *her?* Or because you like *me?*"

The directness of her question surprised him, though it shouldn't have. Her frankness was the first thing he had noticed. He hesitated.

But in that moment she said, "Never mind. You better go. If you want to, come back tomorrow. I'll be here. We can hit some."

"Tomorrow afternoon?"

"Same time?"

"Same time."

They got up simultaneously, stood there face to face. For a moment he felt the impulse to kiss her but he didn't. He was glad, because the look in her eyes said, thanks. He picked up his racket, started down the concrete walk toward the parking lot.

Along the way a car passed him, honked, someone called out his name but he couldn't identify the voice. Possibly Burgess. Or some other actor he had worked with, or some agent. Or just somebody. It didn't matter. There was a freshness in his life suddenly, because of that girl.

That mattered.

When he returned to the Cone house, Joanne was secluded in her room. He went out to the pool area and found the bottle of gin, almost empty. Obviously once he'd gone she had sat out in the air, drinking.

He found her at the dressing-table mirror, examining her face. When she heard him enter she applied herself to her swollen lip and the faint bruise on her cheek. He knew it was intended as a rebuke but he ignored it. He noticed the redness of her skin, from the strong afternoon sun.

"So you finally went out. Good," he said feeling called upon to say something.

"I thought the sun could cure this, or hide it," she lamented, half martyr, half prosecutor. "After all, I don't dare show my face in town this way."

Without answering, he stripped off his tennis clothes, stepped into the glass-enclosed stall shower, and surren-

dered himself to the hot steamy water and fragrant soap.
He washed himself thoroughly, especially around his genitals which seemed more alive since this afternoon. As he
did so, he thought of Charlene, hoping that she might be
an escape from the nagging dullness of being confined
with Joanne in order to avoid gossip. Which obviously
was spreading despite The Doctor's prescribed course of
conduct.

Jeff had finished dinner alone and was ready for bed
when the phone rang. The Doctor was on the line, warm,
affable, and just too goddamned friendly.

"Well, Jeff, find everything okay? The house? Calvin
and Mima?"

"Fine. Everything's fine."

"Have you taken Joanne out?"

"The first few days she said she'd rather stay home."

"Still her face?" The Doctor said sadly.

"Still."

"Well, keep urging her. With a little make-up it won't
look bad. You should be seen together. Especially at
night. And it'll give her a big charge to have people swoon
over her Oscar."

"I'll do my best," Jeff said, hoping that he was exhibiting sufficient determination, all the while knowing that
The Doctor had not called merely about this.

"Okay, then, take it easy. Talk to you in a day or two."
The Doctor seemed about to hang up, but instead he said,
"Oh, by the way . . ."

Jeff listened more intently now. He knew this was Cone's
real reason for calling.

"I hear you ran into Moe Rashbaum's daughter at the
club." Casual, ever the casual Doctor, when he had something on his mind.

"Moe Rashbaum's daughter?" Jeff asked, truly puzzled
for a moment.

"Moe Rashbaum. Rashbaum Theatre Circuit. Out of
Chicago. I understand his daughter's a nice-looking girl.
Tall, dark-haired. Her name is Charlotte or something
like that . . ."

"You mean Charlene. Yes, we played tennis today.
Doubles." That last word made it sound less clandestine.

"Oh? Nice girl? I used to know her father in the old
days."

"Nice girl. Anything you want me to tell her?"

"Just tell her to remember me to her dad."

"Of course."

"And if you can, get Joanne out of the house, be seen around, you know—the usual."

Irritated to have been under such tight surveillance, Jeff exploded, "Look, Doctor, if you want us to be seen around together, that's one thing! But if you want the usual that's something else. Because in recent months 'usually' we do not go out together!"

"Jeff, Jeff, don't blow. Not now. Not when we're so close. Maybe I was trying to be too diplomatic. I'll come right out and say it. As I understand it, Charlene Rashbaum is one hell of a good-looking girl. Playing tennis with her is one thing, but going back to her place for drinks, and etceteras, that's another. In fact, unless you're with Joanne, stay the hell away from the Racquet Club altogether. It's a snake pit for gossip."

"Doctor, as long as we're all being so nice and frank, would you care to enlarge on that 'etcetera'?" When there was no answer, Jeff continued, "*Yes*, we had a drink! *No*, there were no etceteras! Okay?"

"Okay, Jeff," The Doctor said, playing the hurt, wronged father to the hilt. And, of course, he hung up at once.

4

Jeff woke early the next morning. Joanne was still sleeping but her usual soft snoring had stopped. Anxiously, he slid out of bed, stood over her to make sure she was breathing. She was. From his full height he could still smell the gin exuding from her. He went into the bathroom without putting on any lights, guided only by the daylight that seeped in under the closed draperies.

He emptied his bladder, flushed the toilet, then began to brush his teeth. He examined himself in the mirror as he shaved, realizing suddenly that this was in anticipation of Charlene. He was really asking himself, how did he look to a girl twenty years younger than he was.

When he walked softly out of the bathroom Joanne greeted him, "Christ! Can't you be quiet?"

"I didn't make a sound," he protested in an angry whisper.

"Next time, at least have the courtesy to piss against the side of the bowl!" she said, turning over, hiding her head under the pillow, pretending to go back to sleep.

To himself Jeff said, "And now another morning with that lovable all-American couple, Jeff and Joanne, from their love nest high above Beverly Hills. Good morning, Joanne darling. Good morning, Jeff sweetie."

As soon as he reached the Racquet Club he spied her on the far court, reserved for the Pro. She was taking a lesson in net play. Her knit tennis shirt was tight against her body, outlining her breasts, flattering them more than the starched dress she had worn yesterday.

A few minutes after she saw him she pleaded fatigue, asked to call the teaching session short. The pro, affable as all tennis pros are, smiled, and waved her off. She

272

seized a towel and her white sweater from the bench and walked swiftly toward Jeff.

He was holding the iron-mesh fence gate open for her. When she came close he could see the radiant smile on her face.

"I thought you said this afternoon," she said, pretending his sudden appearance was not as welcome as he knew it to be.

"I happened to be free a little earlier than I expected," he lied.

"Shall we play? I'm warmed up and I don't want to cool off."

"Sure!"

"Doubles," she insisted suddenly.

Though his first reaction was disappointment he went to find two other players. He returned to discover her bending over the water cooler, and noticed that her legs, in fact the entire line of her long body, was graceful even in such an unnatural pose. When she turned away from the cooler, there were drops of water on her cheek and her lips. As she tried to wipe them away with her towel he reached out to catch her hand and stare at her. For the first time he knew that he might be in love, that early stage of love where everything that happens adorns the one you love, and where the smallest, most commonplace event becomes, in its way, a miracle of beauty and delight.

She felt it too, and let him know from the gentle way she disengaged her hand and reluctantly wiped away the drops of water. From that moment on, the innocent delight seemed to go out of her violet eyes. She was as lovely, as bright, as pleased with his company as before. But for some reason he did not understand, she seemed preoccupied now.

The two opponents Jeff had rounded up were a producer and a writer down from L.A. to escape incessant phone calls and studio pressure while trying to lick a story. The phrase always irked Jeff. As if a screen story were a recalcitrant child or an enemy which had to be whipped or beaten into submission. No wonder most of the scripts he saw seemed to read that way.

This time Jeff and Charlene were partners. The foursome warmed up quickly, playing two balls at a time, Charlene hitting to the writer, Jeff to the producer. It was soon obvious that the writer was the better of the two, the producer being too heavy to move well, though the remains of a good solid game were evident in occasional shots he made.

They proved not much of a match for Jeff and Charlene. She played well, scoring points that always seemed to surprise her opponents, coming as they did from a woman.

Two sets were all the producer could last and they quit when he suggested it.

As Jeff was helping Charlene on with her sweater, she whispered to him, "Ask them for lunch." He hesitated, not sure he'd heard correctly. So she repeated, "Invite them to lunch!"

Puzzled, he did as she said because it seemed important to her. Lunch was the same all around, Bloody Marys followed by Dungeness crab with a mustard and mayonnaise sauce. Table talk centered mainly on Jeff. The writer, ecstatic over his testimony before the committee, attributed to Jeff left wing sentiments he didn't share, but which he chose not to dispute at the moment. And the producer kept talking about Jeff's great job for the industry.

Their compliments were becoming so profuse that Jeff was relieved when the producer finally said, "Come on, slave! We have work to do!"

They both stood up and Charlene asked, "Same teams for tomorrow?"

They seemed surprised to be invited, but the producer accepted for both of them.

Once they were out of hearing, Jeff asked, "What was the big idea?"

"Otherwise I couldn't have lunch with you," she said simply.

"Why not?"

"Because I got a phone call, too."

"From whom?" Jeff demanded, immediately condemning The Doctor in his mind.

"Dad. Who got a phone call from . . ."

"Don't tell me!" Jeff interrupted. "From Irwin Cone."

She nodded.

"Well, it's not your responsibility what happens to me or Joanne." His voice was growing loud.

"You've got it all wrong," she whispered, deliberately soft now, to quiet him. "He didn't say a word to Dad about your career or the publicity or Joanne. He just used the magic word."

"And that is?"

"*Goy!* He simply called my dad and did him the 'favor' of reporting that his one and only daughter was screwing around with a *goy* movie star. And it was getting serious since we were being seen alone together all the time."

" 'All the time'? One afternoon?"

Quite soberly now, Charlene said, "One afternoon can be a long time. One glance can be a long time. When I turned from the water cooler and found you staring at me, well, a moment like that is a long time. Because that's when I knew. It wasn't *going* to happen, it already *had*. And from that time on my life wasn't going to be the same. It's going to end up hurting. But it's too late to stop it."

She was staring at him, part of her pleading to be let off, part of her pleading to be taken.

"So that's why doubles, and 'Ask them for lunch'?" She nodded. "You were afraid to be alone with me."

"The gossip. I wanted to spare you that."

"Thanks," he said. "I'm old enough to take care of myself." He had spoken too quickly, and he was sorry. "Why does it have to end up hurting?"

"Because it's impossible, right from the start."

"Our ages?" he suggested bluntly. She shook her head. "Then what?" he persisted.

"I told you."

"Would it matter that much?"

"It would to Dad. He's a man who's worked very hard to become important, powerful. And part of being powerful is what he can do for Jews, all Jews. Especially since Hitler. He spends more time working for Israel than for himself. Being a Jew is as important to him now as being rich used to be. It's what he lives for. I couldn't do this to him."

"What about you? Don't you deserve anything out of life?"

"Not at his expense."

"So when The Doctor called him, and he called you, that was it."

"I'm here," she said simply. She had the same look in her eyes that she'd had when he surprised her at the water fountain.

"My car's back up the road. I'll pay the check and leave to get it. In a little while walk back to your bungalow. I'll drive up back somewhere."

"No, please."

"I won't park near your place," he insisted in a low voice.

Her violet eyes smiled. He signed the check and started toward the front exit, more ostentatiously than he normally would have.

Charlene sat there, eyes closed, and finished her cigarette. She drew another out of the pack, lit it and took a few puffs. Then, as if prodded by an urgent chore she'd just remembered, she suddenly looked at her wristwatch, and started back toward her bungalow.

When she reached it he was lying on one of the chaises, facing San Jacinto and hidden from view from the rest of the club.

He didn't rise to greet her, only held up his hand. She took it and he pulled her down to the chaise alongside his own. They sat motionless. Being together was enough for the moment, even though he could feel himself growing larger against his confining jockey shorts. Yet the need to sit quietly beside her was stronger than the need to satisfy his hunger for her.

Suddenly he found himself saying, "I still can't believe it."

"About my father?"

"About you. Being what you are. Looking the way you look. This hasn't happened to me since I was a kid in college. I mean falling in love this way."

He realized, when she suddenly turned away, that it was the first time the word love had been mentioned between them.

"That's what it is," he said. "Unless you know another word for it."

"If that's what it is, then that's enough. If it isn't, talking about it will only make it sound worse afterwards."

He didn't answer. In a moment she drew out her cigarettes, started to light one. He took it away from her.

"You smoke too much."

She laughed. "Now, for the first time, I know it's love.
When they start to worry about how much you smoke."
But she never finished, for a sadness seemed to overcome
her.

She reached for his hand and pressed it against her,
just below her breast. It seemed to mean that now that
they'd found each other she didn't want to risk losing
him. When his hand moved up gently she permitted it,
though she never took her hand off his. They lay that
way a while, facing the sun, silent, eyes closed. Then,
somehow the electricity in his hand transmitted itself to
her breast and in a while she said, "It's getting cold out
here."

"Sun'll be gone in a while," he said, though they both
knew it had almost an hour left.

Still holding his hand she rose, and turned toward
the glass doors, which were completely shrouded by the
closed draperies. She slipped in between the curtains. He
waited a few moments lest he seem too anxious. Somehow,
in this instance, good manners demanded it. Then he took
one cautious look around to see if anyone was watching.
There was no one, no maid, no housekeeper, no garden-
er. He went inside, closed the glass door and turned to
confront her.

She was in the dressing area hidden from his view but
he could hear the rustling of her clothes as she took off
her tennis shorts, and her shirt. Then, as she was removing
her bra, he moved to her, taking it from her hand and
reaching out to embrace her. He kissed her for the first
time and brought her body tight against his own. He could
feel her long legs, her good thighs, and most of all her
breasts which were not pointed but very round and full
and firm.

He held her that way a long time, pressing against her
till his own pain made him release her long enough to
take off his clothes.

When he faced her again, her smile was gone. He embraced her and held her tightly. She gave way gently and
allowed him to ease between her thighs. She was soft but

strong. And young, he realized, as he felt the fullness of her breast. Her nipples rose stiffly to his tongue.

She sank down on the bed, stretched out full length with her eyes closed, as though there might be some risk involved in looking. He stood over her, staring down at her face which seemed almost childlike now that her eyes were shut. He lay down beside her, turning his face so that his mouth was in full contact with her breast. He reached around to lift her to him, pressing his face against her breast till he felt her gasp.

Whatever surges of desire he felt, he could tell that she was responding in kind, for she began to writhe her warm body against his. His hand went gently from her breast, down her slim waist to her thighs, and then subtly between them. He discovered her soft hair was moist. She was ready for him. There was a moment when her hand reached out to stop him but she drew it back and opened wider to him.

He moved over her and slid down slowly, starting to enter her. As he did she gasped slightly in pain. He hesitated, but she reached out to pull him down into her. Then she locked her strong legs around him, and they were one.

For the first few minutes she matched him strength for strength, hunger for hunger, wanting for wanting. She kissed him feverishly, her tongue exploring his mouth. Even at the moment of his climax, though it hardly ever happened that way the first time with any girl, she was with him in intensity. Except that in that ecstatic moment instead of achieving release as he had, she seemed convulsed in a seizure of pain. He rolled off, freeing her to turn and face away from him trying to catch her breath.

He lay on his back quietly, waiting till she recovered. He knew she had when she reached out to take his hand and hold it against her cheek. Only then did he feel free to speak.

"I hurt you. I didn't mean to."

She shook her head, pressed his hand tighter against her cheek and said, "I don't even know what to call you. When people fall in love it shouldn't be so fast. It should take time. They should have pet names. Their own special songs. And favorite dishes. And we don't have time for any of those."

"Then you're not denying it any longer. *We are in love*," he said with a slight pause between each word.

"Yes," she said sadly.

"And I did hurt you."

"Not your fault," she said, seeking to close the subject.

"Next time'll be better," he promised. He heard her head rustle against the pillow as she nodded, her eyes closed again. "Look at me?" he asked.

She shook her head.

"I have to know something," he persisted. Now she opened her eyes, stared across at him in the shadow. "If things could be worked out—I mean Joanne and I, we're through. It's just a matter of how privately and gracefully we can end it. When that happens, would you still feel the same way?"

"I'll always feel the same way about you," she said simply.

"No. I mean about your father, the way he feels about . . . people like me."

"You'll always be my favorite *goy*." She tried to joke, but he refused to let her escape so easily.

"I want to know. It's important. Because whatever differences there are between us, we have too much in common to lose each other."

"Don't, please."

"You know that's true. It was from the first moment."

She didn't answer, only pressed her face into his shoulder. His hand moved across her soft skin, down her long arched back and to her buttocks, resting there, pressing her gently against himself once more. Her arm stole around his neck and she was holding him tight waiting till he came erect, then letting him slide between her thighs. She was content to hold him there a time and he was content to be held.

Then gradually he began to move, pushing gently into her. Their rhythm grew in pace and finally in intensity until they both abandoned themselves to it, each wanting to be closer and closer to the other until, of course, in a burst of explosive passion, it was over.

This time there was no pain and when he looked down at her she was smiling.

"It didn't hurt this time, did it?" he whispered.

She shook her head and leaned back, as content with

the feel of his body as he was with hers.

"You're going to have to answer me," he said. "If not now, then tomorrow. If not tomorrow, then next week, next month."

"I won't be here next month," she said flatly.

"Then in Chicago!"

"No!" she said, angry for the first time. "You must never do that. Promise me!"

"It can't end here, not like this," he protested.

She nodded firmly, fully intending that it would end. He pressed his hands against her breasts, seeking to overcome all her objections by arousing her again. But she got up and crossed the room to the dressing area. He heard a rustle in the closet, and when she came back into the room she was wearing a robe which she had pulled around her naked body and tied just under her breasts.

She reached for the pack of cigarettes on the table and he said only, "Please." She hesitated, but she decided she needed a cigarette more than she needed to please him at this moment.

" 'Did it hurt?' you kept asking. Okay. I'll tell you. Yes, it hurt. But I understand that most times, after a woman has had an abortion, her first few sexual encounters hurt, especially if she has an orgasm."

She paused, waiting to see what effect her startling announcement had had on him. He said nothing, only waited.

"My third year at Northwestern. I was supposed to go East to school but at the last minute my father decided it would be safer for me to stay in Chicago. After all, I was his only child, a daughter at that. So it was Northwestern. The first two years I dated the right boys, from the right Jewish fraternities, boys with fathers just as rich as mine.

"Then my junior year I met a boy by chance, across the lab table in chemistry class. Rashbaum, C. and Robinson, J. He was tall, nice-looking. Not handsome, just nice-looking. In a blond, well, in a nice gentile way."

"Like me," Jeff said almost angrily.

She ignored his question.

"We began to work together. Since it was the last class before lunch, we started to eat together, study together. Then, slowly, we fell in love.

"We both knew it was impossible from the outset.

We said so—many times—and thought that saying it automatically removed the danger. Actually I think that was what caused us to let our guard down. After a while we began to think it *was* possible. Finally I believed that it was not only possible but that I couldn't live without him.

"I even decided to speak to my father. I went to see him at his office. I didn't want my mother involved. She would be too emotional.

"Daddy liked me to come see him at the office. He was proud of me. I was tall, good-looking, wore clothes well. He was as proud of me as I was of him. And that's saying a lot. Because I am proud of him. He is a very good man, kind, very decent. Some people say that in business he's tough, but I am sure he is fair. That's why I went to see him."

She interrupted herself suddenly, "I'm boring you."

"No, please," he protested.

"I know what he expected—that I wanted a new car, or a new fur coat. And his eyes could not conceal that he was ready to grant my wish whatever it was, but only after making a pretense at saying no. I started right out. 'Papa, I'm in love.'

"He got up, embraced me, and said, 'I want you to know that I'm flattered that you came to tell me. Even before you told your mother.'

"I just couldn't let him go on, so I said, 'Papa, he's not Jewish!'

"At first I'm sure he couldn't believe it. The smile was there, fixed on his face like a clown's makeup. Then his eyes began to fill up. I thought, if he cries, I will kill myself for hurting him.

" 'Sweetheart, Charlene, you have to understand about men, all kinds of men. They want only one thing from a girl until they find the girl they want to marry. Jewish boys are bad enough. But *goyim! Goyim* are worse, much worse. And especially with Jewish girls! For them it's a big triumph to get into a Jewish girl! A big joke!'

" 'But I love him.'

" 'So?'

" 'I want to marry him.'

"He never turned back to look at me. He was nodding his head. Not to indicate that he was giving permission.

Nodding in the way Jews do when the worst has befallen them. They nod to confirm that, being Jews, they had expected disaster all along. When he did turn back the tears were quite visible in his eyes, unshed, but clearly there. He said only one thing, but it hurt more than if he'd become angry or threatened or stormed and raged.

" 'No son. And now no daughter either.'

" 'Papa, don't.'

" 'You think I'm going to take you to the door and drive you out like some lousy scene in some of the pictures I exhibit? No, sweetheart. I'm not going to yell and threaten to cut you off. I'm not even going to tell you what a shame it is! I only hope that you won't do anything foolish and that you'll get over this. You could have a beautiful life. It's all there waiting for you. So don't do anything hasty or foolish.'

" 'And your permission?' I asked him.

" 'That's the one thing I can't give you.' He came toward me, kissed me. I knew that from that moment on he would never again kiss me as he used to. No matter what I did or didn't do, something had changed forever between us. He would never again be quite that proud of me.

"At the time I resented it. Being in love, as a girl of nineteen can be in love, I knew only one thing, that he would not give his permission. If he was going to be stubborn, I would be stubborn too. If there was one thing worse than going to bed with a Jewish boy before I was married, it was going to bed with a gentile.

"And after that day with my father I made it happen. We used my car and then the apartment of one of his friends off campus. We were always careful, or John was. Except for one time. And after a few days of worry I knew the truth. I was pregnant. He wanted to marry me. I wouldn't hear of it. He had college to finish.

"So I decided, on my own, there was only one other way. It only became a question of how. There were all kinds of remedies around campus.

"Because I couldn't stand the thought of some butcher digging into that part of me with a scalpel, I decided to try a drug, ergot. And John, poor John, he didn't know what to say or do, so he just agreed. I chose a weekend.

For good reasons. It was a big football weekend in Evanston. Lots of people. All of them with football on their minds. That seemed to afford some protection. And if I started on Friday night and something went wrong or it took some time to recover I would still be okay by Monday and back at class. Most important, I could be gone a whole weekend simply by telling my mother and father that I was staying with a girl friend.

"We got permission to use his friend's apartment. I moved in there Friday night, with the few things I would need in a small bag. John and I went out to dinner, but neither of us ate anything. When we came back I took the stuff and settled down to wait. Nothing happened that night. The next morning, after neither of us sleeping all night, there was no sign of anything happening and John was getting frightfully tense. I could see what was going through his mind.

"Suppose it didn't work. Or worse, that it worked so completely that I hemorrhaged and died, what would happen to him? It could destroy his whole career, his whole life. So I sent him off to the football game. He pretended not to want to go, but I insisted. He was relieved finally that I did insist, and off he went.

"The pains started just before the game. I could hear the bands, the cheers, the car horns as the people converged on the stadium. Then I was beginning to feel the pain. I thought that once it started it would be over rather quickly. Not so. The pain continued off and on. Then constantly, growing worse. And from outside I could hear the crowd reacting to the game, the cheers, the explosions of delight.

"After a while I found myself saying, 'Why isn't he here? He should have stayed, no matter what I said.' Then as the pain grew much worse I found myself saying, 'That *goy!* That's why he left! He's a *goy* and he doesn't give a damn what happens to me!' And I hated him. Forgetting that he was as scared as I was, that he had wanted to stay, that it was I who sent him away, I hated him. And blamed him for being a gentile.

"Then it started. The bleeding. I thought I would welcome the sight of my own blood, but it terrified me. I thought, this is it. I am going to die.

"With a towel between my legs to stop the blood, I lay on the floor of the bathroom crying, fearing death yet hoping for it at the same time. There was a knock on the door and someone calling my name. I thought it was John. I said, 'He came back, he came back! He's not such a *goy* after all.' But the door was locked from the inside. So I pulled myself up and went to open it for him. It was not John at all, but my father.

"Ashamed, but relieved, I cried out only, 'Papa!' I didn't have to say anymore. He knew. He knew it all. He put his coat around me and took me downstairs to his car. He drove me to a doctor friend of his. And there, what was left unfinished by the ergot, was completed. The pain and the danger were over in a matter of hours. He stayed with me through it all, Papa did.

"By Sunday afternoon he was allowed to take me home. On the way back to the house he didn't say a word about it. He wasn't angry or hostile or ashamed. He said nothing, only drove along. And every once in a while he would take his hand off the wheel, reach out and pat me gently. It was only when we turned onto our own street that he said, 'We won't ever tell your mother anything about this.'

"To this day he hasn't mentioned it to me. He must think about it. As I do. He must have thought about it when he called me about you. But he has never mentioned it."

She paused a moment. "I couldn't hurt a man like that again, even if he wasn't my father."

Jeff took her hand, held it tightly. "It wouldn't be the same with me."

"It would be worse," she said. "Marrying an anonymous *goy* would be bad enough. But a celebrity?"

"I need someone like you. Someone who can love me. Someone who needs me. You need me. I can tell."

The tears in her eyes confirmed it.

"Well, then?"

She shook her head sadly.

"What will you do?"

"Oh, some day soon, I guess, there'll be some very 'lucky' nice Jewish doctor or dentist or lawyer who'll do very well for himself when he marries Moe Rashbaum's daughter."

"And that'll be it? The rest of your life?"

"Most people never even have that much. I'll have a home, a husband."

"No children?" Jeff asked.

"We'll adopt some," she said quietly. "That was one thing the doctor couldn't fix."

He reached out, took her hand and drew her close. "A girl as beautiful as you, and as lovely, should have daughters, lots of daughters."

"Well, I won't," she said sadly.

He put his arms about her, but she broke free, saying, "You'd better get back. It must be past dinner time."

He knew it was futile to argue. "Tomorrow?"

"I should be noble and renounce you. But yes, tomorrow. And every day as long as you're here." She smiled, he could see it even in the dark. "There now you know, I'm a girl with no defenses when I fall in love."

He kissed her, feeling the need for her again even as he left.

After he was gone, she sank down onto the studio bed where they had made love and started to weep. She didn't go out for dinner, didn't order anything sent in, just sat in the dark and cried until she eventually fell asleep without ever opening the bed.

For six days it went on. Meeting, always as if tennis were the only reason. Then they disappeared, singly, to meet at her bungalow.

He did not tire of her, which in itself was extremely significant to him. Before, any affair which had been so intense, had always paled fairly quickly. But with Charlene each meeting was a new adventure. He began to show up at the club earlier and earlier.

By the fifth day even Joanne sensed something. She woke when he did and, without saying a word, made it clear she didn't believe him when he said he had to rush off for a match with some of the men at the club.

On the sixth day Jeff and Charlene were in the middle of a set, playing against the tennis pro and his wife when Joanne appeared. Charlene spied her first. Jeff only turned to look once he saw the sudden tension in Charlene's face. They said nothing, played out the match with little more than efficient stroking and no great enjoyment and lost six-four. As they started off the court, Jeff spoke first.

"I never expected . . . she didn't say a word about coming here."

"You better go to her."

"Would you like to meet her?"

"Not if I have a choice," Charlene said. She turned away from him, heading toward the pool to find a table and order a drink.

When Jeff approached Joanne and bent down to kiss her, she did not resist, though she did brush away the dampness his perspiring cheek left on hers.

"So that's her," she said. He turned to glare at her but she continued, "Don't try to deny it. It's too damned obvious to everyone around here. From the minute the girl at the desk saw me, I could tell. If there was an alarm system to warn husbands who are screwing around, it would be ringing all over this place by now."

He didn't answer, fearing her propensity for loud outbursts which might embarrass Charlene.

"I'll say one thing, your taste is improving. And she's young, very young," Joanne said, that fact making her more resentful and jealous than his deception.

"Would you like some lunch? Or a drink?" he asked only to change the subject.

"No, thanks. I think I'll go back to the house," she said, rising. He got up with her.

"I'll get the car and meet you out front."

"Don't bother. Calvin's waiting. Will you be back for dinner?"

"I'll be there."

"Maybe we'll go out tonight. Be seen around, as The Doctor said."

"Okay."

"Or did you have other plans?"

"No other plans. We'll go out," he said. He walked her to the front door, held it open for her, and she was gone.

He wandered back toward the pool where he found Charlene sitting alone, nursing a Bloody Mary. He made a hand signal to the waiter to bring him the same, then turned to look into her violet eyes.

"I'm sorry about that," he said.

"It had to happen sooner or later."

"Did you mind very much?"

"Yes. And no."

"No?"

"No, because she doesn't love you. That's pretty apparent to me now."

"And yes?"

"Because it took something away from us. From me. It isn't so magical anymore. We were like two kids who had fallen in love for the first time. Now it can't be innocent and free anymore. No more pretending."

His drink arrived and she fell silent. Once the waiter was gone, she continued, "That's why she came here. She's a woman. She knows other women. She didn't want to stop it, only to spoil it."

"Don't let her!" he said in a tense whisper.

"It isn't something you control. It just happens. And it did."

They were silent for a time. Then he suggested, "Today, let's go for a long drive up into the mountains away from this place."

"Like criminals fleeing the scene of the crime?"

"Don't say that!"

"Okay, we'll go for a drive."

They each drove their cars away from the Racquet Club. Then they left her car and drove off in his. With the top down, they drove through the town, out onto the open highway, seeking the turnoff that wound up through the arid hills toward the green of the mountains overlooking Palm Springs. She pressed her head against his shoulder.

When they were high up, amid the pine trees, they found an overlook and he parked the car. They sat staring out at the vast desert below them.

"You know now, she doesn't love me," said Jeff. "It will be over soon."

She didn't answer his unspoken question. He said suddenly, "You can't let that one . . . episode in your life change everything!"

"But it did," she said, looking up, wanting him to kiss her.

"No matter how you feel about your father or what happened, you can't let it ruin your life. Or my life. It isn't fair!"

"Fair?" she repeated. "That's one advantage of being born Jewish. From the very first day of your life you know that it's never going to be fair. Don't expect it to be. And don't be destroyed when it isn't. Just pick up the pieces, smashed or scorched though they are, and go on to the next place, the next country, the next life."

He kissed her, hoping to change her mind. She said nothing, just opened her arms and soon she was ready to give herself to him.

It was dark when they returned to where her car was parked. He saw her to it, closed the door, leaned in to kiss her. "I wish we could have dinner tonight."

"We can't," she said, disposing of it.

"Tomorrow?" He seemed doubtful that she would say yes.

"I told you, tomorrow. And every day as long as you're here. But that's all." She kissed him, at the same time reaching for her ignition key. He watched her pull out, turn and go past him toward the club, waving until he was out of the sight of her rear view mirror.

When he arrived at the house, the night lights were on around the pool. Everything seemed peaceful, but when he reached their suite, he found Joanne packing. The sight made him stop abruptly in the doorway. Without turning, she said, "I decided to go back first thing in the morning."

Her tone was matter of fact, as if there'd been no confrontation at the club, no other woman, no anger, no resentment.

"Oh?" he said, all his surprise and disappointment in the one syllable.

"You don't have to go. Calvin will drive me back. It's all arranged."

"Of course I have to go back! Else what the hell did we come down here for?"

"Suit yourself," she said, carefully folding a delicate silk nightgown, placing it in the bag on the luggage rack at the foot of her bed.

"Okay. We'll go back in the morning," he said finally.

Dinner was a silent affair. A hundred times he was

tempted to leave the table and call Charlene but he did not. After dinner Joanne retired to their bedroom, taking a bottle of cognac with her. He waited for a time, finally left the house very quietly and drove over to the club.

When he reached Charlene's bungalow the draperies were closed but there were lights on. He knocked discreetly on the glass door. There was no answer. He knocked louder. Still no answer. He dropped down onto one of the chaises and leaned back, looking up toward the mountain, where the glow of the moon highlighted the snowy crown making it seem brighter and more vivid.

It was past ten when he heard her coming along the path. She was not alone. A man's voice was urging, "At least have dinner with me tomorrow. It can't be fun eating alone all the time."

"It isn't," she said, disarming and frank as usual.

"Then tomorrow?"

"We'll see," she evaded.

His tone became sharper. "Look, it's none of my business, but you and Jefferson. That'll get you nowhere. He's married. And even if he weren't, there'd be no future in it for you."

"You're right about one thing," she said. "It's none of your business!"

"I'm sorry," the man said. "I was only thinking of your own good."

"I know."

"Tomorrow night?"

"I said we'll see."

"If not tomorrow, then back in Chicago? Promise?"

"Okay, Marvin, back in Chicago. Promise."

He must have tried to kiss her for she said softly, "Please, don't." Then Jeff heard him start down the path. She didn't go to her door at once, but stood on the lawn, staring at the bright moonlit snow atop San Jacinto.

"Darling," he said. She turned, startled. Then she began to weep from sheer surprise. He leaped up to embrace her. "Forgive me, I shouldn't have frightened you."

"I'm sorry," she said, "I shouldn't have cried. I promised myself days ago, one thing he's never going to see me do is cry, even when we say good-bye. But here I am." She tried to wipe away her tears with her fingers but did not succeed.

While she was recovering, he asked, "Who was that?"

"Marvin Berg."

"A friend of yours from Chicago?"

"I met him out here. He's been trying to date me for days now."

"He sounded nice enough."

"He is. A nice young Jewish lawyer. With a good firm. A good future."

"All the qualifications," Jeff said, almost bitterly.

"He could be the one. Or else it'll be some other Marvin Berg."

"Anyone but me!" he said.

She put her hand to his lips, pressed hard, saying, "I promised myself *two* things. *I* wasn't going to cry. *You* weren't going to be bitter. Now we've done both."

"Sorry." They stood leaning against each other.

"I know why you're here. You're leaving in the morning."

"She didn't call you," he began furiously.

"She didn't have to. Any woman knows what another woman is going to do in a situation like this. Even if she doesn't love the man."

He kissed her again, arousing her and himself.

"This is the end," she persisted. "Let's not spoil it by talking. When it's over, it's over. Promise?"

"We could still get married!" he protested.

"That's the one thing we can't do," she said, kissing him on the lips so he couldn't answer. He kissed her back, openmouthed, strong, eager.

They made love till just before dawn. Twice he drifted off to sleep and woke to find her leaning on her elbow looking down at him, smiling. He made love to her again, each time.

When dawn began to appear over the mountains far to the east he knew he had to leave. She held his face in her hands and said, "One day when I think of just the right pet name, I'll write you. And you'll know that I'll be thinking of you by that name for the rest of my life."

She kissed him, with closed lips. "Good bye, Jeff."

They were driving out of Palm Springs. It was a clear day with only a fringe of clouds off in the direction of Los

Angeles. They said nothing. There was nothing to say. But he sensed a vindictive satisfaction emanating from Joanne as she sat far away from him, pressed against the door.

To himself, Jeff thought it was the tragedy of his life. He was handsome, and pleasant. All women liked him. Many loved him. But in the end they were able to resist him. In life, as on the screen, he had all the qualities for real stardom. Except one. He had never been irresistible. Like Gable was. Or Cooper. Or John Gilbert had been in his time.

Charlene loved him. Wanted him, very much. But in the end she was able to give him up. Whether it was because of her father, or her own guilt, whatever the reason, it came down to one cold fact—she was able to give him up.

Nor could he draw any comfort from Joanne. She had loved him once, too. And had, in the end, given him up.

He drove on, silently. Ahead lay Los Angeles, The Doctor, and that vague, tantalizing promise about their meeting the day Joanne went back to work.

PART FIVE

1

Joanne had been back at work for four days but Jeff had still not received that anxiously anticipated call from The Doctor. In fact there had been no calls from anyone at TCA. To relieve the tension of waiting, he busied himself catching up on Guild matters which had accumulated during his absence.

The Guild office at least gave purpose to his getting up in the morning. He spent long hours with Abe Heller, drinking coffee, nibbling at Danish, all of it empty activity. At the very moments that he seemed most interested he was least involved. Abe talked studio negotiation and Jeff thought about The Doctor. Abe talked Guild insurance plans and Jeff thought of Charlene. Twice he called the Racquet Club in Palm Springs to make discreet inquiries. The first time that he was told she was not there he thought she was avoiding him. The second time he discovered that she had left the day after he did. Back to Chicago, no doubt, and a life full of Marvin Bergs.

He found her home number and called. She was not at home. "Miss Charlene" had gone to New York with her mother on a shopping trip, and "Who shall I say called?" He left no name.

The next day he decided that as long as she was not home he would fly to Chicago, see her father, convince him that he and Charlene were good for each other, and to hell with religious differences. He even looked up the airline timetables for non-stop flights, LA to CHI, but he realized how futile it would be, and how ridiculous. A man of his age, and a *goy* to boot, trying to convince a man like Moe Rashbaum that what his daughter needed most for a long happy life was marriage to a movie actor twenty years older than she was and without a job to his name.

Which only served to remind him, still no call from The Doctor!

Damn the little bastard! He knew better than anyone that every actor was a puppet dangling at the end of a telephone wire. If there was a delay for some good reason, then call and say so. Say the meeting had to be delayed. Say anything. Just call.

Abe was placing another file before him, concerning actors' rights if the studios ever sold their inventory of films to TV. Would the actors be paid, or would their contracts be interpreted to mean that they had sold their services outright and forever. The lawyers were concerned about it. Still, many actors, Jeff among them, felt that the studios would never sell their films to TV. They would be defeating themselves in the long run. What exhibitor would buy a film from a studio which competed with him by offering free almost the same material to the public on TV? Why become involved in a problem that was never going to arise? thought Jeff.

But there was the folder, there was Abe, and it was a full hour before the next coffee break, so they might as well talk about it. They did. But came to no conclusion. And the folder was put aside for further consideration in the future.

Although Jeff had left word at home that Martha was to forward all his calls to the Guild office none came in. Not from The Doctor. Not even from those people who had courted him in the days immediately after the congressional hearings.

By the beginning of the second week, he had given up hope of hearing from Charlene, though every once in a while he was rudely startled by the sudden appearance of a girl who resembled her. One afternoon when he was leaving his office there was an actress in the waiting room, tall, with flowing black hair, a strong profile, and deep violet eyes. For a stabbing instant he thought she was Charlene. But she proved to be a young Broadway actress who had arrived in Hollywood and was seeking membership in the Guild. In a city where tall, striking girls were so common, Jeff would see many who would remind him of Charlene.

In his worst moments he thought about Doris Martin-

son. Perhaps that would have been the way out or still
could be. If it hadn't been for Charlene. Charlene had
changed him. Going back to Doris would in some strange
way mean being unfaithful. Some other woman, yes. But
not Doris. Charlene would know and she would despise
him.

Which brought his thoughts back to The Doctor.
Where the hell was The Doctor?

2

Most of the time that Jeff was anguished by the absence of any calls, The Doctor was in New York, in consultation with new legal counsel. On most matters, counsel in California was adequate. But on matters as serious as an anti-trust suit The Doctor sought his advice in New York, it was the same with doctors. He was perfectly content to be treated in California, as long as he wasn't sick.

Though Philip Rose was the attorney who had originally warned against the danger of an anti-trust action and had raised the possibility of invoking the Doctrine of Informed Consent, when it came to actually contemplating a possible federal crime The Doctor had decided on another lawyer, an elderly attorney, named Merwin Appleman. Once a mainstay of the Roosevelt administration, he was now a highly respected peddler of influence in the nation's capital.

Appleman said he doubted that TCA could avoid an anti-trust suit if The Doctor followed his plan as presently laid out. As he spoke, Spencer Gould's sinuses began to flow and Freddie Feig tensely tapped his disabled foot.

The Doctor simply fell back on precedents cited by his most eminent teacher in the law, Cat's Eye Bastione. Cat's Eye had said to him more than once, "What I gotta do, I do. Then if the law puts the arm on me, I figure some way. You can always make a deal with the law."

Without quoting his authority, The Doctor said, "I understand the risks. And you've clearly pointed out the dangers. But we have decided to proceed, nevertheless."

The lawyer wet his lips before he gave a judicial reading to his next speech, "Of course this firm has an excellent record in defending clients who have faced similar charges in the past."

That's right, The Doctor thought, circle the killing ground like a vulture, get your sales pitch in early, so I'll know where to come when I want the fix put in. Well, that'll be a long time from now. But I'll be ready, I'll be ready!"

Aloud, he said respectfully, "Counsellor, you may be sure we'll check with you every step of the way."

The Doctor was so positive of what he had to do now that he had Spence and Freddie drive him right to the airport so he could take the next first-class flight back to the Coast.

The next morning he had Alise make a luncheon appointment with Jeff for the following day. Another twenty-four hours of waiting would make Jeff that much more eager and malleable. The place for the lunch? Would Mr. Jefferson mind Hillcrest?

But when Jeff hung up he was troubled. It wasn't so much that he minded Hillcrest. Even if he felt out of place there, he didn't resent the club now as much as he would have before Charlene. But originally The Doctor had mentioned a whole afternoon together, even a drive down to La Jolla.

The next day, at The Doctor's usual secluded table, looking out over the golf course, they met. The Doctor seemed troubled. He said nothing until they'd ordered drinks and the captain had presented menus, which The Doctor waved aside, remarking bitterly, "Eat? You could eat your heart out in this town! The ingratitude! The deceit!"

It was a cryptic statement, thrown out in a torrent of hurt and despair, but up to this moment without relevance to Jeff. Or, Jeff wondered, did it have a relevance about which he was too uninformed to know?

Suddenly The Doctor exploded, "You know, in my time I've done business with the Mob! One thing about those guys, a deal is a deal! A favor is a favor! And they don't forget. But this town! Believe me, they could learn a little about manners from the Mafia!"

He lapsed into silence and Jeff fingered his glass wondering if he were required to say anything.

"I wouldn't mind," Cone continued, "if they hadn't put on such an act when you were out there fronting for them. There are guys working today, producers, writers, directors, who'd be out on their asses if it wasn't for you! You shut up that damned committee before they could really get going. And now, now those bastards at the studios with the big cigars and the fat bellies, who would have kissed your behind a few months ago when they were scared shitless, those bastards are saying to me, 'Sorry, but the name Jefferson, it's got a kind of . . . it's got a kind of smell to it . . . people think he was involved, that *he* was a Communist too, else why did he front for them? Sorry, we can't take a chance.' "

Jeff asked, "You mean that I'm on a blacklist now? For merely getting up before a committee and telling the truth under oath?"

"I mean, kid, that they would rather not have anything to do with anyone who will remind the public that there ever was an investigation," The Doctor said with finality.

"What are we going to do?" Jeff asked.

"What are we going to do?" The Doctor echoed. "Well, one thing we are *not* going to do, and I would advise you to follow my counsel, we are not going to fight. I mean we are not going to explain or justify or insist or make a public scandal about the whole thing. That would only antagonize them more. And I've antagonized them enough as it is."

That last sentence, coming as it did at the end of The Doctor's speech, was not an epilogue but the prologue to a new declaration.

"Kid," he said, leaning across the table and putting his hand on Jeff's, "kid, we've had good times. And bad. And I've always loved you. Maybe more in bad times than in the good. Because you're a gentleman. A man of honor."

Jeff didn't respond, not even with his usual half-smile. What The Doctor was preparing to say seemed too ominous.

"That's why I want to be fair with you, kid. In all honesty, I must say to you, get yourself another agent."

A violent cramp gripped Jeff's stomach. It was the most shocking and castrating declaration that had been made to him in all the years he had been in this town. He could feel the sweat seeping out of his chest and the back of his neck.

"I would be less than honest with you, if I didn't tell you. At first I thought maybe my boys had lost their enthusiasm because you'd been turned down too many times. So I took on the job myself. And I was sure that I would be able to swing it. That's why I was so high on you just before you went down to the Springs."

Suddenly Jeff interrupted viciously, "Did Moe Rashbaum have anything to do with this?"

"Moe Rashbaum? What the hell has an exhibitor got to do with anything. The trouble's right here, in this town!"

"I just thought . . . well, he was . . ." Jeff did not finish.

"What I'm getting at kid, is this. I must have lost my head. I was so outraged by their ingratitude that I told them off! Every studio! Of course I let off a lot of steam, but it doesn't accomplish anything, except make enemies of people. I guess that's what I did. Made enemies."

He reflected a moment then said, "With these whores it doesn't matter to me, personally. The next hot piece of talent I come up with they'll open their doors wide and kiss my feet. But with you, it's a different story. How do *you* get to be hot again?"

"The part," Jeff reminded him bitterly. "The part in that picture would have done it!"

"Maybe," The Doctor conceded. "Maybe I should have let you work for that outrageous price after all."

That was almost as unsettling to Jeff as The Doctor's suggestion about getting a new agent. For Irwin Cone to admit to a serious blunder on behalf of a client was unprecedented. The situation must be as grave as the little man had made it appear.

"I need another drink!" The Doctor said suddenly, and turned to signal the captain.

Until the drinks arrived, both men were silent, Jeff pondering the effect of the news in the industry. It would get out, that TCA had dropped Jeff Jefferson, not that Jeff had dropped TCA. And when The Doctor dropped a star, especially one married to one of their hottest clients, that in itself amounted to the kiss of death.

Midway through his drink The Doctor suddenly suggested, "You should try the stage! Broadway! The right play, the right part, would make you new all over again."

"I haven't been on a stage since college. And even then I was not very good."

"You're a name, a personality. You would be in demand back East."

"Those New York critics are just waiting to clobber any picture star, you know that."

"Not you, Jeff. For political reasons alone they'd be good to you." The Doctor tried to comfort him, but Jeff interpreted the comment exactly as The Doctor had intended, a straw to clutch at, a desperate attempt to glean some hope from a totally hopeless situation.

"You're not the only one," The Doctor said, finishing his drink. "It's the times. If the industry wasn't staggering right now, we wouldn't be having all this trouble. They wouldn't be so afraid to take a chance on you.

"Television!" He spat out the word as if it were an obscenity. "I wish they'd never have invented the goddamned thing! You know what I'm afraid of? Hollywood is going to become a ghost town, all because of television! You can't give entertainment away for free on TV and expect people to pay for it at the box office! And the result? I can name fine respected actors in this town, stars too, who are selling their homes and moving back East. Like goddamned gypsies! High-priced Okies!

"A whole way of life for thousands of actors, thousands of families is going down the drain. It's like being wiped out by a slow earthquake. Everything around you is shaking, trembling, falling apart, and there is nothing you can do to stop it."

The Doctor suddenly broke off. "Look, I don't have to tell you. Even if it wasn't for your personal situation, you'd know from the problems you have to deal with at the Guild."

The Doctor took off his glasses and polished them, which gave Jeff a chance to study his eyes, now watery from emotion or eyestrain.

Though Jeff distrusted Cone, and now had more reason than ever to dislike him, he still felt sorry for him. The man did seem deeply moved on behalf of an industry he loved and clients he represented, some of whom he even liked.

Seeing Jeff's face soften, The Doctor decided that he had accomplished his purpose. "The hell with it!" he said. "Let's have some lunch." He turned to summon the captain with a signal he had picked up in his earlier days booking the Mob clubs, a signal made by the lips, like a loud kiss. The captain was on his way, sweeping the large menus from under his arm like a musketeer unsheathing his sword for combat. Lunch ordered, without anticipation or appetite, both men settled down to wait.

Once The Doctor suggested, "Don't brush off what I said about New York. Broadway. With a good play, the right director, and a long out-of-town tour before you open, you could do it. Maybe play it on the summer circuit for eight or ten weeks."

Jeff did not respond. His thoughts ran in a less hopeful vein. How, for example, would he go about securing a new agent, an agent good enough to handle a star. Good enough so that the changeover from TCA would not seem such a great step down. A good independent agent. Someone who had a certain standing on his own that would lend prestige to Jeff. There were a few. Bert Allenberg. Charlie Feldman. Kurt Frings, one of the newer ones. But would they take on a client TCA had seen fit to cut loose?

Of course there was one graceful way out. He could let it be known that with the impending break between himself and Joanne he had decided it would not be wise for both of them to have the same agent.

But the real fact was that no matter what the public thought, he himself would know the truth. That he had run out the string, that he was no longer worth the time and effort it took to sell him. That the alternatives open to other actors, like going back East, were not open to him. He didn't belong in the East, had no professional roots there, had not the training or the skill for it. If his destiny was anywhere, it was right here. Where no one wanted him.

"There's nothing that can be done?" Jeff asked at last. "If not for me, at least to save the industry."

"Nothing!" The Doctor replied vehemently. "We've

talked about it for months now." Then he added casually, as a throwaway, "The only possible way to save this town, salvage the industry is against the law."

"Law?" Jeff asked. "What does law have to do with it?"

"It's a long story, kid. Too long. Let's go," he said pushing away almost a full plate of food. Then softly, and with the air of a close and considerate friend, The Doctor added, "About not representing you any longer, I'll handle that any way you want. Any announcement you want me to make, we'll make. If you want to make it, anything you say is okay with me. Just because the pressures of this miserable business break up a relationship doesn't mean we have to part enemies. Take a couple of days, think it over, feel free to talk to another agent if you want. Okay, kid?"

"Okay," Jeff said. "Thanks." Then he asked suddenly, "What about Joanne? Does she know?"

"I wouldn't do that to you Jeff," The Doctor protested self-righteously. "You tell her yourself. Whenever and however you want to. And believe me kid, I wouldn't do this if I didn't think it was for your own good."

The little man reached up to pat him on the shoulder, much as his father used to do.

Jeff drove home slowly, for the house was the last place he wanted to go. He thought about dropping by at the Guild office, but for the first time that seemed an even worse alternative. What Guild would want an unemployed and now, it seemed, an unemployable member as its president? Then the thought crossed his mind as it had once before in Amarillo: What if it were possible to retire from acting and devote himself full time to the Guild's business? But that would never work. The president of the Guild had always been an actor, a working actor, and always a star.

Before he reached the house one thing The Doctor had said came back to him. The law. It was against the law. How could it be against the law for a profession or an entire industry to protect itself from extinction? What kind of law could forbid that?

Because The Doctor was right. The whole industry was at stake here. A whole way of life, a good way of life was being jeopardized by television. Whatever law it was, the Guild might do something about it. For years they had sent delegations to Sacramento and to Washington to testify for or against pieces of legislation. They had had some effect, too.

So if it was a matter of law, perhaps the Guild really could do something about it. For the sake of the industry itself the Guild should at least try to stop Hollywood's destruction by live TV.

When he reached the house he parked, went into the pool area, picked up the phone, and dialed TCA. Alise said The Doctor was busy, but not to hang up as he wouldn't be long. And she would know, because The Doctor and every employee of TCA had his phone monitored by his secretary so that if there were any disputes later, or any lawsuits, the secretary could testify on behalf of TCA. Also, it kept his agents from cultivating TCA clients on their own, with a view to leaving the agency and taking them along.

After some restless moments tethered to the silent line Jeff heard The Doctor's voice. "Hi, kid! Got some thoughts about your situation?"

"No, just that . . . what did you mean about the law? If there's a law stopping us from protecting the industry, why can't the Guild lobby to have the law repealed or changed?"

"Oh, that?" The Doctor said, as if speaking of an irrevocable circumstance. "It isn't that kind of law. No congress or state legislature can change it."

"You mean there's nothing that can be done about it?"

"Theoretically, yes. Practically, no."

"What does that mean?"

"Bottom line, nothing can be done."

"Not even if all the Guilds get together? We did get some action out of Congress once."

"I told you, it's not that easy."

"Easy?" Jeff demanded. "We had to send a delegation to Washington four times!"

"Well," The Doctor said grudgingly, as if nothing could come of it, "if you want to discuss it, let's sit down and talk. But it's very involved. It'll take hours."

"I want to talk about it!" Jeff said firmly, on his own

behalf as well as for the craft at large.

"Okay. Let's see, today's Tuesday. What about Thursday? Are you free Thursday for lunch?"

I am free for lunch every day of the goddamn week, Jeff felt like shouting, but instead he said, in business-like fashion, "Thursday? I guess Thursday would be fine."

"I'll pick you up at the house. And we'll take that ride out to La Jolla after all. See you Thursday, kid." The Doctor hung up.

Thursday finally arrived. Jeff was ready before The Doctor's limousine pulled up in front of the house, but he lurked in the pool area so that Martha had to come and find him. He lingered a moment, then finally started out.

The Doctor didn't say anything, until he had raised the glass partition between themselves and the chauffeur.

"If this conversation doesn't go anywhere it might be better if no one knew it ever took place."

It imparted a sense of mystery to what would follow, making Jeff even more anxious to discover what The Doctor had in mind.

"I've thought about this day and night for months, now. What the hell has New York got that we haven't got more of and better? Besides, who belongs on a screen? Stage actors or screen actors? The answer is obvious. Then why has New York got a strangle-hold on television? Because we never put up a fight. The studios didn't want it because it would keep people out of the theaters.

"Result? New York keeps putting out shows, all of which look the same. The cast that was on Kraft last week is on Philco two weeks from now. The same girl who played the lead on Westinghouse last night will be on some other damn show next month! And meantime, our people are going hungry! Our studios are standing empty! Technicians are being laid off. Electricians. Makeup artists. Carpenters. Editors. Musicians.

"Now what if all those people, all those studio facilities, could be put to work? Not in New York, but here!"

"Okay, okay," Jeff said, anxious to get on. "What law says we can't?"

"The law of agency," The Doctor said.

"Law of agency? What law is that?"

"It's what they call Common Law."

"What does it mean?" Jeff demanded.

"Well, there is a thing called 'conflict of interest.' Let's say I represent you and at the same time I represent say, Fox or Warners, and I am making a picture deal for you with Fox. Who would I owe my loyalty to? You? Or Fox? That's the guts of it. An agent can't represent both sides of a deal."

The Doctor ended his explanation by saying righteously, "And it's a damn good law, most times."

Jeff pondered it a moment, then asked, "Exactly what does that have to do with what we're talking about?"

"Well, with the studios handcuffed by the exhibitors, with the networks having such a big investment in television equipment in New York, who's going to make the move to protect the film actor? Who has the power, the resources? Who could go to the banks and get the money?"

"Money?" Jeff asked. "For what?"

"To move television out here!"

"Is that possible?"

"With the right incentive the money could be found. And if the incentive is there and the money is there, it could be done!" Before Jeff could react Cone went on, "Imagine what it would be like! The studios going full blast, turning out both features and TV films! Enough work to keep nine-tenths of your members working. And TV series have an advantage over features. They go on and on. Not like a feature which is over in ten or twelve weeks. Oh, what this could do to the whole industry!" he exulted.

"But where is the conflict of interest?" Jeff asked.

"Let's say I wanted to do it. Let's say that TCA with its leverage wanted to put up the money to produce TV films, to give thousands of actors, writers, directors, and technicians full-time work. The law says no because we would be selling our clients to ourselves."

"But couldn't something be done?" asked Jeff.

"It's too complicated. My attorneys tell me not to bother. They say to hell with the picture business!"

"You can't say to hell with it when so many people are involved. So many of your clients."

"When my own lawyers say forget it, I forget it," the little man proclaimed sadly.

"And there's no way at all?" Jeff asked, reluctant to allow the idea to die.

"Well, there could be a way," The Doctor began. "But it's too impractical, too much trouble."

"As much trouble as seeing a whole industry die? Don't you owe it to your clients to try?"

"Well," The Doctor said wearily. "Well, there's one way. And only one way. If the people who might complain about a conflict of interest, gave their permission in advance, then it might be done."

"Meaning?" Jeff asked.

"Meaning . . . well, suppose your Guild gave TCA permission to produce television films and at the same time continue to represent actors as agents, then it would be possible. There'd be the incentive and the freedom."

Then swiftly The Doctor added, "But it's too complicated. You'd have to explain it to your board. They'd have to explain it to the membership. They would all have to vote on it. It would be nice but impractical. . . ." He left his sentence hanging in mid-air, complete yet unfinished, waiting to be disputed. When Jeff was silent The Doctor felt he had lost an important strategic opportunity.

After a few moments Jeff said, "As long as we're open and honest I don't see why we can't bring it before the board. I think they might go for it."

The Doctor did not wish to betray his eagerness so he did not comment on Jeff's statement. He simply waited. He knew that Jeff's own personal confrontation with the hard realities of the business would work as a powerful leaven.

They said no more until the limousine reached the Victor Hugo, an elegant restaurant looking out on the Pacific from its own green and gardened point.

In deference to The Doctor's request, Jeff passed up a drink in favor of a highly praised red wine. They sipped in silence, studied the menu. Though The Doctor kept his eyes fixed slightly above the top of the ornate red and gold folder, watching Jeff, speculating on how much of an impression he had made.

Once lunch was ordered, Jeff said, "I don't think you should give up. It's 'do something or die!' The Guild has to protect its members or go out of business. If you knew what the figures were. About twenty stars in this town and a few featured players are keeping the Guild going with their dues. It's murder. And it can't get better unless someone does something!"

"You don't have to tell me, Jeff. I've got the figures in my office. Screen actors' earnings this year, a year ago, three years ago and five years ago. If such a disaster happened to any other industry it would make front-page news in the *New York Times*. In fact, if you want to see those figures or use them, I'll give you a copy," The Doctor volunteered. "And then compare them to the figures for the same years for actors in New York. They're cleaning up at our expense.

"I say 'our expense' but I don't strictly mean that. As far as TCA is concerned if we earn our commissions on actors back East we still make money. We can't complain too much. If only I didn't have this damned sense of obligation to the stars who've been with us so long!" he lamented, a man caught in the coils of his own conscience.

"Those figures might come in handy," Jeff said thoughtfully.

"What do you mean?"

"You let me have those figures and I'll get hold of Abe Heller. And then . . ."

"Easy, Jeff. I don't want you to do anything rash. You've got a great obligation to those members of yours."

"What better way to meet it than to see that they keep working?" Jeff demanded.

"Of course," The Doctor agreed. "But slowly. Think about it a day or two. This is not something to plunge into, because if you decide to go ahead, it'll take a bit of doing. So think about it."

The Doctor sensed that Jeff had caught fire. It was safe to urge caution, to appear to be the more conservative influence from now on.

"I'd like those figures!" Jeff insisted.

"You'll have them on one condition!" The Doctor said, reaching across the table, placing his hand on Jeff's in a gesture of restraint. "That you study them. And then talk to me before you say a word to anyone else."

They lunched on sand dabs in a wine and cream sauce which appeared on the menu as Filets de Mer à la Bonne Femme. They passed up dessert, settled for coffee and were ready for the drive back.

They sat in silence for the first half hour, looking out at the pleasant day, insulated from the heat by the air conditioning which hissed efficiently.

The Doctor was aware how deeply immersed in the idea Jeff was.

At what he deemed the strategic moment, The Doctor observed casually, "Of course, with actors you never can tell. You try to do something for their own good and they can't see it. When I first mentioned television to some of our clients they wouldn't touch it. The prices were too low. The shows were too slipshod. It was a cheap medium that would always be cheap. They wouldn't believe that it would ever threaten the picture industry. They learn hard. They'll have to be convinced."

"Convinced to save their own skins?" Jeff asked, almost amused.

"Don't laugh, kid. I can tell you from my years as a doctor, sometimes the patient is the last one to believe that he's seriously ill. And in show business it's even worse. In this business we live by illusion and we're the first ones to be deceived. The biggest sucker for a con game is a con man."

"The figures will do it!" Jeff said.

"It's going to take more," Cone predicted sadly.

After a long pause The Doctor said, "You know what it could take? It would be a magnificent gesture. An act of confidence. An act of personal sacrifice, too. But it would convince them."

"What?" Jeff asked.

"You're not going to like this. But if you believe that something can be done, that something must be done, then you're the one who may have to do it," Cone said, appearing reluctant to exact a sacrifice of such gravity from a friend.

"Do what?" Jeff persisted.

"Offer to devote the next few years to proving it."

"Proving *what?*"

"That you believe in television enough to give it a few years of your life."

"I don't understand," Jeff said, turning to The Doctor.

"What I mean, kid, is this. To prove how much you believe in the idea, you would be willing to become the first real picture star to be the lead in a TV series owned and produced by TCA. It would be the best proof of sincerity that you could give your members."

Before Jeff could answer, The Doctor continued, "It'll be hard work. It could take five days a week, fifty weeks a year to shoot a series. I don't know if you want to work that hard. And for that kind of money." The Doctor paused, then said disparagingly, "It couldn't pay more than four or five grand a week at the start."

He paused again, giving Jeff time to multiply five thousand by fifty weeks and come up with a round quarter of a million dollars a year.

"Of course, to make up for the short money, there would be a piece of the show. I'll get resistance from my own boys, but I'll insist on it. You'd get no less than twenty percent."

He leaned back a little, giving Jeff time to absorb that much of it. "I'm not saying you'll like it. But by giving up two or three years of your career, you may be saving thousands of your Guild members from years of hardship and poverty. Two or three years, Jeff, that's all it would take."

Having thus tripled the quarter of a million dollars, and held out the prospect of three years of continuous work to a Jeff Jefferson who hadn't worked in over a year, The Doctor felt free now to lean back, completely at ease.

He had never baited a trap better, nor initiated a gambit with more precise care.

Jeff sat back figuring five thousand times fifty times three. Seven hundred and fifty thousand dollars over three years. On top of that, something he had never been able to obtain on any of his pictures, a piece of the action, a share of the net.

The offer became more and more attractive. There was only one thing wrong. The better it sounded the worse he felt about it.

Finally he knew why.

Call it sacrifice as The Doctor had done, or call it an act of courage on behalf of his fellow actors, its rightful name was bribe. Suddenly Jeff knew that. But the size of the offer weighed heavy in his thoughts.

If this were a scene in a picture and such an offer had been made to the hero, Jeff knew he would have been called on to reject it forthwith. But in real life there is time. One need not answer immediately. Such proposals can die by pocket veto or else be allowed to linger long enough to find justifications, of which The Doctor had supplied many.

And not only The Doctor. The past year of defeats, the loss of Joanne, and Charlene, even the insult implicit in Doris Martinson's proposal, all conspired to make him say yes. And The Doctor's announcement that TCA would no longer be able to represent him had left him vulnerable, wide open.

Even if he profited himself, the benefits to the rest of the Guild still held. If television could be brought West, careers would be preserved, families enabled to remain in their homes instead of being uprooted and shipped across the country to uncertain jobs and to all the other problems which living in New York entailed.

By the time he had reached home and was getting out of the car, Jeff had almost convinced himself he could accept in good faith. It would take a day or two, but he had the ammunition.

The Doctor knew enough to drop the subject gracefully, saying only, "Jeff, it's three years of your life. A man should think carefully before he gives away three years."

By the time Irwin Cone reached TCA's Colonial mansion on Santa Monica Boulevard, he had assured himself that he had succeeded with Jeff Jefferson. Within forty-eight hours, twenty-four if Jeff was even more anxious than he suspected, the phone would ring and it would be Jeff suggesting another meeting. Cone, of course, would agree. What was said at the meeting wouldn't matter. The mere fact that Jeff called would mean that his answer was yes.

The Doctor's barber and the manicurist were waiting for him when he arrived in his office. It was the end of the day and The Doctor liked to leave the office prepared for the combined business and social events of the evening. He surrendered himself to the barber while Alise stood by reading him the list of phone calls and problems that had accumulated in his absence.

The Doctor nodded routinely to the routine troubles. Every problem was major, so there were no really serious ones. When dealing with creative people there were never minor crises.

Alise had completed her list. He dismissed her, saying, "Okay, dear. And don't interrupt me for any calls. Except Jeff Jefferson."

Alise swung around to stare at him, delighted, but surprised that he would be so concerned about a call from Jefferson. Then she continued out of the room.

At the barber's urging, The Doctor leaned back in the chair. He closed his eyes, only to open them moments later to stare at the manicurist, who was exactly the kind of fleshy girl he coveted. Her breasts swelled high above her pink uniform. And the fragrance of her perfume, inexpensive, far too obvious, proclaimed her lack of taste. Her hair, auburn now, had been blond only two weeks ago. True, her ass was a bit too broad for her height. She was probably the kind of girl who had been had easily and often by many customers. Nor was she averse to accepting a gift on the side, he speculated.

Ever since his days as an intern he had had this weakness for girls in any kind of uniform. In all respects, she suited his taste and she would also provide the proper sense of guilt and self-reproach, for he was like an alcoholic, hating the very thing he craved.

He would have begun scheming how to rid himself of the barber and keep the manicurist, but the phone rang. He lifted it, asking, "Yes, Jeff?"

But it turned out to be Spencer Gould from New York. Irritated as he was by a call that he suspected could have been avoided, he asked brusquely, "What is it this time, Spence?"

It turned out to be a bit of casting trouble with ALUMCO Television Theatre. The rating had dropped and the sponsor was insisting that TCA deliver bigger stars to build it up again. The Doctor suggested perhaps they could convince some studio to let one of their actors do an ALUMCO show in exchange for promoting a new film on Network TV.

Then, almost as an afterthought, The Doctor said, "What would they say to getting Jeff Jefferson?"

"What would they say? They would say, but in polite terms, What the hell do you think we are, crazy? No, they're thinking in terms of Jimmy Stewart, or Cary Grant, or maybe Deborah Kerr."

"Oh, they are?" The Doctor bristled. "We'll see about that!"

The challenge had dispersed the feeling that had been stirring in his crotch. As soon as he could, he dispensed with both the manicurist and the barber. He summoned Buddy Black and Freddie Feig to his office, Feig being in town from New York for the week.

Both subordinates took their seats gingerly at the conference table at the far end of The Doctor's huge office. The table itself was a single piece of magnificently grained walnut fashioned into a graceful oval by English craftsmen in 1804.

"Boys," The Doctor began, relaxing into his old Chicagoese in which "boys" became a two-syllable word, "we have a problem. Not a problem exactly. But a phase in a campaign which, if we win, can net us hundreds of millions of dollars. But if we don't accomplish this step, we can wind up with zero."

Since Buddy and Freddie, along with Spence, each had a small stock interest in TCA, the phrase "hundreds of millions" had already set their minds spinning.

"The problem has to do with our getting into TV film production. The phase I am referring to is Jeff Jefferson."

"He said yes?" Freddie asked eagerly.

"He's thinking it over. That means yes."

"So what's the problem?" Freddie asked.

"The problem is, I have to find a spot for him as the guest star on a prestige television show. What do you think?"

Freddie got up, saying, "I think we could find a cure for cancer first."

"No wisecracks, Freddie!" The Doctor said sharply. "I want that guest shot! I need it! It's part of the deal."

"Part of the deal," Freddie mused and began pacing.

Until The Doctor called out, "Will you and your god-damned 'service-connected disability' stop limping up and down this office? I want thought, constructive thought! Not mileage!"

"A guest shot . . . a guest shot . . ." Freddie said. "What about Kraft Music Hall?"

"He doesn't sing. He doesn't dance. He doesn't make jokes. I want him on a dramatic show. A high class, dramatic show!" The Doctor exclaimed.

Buddy ventured, "In addition to not singing, dancing, and making jokes there's one other thing he doesn't do—act!"

"Okay, okay," The Doctor said impatiently. "Now get out of here and think!"

Freddie and Buddy nodded, promising to check with each other later in the day, though each one knew damn well that if he had a good idea he would take it directly to The Doctor. For hanging in the balance always was the prize that The Doctor deliberately dangled before them. When he retired, Spencer Gould would take over the New York Office. Which would leave the motion picture end wide open. Freddie Feig or Buddy Black would inherit that power. Thus the two junior cobras were always scheming which eggs to suck next.

The Doctor was aware of all this. And confident one of them would come up with a solution to his current problem.

A few minutes after ten the next morning The Doctor's phone rang. Jeff tried to sound businesslike. He spoke with deliberation, knowing that his words were being monitored by someone besides Cone.

"Doctor, I've been thinking it over. Very carefully. One thing is sure. If we do nothing and things go the way they're going, this place will be a ghost town in another year. Two at the most," Jeff said.

"If I ever saw handwriting on a wall, this is it!" Cone agreed.

"So something has to be done."

"Of course," The Doctor said mildly. This was an exercise in self-justification that he knew Jeff must accomplish alone.

"I studied the whole picture," Jeff continued. "We have

actors, writers, producers, directors, technicians, and studio help. Who's going to lead in taking action? The writers? The producers? The directors? A writer can write anywhere. He can mail it in, if he wants to. A director? He can work on location easier than an actor can, because he decides on the location. The producer? He makes his deals in New York anyhow. So what does it come down to? The group with the biggest stake professionally and economically are the actors. Screen actors. The kind who came up the hard way to achieve a little security, a home, a decent way of life. It will be up to the actors to lead this fight, if anyone will."

The Doctor listened, glanced across at Alise who was on the extension. She was delighted and proud to hear such cogent arguments from Jeff Jefferson.

"Exactly what I was trying to say yesterday, Jeff," murmured The Doctor. "Only you just said it a hundred times better than I did!"

"Now as to going on TV myself," Jeff hesitated, "I don't know. . . ."

The Doctor sat up, for this was a development he had not expected. But he did not interrupt, only listened more attentively.

"Three years is a long time. Especially when a man has hit forty. For a star the gap between forty and forty-three is a serious one."

And, The Doctor thought, the gap between forty-two and forty-five is even more serious. But he said nothing.

"I mean, if a man removed himself from the picture market for three years it might be impossible to come back at all. You know what I mean?"

"Of course I do," The Doctor ad-libbed swiftly. "That's why I was sorry we didn't have more time yesterday to go into the details of the deal. What I had in mind was this.

"First, you do a pilot show. That proves your good intentions to the Guild. Who knows? If you're lucky, the pilot doesn't sell and you're a free man. Of course nobody is going to put up all that money to do a pilot unless they have a firm option on your services in case the series *does* sell.

"Now we have to take into account the fact that the odds are that it will sell. After all, what sponsor is going to pass up an opportunity to have Jeff Jefferson on TV week after week? You have to be prepared for that eventuality. So now you're asking, What's the protection? Hiatus, my boy! Hiatus! Time off from the TV show. We will make it a part of the deal that you are to have at least three consecutive months off each year to make a feature film. Got it?"

"But yesterday you said it could take up to fifty weeks a year to do a series right."

"And what do you think I've been doing since yesterday, sitting on my ass? I could tell when I mentioned fifty weeks that you were unhappy. I said to myself, how can I make it possible for this man to do what must be done? And still keep him from making too big a sacrifice? This morning it came to me—time off. We can work it out. For example, what if you don't appear in every show, but we use guest stars instead. Then you have time to do a picture."

"That sounds reasonable," Jeff agreed, meaning that it sounded much more than generous. "Do you think you could get a sponsor to go along with that?"

"Either they go along or they don't get Jeff Jefferson!" The Doctor retorted.

Jeff was almost tempted to say, remember the last time when you said hold out, be tough, and I lost the part. But instead, since he was on such delicate ground, he said, "Whatever you think. You're the Doctor."

"Jeff, Jeff, I know you're concerned. This is an important step. You could jeopardize your whole career. But I give you my word, if I feel that you're taking too big a risk, I'll put my foot down. You're not going to be the fall guy for the whole industry again! Not while I'm around!"

"Okay, Doctor!" Jeff agreed.

"We'll talk again tomorrow, Jeff. And think about the best way to approach the Guild. Right?"

"Right!"

"Good boy!" The Doctor hung up.

3

At two o'clock the same day Freddie Feig returned from lunch at the Beverly Hills Hotel where he had entertained an advertising executive from New York. An executive whom TCA had brought West ostensibly to discuss a deal, but actually because they had promised him a trip West as a little under-the-table consideration for a TCA show the executive had bought for one of his clients. The lunch was to welcome the executive and his wife to California, but just before Freddie left the hotel he slipped the executive an envelope containing three thousand dollars in cash, "For expenses. And have a good time, long as you're here."

Then he raced back to the office. For during lunch Freddie had come up with a possible solution to the problem of Jeff Jefferson.

When he was sure that Buddy was off making a call at one of the studios, Freddie pressed down the button of his intercom, asked, "Allie, is he free?"

"In. And free," came Alise's clipped British reply.

"Let me talk to him, sweetie."

A moment passed. The Doctor's voice came over the intercom. "Yeah, Freddie?"

"I think I got it."

"What?"

"Jefferson. I think I got it."

"Then come in!" The Doctor said briskly, making no effort to conceal his interest.

Freddie found him poring over the market listings in the *Wall Street Journal.* He knew enough not to interrupt.

Finally, The Doctor said, as if uttering a private thought aloud, "Some day soon *we* got to go public, too." He put aside the *Journal,* looked up at Freddie. "Nu?"

"There's only one show where we got such leverage

that we can spot Jefferson and make it stick!" Freddie said.

"Yeah?" The Doctor asked, skeptically.

"ALUMCO!"

"ALUMCO?" The Doctor answered, visibly disappointed. "Two days ago Spence called and said they're talking about canceling, because we're not delivering the right stars. They expect a Clark Ford every week!"

"I know," Freddie conceded, "but I've got such muscle with Carl Brewster that for me he'll do it, as a personal favor."

"I've told you a thousand times," The Doctor remonstrated. "We don't *ask* favors. We *do* them. I don't like any unpaid debts. If there was something we could do for Brewster."

"If we get him out there, you can sell him the idea."

"But how?" The Doctor demanded.

Freddie smiled, his hairline mustache drawn even thinner than usual. "I'll do him a 'favor.' I'll do him such a favor that he'll be out here day after tomorrow! Maybe even sooner!"

"What kind of favor?" The Doctor demanded.

"May I?" Freddie pointed to the telephone. Then he looked at his watch, "Two-forty here. Five-forty in New York. He should still be in the office." He lifted the phone. "Alise, honey, get me Carl Brewster S.S. . . ."

Alise interrupted, "Yes, I know! S.S.D. & O!"

In minutes the phone rang. When Freddie answered The Doctor picked up the extension.

"Carl-baby? How's Eleanor? And the kids?"

"Fine, Freddie, fine. Just leaving the office now to catch the six-seventeen. Oh, by the way, thanks for that gift from F.A.O. Schwarz. Junior loved it."

"Carl, if we can't bring a little joy into the life of a kid, what's it all about? Right?"

"Right." By now Brewster was wondering why Freddie had called.

"Carl, I don't want you to worry. I want to assure you right now no matter what you hear, we've got the situation covered," Freddie said. The Doctor sat up a bit more sharply in his huge red-leather wing chair, circa 1815. Brewster's reaction on the other end of the line was equally as surprised and puzzled.

"What situation?" Brewster asked, obviously alarmed.

"Well," Freddie ventured reluctantly. "You might hear a rumor in the next week or two that Robbie Richards won't be re-signing for next season."

"Richards won't be . . ." Brewster did not even dare utter the words, as though to do so might bring down the worst curse possible to be visited on an advertising agency, losing its most highly rated television show.

"That's his present thinking," Freddie said, at the same time gesturing to The Doctor that there was no shred of truth in what he was saying.

"What did he *say?* What did he *do?*" asked Brewster frantically.

"Carl-baby, listen to me! I didn't say it was definite. I was merely calling as a favor, to tell you not to worry. If Robbie does walk we've got four replacement shows ready, any one of which would be acceptable to the network, so you won't lose your time spot."

"Screw the time spot!" Brewster shouted. "We've got a fortune tied up in that guy! Don't forget we took him from being a second banana, a mere kid, and built him up to the top ten!"

Freddie and The Doctor knew this was precisely what Brewster had been telling his client every week.

"And now the sonofabitch wants to cut out? Did somebody make him a better offer?"

"No. He just wants to take a year or two off. He's had it," Freddie said, his reading of the line exhibiting great sympathy with Brewster, great puzzlement about Robbie's decision. "You know comics."

"*He's* had it? What the hell does he think *I've* had, putting up with his fucking temperament week after week? Believe me, if the client didn't like him so much I'd cancel the bastard quicker than you can blink, rating and all! Christ, we've got our whole magazine campaign built around him for next fall!"

The Doctor glanced sharply at Freddie, who nodded, indicating that he had known this all along.

"Look! We got an option on him for next season," Brewster was saying, "and we're going to hold him to it! You can tell that cocky sonofabitch that we are going to hold him if we have to go all the way to the Supreme Court!" Having made the ultimate threat, Brewster took time now to recover his breath.

Then he started up again, "You know what I'm going to do, I'm going to call that bastard and tell him myself!"

"No, no, Carl! That's the one thing you mustn't do! You call Robbie direct and you'll ruin everything! In the first place, he's only thinking about it. In the second place, he doesn't even know that I'm calling you. It's strictly confidential between him and me. I mean, I broke my solemn word as an agent to him in order to protect you. You can't repay me by telling him. Christ, Carl, after all we've done for you!"

Freddie was practically crying when he finished. Even Brewster felt abashed, remembering the things Freddie and TCA had done for him, for the kids, for their college educations. Instead of remonstrating further, he said softly, "Don't do a thing. And don't let Robbie do anything. I don't want any rumors starting. I'll fly out tomorrow. Meet you at the Bel Air for breakfast on Thursday. Eight o'clock."

"Eight o'clock," Freddie agreed.

He hung up and turned to The Doctor who was smiling approval. He had trained Freddie well and it was yielding dividends, important dividends.

Thursday at eight o'clock when Freddie Feig's car pulled into the parking lot at the Bel Air it was one of those cool mornings when anyone but a native Southern Californian would have worn a topcoat. The gardeners were spraying the walks and watering the trees and lawns. Freddie walked along the concrete path, crossed the little bridge that spanned the man-made lagoon and entered the main building which could, to all intents, have been a large private home. Intending to call Brewster on the house phone, Freddie discovered there was no need. He was in the lobby, waiting for him. That was a good sign.

They greeted each other with the apprehension two relatives might display prior to discussing the serious illness of a third member of the family. Brewster had arranged a secluded table by the pool. They ordered breakfast. After a few opening remarks, none of which had to do with Robbie Richards, Brewster could no longer avoid the issue.

"Well? Anything happen? Any clues to what's going

through that madman's mind?"

"Not a word. Except he seems more determined than ever to quit," Freddie said, sounding as desolate as he could.

"I've been thinking about it, Freddie." Brewster paused, considering the wisdom of what he was about to say. "You know what I think? I think you guys have got a better offer from somebody else."

"Carl, Carlie, what a hell of a thing to say!"

"No, I've been thinking about it for two whole days and nights now. It doesn't make sense. What's he got to gain? He's in the top ten every week. If he takes a year or two off and loses his following he may never get back up there. He knows that. So what is the logical conclusion? He wants out because he has a promise of a deal from someone else, in the same time spot, but for more money!"

"Carl-baby, I give you my word. I swear on everything I hold holy, that's not true." As vehemently as Freddie made his declaration, so perfunctorily did Brewster shrug it off, TCA being notorious for holding nothing holy.

"Now, I talked it over with my own boys," Brewster said. "And this is what we're prepared to do. You make full and complete disclosure to us of who is interested in Richards, and what the deal is, and let us decide if we want to match it. Else there's going to be trouble. Big trouble!" Brewster threatened.

"I tell you there's no other offer!" Freddie insisted, which only served to convince Brewster that there was.

"We even talked about going to the Justice Department!" Brewster said in a moment of angry despair.

"Justice Department?" Freddie repeated, startled for the first time.

"Right! Our legal counsel says you guys may be in a monopoly situation," he said giving Freddie a hint, for the first time, of the consternation stirred up at S.S.D. & O. by his phone call.

"Look, Carl, before either of us does anything rash or says anything rash, why don't I call The Doctor? Let him handle the whole thing."

"You'd better!" Brewster said, both angry and self-righteous.

"Look, sit still. Don't leave here. Don't call anyone. Just wait till The Doctor calls you. Okay?"

After a moment Brewster agreed.

By the time Freddie Feig reached the office the back of his white shirt was soaked through with sweat. He parked his car, slipped into his shiny black mohair jacket and started toward The Doctor's office.

Cone listened, not revealing any undue concern, even when Freddie repeated Brewster's threat about the Justice Department. Freddie finished and waited for the abuse that he felt he deserved. But The Doctor only asked, "Did I ever tell you about a guy I knew once named Cat's Eye Bastione?"

Freddie nodded, for he had heard The Doctor refer to Bastione a thousand times, and he always introduced the subject precisely the same way.

"Well, Cat's Eye used to say, 'When some prick threatens me with the law, then I know I really got the bastard up against the gun. Because I don't do business with nobody who ain't outside the law himself!' "

Freddie, confused by this bit of street philosophy, merely stared.

Impatiently, The Doctor explained, "Brewster opens his mouth, he goes to jail! It's a crime, taking payoffs the way he has. That consulting corporation, you don't think that would stand up for a minute in court, do you? He's not running to any Justice Department. But at least we know how desperate he is. Okay, okay," The Doctor mused, contented when Freddie had expected he would be irate.

Then he called Brewster and arranged for lunch at Hillcrest. When he hung up, Freddie asked, "Hillcrest? Robbie'll be there."

"I know," The Doctor said. "But Brewster likes kosher corned beef and blintzes. Jew food, he calls it. So I'll take him to Hillcrest." The Doctor was pensive as he spoke.

Groucho Marx, George Burns, Lou Holtz, Milton Berle, and Robbie Richards were seated at the large round comedians' table when The Doctor and Carl Brewster entered the men's dining room. One of them had just told a joke, and a fairly good one, for there was an outburst of

wholehearted laughter just as Cone and Brewster came into sight. At which point, Robbie Richards, who sat facing
the entryway, spied them and leaped up. Assuming a
Southern accent, he started toward them, got down on
his knees and wailed, "Don' beat me, Mr. Bossman, don'
beat me. I ain't never goin' to do nuthin' wrong again. I
just gonna sing dem spirichals, tell dem jokes, beat my
feet on the Mississippi mud, tote that barge, lif' that bale
and do whatever Massa Carl says to do!"

It was the way comedians, earning ten thousand dollars
a week, ingratiated themselves with important advertising
executives who earned a tenth that much. But today
Brewster was too upset to respond, so The Doctor helped
Robbie to his feet, rewarded him with considerable laughter, and sent him back to his fellow comics.

The Doctor's table was at the other end of the
room. When they had been seated, and had one drink,
The Doctor said, "Well, I guess you know now, what
Freddie told you is true." Brewster looked across his
glass, puzzled. "Robbie doesn't have any idea that we told
you. You could see that for yourself, couldn't you?"

Grudgingly, Brewster nodded.

"We brought the whole thing up only to protect you,
to give you a preferred position in this situation out of
loyalty to our past association. So you've got to protect us
by never mentioning a word of this to Robbie."

"Okay, okay," Brewster said.

"And one other thing, those threats about going to the
Justice Department. I can understand how you feel. If
you lose the Robbie Richards show, you could lose the
account along with it. Still, if on top of that there was
any scandal involving the Justice Department, with all
the stuff that they would dredge up, you'd lose your job.
Now, I wouldn't want that to happen. Not to you, Carl.
You're one of the true gentlemen in this business.

"Of course," continued The Doctor, "you *were* right
about one thing. Though we never suspected until after
Freddie called you. There *is* another interest in Robbie Richards. Another agency, another sponsor. I tracked
it down this morning.

"But I will tell you now, before I let him walk out on
you and S.S.D. & O. I will throw an injunction against

him that will keep him from working in TV or any medium for the next ten years! Such duplicity! Such deception." He became as irate as only The Doctor could become in such situations. "I don't care if we lose him as a client, he's not going to get away with it!"

"Look, Irwin, at the same time we don't want him to be unhappy," Brewster said. "You know what it can be like doing a show with an unhappy star. Especially a comic."

"I'll take care of everything. And he won't be unhappy. Sonofabitch! When I think of the greeting he gave you just now, as if he was your best friend. Christ, comics have no gratitude, no shame!"

The Doctor drained the last of his drink. "No, Carl, I give you my word. You'll have him for next year. You may have to up the ante, give him a little more than his escalation clause calls for, but take my word, you got him! Don't give it another moment's thought!"

Thus, The Doctor had not only advanced his own cause but had secured for Robbie an added raise.

As they were ordering lunch, The Doctor proceeded to introduce his true purpose for the meeting. He was glancing down the list of delicacies, Nova Scotia lox and sturgeon plate, kosher calves' liver and bacon, pastrami flown in from New York, shrimps scampi, pot roast and potato pancakes, blintzes, either as a main dish or dessert. Without lifting his eyes from the impressive card, he observed, "You know, Carl, about ALUMCO, I've been giving that great thought since Spence called. About new stars, I mean. You know, there are only so many top stars and we like to feed them into the show on a carefully planned schedule, saving the best for the rating weeks, so ALUMCO can stand up against any competition. We have to use them sparingly, but that doesn't mean we're not aware.

"In fact, only last night when I couldn't sleep I was making up a list. For instance, how would you like Henry Fonda? In the right vehicle, of course."

"Fonda?" Brewster sparked immediately. "You think you could get Fonda to do TV?"

"I think so. As I said, in the right vehicle. And during a rating week."

"That would be something to tell Pittsburgh!" Brewster exulted.

"But they'd have to trade off. They'd have to take a not-so-top-drawer star another week."

"Such as?"

"Well, such as Jeff Jefferson," The Doctor suggested casually, waiting for a reaction.

"Jeff Jefferson," Brewster said, unenthusiastically. "I'd never get him okayed by the sponsor."

"Why not? He's a good name. Been a star a long time."

"No pizzazz," Brewster said, still unhappy.

The Doctor smiled. "Look, as we say at the track, they'll be an entry. Jefferson and Fonda. If the client wants Fonda, he's got to take Jefferson. Fair?"

"I'll try it out."

"Call Pittsburgh. Find out. Maybe we can wrap up everything before you leave town," The Doctor suggested.

"I was figuring on going back tonight. On the red-eye special," Brewster said.

"And leave the Richards situation hanging fire? I don't know . . ." The Doctor allowed his words to trail off ominously.

"You think I should wait?"

"Give me forty-eight hours," The Doctor proposed. "Look, take two days off, lie around the pool at the Bel Air. Or better still go down to my place at the Springs. But take two days off, get a little tan, a little rest. You guys work under too much pressure. In forty-eight hours I think I'll have the firm answer on Richards for you."

"Well, if you think we can have a definite answer," Brewster considered, though The Doctor knew that he had already decided to stay.

"Just take it easy for a couple of days. Of course, you could call Pittsburgh about Fonda, if you want," The Doctor suggested, not wishing to repeat Jefferson's name.

"Okay!" Brewster agreed after another moment's hesitation.

Carl Brewster stayed on at the Bel Air, since it was politic not to have his New York office constantly trying to reach him in Palm Springs. Also there was an actress he knew who was divorced again for the third time, and always willing to resume their affair whenever Carl was in town and when she wasn't involved with anyone else.

At the end of the second day, needing a pretext to call The Doctor without revealing too much anxiety, Brewster placed a call to Pittsburgh, spoke to the sponsor personally, was able to secure an okay on both Fonda and Jefferson.

The Doctor was expecting his call. "Carl? Hi! Having a good rest?" he asked, though he knew that Carl Brewster had been screwing his head off for the past two days.

"Goofing off. Getting a little sun. By the way, I talked to Pittsburgh. They said okay to Fonda *and* Jefferson."

"Great!" The Doctor beamed.

"Of course they're going to want some guarantees on Fonda."

"Of course. I'll send you a confirmation. Fonda in any vehicle he approves," The Doctor promised, knowing all the while how unlikely it would be that Fonda would approve any script. "I'll send you a letter of intent so we nail it down."

"Right!" said Brewster, then feeling he had prepared the ground he ventured to ask, "Any word on Robbie?"

"I'm waiting for his call right now," The Doctor lied. "He met with his business manager this morning. I'll be back to you the moment I hear." He hung up, this time feeling that he had achieved the next important step in securing Jeff Jefferson's cooperation.

Just before he went to lunch, The Doctor called Brewster, and told him, "It's all set! You got Robbie for another three years! At a slightly higher price than we figured, but you can live with it. I'll get the details into the mail for you as soon as the boys finalize them."

"Good!" Brewster said. "And thanks, Doctor. I won't forget this!"

"Carl, I told you, you're a gentleman. And in this business that's so rare that I feel it's a privilege to do a favor for you. I'll get both things in the mail to you, the confirmation on Robbie, the letter of intent on Fonda and Jefferson."

"Right. And thanks again!"

As he hung up, one fact stuck in The Doctor's mind. The threat that Carl Brewster had made about going to the

Justice Department. The Doctor didn't hold it against Brewster. In a way he was grateful to him. The question had finally come up. Much sooner than he had anticipated. But it had come up. One day it would be raised officially.

He must begin to prepare his defenses. As Cat's Eye was wont to say, with the law you can always make a deal. But in order to make the deal you needed intermediaries, connections. The Doctor determined that soon he would begin building his strength in both political parties. After all, who could know which party would be in power when the whistle was finally blown on TCA. But whoever was in the White House, The Doctor intended to have leverage there.

4

The date for Jeff Jefferson's guest appearance on ALUM-CO Star Theatre was firmly set. The place, New York, of course. All that remained to be agreed on were the vehicle and the director. The Doctor sent word to New York that he wanted the very best director in live TV, even if TCA itself had to pay the difference between the budgeted price and the director's price.

As to the vehicle, The Doctor had given specific instructions. It was not to be an original. It must be a piece of proven material—an adaptation from a successful play, novel, or short story. The lead role must be that of a handsome, charming young American whose sincerity and convictions were beyond question, who would in the end endear himself to the audience by making a great sacrifice to achieve some purpose which the audience would emotionally endorse. If the hero's purpose was unselfish besides, so much the better. Perfect, in fact.

While the hunt was on for the best director and the proper story, The Doctor turned his full time and attention to Jeff's dealings with the Guild.

The first step, Jeff felt, was Abe Heller.

"Abe has an uncanny knack of knowing how people who work for a living will react to any idea," Jeff explained. "His speeches work. His ideas work. And his suspicions work. If there's going to be trouble, Abe'll spot it first."

So, for several days, The Doctor and Jeff rehearsed carefully how to broach the subject to Abe, how to develop it, how, finally, to assign Abe a role that would win him over. When The Doctor was satisfied that Jeff was ready, he permitted him to begin discussions.

Abe arrived at Jeff's house as arranged, bringing with

him a thick file on Guild finances, falling membership, and rising expenses.

Jeff began outlining the grim future for the Guild and its members while Abe nervously ate from the plate of Danish that Martha had prepared for him.

"Jeff," he interrupted finally, "I know what you're leading up to. And I don't blame you."

"What I'm leading up to?" Jeff asked, startled and somewhat guilty as well.

"You want to resign. Right? I don't blame you. You've had enough. *Done* enough. But please, I ask you, I beg you, don't quit! It'll undermine our position in the entire industry!"

Jeff was silent for a moment. Then, imitating in a small way The Doctor's approach, Jeff asked, "And if I don't resign? I mean, if things are allowed to continue as they are? Then what? What I mean is, Abe, if I'm not going to *do* anything, maybe the Guild would be better off if I did resign."

"Do?" Abe lamented. "Do what? The walls are crumbling all around us! The studios are just as shaky as we are! What can anyone do?"

"That's just the point," Jeff said. "I've been thinking about the studios. They're running scared. The other unions are not as much affected as we are. But we don't have the power. We need help. We need money to revolutionize this whole industry." He knew that somehow the word "revolutionize" would have the right effect on Abe.

"And if there *was* money, what good would that do?" Abe asked.

"We need someone, or some group, that can bring in enough capital to convert live TV to film! TV should be on film! And that film should be made in the picture capital of the world! Hollywood, USA!" Jeff declared.

"The majors won't touch TV, you know that, Jeff." Then Abe proceeded to raise precisely the same objections as Jeff had when The Doctor first mentioned the idea to him. And Jeff countered with the very same arguments that The Doctor had used on him.

By the time the sun had passed behind the tall palm tree so the whole pool area was in shadow, Abe Heller was saying, "If it worked that way it would be fantastic.

We would be able to recapture the jobs from the East and from AFTRA. It's a hell of an idea, Jeff!"

"What about that conflict of interest angle I mentioned?" Jeff asked cautiously.

"We got lawyers on retainer. Let's talk to the lawyers!"

Together Jeff and Abe consulted the Guild attorneys, who could find no legal reason why the Guild could not vote TCA immunity from a conflict of interests charge. But as one of the attorneys cautioned, "That would be a pretty broad power to give to TCA. I'd feel better with some guarantees."

"Then we'll find some guarantees," Abe promised, more aflame with the idea even than Jeff.

Meantime, the attorneys agreed to draw up a Memorandum of Law authorizing Jeff, as president, and Abe, as executive secretary, to proceed with the plan.

The Doctor listened with satisfaction as Jeff related the events of the meeting.

"Good! Soon as you get the Memorandum, let me know what it says. Or if you want, I'll have our own lawyers check it out."

"I'd rather not," Jeff said quickly.

"Of course!" The Doctor responded just as quickly. "It's confidential Guild business. And now," The Doctor reached for an envelope that lay on a corner of his otherwise empty desk, "*I* have something for *you*." He handed Jeff the envelope.

Jeff took it, drew out a script with the name ALUMCO STAR THEATRE emblazoned across the top in aggressive script. Below in capital type was the title, ALIAS JIMMY VALENTINE. Four lines below appeared the word, "Starring" and below that, "JEFF JEFFERSON."

"*Jimmy Valentine*," Jeff said, "Christ, that's been around for forty years. They've made it into a picture three different times! Besides, it's a costume piece, from the eighteen-nineties. I thought they'd come up with something bright and fresh. I'll get murdered in New York by those smart-ass television critics."

"Jeff, would I let you do something that wasn't good for you? Take it home. Read it over a few times. Then we'll talk."

"*Alias Jimmy Valentine,* Christ!" Jeff repeated.

Nevertheless he took the script home and read it over. He read it twice. The first time to refresh his mind on the story of the young ex-con with a great skill at cracking safes. He is paroled, violates that parole by changing his name and gets a job in a bank, of all places. Of course the banker has a pretty daughter, and, of course, Valentine and the daughter fall in love. The banker also has a son, a nice kid who forms a hero-worship relationship with Valentine, under his new name, Will Carter.

Then one day a detective shows up. Naturally no one in town suspects that Will Carter and the bank robber are one and the same, certainly not the banker's beautiful daughter, at least not until her kid brother manages to get himself locked in the bank vault. Naturally it has a time lock and is impossible to open until nine o'clock in the morning. And naturally, too, there is only a limited supply of oxygen, far too little to keep the boy alive through the night. What to do to save his life? Blast? The impact would kill him outright. What else?

There is only one solution—if such a man were available—an expert safe-cracker!

So now Jimmy Valentine has to face the greatest decision of his life, save the boy and expose his real identity in the presence of the pursuing detective, or let the boy die? Well, naturally Jimmy is going to sacrifice himself. And he does, racing against time to pick that lock.

Of course the detective, in a matching gesture of sacrifice, agrees to go back to the city and forget that he ever found Jimmy Valentine—leaving Jimmy, the girl, the worshiping young brother, and the grateful father all happy and forgiving at the fadeout.

Corny, corny as hell, Jeff thought when he finished reading it for the second time. There was only one thing to do, turn it down. He was tempted to call The Doctor at once. But then decided to read it again in the morning.

But before he had a chance there was a phone call. Abe Heller again. He had the memo from the lawyers. They should get together and discuss it. And Abe had an idea about how to protect the actors if they voted to allow TCA to hire as well as represent talent. Could they meet right away?

Dolores was the place. Abe handed Jeff the memo, very

official looking, in a light blue binder. The legal language and the references to previous cases including excerpts from judges' decisions, were difficult to follow. But the summary was clear. As long as the dual activities of TCA were out in the open, as long as full disclosure had been made, the Doctrine of Informed Consent would apply.

Abe had been eating Danish and drinking coffee all the while that Jeff plodded through the memo. He had so timed his consumption of both that he was finished when Jeff looked up.

"Then it's okay," Jeff said.

Abe nodded. "Now here's where my idea for protection comes in."

"Yes?" Jeff asked.

"It's very simple. We go to the membership on this issue. And I think we got a good chance to get the idea accepted. So we vote TCA the power. Now, what's our protection? Our ace in the hole in case they begin to play fast and loose? Countersigning."

"Countersigning what?"

"The Guild can exercise control by having the right to countersign every deal made between TCA and any TCA actor." Abe was smiling. "In the end the actors have control in spite of the waiver."

Jeff nodded. He welcomed the suggestion, for he was still not entirely easy with the situation.

"Next move is hold a meeting of the Executive Committee," said Abe.

"Try for Thursday night," said Jeff and went back to his car to drive to TCA.

When Alise showed him into The Doctor's office he came straight to the point.

"We saw the lawyers' Memorandum on the Law of Conflict of Interest this morning. It looks like we can go ahead," Jeff reported.

The Doctor sat up, leaned forward, smiled. "Good, good! Then you'll go right to your Executive Committee."

"There's a little hooker, Doctor."

"Hooker?"

"Somebody came up with the idea that the Guild would have to countersign every contract which involved a TCA client working on a TCA production."

"Oh?" The Doctor grunted, revealing that he had not expected that development. "Well, our lawyer will talk to your lawyer and we'll get it all straightened out."

"It wasn't one of the lawyers. It was Abe Heller."

"Abe Heller? Well, we'll talk to him. The main thing is to get things moving before the whole damned industry falls apart. Talk to your Executive Committee, but leave out details like countersigning. They'll have enough to grapple with without complications. Right?"

Jeff didn't answer directly, instead he changed the subject to one that had been irritating him since early morning.

"Doctor, about that script . . ."

"Yeah?"

"It's a pretty corny piece."

"Corny? It's a classic! A heart-warming classic! A part of traditional Americana!"

"You expect me to get by Gould in the *Times* and Crosby in the *Trib* with that?"

"I am not interested in what two pretentious idiots think. It's the people across the country who count."

"I never heard of anybody who reads reviews by one of the 'people'!" Jeff said. *"Variety, The Times,* the *Trib* and maybe the *LA Times,* that's it! And with this script we'll lose at least three out of four! I won't do it."

"Jeff, Jeff." The Doctor rose, placed his hand on Jeff's shoulder. "Kid, you know the difference between you and me?"

Jeff could think of many but refrained from answering.

"You think about today," The Doctor said. "I think about tomorrow. Would I ask you to do anything that would hurt your career at this delicate stage of . . . things? I told you I have plans. Great plans. And while there are sacrifices at the beginning, you'll be amazed at what's waiting for you at the end. A lousy fortune, that's all!"

Having made that enigmatic statement, The Doctor turned back toward his desk. He was silent for a moment, brooding.

"Doctor, surely it's not impossible to find another script."

"Not that fits the qualifications."

"What qualifications?" Jeff asked.

"I want to give you a TV image that will launch you on a whole new career! And you think only in terms of one play! I had this written to my express demands by the best TV writer in New York! Why? Because I want you to fail? What good would that do anyone? Especially you?"

"What about *you?*" Jeff asked, a bit more sharply than he had intended.

"What does that mean?" The Doctor demanded.

"Some day we're going to have it out, Doctor!" Jeff said in a voice as cold as he could command.

"Have it out?" said The Doctor suddenly anxious that his entire carefully worked out plan was in jeopardy.

"You want the Guild's permission. And this TV shot is my payoff. Right?" Jeff demanded. "And if I fall on my ass then you've done your part and you don't owe me anything anymore. Right again?"

The Doctor did not change expression. He merely turned away, and in doing so revealed, deliberately or not, his age and his sheer exhaustion in dealing with such problems. He moved to his desk, opened the middle drawer, took out a sheaf of typed pages, weighing the advisability of showing them to Jeff.

"So I'm looking for a cheap out, is that it?"

To himself, Jeff said, If this is another of The Doctor's acts, it's the best one.

"First," Cone said, almost trembling with indignation, "first I will tell you what I expect that script to accomplish for you. Then . . . then I'll let you see this." He dropped the pages to the desk and spoke as if to himself.

"Critics, audiences, fuck them all! *I* am interested in only one old man with a hearing aid screwed into his ear who sits out in Detroit and watches TV shows like a hawk. And the morning after he sees a show he likes he calls his agency in New York and tells them, in detail, what he liked. And he orders, 'Find me a show like that!' I want *that* old man to like *this* show! I want that old man to like *you!* And I know what he likes from the reports I get from his agency in New York. He likes corny stories. He likes stories with uplift endings. In his world, all marriages are happy, virtue triumphs, all criminals see the error of their ways.

"And if there is a child in the story who is saved from danger, that old man with the hearing aid cries like a baby.

"I want that man to see you, in this part, to sympathize with you. Most of all, I want him to go to bed with the beautiful memory of Jeff Jefferson, handsome, blond, sincere, saving the poor boy from a terrible death by suffocation. That's what I want!"

Now the Doctor turned on Jeff and demanded, "And *why* do I want him to feel that way about you?" He snatched up the pages from the desk. *"This is why!"*

Jeff hesitated, took the pages, glanced down at the words typed in the jumbo-size type used for live TV scripts.

JEFFERSON: GOOD EVENING AND WEL-COME AGAIN TO CONSOLIDATED STAR THEATRE. I AM JEFF JEFFERSON, YOUR HOST, ON BEHALF OF CONSOLIDATED MO-TORS, THE FAMILY OF FINE COMPANIES THAT PRODUCE THOSE FINE CARS AND TRUCKS THAT SUPPLY YOU, YOUR FAMILY AND YOUR BUSINESS WITH THE BEST, THE SAFEST, THE MOST ECONOMICAL TRANS-PORTATION IN THE WORLD! JUST AS OUR MOTTO HAS ALWAYS BEEN BETTER SAFER CARS FOR YOU FROM THE COMPANY THAT CARES, SO WE BRING YOU AND YOUR FAM-ILY THE FINEST IN HOME ENTERTAIN-MENT ON CONSOLIDATED STAR THEATRE. BECAUSE WE CARE. AND NOW, OUR STAR THEATRE PRESENTATION THIS EVENING . . . A TOUCHING AND HEARTWARMING STORY, AN AMERICAN CLASSIC, "ALIAS JIM-MY VALENTINE!" BUT FIRST . . .

Jeff flipped through the other pages, they were act breaks, material for him to read leading into the C.M. commercials and then out of the commercials back into the play. His last piece was a farewell and a teaser for the following week's show.

Completely bewildered, Jeff asked, "How can you put another sponsor's message on an ALUMCO show?"

"I'll take care of that," The Doctor said. "It'll be a pilot. We'll cut your host announcements into the kinescope of *Jimmy Valentine*. The only one who'll ever see it is that man in Detroit. And he'll understand."

But Jeff was still gnawing on the word The Doctor had used. "My host announcements! You're turning me into a TV announcer! A lousy commercial announcer!" Jeff protested.

"I'm making you a Master of Ceremonies so that you will have continuity even during those weeks when you're off doing a feature!"

"Still an announcer!" Jeff persisted.

"I'm giving you a whole new career," The Doctor corrected.

Jeff tossed the pages onto the antique desk. They slid across the highly polished wood to flutter to the carpet.

Instead of becoming angry or indignant, The Doctor shook his head in the way that he adopted to nourish uncertainty in the minds of clients.

"What's wrong?" asked Jeff as expected.

"I'm ashamed of myself," The Doctor said, self-effacingly. "I've made mistakes in my time. Picked the wrong vehicle, backed the wrong youngster, put together the wrong combination of a male and female star. But if anyone had told me that I was making a mistake with you, I wouldn't have believed it." To give Jeff time to worry, The Doctor bent down and slowly picked up the script.

"What do you mean, you wouldn't have believed it?" Jeff asked, like a chastened child already prepared to admit his error.

"What is there left to say?" The Doctor asked rhetorically. He went back to his desk, carefully replaced the pages in the middle drawer and closed it. Then, resigned, he said, "Jeff, go to New York, do the show, and we'll forget it. If you don't want to go through with the proposal to the Guild, you can forget that, too."

From all appearances, the meeting was over. Then Jeff did precisely what The Doctor had expected he would do. Dismissed, he did not move. Instead he waited, hoping

The Doctor would break the silence, but that would have been contrary to The Doctor's strategy.

Finally, rather than put self-interest first, Jeff began by saying, "The proposal to the Guild is good. It's the only thing that can keep actors working in California. We don't have to drop the idea just because I don't like *that!*" Jeff pointed in the direction of the desk drawer with the offending commercial copy.

"If you want me to go through with the plan," The Doctor said, pretending not enthusiasm but obligation, "I'll go through with it. But it won't be the same."

"Why not, if it works?"

"Because," The Doctor seemed ready now to give way to his emotions, "because I started the project partly out of concern for you, for your career.

"This script was *my* idea created especially for *you.* Jeff, the rewards are for the pioneers, the trailblazers. Berle is 'Mr. Television'! Why? Because he was the first comic to do a weekly variety show as the MC. Anybody who comes along now is only Mr. Imitator. There is only one Mr. Television. That's what I had in mind for you. But you didn't like it, didn't want it. All right."

"What you had in mind for me . . ." Jeff repeated, hoping to keep the man's interest alive.

"What I had in mind for you," The Doctor reiterated, "was a situation where you, an actor, would have a steady job for as long as you wanted it. For once, the actor would be calling the tune! For once, the actor would be so solidly entrenched that *he* would decide if he wanted to work, not someone else.

"You take a star, the biggest, Gable, Garson, Cooper, Lancaster. You ever hear of them really holding out these days? Oh, sure, they balk, they walk off. But they *always* come back. Why? Because time is running against them.

"Well, I wanted to free you from that tyranny. I wanted to make it possible for you to mature gracefully. Profitably. And to decide how long you wanted to work. But no."

Jeff felt humble now, and stupid as well. He hadn't seen such dimensions in what The Doctor had proposed. He had reacted only out of vanity. A recognized star, no matter how hard the times, did not become an announcer, a TV pitchman for any company.

Jeff's silence encouraged The Doctor to move into the more open phase of his offensive.

"There's a different world coming, Jeff. Companies that previously spent their energy building plants, making products, selling them, are beginning to worry about what the public thinks of them. Public relations is no longer simply advising John D. Rockefeller to give away dimes. Companies are becoming conscious that the thing now is Image. A company has to be human, has to be able to meet the people on a level they understand and like.

"Now that stuffy old bastard in Detroit who knows how to make cars and sell them better than anyone else in the world, if he were to go before the public on TV they'd take one look at him and scream, 'Scrooge!' Because that's what he looks like. What he needs, what that company needs is a nice-looking, intelligent, honest front man to go before the public and say, 'I am Consolidated Motors. We're all like this at our company. Nice, human, warm, friendly folk. You can buy our product and feel good about it.' "

The Doctor spun about suddenly to point at the carved linen-fold oak panels that hid his own television screen. "That box is creating a revolution! Because it *seems* to present the truth. They used to say, 'No one can fool a camera.' But you know damn well that *any* good actor can fool a camera. Now they're saying, 'One thing about TV, nobody can fool that camera.' Horseshit!

"And it's not going to end with advertising. One day soon, if you want to elect a man to public office you're going to need a politician who looks like an actor, *or* an actor who looks like a politician."

Jeff moved back toward the desk in such manner as to make The Doctor reach into the drawer and produce the offending pages again.

"Jeff, I couldn't give better advice to my own son. Read these over, calmly, carefully. In fact, do it at home in front of a mirror. See if it's really as bad as you think."

Jeff went back to the house. He locked himself in the guest room, stood before the mirror, began to read the copy aloud. During the first reading he discovered, because the copy was in such large type, there seemed to be infinitely more words than there actually were. Then, after he had tried it four times, with a different attack each time, he found that he could summon a certain degree of enthusiasm.

After an hour of reading in one attitude, then another, he finally evolved a style that made him say to himself, Any company would be damned lucky to have a man like me represent it to the public. And when he thought about it, it wasn't so demeaning. For example there was already a distinguished tradition for this sort of role in radio. C. B. DeMille had done it for years. Orson Welles, in the days of the Mercury Theatre, had done it too, as well as playing the leads in many of the dramas. So the job could be justified. In fact, it only proved again what foresight The Doctor had. He owed the little man an apology.

Rather than delay it, he went to the phone, called and was put through at once.

"Yeah, kid?" The Doctor greeted him genially.

"I've been going over it. It's not as bad as I thought. I can do it," Jeff admitted. "I can do it goddamn well! Of course the copy could be changed somewhat."

"Before the time comes for you to do it, it will be put into your own style," The Doctor assured him.

"There's one other problem. I don't want to give up acting to do this."

"Of course not!" The Doctor agreed vehemently. "But *we* are not going to bring up the issue."

"Why not?" Jeff asked, disappointed.

"We are going to let Old Trumpet-in-His-Ear suggest that. And what's more, we are going to say no the first two times. Then the third time, when he is begging to have you act in every other show we are going to graciously give in. At a price. An extra five thousand a week. Five thousand a week when you host the show. Ten thousand a week when you act, as well. By that time he'll want you enough to agree to anything!"

"I see," Jeff said, in awe of The Doctor's mind that worked constantly in undisclosed convolutions which always provided the right answers.

While The Doctor had previously regretted having to expose his plan so fully to Jeff, he consoled himself now that it might prove fortuitous. Better to face Jeff's inhibitions here than in New York when it came time to shoot, which reminded him to call the network in New York. It was a duty he did not wish to entrust to anyone else. He needed studio facilities for two extra hours, right after ALUMCO STAR THEATRE was off the air.

He would make this arrangement on his own. After all, Anson Taft, president of the CBN network, owed him a big favor. Thanks to The Doctor, Taft had remained solvent, secure in his job, and able to divorce his wife and marry his onetime secretary. Yes, Anson Taft would always feel that he was beholden to TCA. He would readily agree to having the studio and the camera crew at The Doctor's disposal, for two hours or for ten.

5

Once Jeff had steered The Doctor's proposal through the Guild's Executive Committee, Abe Heller rented the ballroom of the Beverly Hills Hotel for a meeting of the general membership. It proved to be a larger gathering than any other in the history of the Guild. Since it was a special meeting on a single issue, no other business was on the agenda.

From his long experience in organizing, Abe knew that in crucial labor meetings one did not leave anything to chance. He had seeded the group with half a dozen actors who were close personal friends. They were primed to speak any time the issue seemed in doubt. Abe had even written out the arguments each should use so that there would be variety as well as power in their speeches.

For this reason Abe was much more confident than Jeff was, as he rose to open the meeting. The tension in the crowd was evident from the difficulty he had in securing silence. When they were finally quiet he began reading from a text contained in a black binder. He wore glasses, not because he needed them but because they made him appear more dignified.

He laid the foundation for his proposal by citing the unemployment statistics which had grown even worse in the past month. Planned feature productions to be done in Hollywood were now down fourteen percent from the previous month, and down thirty-seven percent from the same month in the previous year. The increase in TV jobs in New York and Chicago during the past three months was up twenty-six percent over the preceding six months.

Just before presenting the TCA proposal, Jeff paused, took off his glasses, and wiped them. It was a sincere gesture. The effect of the speech was as emotionally un-settling to himself as it had been to everyone in the room.

That a part of his emotional reaction might have been guilt did not occur to him at that time. He was ready to launch into the hopeful part of his speech.

"It is strange that in a time when the studios cower in fear, when the other Guilds content themselves with hand-wringing, when everyone is willing to desert this city, only one group has come forward with a plan to save us. And that group is one about which we have made some pretty cruel jokes for many years.

"We have called them flesh peddlers, Shylocks, and worse. We have accused them of getting ten percent of what *our* talent, *our* sweat and *our* devotion produces, without any talent or sweat or devotion of their own. This may all be true. But I must say for them now that at least one agency has come forward with a plan that has a chance of saving us from disaster.

"The plan we are here to discuss tonight is the product of a large agency—to be exact, TCA!"

When he enunciated the letters, he could feel a surge of cynicism sweep through the room. Remarks that he could not hear evoked sarcastic laughter.

He rapped his gavel and forced them to listen to the en-tire plan, concluding with, "Your Executive Board, your officers and your president place before you, with their strongest and most urgent recommendation, this pro-posal: that Talent Corporation of America be empowered by this Guild to function as producers of television pro-grams, as well as agents, without being placed in the position of being guilty of a conflict of interest."

The rush of members to their feet, the outburst of en-raged voices, made clear to Jeff and Abe how strong the opposition was. Whatever Jeff had feared, the first tor-rent of outrage far exceeded it. He doubted that he could even bring the meeting to order again. Finally, simply by expending its hostile energy, the crowd quieted down. Small groups formed, like hostile camps. Jeff began to acknowledge objections from the floor.

The first person he recognized was Edgar Berry, a short, stoutish man who had made a reputation for himself in character roles. He was a highly skillful actor and a political militant whose name had been mentioned a number of times during the loathsome days of the investigation. When he spoke many of his colleagues listened respectfully and with a tendency to endorse, in advance, any of his views.

"I've been around a little in my time," the actor began. "I've been a member of"—and he raised his hands to count off the fingers of his left hand with his right—"the Bagel Bakers Union in New York." With that he drew a laugh which encouraged him. "The Furriers Union. The Department Store Clerks. You can't be an actor without having some other visible means of support. Otherwise, between jobs, you could be accused of being a bum!"

He drew an even bigger laugh.

"I have also been a member of the Yiddish Actors Guild, to say nothing of AFTRA, Equity and Screen Actors Guild. In all my experience I have never heard such a dangerous proposition as I've just heard here tonight. And if it wasn't for Jeff Jefferson, who was so magnificent during the black days of the hearings, I would say it was a deliberate plot to destroy this Guild!"

He sat down to a surge of applause which served to encourage those other actors who objected to the plan, but who normally would have been reluctant to speak out.

Jeff, shaken, but maintaining at least an outward appearance of dignity and control, recognized the next speaker, a woman.

She had all the attributes that men usually admire: good breasts, firm legs, clean neat features and golden blond hair, long and shiny. Yet her very strength and intelligence had always served to discourage men. Though she would have welcomed their attentions and their love, she suffered the unearned reputation of being a lesbian. The roles she played were generally female villains, neurotic killers, Teutonic heavies who had run Nazi concentration camps.

When she spoke she was soft-voiced, but she could not disguise her underlying strength.

"I almost wish I hadn't been here tonight," she began. "I would rather have heard about this meeting second hand, so that I could have doubted that it ever took place.

"This proposal is like asking the Jews to agree not to

attack the Cossacks or the Czechs to apologize to the Nazis. Now I know that the Bible says that one day the lamb will lie down with the lion. But it also says this will not occur until the Messiah comes. And unless the rapacious, scheming little monster named Irwin Cone *is* the Messiah, I say this proposal comes either two thousand years too late or two thousand years too soon! As for myself, I think, too soon!"

She sat down, but the applause for her was so sustained that, being an actress, she rose again to acknowledge it.

Jeff tried to quiet the crowd by recognizing another actor who, he hoped, would be less hostile. He was an older man and though his name had never appeared above the title of a film, he was considered a minor star.

"I'm an old hand at this kind of thing," he said softly, restoring order simply by his moderate tone. "I tramped a picket line for Actors Equity back in the twenties. And even in those days I did not like subterfuge."

The word subterfuge made Jeff's cheeks burn, for it seemed a personal accusation.

"What do I mean by subterfuge? I mean 'Actors Equity.' Why not come out and call it what it is—a union! Just as this is a union of actors! No Guild. No exclusive gentlemen's club. We are workers. When there are jobs we get hired and we get paid, by the day or the week. And we are only fooling ourselves if we think we are any different from a group of plumbers or bricklayers."

The militants in the room began to nod in agreement.

"So, I say, let's act like a union. Let's take into account the real issue at stake—jobs for workers! Speeches won't feed your families, nor will smart remarks about Cone and his Cobras. We are talking about jobs. Will we have a viable industry here a year from now? Or will we all have to Okie our way back to New York and start the endless rounds of theatrical offices and casting agencies for live TV shows?

"For myself, before I desert my house and rose garden, I am willing to listen, think, and vote in my own best interest."

Though he did not elicit any applause, he changed the entire tone of the meeting. Even the later speeches which viewed The Doctor's plan with great suspicion were more temperate and evoked fewer nasty laughs.

After the old man was seated, Jeff called on two of Abe's plants. They spoke moderately and well, insisting that at least Jeff's presentation was deserving of sincere and intelligent consideration.

Jeff breathed more easily. He became aware of the damp chill on the back of his neck from his wet shirt collar. But there were more objections from the hard core dissidents who hated and suspected any entrenched power but their own.

The gravity of the situation was underlined, if it needed underlining, by the fact that for the first time during the evening Abe Heller signified with an economical gesture of his forefinger that he wished to speak.

Jeff asked the meeting at large, "Is there anyone here who would object to hearing from our Executive Secretary?"

The audience remained silent and Jeff gave the floor to Abe, who got up, hitching up his pants which had slipped below his belly.

"I know that strictly speaking I am not a member. I am not even entitled to vote. But if the qualifications here tonight are previous union activity then I yield first place to no one.

"Does anyone in this room want to match arrest records? I'll beat him. Does he want to match injuries? I have left more blood in Union Square than any man here has left anywhere. I, too, have paid my dues. I say this only because I do not want to have my motives challenged by anyone in this room!"

His chubby face was angry and strong. Then suddenly he broke into a smile.

"Some of you may have noticed, in fact I'll bet that behind my broad behind you make jokes about it, this affinity I have for coffee and Danish. Would you like to know how I acquired it? Because for nine years, that's right, nine years, I did not sit down to a single complete meal. I lived out of cardboard coffee cups and waxed paper. I ate in meetings or sitting at a typewriter or on cold winter days I ate standing by a fire burning in a garbage can while I was supervising a picket line. I gave up a lot. Eating was only symbolic. I married late, so I have a wife and kids who are too young for me. They deserve better.

Yes, I have sacrificed a great deal for labor. And I have fought bosses and employers more bitterly and consistently than any of you."

There was a hush in the room now. Abe continued.

"From it all I learned one thing. We are in a peculiar position, we workers. No matter what field we are in. Much as we hate and distrust bosses, and much as they hate and fear us, it is a marriage of necessity from which there can be no divorce.

"Now my conviction is that we have to concentrate on the major issue at hand—jobs for actors in a declining market! Years ago when I was associated with the International Ladies' Garment Workers we had a huge fund set aside. The purpose? To lend money to bosses who came on hard times financially. Why? Because without them we had no jobs. It was *our* business to keep *them* in business.

"The same reasoning applies here. The industry is disintegrating before our eyes. The facts speak for themselves." Abe pointed in the direction of Jeff's black speech book.

"So it all boils down to what can we do as working men and women to keep the studios open? And when we know the answer to that, we *do* it!"

Abe paused to let the audience absorb his indignation. Then he concluded with, "The one thing we should *not* do is cast aspersions on the one man who is trying to help us."

For the first time it was out in the open, the doubt that some of the members felt about Jeff. With all eyes on him, Jeff stood up. Whatever Abe's purpose had been, he had focused the debate on Jeff Jefferson and there was no way Jeff could avoid it.

"I hadn't wanted to make this a personal issue because it affects us all equally. Star or bit player, we are fighting for our jobs. I as much as you.

"Because a worker without a job is powerless. A worker without a job cannot strike. He cannot bargain. That's why I am for this plan, why I presented it to the Executive Board and asked their approval to present it to you. Now that isn't all that I have done about this."

Jeff hesitated as if trying to decide whether to make a damaging personal admission. It was a studied pause, to give maximum effect to what would follow.

"Next week I am making a trip I do not wish to make. To a city I do not wish to visit. To do a job I will hate doing. I will spend three weeks there, rehearsing and then playing in a live television show!

"Yes, that's right! I have become one of the gypsies. Not because I want to or because I have to. Pictures can go to hell and I will remain solvent. I am going because TCA forced me to sign the contract before they would make this proposal!"

Then, intoxicated by the effect that statement had on his audience, Jeff decided to exploit the mood to the full.

"And not only did I have to sign, but I had to make a gentlemen's agreement with them that if this motion passed tonight I would give them a three-year option on my services for television. That's right! If this motion goes through it will probably mean that I am through in feature pictures. Because I will be the first movie star to break the unwritten agreement between the studios and exhibitors that no star will be welcome in a picture if he works for the enemy, television!"

He could feel it growing, the belief, the acceptance, the empathy of this audience of actors who understood the enormity of his sacrifice.

"I hope that gives you a small idea of how deeply I believe in TCA's proposal. What I think it means to our craft, to this Guild and to our entire community."

He sat down, a modest, humble man. The audience apparently believed his act. After an instant of silence, they burst forth in sustained applause that assured him that, for tonight at least, they were behind him.

Immediately thereafter there was a motion from the floor to put the question to a vote. The result was four hundred sixty-two for TCA to seventy-three against. After the count, Edgar Berry, who had voiced the most vehement opposition, asked for the floor. Jeff hesitated, but gave it to him.

"In view of the outcome and the things I have heard since I first spoke, I would like to change my vote and move that the decision be unanimous."

Berry's change of mind was greeted by cheers. Shortly after midnight, when Jeff left, he had the Guild's unanimous approval allowing The Doctor and TCA to proceed with their plan.

He drove home, his clothes so damp that he raised the windows of the car to keep out the cool night air.

When he reached home he didn't even bother to go upstairs to see if Joanne was there. Since Oscar night they had had no physical contact and very little conversation. They were, as the leasehold declared, only tenants in common. The lawyer had advised that they remain so for the time being since California was a community property state. There were moments though when Jeff felt the only thing they shared was contempt for each other. But he was following The Doctor's advice—no divorce, no scandal until Jeff's future career was more settled.

He was too exhausted to call The Doctor. He went out to the kitchen to get some cold milk and any snack that might be in the refrigerator. The emotion of the evening had drained him, left him as empty and hungry as he used to be after a football game at college. The antidote now as in those days was cold milk and lots of food. He was having his second glass of milk and some cold chicken when he heard Joanne.

She didn't seem surprised to see him. Her entrance was deliberate. She stared at him with that enforced focusing of her eyes which indicated that she was drunk and that she knew it. There was always something aggressively lady-like about her when she was drinking. Until she opened her mouth.

"Do you have to make so fucking much noise?" she demanded.

"I thought I was pretty quiet," he said, seeking to avoid any confrontation.

"From the minute you drove into the driveway it's been one goddamn door after another. The car door! The front door! The den door!"

"Sorry." Follow The Doctor's advice, he kept reminding himself, no trouble, until the right time. He hoped that lacking any opposition she would leave him and go back to bed, but she did not move.

"*She* called!" Joanne said suddenly.

Turning as he spoke, "*She* called? Who?"

"Not that Martinson broad from Texas!" she said, glad

to let him know that she had heard about her.

He didn't like to give her the satisfaction of asking, but it was her price and he finally paid it. "Who called?"

"That Jew bitch from Chicago!"

Trying to conceal the startling effect the news had on him, he asked, "Did she leave any message?"

"Only to say that she called. I guess she didn't have much to say to me," Joanne said.

"Okay," he said, wanting to end the conversation.

"She sounded upset," Joanne continued.

"I said okay! I got the message! Now let's drop it!"

"Okay," she said sweetly now that she knew she had succeeded in infuriating him. She turned to leave, but before she reached the door he stopped her.

"You bitch! Your idea of possessing something is not to enjoy it yourself, only to keep someone else from having it!"

She turned, smiled sweetly, and said, "Fuck you, Jeff Jefferson, movie star!" She exited, letting the kitchen door whisk closed behind her.

His first impulse was to turn to the phone. He lifted it, began to dial long distance but then realized that Joanne would probably pick up one of the extensions. Besides, he cautioned himself, it was well past two o'clock in the morning in Chicago. Something must be wrong, terribly wrong for Charlene to call him.

Perhaps, he began to fantasize, perhaps her father had died and she was calling to tell him. Why else would she call? To say that she had changed her mind by herself?

In the morning he would call. At seven L.A. time it would be nine in Chicago.

He was up before seven. He went out to the foyer, stood at the foot of the stairs and listened. There was no sound from the bedroom, no sound of rushing water from Joanne's first shower of the day. She must be asleep. Perhaps she had a late call today and wasn't due at the studio until mid-morning. He went into the den, closed the door with exquisite care so as not to make any sound, lifted the receiver, dialed long distance. He placed the call person to person to Miss Charlene Rashbaum and waited.

In moments there was a ring.

"Miss Charlene Rashbaum," the operator said. "Long distance calling."

"Miss Charlene is not up yet." It was obviously the maid.

"Do you have any idea what time she will be able to answer the phone?"

"After the party last night, I don't rightly know."

"Shall I leave word, sir?" the operator asked Jeff.

He hesitated an instant. "Yes. Ask her to call Mr. Jefferson in Beverly Hills."

"Yes, sir." The operator transmitted the message.

"I tell her soon as she get up. Though I say, after las' night I don't know when that be."

He hung up and settled down to wait.

By the time it was noon in Chicago he had given up. Might as well call The Doctor and report on last night's meeting.

The Doctor was on the phone instantly. He listened to Jeff but seemed to know everything about the meeting, for he said, "I understand the way you handled your New York trip was very electric!"

"You understand how?"

"I got reports, two different sets of reports last night. You should have called," Cone reproved him, but pleasantly.

"I thought it was too late."

"It's never too late for you, Jeff!" The Doctor assured him, though Jeff could remember a thousand times when he tried to get through to Cone at the office even during the day.

Oh, the joys of being wanted, especially for an actor, even when he knew he was being used. It was reassuring just to know there was someone who wanted to use him.

"You know, Jeff-baby," said The Doctor, "you have a way with people. When you let yourself go, you really have a way with people."

"Who called?" Jeff asked suddenly.

Though The Doctor resented such a naked direct question he answered it, "Abe Heller."

"Abe called last night?" Jeff was startled.

"No, this morning. Last night it was Ed Berry," The Doctor volunteered. "He loved the way you handled the meeting."

"He sure went all out to murder me!" Jeff responded.

"He said he didn't want it to look like a set-up."

"Yeah," Jeff answered, wondering, Does The Doctor ever go into any deal without having the game rigged?

"I asked Abe Heller to call you this morning," The Doctor said, "about releasing the news. I'd rather it didn't just leak. I mean it should break with an official statement from you as president of the Guild. Maybe you should call a news conference. Yes, that's the way to do it." He was trying to make his thought sound providential. "A news conference."

"I'll drive down to the office. Abe and I will discuss it," Jeff said.

"Good. Good," The Doctor said. And he hung up.

The press conference late that afternoon went off very well. Between them, Abe and Jeff had prepared a number of responses to the most logical and troublesome questions. Jeff had picked up some of Abe's pungent phraseology and used it most effectively when confronted by the press. The reporters' major doubts centered on the risks that were involved in giving TCA such a free hand. But instead of backing off, Jeff lauded The Doctor for his foresight and courage in risking so much to save an industry that others seemed willing to watch die.

When the last reporter had left the Guild board room, taking their photographers with them, Jeff felt that the deed was finally fact. He was glad that it was over, that he could turn back to his own career, to the challenge that lay ahead in New York. Throughout the day he had wanted to ask Abe Heller what deal he had made with The Doctor. But he didn't dare, for fear that Abe had made no deal, that he had taken his stand because he honestly believed it was the best and most logical move for the Guild to make.

As for Edgar Berry, that mystery was cleared up later without Jeff's ever asking. Within eight months of that crucial meeting, Berry was signed to play the lead in a TV series produced by TCA. One thing about The Doctor, he possessed Bastione's dedication to paying off both debts and transgressions.

The flight out of L.A. was smooth for the first hour. After that, and until they set down in Chicago to refuel, it was bumpy all the way. But Jeff hardly noticed the turbulence. He was thinking about Charlene. There might be time to call during the layover.

Any doubts he had about phoning were dissipated when they began their descent. The pilot announced that everyone would have to deplane for twenty-five minutes. Jeff reached into his pocket to find as many dimes as he could. They were hot in his hand by the time the plane had come to a stop. He was first at the door, first down the steps. He ran across the windy landing area to the terminal to seek out the row of telephones.

He reached the booths, selected the one at the end where he would be least likely to be overheard, swung the door closed, dialed. Only then did he realize that he was sweating. Finally there was an answer, the same voice he had heard before. No, Miss Charlene was not home, though she was expected any minute.

Jeff hung up and glanced at the large clock on the wall over the boarding gates. Twenty minutes. He still had twenty minutes and if she was expected home so soon . . . He started pacing between the gate and the telephones.

Four times he was stopped by passengers who recognized him. Two asked for autographs, one for a daughter, another for a grandson. Jeff smiled, tried to seem interested, but kept thinking about Charlene.

With eight minutes left he decided to try again. He went into the only free booth, dialed so hastily that midway he had to stop and start over again. This time the call went through but instead of a ring he heard only the discouraging and frustrating buzz of a busy signal.

She was home. She was on the phone. And being a woman, she would be on it a lot longer than eight minutes. He hung up, retrieved his dime, dialed again. Again there was a busy signal, but he kept at it, glancing at his wristwatch. Four minutes had gone by. They would be calling the passengers back to the plane.

The dime had just been returned to him again. He inserted it, fumbling, his fingers damp and slippery. He dialed, carefully, deliberately, so that he would not foul up. This time the phone rang.

"Miss Charlene? Yes, yes, Miss Charlene is home, just a moment, who shall I say is calling. Oh, I see, just a moment, please."

He waited, his eyes staring at the large clock over the gate. Two minutes left, if they were on time.

Then for the first time in many weeks he heard her voice. It was guarded, but she wouldn't have been so painfully breathy if she didn't feel the same urgency he did.

She barely managed, "Jeff."

"Yeah. It's me. I'm in Chicago at the airport."

"Don't come to the house!" she pleaded fearfully.

"I'm on my way to New York. I've got to be there tonight and I'll be staying for a few weeks. Why didn't you ever call back?"

"I . . . I couldn't. . . ." was all she said as if she dared no more.

"Can you talk, are you alone?"

"Yes, I'm alone." But she still seemed restrained.

"Then why didn't you call back? I waited all day."

"I know." She sounded frightened.

"Charlene? Darling, what's wrong?"

"I never should have called you!" she said suddenly.

"Why? What happened?" When she hesitated, he insisted, "You've got to tell me!"

The voice over the loudspeaker was announcing, "Passengers for American flight number three please board the aircraft. All passengers for American flight number three! All passengers!"

"Don't waste time! They're calling the flight. Tell me!" he persisted.

"I should never have called you. It was . . . I was a little drunk. It was the party."

"What party?"

"My . . . my engagement party." Then he heard her sobbing.

"Engagement? Who, Charlene? Talk to me!"

The loudspeaker began again: *"Will passenger Jeff Jefferson please report to gate seventeen, American Airlines paging passenger Jeff Jefferson."*

"Charlene, honey, listen to me. I have to run. Promise me one thing. You'll come to New York. I'm at the Plaza. Promise me you'll come."

"I can't, there's Marvin and everything," she pleaded.

"Marvin? Marvin Berg?"

"Yes. Marvin Berg," she enunciated carefully.

"Say that you have to come to New York to shop for your trousseau."

"Will passenger Jeff Jefferson please report to gate seventeen American Airlines."

"My mother will want to come along."

"Find some reason, some excuse, tell her anything, only come to New York, alone, darling, please?"

"Passenger Jefferson . . . passenger Jefferson . . ."

"I have to board now or I'll miss the flight. Promise me you'll come to New York. Promise!"

"I can't say now . . . but I'll think about it."

The stewardess was at the phone booth now, "Mr. Jefferson! We'll have to take off without you!"

Charlene overheard, for she said, "Go on, darling, catch your flight. I'll, I'll see you in New York."

"Good, good," was all that he could say as he hung up and turned to the stewardess whose anxiety was apparent.

He smiled at her and started back toward the gate. The stiff wind blowing across the landing area reminded him how heavily he had been sweating. But with Charlene's promise he could relax now. When she arrived he would change her mind about Marvin. Mrs. Marvin Berg. Ridiculous! He could laugh at it now though minutes before it was a pain in his gut.

He felt so good that he even forgave American Airlines for keeping the plane sitting at the gate for fifteen minutes after their damn rush to get him off the phone.

As soon as he landed in New York he spied Freddie

Feig among the waiting crowd. He remembered The Doctor had said he would be met at the airport, but Jeff never expected that Feig would come himself. He was flanked on one side by a uniformed chauffeur and on the other by a photographer with heavy camera and flash equipment. Freddie was smiling broadly, making his way through the debarking passengers like a salmon swimming upstream. He reached Jeff, held out his hand and asked, "Where are your baggage checks?"

Jeff surrendered them to the chauffeur. Then Freddie took Jeff by the arm, turned him around, led him back toward the aircraft.

"What the hell," Jeff said.

"Publicity shots!" Freddie said. "We're going to blanket the country with them."

"For a lousy television show?" Jeff asked.

"Jeff-sweetie, The Doctor says he wants Grade A star treatment for you. Okay, that's what you're going to get!"

They had him pose on the top step of the landing platform, holding his script in hand, waving at New York, smiling at the willing stewardesses. Then they posed him coming down the steps, and again at the foot of the steps.

The photographer even raced backwards across the landing area before them to take candid shots of Jeff and Freddie as they approached the building. When they reached the gate the chauffeur was there ready to lead them to the limousine.

On the way into Manhattan, Freddie asked, "Like a bite of supper or a drink before you turn in? We could go to the Stork. Or Twenty-One."

"No, thanks, I think I'll just go to the hotel. If I want anything, I'll order room service." Then in as casual a way as he could, he added, "I'll have some time to myself once I get settled, won't I?"

"Sure, sure," Freddie anticipated. "In fact, I got a couple of broads lined up."

"I didn't mean that," Jeff said. "I just want to be alone. I want privacy." Then he added, "After all, I have a lot of work to do." To himself he said, broads, they certainly are giving me first-class star treatment.

He wasn't sure that he had deceived Freddie, but it

didn't matter, just so long as he had time alone with Charlene.

He awoke to the phone ringing. When he heard Feig's voice he realized that he had been hoping that it would be Charlene.

Cheerfully, Freddie apologized, "Sorry, if I woke you, Jeff-baby, but I figured you're still operating on Coast time and you might be late for the first rehearsal."

Jeff reached for his watch, saw it was eight thirty and he was due way across town for the first reading at ten. "Oh," he grunted. "Thanks. I'll make it."

"Pick you up at nine-thirty," Freddie said.

"There's no need," Jeff began.

But Freddie intervened cheerfully, "My pleasure, sweetie, my pleasure."

Jeff hung up. Evidently Cone had given orders that Jeff Jefferson was to be shepherded every step of the way. It indicated how important this event was to The Doctor. That was reassuring as long as it didn't interfere with his free time once Charlene arrived.

The rehearsal hall was a huge ballroom in an old West Side hotel. The rest of the building operated mainly as a whore house. Although the director was already at work, the cast had not yet assembled. It became evident that this early call was only for Jeff.

The director was a gnome of a man, with wild hair and thick glasses. When the elevator door opened, Jeff's first sight of him was standing with his arms on his hips, surveying the area where the boundaries of every set and each large piece of furniture were marked off on the floor with masking tape. Suddenly the director asked the script girl who stood beside him, holding a big black leather book, "What the hell is *that?*"

"That's the bank vault," she said. "Where Valentine rescues the boy."

"Stinks!"

"It's exactly like the sketch you okayed," she said.

"Stinks! Get that designer up here right away!"

"He's out at the scenery shop on Long Island," she explained.

"Get him the fuck up here before they drive one single

nail into one piece of wood!" he commanded.

Spying Jeff and Freddie, he acknowledged their presence with a single forbidding gesture of his tiny forefinger, which said, wait and I will get to you in due time. He continued his inspection of the taped sets, asked the girl a few more questions, then dispatched her to call the designer. Finally he started toward Jeff and Freddie.

He held out his hand. His grip turned out to be far stronger than Jeff anticipated.

"Let's start out being friends," the gnome said. "We can work up into a fine keen hatred later. But for now we're friends. Jeff. And Bernie. Okay?"

"Okay."

"Now, pretty soon the cast'll come trooping in here to take a look at another Hollywood celebrity. Whom they have made up their minds to hate. Expect it. Don't resent it. On the other hand, don't pander to them. That's like feeding wild animals in the Central Park Zoo. They'll bite your hand off. Just be a *mensch*." He stopped to stare at Jeff. "You know what the term means?"

"Yes, I know."

"Good. Be a *mensch,* but still a Star. Don't try to be one of the boys. Be the Star, but a nice Star. If some bit actor goofs, don't blow. If the scene has to be done over again, do it. Don't complain. Because the poor bastard who blew his line is depending on this for his livelihood.

"Times I'll say something that mystifies you, don't react, don't question. I mean, if some other actor is lousing up the scene I may suddenly change my shooting plan to keep him off camera. That'll mean a change for you. If you don't like it, let me know during a break, not during rehearsal."

"Fine," Jeff said, remembering his own days as an extra.

"Above all," Bernie said, his diction quite precise now, "do not get into any test of strength with me in front of the company. I'm a little man, a funny-looking little man, but I can be the most vicious sonofabitch you ever met. So don't pull rank on me. You're the Star. I know that. But I'm the director. I want *you* to know *that*. Okay?"

Jeff hesitated, "Okay."

"Then we can be friends," Bernie said, starting toward

the script girl who was returning from the telephone.

When he was out of earshot, Freddie said, a bit embarrassed, "He's the genius of television. A prick. A mean, nasty prick. But a genius."

"I've met my share," Jeff said, letting his tension dissolve, though he still resented Bernie's lecture.

The rest of the cast began to assemble. Freddie made the introductions since the director was busy reviewing the set design. Over coffee Jeff met the girl who was to play the banker's daughter and his love interest. He also met the banker, a dignified actor named Homer Clinton, and the other minor characters in the play. The boy, the girl's young brother who was to be the object of Jimmy Valentine's heroic self-sacrifice was not there, having to attend school in the morning.

The girl, Claire Colton, was a fairly tall young woman. She had a pretty face, strong, with warm, intuitive eyes. If she hadn't been blond she would have reminded him of Charlene. But she was blond. And nicely built, he noticed at once. She came over to him, held out her hand. "I always think it's nice to shake hands with someone before you kiss them."

Jeff smiled. He would have liked to say something funny or bright but nothing came to him. That made him realize how tense he actually was. Perhaps she realized, too, for she held his cold hand a little longer than necessary.

Now the director was approaching them, calling out in his high, irritating voice, "Okay! We've wasted enough time. Let's get this show on the road." He signaled them to the long rehearsal table, ordered all paper coffee cups out of sight and set his stop watch before him.

"Now, I don't want a performance! But I do want a fair approximation of the pace. So off your ass and keep it moving. Okay!" Without waiting, he started his watch, mumbled words that sounded like, "Up on one . . . opening logo . . . music . . . . announce . . . title . . . billboard . . . first commercial . . ." all the while allowing the proper number of seconds to tick off. He continued to himself, a low mumble of key words: "Commercial . . . commercial . . . commercial . . . and into playoff . . . playoff . . . segue into Jimmy Valentine theme . . . then up on Cam-

era One for long shot of bank . . . move down the street
. . . (Some street! I'll rip that fucking designer's head off
and use it for a postage stamp!) . . . now, to the bank
door . . . and pan the bank interior from the door . . .
establish bank . . . now pick up reverse shot on Four, a
young man standing in the doorway, holding his suitcase,
to establish in our very brilliant way that he has just arrived in town . . . and is our *Star!"*

Mockery was evident in the ugly little man's reading of
that last line. But Jeff did not look at him or at anyone
else, though he could feel Claire stiffen a little beside
him. Then the director said suddenly, "Cue and first line.
Hit it!"

Without referring to his script Jeff read his first line of
dialogue to the girl. He made no special effort to perform, but by the time he had finished his first scene he
had let them all know that he had come here prepared,
that he knew his lines and his character, that he was
serious about the business of acting. The reading went
well. His confidence put the rest of the cast at ease. He
was not another Hollywood *lox* they would have to carry
through rehearsals.

The only problem during the reading arose when the
director had to stand in for the absent boy who was to
play the banker's son. Bernie read the lines in an intentionally bad imitation of a young boy's voice, letting
them all know his low estimate of the story and the script.
After that the reading became more tense, but Jeff controlled his anger and finished the scene, despite Bernie's
hammy outcries as the terrified boy trapped inside the
locked time vault.

All the while Freddie Feig sat at the end of the table,
his face growing redder and redder. Jeff felt his own face
burning, too, but he said nothing.

When the reading was over they got up from the table.
The Colton girl let her script book fall to the floor, scat-
tering the pages. While Jeff was helping her pick them up,
she took the opportunity to whisper to him. "Don't let this
snotty little bastard get on your nerves. You're fine. I'm
going to like falling in love with you."

But her encouragement was strictly professional. Before
the day was out she told Jeff about her children and her

husband, a successful dentist who only indulged her acting because both kids were now in nursery school and it
made her happy to be working.

Meantime, Freddie had gone over to talk to the director. What Freddie said to him, Jeff never discovered, but
it was obviously about his attitude, for when that little
session was over, Bernie rejoined the group in a more affable mood.

"We're about on time so there won't be any extensive
cutting, just a little tightening here and there for pace and
to suit the cameras. Otherwise, great!"

Jeff knew that his studying had not been wasted. During the breakdown of the scenes it was Jeff who was the
first to work completely without his book. Yet, in some
way, Jeff's very preparedness seemed to irk Bernie. Twice
when Jeff did not respond instantly to a floor direction,
Bernie took him by the arm and moved him to the right
spot.

The third time, Jeff said in a voice loud enough for the
entire cast to hear, "I'd heard you were a nasty little jerk,
but they never told me you were queer."

"What the hell does that mean?" the director asked viciously.

"I had a masseur once," Jeff continued calmly. "He
was always touching me that way, too. I never knew why,
until he made a pass. That's why I pull back every time
you touch me."

"Oh!" Bernie said attempting to appear satisfied with
the explanation.

"So if you don't mind," Jeff said, "don't touch me. Just
tell me what you want. I think I can manage it."

He sensed that the rest of the cast was with him after
that. He knew it at lunchtime when Claire and Homer
Clinton asked if he had any plans. Since Freddie had gone,
Jeff joined them at a large restaurant around the corner
on upper Broadway. On the walk over Claire said, "You
irritated him."

"How? I tried not to."

"By knowing your lines, for one thing."

"Is that wrong?"

"Bernie likes to have actors come in from the Coast
unprepared and inept. It gives him a sense of mastery,

and it adds to the repertoire of stories he tells at parties about how he taught this big star how to act, or saved that one's performance from being a complete disaster. It's his only chance to be a big man," she said sadly.

"I know the type."

"But he's a good director," she added. "And I don't think you're going to have any more trouble with him." Then she asked suddenly, "Did that really happen? With the masseur?"

Jeff laughed. "Of course not."

"Good," she said.

"Why?" he asked.

"I don't know. I'm just glad that queers don't get their hands on men like you. There are so few of you left."

"What do you think would have happened if there *had* been a masseur like that? And he *did* make a pass?"

"I just don't like the thought," she said. "It makes my skin crawl. I've got two sons."

"Okay, Mother, I will not ever fool around with fags. That's a promise." They laughed together. It felt good, having a woman beside him with whom he could be friendly without being involved.

When they reached the restaurant, he excused himself, went to the phone booth, called the hotel. No word about Charlene. She had not checked in. She had not called. He tried to make himself believe the reason was that she was on her way from Chicago, but before they left the restaurant he called the hotel again. Still no word.

During the afternoon they continued to break down every scene into the smallest bits of business—moves, indications of camera location, prop placement, the entire detailed process that makes it seem that the scene will never again coalesce. But one thing Bernie always did. After each breakdown he had them run the entire scene from start to finish, twice. That helped.

Freddie Feig had been right. The gnome was a mean, nasty prick but a very thorough competent director. That fact enabled Jeff to endure the first day which at the outset had seemed to justify all the fears he had first suffered when The Doctor mentioned doing a live show in New York.

Just as they were running the last scene, Freddie Feig

THE KINGMAKER   363

appeared in the rehearsal hall. He was accompanied by a tall, executive-type who watched the proceedings skeptically. When the run-through was over, Freddie came across the floor, the man trailing at his heels. Obviously Freddie was intent on saying something to Jeff before the man reached them. Just as obviously the man intended to prevent it.

When they reached Jeff he was buttoning his collar and putting on his tie. Freddie had to make his introduction with no prologues or explanations. "Jeff, this is Carl Brewster of S.S.D. & O. He's the ALUMCO account executive."

Jeff smiled, shook hands with Brewster who smiled, too, but could not conceal his inner concern. After a moment of polite conversation, Brewster drifted over to speak to the director. It was obvious Brewster was asking some important questions. And just as obvious that the questions related to Jeff. Jeff remembered now, Brewster was the man The Doctor had warned him about.

"What's he so worried about?" Jeff asked Freddie.

"First thing you got to learn about television," Freddie explained, "account executives are always nervous. Every show, they're all over the director. How is the script? Is it too long? How is the cast?"

"How is the *star?*" Jeff interrupted angrily.

"Nothing personal. They ask about every star. We had Olivier do a guest shot and they were even worried about him. It's the name of the game. Without their ulcers those guys would be very lonely."

Just then Claire came over to say good night. Unexpectedly, she kissed Jeff on the cheek.

"I did that," she teased, "so that I can go home and tell my husband, Today I kissed a big movie star. That'll make him jealous! And nothing makes a Jewish dentist more passionate than being jealous."

They both laughed, till Jeff asked, "Are you married to a Jew?"

Claire's smile was suddenly gone. "Yes, why? Do you mind?"

"No. I just want to know, if you don't mind talking about it. Does it work? I mean, really, deep down, does it?"

"It works. Believe me, it works." She said it with a
compassion that let him know instantly that she suspected
why he was asking.

"Thanks. Good night. See you in the morning." He
reached for her hand, held it, then kissed her full on the
lips.

"Now you can tell him the star kissed back. He won't
let you get any sleep at all tonight!"

Jeff and Freddie took the limousine across town. On
the way Freddie told Jeff that the director would call him
every evening at the hotel. That way each could bring up
problems and gripes without airing them in front of the
whole cast.

When the limousine pulled up at the Plaza canopy
Freddie volunteered, "Don't forget. If there's anything else
I can do . . ."

"There *is* one thing. . . ." Jeff started to say.

"What?" Freddie snapped, eager to please.

"Stop all this bullshit! This Grade A Star treatment! I
am a star, but not an idiot. I can find my way crosstown
in a cab. I don't need to be taken and brought back like
a two-year-old. And I don't drink too much, so I don't
have to be checked on every night. I am regular in all my
habits, from bowel movements to showing up at rehearsals.
So just leave me alone!"

Without waiting for an answer, he bolted out of the
limousine, started up the stairs into the Plaza.

There was no message waiting at the desk. Jeff went
to his suite, deciding to order a few drinks, but saw that
someone had sent up a bottle each of scotch, bourbon,
and vodka, complete with a thermos of ice and plenty of
soda and tonic. There was a neat card reading, "Courtesy
of the Plaza."

More Grade A Star treatment.

He did not turn on any of the lights in the room. He
mixed himself a drink, went to stare out at the Park and
think about Charlene. Even when the call came through
from Bernie, Jeff barely reacted. He murmured assent, let
the director talk, then hung up without expressing any
opinions of his own.

More than an hour had gone by and there was still
no call from Charlene. He was ready to go out to dinner,

except that he wasn't hungry. Even if he were, he did not want to eat alone. He thought of looking in the phone book, finding Claire's number and calling her. But he had no idea what her married name was.

Still, he picked up the Manhattan book, started to search under the C's, Cohen, Cokins, Colsten, Colton . . . he found it, *Colton, Claire.* And right beneath it, *Colton, Irving, Dr.,* same address. So that was her married name. He decided not to call after all. He would wait.

By eight o'clock Jeff found himself threatening Charlene. If she didn't show, he'd take Freddie up on that offer of the broads. But he knew he really wouldn't. Instead he decided he would call Claire. She'd know, she'd understand. She knew immediately this afternoon when he asked how it was to be married to a Jew. He lifted the phone but the operator was already on. "Mr. Jefferson?"

"Yes."

"I never had a chance to ring. Call for you, Mr. Jefferson."

"Okay!" he answered swiftly. Then he heard Charlene's voice.

"Jeff, darling, is that you?"

"Charlene! Where are you?"

"Thank God you're still there! I thought you'd gone out to dinner or something."

"Where are you?" he persisted.

"La Guardia," she said, giving him the whole world in those few syllables.

"I'll be right out to get you!" he said.

"That's silly," she said, laughing, relieved now that she had found him. "By the time you get out here, I can be in New York."

"Okay," he said. "Get right into a cab. I'll be downstairs."

"No you won't," she said more soberly. "Let's not have any big scene where a dozen of my father's friends might see me."

"Okay. I'll wait here. Suite Twelve-O-Four. But hurry!"

Charlene reached the Plaza in less than half an hour. She checked in, had her luggage taken up to her room which was on Jeff's floor. After freshening up, she picked up the phone, asked for Twelve-O-Four and said softly,

"I'm here. Twelve-Ten." She hung up and began to tremble.

If he hadn't knocked on the door within seconds she would have started to cry. They embraced even before the door was closed.

He held her close to him. It felt every bit as good as he had remembered. "You're not disappointed?" she asked.

"God, no!"

"I thought you would be. After all, now it's just me. No romantic desert. No seclusion. Just us."

"What's wrong with just us?"

"I meant, sometimes you meet someone at a party or during the summer at some hotel and get a crush. You can't wait for them to call. But when you see them, you wonder, What did I ever see in him?"

"What *did* you ever?" he asked.

She kissed him. Her excitement made her ramble on.

"And there was the plane trip! We had a storm in Chicago. More than two hours late getting off. I thought, he'll think I'm not coming. He won't wait. He'll be angry. And it isn't my fault. It's United Airlines. And the weather. But he'll blame me. I wanted to get off the plane and call. But of course I couldn't. So I sat there tense, hot. They don't put the air conditioning on when they're sitting on the ground. I thought to myself, take this damn thing up in the air! Let's get going! I don't care if we crash! Then I said, Before we crash, I want to see him. Just once. Just once more."

She held him tightly, her tall strong body against his, eager, trembling again. He looked into her face, at her violet eyes, moist now. She was more the little girl than he had ever seen before. She seemed ashamed and embarrassed at her own weeping. Then she broke from him saying, "I have to unpack." While she did he sat on the edge of the bed admiring the way she moved.

When she reached the bottom of the suitcase she took out something and threw it to him. He caught it in one hand, a bottle of his after-shave lotion, from Dunhill's.

"You don't know how many men I had to ask, how many shops I had to go to, how many fragrances I had to test till I found out which brand it was." She laughed. "So I bought some. I said to myself, If he's changed brands I don't want to know it. Put some on!"

"I have some on," he protested, laughing.

"Put some on out of my bottle."

He poured some on his hands and patted it onto his face. She kissed him, then let her face rest against his cheek.

"That's better, much better," she said.

He whispered softly, "There's a girl on the show. She plays opposite me."

"And she's blond and good-looking and I hate her," Charlene said, kidding.

"How did you know?"

"All my life, from the time I was eleven I was always running second to some blonde," she joked, secure in his arms.

But he said quite seriously, "She's married to a Jew."

"So is my mother," Charlene said, trying to avoid the subject.

"You know what I mean. She's not Jewish. He is. And she says it works just fine."

She slipped from his arms, "Let's go to dinner, or have a drink, before we start talking about that. Please, Jeff?"

"Okay," he said in a whisper.

She changed clothes. He watched her, her long graceful legs, her good thighs which had embraced him so many times, her breasts, very round and high, but he did not make any advances. He was eager, hungry for her, but it would be even better if they waited.

They walked down Fifth Avenue to a small, expensive French restaurant that Charlene remembered. She had eaten there once with her mother.

On the way he asked, "What did you tell them?"

"Nothing," she said.

"Then how did you arrange to get away?"

"I thought you meant about you," she said, then explained. "I used the most convenient excuse. I had to do some shopping in New York."

Because she had so carefully avoided the word, he asked, "What *kind* of shopping?"

She hesitated, then forced herself to say, "Trousseau shopping." She turned to face him. "I didn't want to think

about that. Until afterwards. Maybe not until I was at
the airport and starting back. Don't make me talk about
it now."

"We have to. That's what it's all about. Not just making
love. Not just going to bed. But you and me. Together.
Married."

"Jeff, please, not now." She looked around at the people who were staring. He nodded almost imperceptibly
but enough to let her know that he was not going to
embarrass her. "Not till I'm ready to talk about it,
please?" she begged.

"Okay, okay," he said.

He tried not to talk about it through dinner. She asked
about his show, but because he was far from sure about
the outcome he didn't welcome any discussion. He said
the show was "Okay," the director "pretty good, I guess."
When she suggested coming to a rehearsal, he demurred.
Visitors made the cast self-conscious, and, under the circumstances, it would be embarrassing to identify her.

They walked back to the Plaza slowly, as though
neither of them wanted to reveal how much each wanted
the other. They picked up their keys at the desk and she
went up to her room first. He followed after lingering at
the newsstand in the lobby for a few moments. When he
reached her room she was wearing a lacy peignoir.

There was no time, no patience now for talking. They
were naked in each other's arms, moving against one another, with hands that could barely restrain themselves.
Once he was in her and felt the strength and urgency of
her desire he knew at once that since those days in Palm
Springs there had been no one else. No man had as much
as touched her since then. It made him feel good to discover that he had been wanted for so many weeks.

But there was an uneasy undercurrent that scratched at
his consciousness all during their first encounter. If she
had wanted him this much yet refused to call, except that
one hasty time when she was a bit drunk, then her need
alone would not determine her decision. It seemed to him
that somehow the more she loved him, the more intensely she gave herself to him in her moment of orgasm,
the less chance there was of his winning. Whatever spell

her father held over her, it was stronger even than her desires.

It was after midnight. The room was dark and from the outside only the sound of an occasional car could be heard. They lay side by side on their backs staring up at the ceiling. He felt for her hand and held it.

"That night," he began.

Though she knew very well, she asked, "What night?"

"That night you called."

"I told you, I was drunk."

"You don't drink enough to get drunk."

"I did that night."

"That's what I mean. If you had to drink that much, your engagement was wrong. You knew it was wrong. And if it was wrong then, it's wrong now!"

Instead of answering she turned her long warm body to him. When she sought his lips he kissed back and lost again the chance to convince her. She had seduced him into silence.

When he woke it was morning. He eased out of bed gently so as not to wake her. She slept like a child, the wrinkled sheet drawn up between her legs, the topmost corner pressed against her face.

He returned to his suite, took his shower, ordered coffee, dressed and then wrote her a note, "Darling, sleep well, have a good day. Back about six. Love! And *think*, for God's sake, *think!* about *us!*"

Rehearsal was a repetition of the first day, except there was no reading at the outset. They blocked scene after scene until the lunch break. He made pleasant conversation with Claire, teasing her about her love life the night before. Only when he asked after Irving did she look up from her coffee and remark, "I never told you his name."

He confessed he had looked her up in the phone book. "Then *she* called," said Claire, "and you didn't need me or Irving anymore. I'm glad. All day yesterday you seemed like the loneliest man in the world. That's one of the reasons I kissed you." Then she added, "She's the reason you were asking yesterday about mixed marriage."

He nodded again.

"Well, a marriage isn't between Jews and gentiles. It's between two people. And if either one of them has strong guilts about it, it won't work. I know couples who were very much in love, but the guilts were stronger. For your sake I hope it works."

"I wish you would talk to her," Jeff suggested suddenly.

"Uh uh," she refused. "That's not something an outsider talks about. You talk to each other. That's the only way. Even then, it doesn't work out the way you think. With Irving, the problem was children. He insisted his children had to be brought up Jewish. So I agreed. When the time came, *I* was the one who had to take them to Hebrew school and synagogue for holidays. It turned out Irving didn't really know much about being Jewish. Now I'm a better Jew than he is. I'll tell you one thing, his sons are certainly going to be better Jews than he is!

"So you can't plan it all in advance. You have to want it enough, be free enough to make it work."

They went back to rehearsal. At the end of the day Carl Brewster showed up again with Freddie Feig. Freddie was obviously the nervous one today. Jeff could tell from the way his tiny hairline mustache flickered as he tried to smile. Whether it was Carl's presence or his own self-consciousness after the way Jeff had read him out yesterday afternoon didn't matter. Carl was anxious. Freddie was nervous. And Jeff hated them both.

Then the rehearsal was over. Jeff was free to go. He and Claire shared a cab. She dropped him at the Plaza on her way to East End Avenue where she lived. Just before he got out she said, "Maybe you'll bring her up to the house one night before you go back."

"Thanks, I'd love to. It might help!"

He ran up the steps, hurried into a crowded elevator, stabbed some poor overdressed woman in her large bosom with his rehearsal book, apologized and finally reached the twelfth floor. He went to Charlene's room first, almost knocked, listened instead. She was there. His fear that she might have gone dissolved and he went on to his own suite, got out of his clothes and took a long hot shower.

He dried himself, glancing at his body in the mirror. He was in damned good shape for forty-two. Then he slapped on lots of Dunhill, and settled down on the sofa to call. She answered on the very first ring.

"Come to my place for a drink?" he asked.

"Uh huh," she whispered.

In a moment there was a knock. He opened the door and she clung to him. "You're going to try to seduce me," she said. "No man uses that much after-shave without an ulterior purpose."

"You gave it to me."

She kissed him again and said, "You lured me here on the promise of a drink."

He turned to make two drinks at the small portable bar. She said very sadly, "We can't even joke about us. We don't seem to come up with very funny lines. How was rehearsal?"

"Okay. I talked some more with Claire."

"The lady with the Jewish dentist."

"The lady with the Jewish dentist. And the two Jewish kids. She told me all about that. It didn't sound so difficult. I mean if that's a requirement of yours, or your father's, I can agree to that. I'll even take them to synagogue on holidays."

She tried to treat it as a joke and laughed. But he didn't. In a few moments neither did she. They sat, stared at each other across the darkening room, glasses held in icy hands, untouched. Then she turned away, rose, put aside her glass, stared out of the window down at the park, at the lights, the cars and a whole city going back to where it had come from this morning. He went to her, put his arm around her, pressed his cheek against hers, stared out with her. She inhaled so deeply and exhaled so tensely that he thought she was crying. His fingers found her eyes but they were dry.

"The whole world's going home, except us," she said sadly.

"We could," he said.

She didn't answer. They stared out until the room was in complete darkness and the park lights came on.

"What else did she say?" Charlene asked suddenly.

"Claire? All about how she had to take over and make Jews of their kids. How much she enjoyed it. Mainly, that if two people want it enough, it works."

Charlene didn't answer. When he was convinced that she wouldn't, he said, "I'll get some clothes on and we'll go to dinner."

"Can't we have dinner sent up?"

"Of course," he agreed quickly.

It was hours later. A steady rain was attacking the windows, driven by a strong east wind. They lay on his bed, he on his back, she on her side, facing him. She laughed, a quiet personal little laugh.

"What's funny?" he asked.

"You. In synagogue. And in *cheder*," she teased.

"*Cheder?*" he asked, having trouble with the harsh *ch* sound.

"Hebrew school. You see, you don't even know the simplest words."

"I could learn. I could even get that little gnome Bernie to direct me in the proper pronunciation. I'm sure he'd love that. A few lessons and you could pass me off to your father as a rabbi."

"You, Barry Fitzgerald and Bing Crosby," she said, laughing.

He kissed her. It was the end of the conversation.

Rehearsals had settled into a routine. Jeff and Claire always went home in the same cab. She would drop him at the Plaza, he would protest, wanting to pay his share. But she would laugh and say, "I'm married to a rich dentist. I can afford it. Besides, I don't get many chances to be seen at the Plaza with a movie star. Some producer might discover me and make me famous. I'm using you."

In the evenings he and Charlene began going out. They went to the Stork, sat in the small, very exclusive Cub Room. Billingsley sent over champagne and sat down a moment to check out Charlene. He didn't like strangers in his Cub Room, especially very attractive girls. He didn't want the place to get a reputation as a hangout for call girls. Kept women, okay. Adultresses, okay, as long as their husbands weren't likely to drop in and create a scene. An attractive young girl from Chicago, whose father Billingsley knew was certainly okay.

Another night they went to the theater. Between acts people recognized Jeff, nudged each other, slyly pointed him out. Charlene loved it. Especially when people whispered "Course we've seen her in pictures. I just can't remember her name." They both laughed over that. He joked, "Will you still love me when you're a star? I've heard all about those show business marriages."

One night when they stopped at the message desk Jeff found several notes. One from The Doctor. Urgent. Call back. Jeff decided he wouldn't. If The Doctor was concerned about Charlene, Jeff didn't want to know it. Charlene had a couple of messages which seemed to bother her. When they got out of the elevator, instead of going to his suite, she pleaded having to make a phone call. She started down the hall toward her own room. He went after her, took her hand, glanced at the message slips.

Her father had called—and two school friends. There was one more message. "Mr. Marvin Berg. Please call back. Urgent. Says you know the number."

"You going to call him?" Jeff asked.

"I have to."

"What are you going to say?" he demanded.

"I'll find something to say."

"He's going to want to know when you're coming back. What will you tell him?"

"That I have to stay in New York . . . fittings and things . . ."

" 'and things'? Is that what I am?"

"What do you want me to tell him?" she asked.

"The truth. The engagement's over. You're staying here with me. And we're getting married."

"That'll come later. I have to find some way of telling my folks first."

"There's only one way. You pick up the phone. You call your father. You say, 'Papa, I can't marry Marvin because I am getting married to Jeff.' That's all you have to say."

She hesitated, and he urged, "Do it now! Tell him!" He was so sure she would that he released her hand, watched her go down the hall to her room.

As he let himself into his suite his phone rang. It was The Doctor.

"Christ, kid, where you been? Why didn't you call back?" Cone asked, pretending to be jovial. Before Jeff could answer, he continued, "How's it going?"

"Okay, I guess. We work hard, get along okay, even though the director is a prick."

The Doctor laughed. "From the reports I get it's going

a hell of a lot better than just okay. Can't wait to see it when I get there." Jeff knew that wasn't The Doctor's reason for calling. "That other material, you're working on that, aren't you? Rehearsing it by yourself? At night?"

That last phrase told the story. The Doctor had learned about Charlene. Jeff had no patience for fencing. He said, "I know that material cold. I don't have to spend my nights on it."

"I know," The Doctor said somberly. "Well, what I really called to say, I had a long talk with Joanne today. I convinced her that the minute we sell your series, she should discuss the divorce. A lot hangs on next Saturday."

"I know, Doctor," Jeff said and The Doctor was content to hang up. Without ever mentioning the subject he had indicated that he knew all about Charlene and he was using the information for his own purposes. Okay, Jeff said to himself, okay. I don't care, as long as it works for me!

There was a soft knock at his door. He crossed the room and flung open the door. "Well, did you tell him?"

"He wasn't home. Some Bar Association meeting, his mother said."

"I don't mean Marvin! I mean your father! After all, that's really who I'm taking you away from!"

"Jeff . . ."

"Even before you ever thought seriously about Marvin we had *the problem*," which is what they had come to call it.

"Jeff, don't do it," she pleaded.

"Do what?"

"Don't be angry with my father. You'll destroy something if you do. It's not his fault. We created this. Don't become angry with him."

He held her, his cheek against hers. "All I know is that the night you got engaged you couldn't face it without getting drunk. And when you got drunk, who did you call? Your father? Or Marvin? No! Me! That has to mean something." When she didn't answer, he persisted. "It has to!"

"Only don't hate my father," she said.

"Okay," he agreed readily. "I won't hate him. I'll love him if he'll just get out of our way. If you marry me it won't destroy the whole State of Israel. I can't tell you how many Jewish men in Hollywood are married to gentile girls. Half the producers and writers I know."

"That's different. For some reason that's not considered as bad as a Jewish girl marrying out of the faith."

"I'll talk to Claire. Arrange for us to visit them Sunday night. Then you'll see. Okay?"

"Okay," she said, not agreeing so much as closing the subject.

He kissed her to seal the bargain. Their kiss grew into a mutual seeking for each other. This time she seemed to be the aggressor. He felt that she had made her decision and, having done so, rid herself of all guilts and restraints. The night at Claire's, he thought, would turn out to be a little celebration.

Next morning, as soon as Claire arrived at rehearsal Jeff spoke to her.

"Would Sunday be all right, after we get the show out of the way?"

It took her a moment to realize what he was asking, then she broke into a big smile. "Progress? Good! Sunday would be fine. In fact, come for dinner. I'll order a brisket and make pot roast and kashe. If you don't know what it is, I'm sure she does. If she doesn't know then she's not the right Jewish girl for you. Sunday, at six. My two *yeshiva bochers* will still be up."

"Yeshivah . . ." But he couldn't manage the second word. "What does that mean?"

"To explain what it *used* to mean would take forever. These days it means they go to a very progressive nursery school that's affiliated with a very reformed synagogue."

As the day of the show grew nearer Bernie became more sarcastic than ever. Brewster began showing up at rehearsals right after lunch. On the last day in the rehearsal hall when Jeff went up in his lines, Brewster no longer made any attempt to hide his fears.

After a long, heated discussion with Brewster and Freddie, the director came over to Jeff.

"Look, Jeff, if that happens on air, don't worry about it. The stage manager is always handy to slip in under camera and feed you the line. So don't worry. Just don't freeze."

"Tell Brewster to relax. I'll be okay," Jeff snapped back.

"He doesn't get paid to relax. Account executives are the Jews of the advertising business. One mistake and they have to put their packs on their backs and start moving."

"To avoid a *pogrom*," Jeff volunteered.

Bernie seemed surprised, but pleasantly so. "Hey, you're okay," he said as if he had just made a discovery. Then he added confidentially, "Look, I'll keep that bastard off your back the next four days. Just hang in there. You're going to make it. And you'll be fine."

But, despite all assurances, once they started to work in the studio, things became even worse. Confronted by the reality of multiple cameras, Jeff's performance gradually disintegrated.

The morning of the second day he went up so completely that Bernie had to interrupt rehearsals with a ten-minute break.

The word must have got out. Before they broke for lunch Carl Brewster showed up. He had spies in the control room. Ten minutes after Brewster, Freddie Feig appeared with Spencer Gould. Freddie, too, had his spies among the technical crew. At the lunch break, Freddie and Spence came onto the studio floor. The presence of two cobras at the same rehearsal signaled a full-scale alert. Jeff knew his performance was the cause of it.

As soon as rehearsals resumed, Freddie and Spence were able to have a quiet word together. They agreed there was only one thing to do—call The Doctor. Have him fly in tonight! They could not afford to wait.

Toward the end of the next day The Doctor strode into the studio which put everyone on notice both as to the importance of the show and the degree of the emergency.

When rehearsal was over The Doctor invited Jeff to dinner, but he refused. Cone settled for a drink in the Oak bar at the hotel.

He never mentioned Charlene but talked only about the show. He touched casually on the not unexpected difficulties that had developed and dwelt on the high hopes they all had for the play and the intense interest on the Coast among Jeff's friends. Many of the Guild actors were waiting for a Jeff Jefferson TV Series and the parts it would provide.

In his own understated way, The Doctor was saying

that Saturday night *had* to work—not just for Jeff or TCA, but for all the actors, directors, and writers who were depending on him.

Jeff listened and the burden only became greater, the tension worse. At which point The Doctor, sensing that, said, "Jeff, remember, if this works, it will solve all your other problems too."

It was as close as The Doctor ever came to mentioning Charlene. But he knew that would give Jeff enough incentive to see him through Saturday night. With a slap on the back, he sent Jeff up to her.

In the elevator, Jeff said to himself, Strange about that little man, even when you didn't believe a word he said he had a strong influence on you. The fear was still there but somehow it seemed easier to bear, even possible to overcome.

7

Saturday morning dawned gray and chilly. He rose earlier than he needed to, left Charlene still sleeping on his side of the bed. He dressed quietly and walked crosstown to the studio. He was the first cast member there. He went to his dressing room feeling cold and stiff. When his dresser brought him hot coffee he didn't drink it, just held the paper cup to warm his hands.

At last the speaker in the room crackled to life and Bernie announced, "Cast onstage, please! Entire company onstage!"

They assembled at the bank vault. For once Bernie did not raise his voice. He spoke softly, addressing himself more to Jeff than anyone else.

"Okay, kids. This is *Der Tag. N* day for Bernie. *I* am the one entitled to be nervous today. You all know your lines, your moves, your interpretations. But me, I have to worry that every idiot cameraman makes the right move at the right time, and if one of them doesn't, what the hell do I improvise for Bernie. The mean, nasty little prick who tortured you for weeks is going to go through hell. Say a prayer for me. And thank your lucky stars that you're actors, not directors."

By taking the tension, the risks, and the blame onto himself, Bernie had served to ease their tension, especially Jeff's.

And he had done it in precisely the way The Doctor had instructed him to do.

Throughout the day Jeff was kept constantly active. When they were supposed to break for lunch, Bernie found a camera move that he claimed did not work. He imposed on Jeff's cooperative nature to do the scene over twice until the problem was straightened out. There was no time

for Jeff to go out for lunch, but he found hot soup and a
sandwich waiting on his dressing table. While he was eating The Doctor dropped by with a handful of yellow envelopes. He'd taken the liberty of opening them. Telegrams, scores of telegrams from Jeff's friends, actors, other
unions, from The Doctor's secretary Alise, from two writers who'd been involved in the congressional hearings, even
from Lee Mandell in Washington who said his whole law
office would be watching tonight.

The entire world, The Doctor was saying, was rooting
for Jeff to succeed and was sure that he would.

The Doctor was beaming.

"You were just great, Jeff! Great! The whole company says they've never seen a Hollywood Star put himself out for a show the way you have. A few more hours
and it'll be over. Then we do our piece and you're a free
man. With a fortune staring you in the face. And a whole
new life!"

He eased Jeff onto the cot. "Now lie down. Take a little rest. Nobody's earned it more. We'll call you when
they're ready." The Doctor patted him on the shoulder
and left.

Once Jeff was safely back on camera again, The Doctor took Freddie and Spence aside. "It's working. Bernie
just has to keep him busy until air time. He must not be
allowed to have a minute to think."

"But he's so cold, he's not giving," Freddie moaned.

"He'll give, he'll give," The Doctor said. "Meantime,
Freddie, it's your job to get Carl Brewster the hell out of
this studio when the show is over so Jeff and I can cut
those other pieces."

"Don't worry. I've got a table at Twenty-One. By the
time this is over he'll be so damn glad to get a drink in
his hand I'll have no trouble at all."

"Good! That's all I'd need, to have him around when
I'm trying to get Jefferson relaxed and folksy and warm
for his host spots."

They had finished the last dress rehearsal. Bernie dismissed the cast and turned to The Doctor, Freddie, Spencer,
and Brewster. "Okay, bosses? Any complaints? Last minute
flashes of genius?"

The Doctor said mildly, "Fine. It's just fine, Bernie."

Freddie and Spence murmured their agreement. Carl Brewster was the only one who objected.

"You call that a performance?" he demanded. "He's a zombie! You didn't have to send all the way to Hollywood for that!"

"He's going to be okay!" The Doctor insisted. "He's saving it for the air."

"And if he gets on air and we find out that he's got nothing to save, then what?" Brewster demanded.

"What do you want us to do?" The Doctor shot back.

"Well, do something, say something. Somebody talk to him!" Brewster half commanded, half pleaded.

"Would *you* like to talk to him now? Would you like to go into his dressing room and bawl the shit out of him twelve minutes before air time? Be my guest!" The Doctor invited, knowing full well that account executives never *do*. They only suggest or ask others to do. On their own, they are eunuchs. "I say we don't upset the man. He is a pro and a conscientious actor. When the moment comes he'll rise to it."

The Doctor turned to Bernie. "He's in your hands. If you feel he should be talked to, you talk to him. If you think he's best left alone, leave him alone."

Bernie hesitated a moment, then pressed down the key. "Cast, please? I want a moment of your time."

They gathered, exhausted, nervous, lending themselves to touch-ups by makeup men and hairdressers while Bernie talked.

"We've got a nice comfortable show. I mean, we're on time. We don't have to stretch, we don't have to race. If we slow down, the floor manager will give you a speed-up. If we're racing, he'll slow you down. For the rest, you're ready. Believe me, I've seen casts in my time and this one is ready! And no small part of it is due to Mr. Jefferson. I've never seen a star work so hard for a show as he has for this one. I want to tell him now, in front of all of you, how much I appreciate it.

"I wish you could have been in the control room after the last dress and heard the comments. Fabulous! Just fabulous!"

He shook Jeff's hand, kissed Claire on the cheek, said to the group at large, "Break a leg!"

They were waiting tha. last sixty seconds before air. Jeff stood just outside the bank set in which he would make his first appearance. Claire moved silently alongside him and whispered, "If I kiss you on the cheek my lipstick will show, so!" She raised his hand and kissed it. "You'll be great!"

Suddenly they were on air. Jeff remembered moving into position at the door of the bank and that was all he remembered. Then that special providence which looks after drunks, fools, and actors took over. He went through the rest of the show instinctively. The only thing he was aware of was that he was not trembling and that he didn't hate it as he had expected he would.

Then it was over. Claire was at his side, kissing him, this time as Claire, not the banker's daughter. She was saying, "We'll have a double celebration tomorrow! The show *and* Charlene!" The other cast members crowded around to say their good-byes and thank Jeff for making it a pleasant experience. Even Carl Brewster looked relieved and happy. Bernie actually kissed Jeff on the cheek, betraying the enormous doubts he had felt during rehearsals about Jeff's ability to deliver. But this was no time for recriminations, even unspoken ones. It was over. He'd made it. Now if he could get away long enough to call Charlene. But The Doctor had a tight grip on his arm. When he tried to free himself, The Doctor only shook his head in a gesture of warning.

Freddie was urging Carl Brewster to come have a drink at Twenty-One, but Brewster, in the exhilaration of relief, kept insisting that they wait for Jeff. They would all go out and celebrate together!

"It'll take him a while to get out of costume and make-up," Freddie argued. "And he'll probably want to shower. He'll catch up with us later. Right, Jeff-baby?"

Jeff nodded, but Carl said, "After the performance he delivered tonight, *we* wait for *him!*"

The Doctor's face was taking on that stiff immobile look that he reserved only for times of greatest anger and frustration. Freddie could read it. He took Carl by the arm. "Come on, Carlie, let's go! I need a drink!"

Unfortunately, by this time Brewster had noticed that the crew had not turned off their cameras. They were having their cigarettes as they did during a break, but were not retiring their equipment as they normally would after a show. Instead of the strong overhead lights going off to allow the studio to cool down from the intense heat, the lighting was actually being intensified.

"Carlie?" Freddie was insisting.

Suspicious, Brewster demanded, "What the hell's going on here?"

Spence tried to intervene. "Go on, Carl, we'll join you at Twenty-One."

By now Brewster had become so incensed that he looked around, saw the floor manager writing large crayon letters on cue cards. Pushing Spence aside, Brewster rushed across to stand over the floor manager and read Jeff's copy as Host for Consolidated Motors. He wheeled, turning on Spence, Freddie and The Doctor. "You bastards! What the hell is the meaning of this? Are you pirating my show to make a pilot for C.M.? Of all the fucking nerve!"

"Carl, please?" Freddie tried to calm him.

Brewster brushed aside Freddie's hands. "This whole thing is going to stop right now!"

Whereupon The Doctor moved between Freddie and Brewster and said, "Carl, for your own sake, I say get out of here! But if you insist on staying, get into that control room and shut up!"

Small as The Doctor was, when he spoke in that tone people obeyed. Brewster said like a chastised little boy, "Yeah? We'll see about that." But he started toward the control room, with Freddie following. Feig looked back only once, apologizing for his failure to handle Brewster in this critical moment.

Through it all Jeff stood by, embarrassed. The scene had made the whole plan seem even more clandestine, his participation in it more shabby, but The Doctor had no intention of giving him time to think.

"Jeff, I want you to go to your dressing room. Get out of that costume. Wash, shave, and put on the suit I had sent over from your hotel." When Jeff protested, The Doctor explained, "I didn't want you to bother with details today so I called Charlene and had everything sent over. Now go. I want the real Jeff Jefferson, not Jimmy Valentine."

"I have to make a call," Jeff protested.

"There's no time," said The Doctor, sending Jeff off to his dressing room.

When he had changed and shaved, The Doctor appeared with the makeup man. Evidently they had a pre-discussed plan, for at various stages in the process he would turn to The Doctor and ask, "Okay, sir?" The Doctor would nod or else make a cryptic suggestion.

"Darken the hairline," he said at one point. "Blonds wash out." Later he said, "Don't take anything away from his strong jawline. . . ."

Each time the makeup man complied, with a touch, a dab, a pencil mark. Then he stood back waiting The Doctor's approval. Finally the little man was satisfied. They were ready. When they went back to the studio, the technical director was calling over the intercom, "Cut the smoking. I'll turn on the air conditioning just long enough to clear the air. Then I have to cut it because we're going right for a take."

"First time?" a surprised cameraman asked toward the hanging mike.

"On this job, every time is a take!" the technical director called back.

The Doctor walked Jeff to the vault set, where three of the four cameras had now been grouped. The floor manager had just completed neatly lettering all of Jeff's copy on the huge cue cards.

"Now, kid, listen to me," The Doctor said softly. "I want you to relax. I want you to be Jeff Jefferson, a nice, decent man, friendly, intelligent, and warm. Above all, warm. When you see that camera move in on you, I want you to smile, and start your speech. Don't look at the cue cards unless you absolutely have to because the audience will notice you reading. The main thing is to be warm and relaxed."

The Doctor patted Jeff's arm, went back into the control room. When he entered, he spotted Brewster scowling in the corner. He and Freddie had obviously had words. The Doctor took a seat alongside the technical director and said, "Okay. Let me see!"

The technical director punched up all three cameras on monitor screens. Camera One was on the screen directly overhead. Seeing the red light, Jeff looked into it and said, "Okay for me."

At that point Brewster shouted at The Doctor, "Well, it is not okay for me! I want everyone in this control room to know that I dissociate myself from the whole damned thing!"

"Carl," The Doctor interposed, "shut up!"

Brewster turned on the little man. "You engineered this! The client never wanted Jefferson on the show to begin with! If they find out now that you did this just to get a free pilot they'll cancel this show! You'll see!"

"I said shut up!"

"You have no right to let him read another sponsor's copy and cut it into a show that belongs to ALUMCO! No legal right!" Brewster continued. "We are going to sue TCA! We are going to sue this network!" He directed his attack at the technical director, "Unless you close down this console and shut off those cameras."

The technical director flushed, looking to The Doctor.

"This is going to cost you your job!" Brewster threatened.

The Doctor placed a supporting hand on the technical director's arm to reassure him. Without turning, he said to Freddie, "Unless he shuts up, I want you to kick him out of this control room! Get the stagehands to help if you need to!" Then he calmly turned back to the console, and asked, "Where is the talk-back button?" The technical director pointed and The Doctor pressed it saying, "Okay Jeff, when you get the next word, go!"

The technical director alerted his camera crew, demanded silence. He pressed down the key, "Mr. Jefferson!"

The Doctor watched as Jeff appeared on the monitor. He smiled, but stiffly. He spoke correctly but unnaturally. The technical director asked, "Shall we keep going?"

"Keep going," The Doctor said, though he was equally dissatisfied. "I don't want to stop and start with him. Let him run it and run it and run it. For familiarity, if nothing else."

But when Jeff had done it for the fourth time, and it seemed more ragged than the first, the technical director said, "He's beat. After all, he did a show tonight. He'll only get worse."

The Doctor calmly left the control room, took Jeff by the arm and gently led him off the set.

"Jeff, you're starting to tighten up. Why? Because you're tired? Or you don't like the idea of being what you consider an announcer? Well, you are not an announcer. An announcer sells merchandise. You are the first of a new breed. You are a corporate representative. You sell companies, whole industries. Because people like *you*, they are going to like the company *you* represent. But first they have to like *you*. They can't if you're tense and uncomfortable.

"So I'll tell you what. Instead of the camera picking you up standing in the set, I want you to walk into it, look around, as if you're seeing it for the first time. Discover it as the audience will be discovering it. Then turn and notice the audience, as you would if I walked into the room and you didn't realize it 'til you turned around. As you talk, move around, touch the vault door, fool around with the time lock. That'll do two things. It will get the audience interested in the set and the story. And it will give you some business to do. That will help you relax.

Jeff ran his entrance a few times. It kept getting easier, more comfortable, especially when he timed his bits of business to certain key words in his material. The Doctor went back into the control room. Jeff tried it again. And again. But it still didn't satisfy The Doctor.

The technical director kept saying, "He's shot, exhausted, he can only get worse."

The Doctor, however, displeased as he was, was not dissuaded. Finally he said, "Give them five." The technical director complied. Everyone relaxed, though one cameraman called back, "We're overheating. We better turn these cameras off."

The technical director was about to say okay when The Doctor wheeled on him. "Don't touch that key! If they turn them off and then have to heat them up again he'll never make it. Just give me a minute. Just give me a . . ." He didn't finish the sentence. Instead he went to a corner of the dark control room, chewed on his upper lip in a moment of desperate thought. When he turned back it was only to say, "This time I'll be out on the floor. And I want a take."

He went straight to Jeff who was silently going over his lines and led him into the darkness behind the set.

"Jeff, you know what the trouble is? You're talking to the whole world. Don't do that. Talk to one person. I'll stand right alongside the camera. You talk right to me. Okay?"

"It isn't working, it won't work, I don't like it!"

"It'll work," the little man persisted. "Just talk to me!" Because The Doctor seemed so confident, Jeff agreed to try it again.

The Doctor positioned himself just alongside Camera One so that if Jeff looked at him he would be looking into the lens as well.

Jeff made his entrance, smiled at The Doctor, played his opening speech to him. It was not the take The Doctor had envisioned, but when it was done the technical director pressed down the key and said, "Now, we're cooking!"

They did it again, then again. Jeff grew better each time. After that it was simply a question of putting all the breaks together including the last scene in which Jeff bid the audience good night after telling them what a fine exciting show he had in store for them on next week's C.M. Playhouse.

The limousine was waiting when they stepped into the cool air—The Doctor, Jeff, Freddie, Spence, and Carl Brewster. It was after two o'clock, too late to go to Twenty-One. Brewster started down the street ahead of them. The Doctor gestured to Spence and Freddie to try and calm him down.

"Jeff," he said, "Reuben's is still open. How about some scrambled eggs and coffee?"

"I'm going back to the hotel. I have a cold supper waiting," Jeff started walking. The Doctor followed, the limousine trailing just behind.

"You were sensational tonight," said The Doctor. "You did everything I asked of you, everything! If there's ever anything I can do . . ."

"There is!" Jeff interrupted sharply. "Soon as you get back, talk to Joanne. I want a nice, clean, quick divorce."

"I told you. The minute the show gets sold," The Doctor said. "And it's a smart move. With what you stand to make out of this, it's smart to get it over with early."

"That's not the reason," Jeff said. "I want to get married. Right away! So talk to her *before* the show is sold!"

"Of course, Jeff, of course!" The Doctor promised. He signaled the limousine. Jeff got in, but The Doctor did not, saying, "I have to straighten out that sonofabitch Brewster. See you on the Coast in a day or two?"

"I don't know. I have to stop off in Chicago," Jeff said.

The Doctor nodded, and hurried down the block. He caught up with Brewster, Freddie, and Spence as they waited for the light to change on the corner of Second Avenue. The Doctor began his attack at once, overwhelming Brewster's mounting anger.

"For Christ sakes, Carl! Do you realize what you almost did? To all of us, but to yourself most of all!"

"Look," Brewster exploded, "if it comes out that you guys stole my client's show to dummy up a pilot for another sponsor . . ."

"Stole, stole? What kind of language is that? Protect! 'Protect' is the operative word, Carl! Protect *you!* Protect TV Consultants Ltd!"

"How the hell are you going to protect me by stealing a show that my client just laid out eighty thousand bucks for tonight?"

"First," The Doctor said, "by never letting you know about it. You supervise the show on air for ALUMCO, do your job, everything is okay, you go home. You were not supposed to know a thing about what happened after that! We wanted you in the clear. *We're* the bastards. *We're* the thieves. Not you."

The light changed. Brewster stepped down into the gutter to cross but The Doctor seized him by the arm. "You could go before the Supreme Court of the United States and take an oath—'I, Carl Brewster of S.S.D. & O., never knew a thing about it.' Now, about TV Consultants Ltd., that's another matter."

The Doctor turned Brewster around to stare directly into his face. "Carl, let's face it. The ALUMCO show has a very limited life. When they start asking for bigger and bigger stars that's the tipoff. Cancellations follow like winter follows fall. And if that show's canceled, TV Consultants is finished. *Unless. . .*" He let the sentence dangle deliberately. The light changed and he marched Carl across Second Avenue.

When they got to the other side, The Doctor said, as if there'd been no pause at all, "Unless there's a replacement. Another show that can retain TV Consultants Ltd. And it also wouldn't do S.S.D. & O. any harm to have billing to replace the commission you lose when ALUMCO goes off the air. So," and The Doctor paused again, "how would you like to have a piece of the Consolidated Motors account?"

"C.M.?" Brewster asked, afraid to embrace such an ambition.

"I know you guys have been after a big automobile account for a long time now. Suppose it walked into your shop? Over the transom, so to speak?"

"You mean . . ."

"I mean, Carl, that if we sell the Jeff Jefferson show to C.M. we are going to make a strong pitch to have it done through S.S.D. & O.!" Spence and Freddie tried to control their astonishment. "You know, Carl, I'm surprised, you of all people. Other guys in the agency business call us thieves and cutthroats because they don't know us. But you do. You know we'd never pull a fast one on you, Carl. We've done business together too long. You almost made an ugly episode out of a big favor we were trying to do you."

"I can see that now," Brewster said, seeming apologetic. But all the while he was saying to himself, You Jew bastard, don't you ever try to pull one like that on me again! Aloud, he asked, "When are you going to make the presentation to C.M.?"

"Just as soon as we can splice Jeff's host spots into the kine."

"Good," Carl said. "Good!"

8

When Jeff got out of the limousine in front of the Plaza with his battered script under his arm, and his coat collar up, he looked more a refugee than a Star. In the elevator, the operator said, "Evening, Mr. Jefferson. Quite a nice show tonight, I heard."

"Thanks," Jeff said. But the show seemed a long time ago, so much had intervened since. She must be asleep by now, he thought. Poor Charlene, ordered a magnificent cold supper, iced champagne, and then waited, and waited, until the ice turned to water and the little sandwiches grew so dry that the edges must have curled up. He would wake her, by rubbing his stubbled face against her soft cheek. She liked that.

He unlocked his door as gently as he could. There was a single light on in the sitting room. The room service cart was there and the champagne cooler, but not Charlene. She must have gone into the bedroom to lie down. He walked over and opened the door. The bed was empty and there was a note on the pillow.

Before he opened it, he knew.

Jeff, darling, I decided days ago, but I couldn't leave you before the show. If I ever had any doubt, I knew I had to do this when you said you were taking me to Claire's for dinner tomorrow night. I knew then it had gone too far. What we have, or had, was wonderful. But there's a lifetime to think about. I am not a Jefferson, I am a Rashbaum. I am a Berg. I am what I was brought up to be, my father's daughter. So I will become Mrs. Marvin Berg and have the honeymoon in Israel which my father will pay for. And we will visit the orphanage he estab-

389

lished there. And accept the gratitude that he earned.
Then I will come back and take my proper place in
society as Mrs. Marvin Berg. People will admire me
and like me and envy me. And they will never know
that every time Marvin Berg makes love to his wife,
she is making love to Jeff Jefferson.

There was only one moment when I would have
dared. The night of my party when I was drunk, if
you had been home . . .

Don't hate me. Just say that I'm a coward. Which
I am. I couldn't even tell you to your face. I did wait
to see the show, though, and you were fine.

I'll always follow your career. I'll always be thinking of you, but please, don't call me. Ever. All my
love, Charlene.

She had appended a postscript:

Here it is, a love affair brought to full bloom and
ended, with all the passion, joy, and torture, and still
I have no nickname for you. . . .

He sank down on the edge of the bed. His first thought
was to call the airlines and inquire about the next plane
to Chicago. But if holding her in his arms hadn't convinced her, flying after her certainly wouldn't.

Suddenly the whole venture, the fight at the Guild, the
show, all of it seemed to have been only for Charlene.
Now it was worthless. Worse yet, he had compromised a
part of himself that he did not even dare to think about.

He sat alone in the room, not touching either food or
champagne, until the dawn came up across the park. Then
without undressing he fell asleep.

That morning when Freddie and Spence drove The Doctor to the airport, he explained that he hadn't originally
meant to include Carl Brewster in the deal. And if Consolidated Motors really objected, he would forget about
S.S.D. & O. But it was the only way to square the rap.

The Doctor said, "The minute the kine is ready, let me
know. But I want it perfect. Perfect, you understand?"
He said this to Spence, as if he felt he could not trust
Freddie.

"It will be perfect, Doctor, believe me!" Freddie volunteered.

But The Doctor only said, "Call me when it's done. The Old Man's waiting to see it."

"The Old Man," Spence echoed. There was no need to identify him any further. When one talked of automobiles and Detroit, The Old Man meant only the Chairman of the Board of C.M.

"I called him and asked him to watch last night's show. By the time I got back to the hotel I had a wire. He's ready to talk. When he sees the kine, with Jeff selling C.M. he'll grab the idea. The pitch is simple enough. Wouldn't he like America to think of C.M. not as a big heartless corporation but as honest, decent, friendly men like Jeff Jefferson. 'C.M., the company that cares.' He'll buy it," The Doctor said, quite sure of himself.

"We'll have our first owned and controlled package of film. That's only the beginning. Within three years I want twenty series on the air. I want a vault full of films that will be worth millions. Hundreds of millions! I want to get as many hours and half hours of film in the vault as I can before the government cracks down.

"As long as we represent the best stars, producers and writers we can use them, where it will do us the most good. But the time will come when somebody will blow the whistle.

"Then we will have to cut the operation in two, separate the agency business from the production business. When that time comes I want muscle in both political parties."

Spence and Freddie both nodded.

The Doctor continued somewhat cryptically, "We'll work the political parties the same way you boys handled the networks, one man covering each. I want a powerful contact among the Democrats, another among the Republicans. Because when the anti-trust issue comes up we don't know which party will be in the White House and I want to make sure I can reach the man at the top."

He turned and started toward the plane.

Later the same morning, Jeff Jefferson woke with a massive sense of loss. The day passed in a blur of misery and it was six o'clock when he remembered Claire's invitation, too late to call it off.

He went through the routine of showering, shaving, dressing. He stopped at the florist's in the lobby, picked out some flowers, got into a cab, gave Claire's address on East End Avenue.

She opened the door dressed in a bright-colored sari which enhanced her beauty. Her blond hair was done more flatteringly than it had been during rehearsal. She was smiling, an expectant, welcoming smile.

Then she realized that Jeff was alone. Without a word or a question she knew. She reached for the flowers, saying, "How nice!" But she couldn't carry the pretense any further. She said softly, "I'm sorry, Jeff. Really, I am."

She kissed him on the cheek, in exactly the way she would have done if he'd brought word of the death of a close friend.

Two weeks later, Irwin Cone, looking his dapper best, was picked up at the exclusive Detroit Club where he had been quartered overnight as a guest of Consolidated Motors. He was driven in a company limousine to corporate headquarters. Resting alongside him in a flat metal container was the kinescope of the new C.M. Playhouse Series hosted by Jeff Jefferson.

The limousine drove down into the building and The Doctor got out at the elevator which took him to the top floor, half of which was devoted to the huge paneled board room. A projector was set up. The Doctor opened the metal container and handed the reel to the projectionist. The man threaded the film into the machine, ran a few feet of it to make sure of the sound level and the sequence.

"Take down the level," The Doctor said.

"I know it's too loud," said the projectionist. "But *he* likes to tell me that. Makes up for his having to wear that damned hearing aid."

A few minutes later the Old Man entered. He was tall, very slender, somewhat stoop-shouldered, as if from bending to let shorter men speak directly into his one good ear. He wore an almost imperceptible hearing aid.

Harvey Beecher was not a man given to smiling or pleasantries. His thin face was always grave, even when he wanted to seem pleased.

"Mr. Cohen," he said, acknowledging The Doctor.

Cone let it pass. Beecher gave a signal to the projectionist, but before he could kill the lights and turn on the machine, The Doctor interrupted to ask, "Aren't any of your other executives going to see it?"

"If I like it, they'll like it," Beecher said. The projectionist turned on the machine which threw a strong white light onto the screen at the far end of the room. The dubbed-in music began, far too loud.

"Can't you make that lower?" the Chairman asked, somewhat irritated.

"Yes, sir!" The projectionist turned down the volume but it was still too loud for The Doctor's taste.

Beecher said, "Fine! That's much better!" And he settled back to watch.

All trace of ALUMCO's name had been removed. In its place Jeff Jefferson appeared, gracious, warm, and friendly. He spoke well of C.M. and welcomed the audience to the exciting and heart-warming drama which would follow C.M.'s brief commercial message.

The Doctor who had already seen the kinescope four times, studied Beecher's face which was bathed in the reflected light from the screen. It was immobile, but The Doctor was sure the man was not displeased.

During the act breaks when Jeff Jefferson was speaking for C.M., Beecher did exhibit a slightly increased degree of interest. When it was over, he waited till the projectionist had left the room.

"That's a nice young man," he said, thoughtfully. But his very thoughtfulness made it clear to The Doctor that there were reservations attached. Suddenly Beecher asked, "We'd get the same kind of show every week?"

"Better, since we'd be on film. We'd have greater control, no chance of an accident on the air."

"I meant the kind of stories. I don't aim to please the critics. I am to please people. I had my boys take a survey once. Do you know how many critics there are in this country?"

Totally unprepared, The Doctor ventured, "Three thousand?"

"Not half that many. Thirteen hundred and fifty-two. Put them all together they can't buy many cars or refrigerators or washing machines. As far as I'm concerned, critics don't count. Most of them are Reds anyway!

"I want stories, with values, like that story we just saw. Any man can be redeemed, no matter what he's done. That's what it's all about. Religion, I mean." Suddenly Beecher asked, "Is he a religious man?" The Doctor didn't answer until the chairman repeated. "What's his background?"

"He's a Methodist. Born in Iowa. Lived there till he came to Hollywood."

"You don't find a Methodist straying too far from what he was brought up to believe." Beecher seemed pleased until he announced quite unexpectedly, "It hasn't all been favorable."

Taken aback, The Doctor made no attempt to answer. If the Old Man had anything on his mind it would come out without prodding.

"You understand before I could put the name C.M. in anyone's hands I have to be sure he's clean. So I had a check made on him. There are two things."

The Doctor sat up alertly.

"I understand that his marriage is in trouble. There might be a divorce. Well, we sell our cars to families. Family people don't like divorce.

"Then there's his affair with that Jewish girl."

Surprised as he was that Beecher knew, The Doctor could at least say firmly, "That's over!"

"Good!" Beecher approved. "I don't mind Jews, you understand. It's just with intermarriage you alienate both groups. So it's really just his divorce we have to worry about."

The Doctor realized now that when the Old Man bought someone he bought them totally.

"And, of course, one other thing . . ."

The Doctor waited, unable to guess what was coming.

"That Red business. Why would a nice clean-cut young man front for a lot of Commies?"

"I wouldn't say he was fronting for anyone," The Doctor answered. There was a sudden flush of anger in the Old Man's face. People rarely disagreed with him directly. The Doctor knew he would have to talk fast and well to be convincing. "If you saw his appearance on television, you will remember that when he testified, he only testified to what had happened to *him*. He wanted to explain how young men in the thirties were shaken, easily misled by false ideologies. *He* wasn't. But he was concerned about those who had been and were sorry. As you said yourself, redemption is what it's all about. He didn't want them judged and condemned without the chance to repent."

"He never did come out for the ten who were convicted," Beecher conceded.

"No, he didn't."

"It would be better if he didn't take part in *any* kind of politics from now on," Beecher concluded.

"Once his term as president of the Guild expires I don't think he means to run again," The Doctor said, without the vaguest notion of whether Jeff had given any thought to that question.

"Good. Good," the Old Man said thoughtfully. Then he added, "There are ways of handling divorces, quiet ways. My own daughter's been divorced twice and there was hardly a ripple. If I could be assured . . ."

"It will be handled very quietly."

"I don't like a lot of accusations and counter-accusations. Professional differences, people seem to understand that, forgive that. . . ." He was laying out the way in which he wanted Jeff's divorce handled. The Doctor understood, and agreed.

"He knows what's expected of him when he becomes C.M.'s public image. Else he wouldn't have done this," The Doctor said, tapping the can in which the kinescope reposed.

"Public image," the Old Man said. "Leave the film here, Mr. Cohen. I want my entire board to see it."

The Doctor smiled, understanding that the statement was a stronger commitment than a signed contract. When the Old Man asked his board for approval there was not the slightest chance of any objection.

Within four days a letter arrived at the TCA offices in Beverly Hills committing Consolidated Motors to the Jeff Jefferson show on film for a firm fifty-two weeks. There were two provisos: one that the show be called C.M. Star Theatre; the other that it be conditional on the good personal and political conduct of Jeff Jefferson. Any act on his part which served to embarrass or compromise the sponsor would be cause for immediate cancellation of the series. Beecher's telephone call which followed the letter made it clear to The Doctor that the sooner the divorce was over the better.

The day after her picture was finished, Joanne flew down to Mexico. Within four days she returned, practically unnoticed by the press.

Three weeks later, with greater than usual fanfare, TCA in cooperation with S.S.D. & O. gave a joint cocktail party for the press to announce the first of a series of filmed TV dramas to be made in Hollywood by the new production division of TCA. It had the enthusiastic approval of the Screen Actors Guild and all the other unions in the Motion Picture Industry.

Innumerable toasts were drunk to the success of the new venture and to the renaissance of Hollywood as the film capital of the world.

During the interrogation that accompanied the press pictures, Jeff Jefferson made it clear that with his heavy duties as both host and star of C.M. Star Theatre he would be forced to forego his activities with the Screen Actors Guild and he would not be a candidate for re-election. He felt that having brought film TV to Hollywood he was leaving the Guild in a much stronger position than when he first assumed office some years ago.

Only The Doctor did not appear in any of the publicity photos. He chose to remain in the background.

In the twelve months thereafter, TCA created twenty-six new filmed TV concepts and sold eight of them. By the end of its first full season, TCA-Films owned over four hundred TV films with a market value, after their first exhibition on television, of eight million dollars.

PART SIX

1

C.M. Star Theatre, hosted by Jeff Jefferson, was just beginning its fourth season.

The first annual show in any series was always an event, because this was the one which would be reviewed by the press.

In the three years since TCA started the stampede from live TV, the critics had decided that film series were not worthy of the meticulous weekly critiques they had given the live shows broadcast from New York. Whether this was geographical snobbery or unconscious resentment of the fact that TCA had made Hollywood the TV capital of the world was never clear. But the custom had become established. Film series were reviewed once, on the first show, so you led with your best script and cast.

In his dressing room at Central Studios, Jeff Jefferson was being made up. The script was a far cry from the corny costume piece, *Alias Jimmy Valentine*. This was a modern story, written to give Jeff the opportunity to play the type of role always denied him in features.

Jeff had played a variety of parts since the series began—returning veteran from World War II, a doctor, a lawyer, a father to an adopted child, more doctors, more lawyers, a courageous businessman, intended victim of mob practices, a senator, twice.

But always the roles were written to portray Jeff as the sincere, honest, fine-looking American with whom the Old Man wanted Consolidated Motors' name associated. And always the shows wound up reflecting a distinct lack of dramatic perception.

At the close of each season, armed with sarcastic reviews from Jack Gould in the *New York Times* and John Crosby in the *Herald-Tribune*, Jeff would have a confer-

ence with The Doctor about "next season" and the need
for fresh and important scripts.

"Next season" in television, and the ambitious plans
made for it, always reminded The Doctor of his childhood
when he used to go to his grandfather's tenement flat for
Passover. At the end of the Seder everyone always intoned
"Next year in Jerusalem." Even as a little boy, Isidore
Cohen sensed that it was a ritualistic wish all Jews made,
with absolutely no expectation of fulfillment.

Yet now, after two thousand years of dispersion, behold
there was an Israel. And today when Jews said "Next year
in Jerusalem" they not only meant it, they could call El
Al and make reservations.

Secretly The Doctor felt the same way about the im-
provement of television. In two thousand years it, too,
could change. But in the meantime at the end of each
season he went through the same ritualistic discussion with
Jeff Jefferson.

The Doctor always pretended to give Jeff's complaints
more than lip service. Each year he would authorize the
writing of two scripts with "real content," "significance,"
"depth."

Each of the two scripts would have a fat, meaty
part for Jeff. Each would take a strong stand on some
social issue. Each would delight the producer and set
Jeff dreaming about getting reviews and awards. Each
script would then be sent to the network, which was now
the final "responsible authority." Neither script was ever
rejected outright.

The network executives were more devious. Though
they claimed to approve the social stand taken in the
script, they suggested that due to geographical pressures,
certain aspects of that stand be toned down. By the time
the script had been sent back for the third re-write even
the writers felt it was no longer worth saving.

But The Doctor always made the entire procedure appear an honest effort to uplift the medium. So, for the few
thousand dollars that the scripts cost, The Doctor succeeded in keeping Jeff and TCA's other stars happy and
willing to turn out the usual unexciting fare to which
television audiences were now accustomed. And which, it
seemed, they loved, if one could judge from the enor-

mous growth in the number of television sets that were being bought.

Now at the start of C.M. Theatre's fourth season, The Doctor was in Jeff's dressing room to wish him well, and to console him about the fact that both their "new" and "daring" scripts had again been turned down.

"Look at it this way, kid. Every time you make a film it becomes a piece of property, an asset. In addition to being paid up front, you've got thirty percent of each film. When we get two hundred films in the can, as we will by the end of this season, we can sell the whole bundle for a capital gain. On your end alone that's two-three million dollars. And at a twenty-five percent tax rate. So keep the Old Man happy, and believe me, when you're ready to quit, he'll be keeping you happy for the rest of your life."

"But the negatives will be worth even more if we make good films," Jeff protested. "And good films would give me a chance to act for a change!"

"Jeff, Jeff, being an actor isn't an end. For a man like you, it's a beginning. Now you're a host, a personality. But do you know what else we've been doing. We've been turning you into a producer!"

That speech always worked well with stars. The Doctor had never met an actor who didn't feel that he knew more than any producer. Or a writer who didn't feel that he knew more than any director.

"Why do we get your approval, your story suggestions on every play? Why do we have you sit in on production conferences? Same reason. Because the day is coming when you're going to say, I am through being an actor! When that day comes, I want you to be ready!"

Jeff nodded, somewhat abashed that he hadn't taken the same long view of his career as The Doctor had.

"Of course, to do that," the little man continued, "you need four or five years of the series under your belt. So let's not rock the boat now."

Jeff nodded. The Doctor patted him on the shoulder, wished him well, and left.

What The Doctor had really meant was that three years of inventory of a filmed series was not quite as profitable as five or six years. With that much inventory

on hand those films could more easily be sold and re-sold
to those small American stations which liked to know at
the outset that once they bought a series they had filled a
programming need not for weeks or months but for years.

Leaving Jeff's sound stage, The Doctor started on his
way to the next one, to play the same scene all over again
with another star. As he walked, the little man ticked off
his assets—number of profitable TCA-owned series on the
air, inventory of films already in the vaults, the studio and
the land. . . .

He was forced to interrupt his thought flow. He kept
forgetting that the studio and the land did not belong to
TCA yet.

Central Studios was the place The Doctor had chosen
to film most of TCA's shows. In fact, it was commonly referred to as "the TCA lot" by most people in the industry. For TCA used three quarters of the facilities, and
but for the rentals from TCA, Central Studios would have
been forced to retrench severely. Even now, one big feature
that bombed might put Central out of business completely.
The Doctor had even considered seriously making them
an offer for the whole works, studio, back lot and all, but
he knew they would ask fifty million and be justified.

So there had to be a more roundabout way, to acquire
it all. And there was. Thanks to Spencer Gould.

Several years ago Spence had recommended that
TCA acquire a small St. Louis bank which had gotten into trouble. It had been a very smart move, that bank
acquisition, the kind of move that The Doctor himself
should have initiated. Cat's Eye Bastione had done a very
similar thing years ago.

"Money is muscle," Cat's Eye used to say. "But to use
it right it got to be clean money, so the government can't
ask nasty questions. Well, where you going to find nice
clean money easier than in a bank? So I got me a bank."

The St. Louis bank financed all TCA's series between
shooting and final payment by the network or sponsor.
And when it came time for TCA to take over the studio,
the bank would prove invaluable. But things had to mesh,
or The Doctor's big plan might collapse under sudden
anti-trust pressure from the government, for selling off
films was only a small part of Cone's program.

Actually his overall plan was far more ambitious since

it involved establishing a base in both political parties. He had already made inroads on the Democratic side, perhaps because California was basically a Democratic state. With the exception of Earl Warren there hadn't been a strong Republican in power in almost a generation. Though perhaps his failure to penetrate the Republican ranks was due to a different reason. Buddy Black had once touched on it in a wisecrack. "Doctor, deep in his heart, no Jew is a Republican."

If indeed that was the reason, it was not enough to convince The Doctor that it could not be changed. Now, as he walked from one stage on the lot to another, making sure that all his TV stars were being launched with the proper enthusiasm, he worried about his yet-to-be-established Republican contacts.

Given enough time, that is, given enough time without government intervention, The Doctor's Big Plan was assured. Of course, one factor could upset his timing—color television. The huge TCA film inventory was all in black and white. If color television came too fast, or if The Doctor's political connections matured too slowly, the black and white film would decrease in value, and very sharply. So The Doctor realized that he would have to accelerate his move into the Republican party.

But now he was at Stage Seven where Joanne West was at work on the very first film of her new television series. Her drink-coarsened features had proved unphotographable for the new wide screens and her irregular habits had made her theatrical films too costly so television was her only hope. Perhaps the long working hours and the tough demands of a series would make alcoholism impossible. With the dawn-to-dark, day-after-day, pressure of TV she might not have either the time or the temptation to drink so much.

This was the start of The Doctor's own "noble experiment." It hadn't been easy to convince Jeff to give Joanne a guest shot on his series so they could have a pilot film with which to sell her. But finally Jeff had agreed. And today Joanne was shooting the first of her own series.

For the moment, The Doctor banished all thoughts of political contacts to concentrate on flattering her. He calculated, if she could make it, and could run three years or more, it would mean another hundred-odd films in inventory, with a value, easily, of two to three million dollars to TCA.

If she didn't make it, TCA's loss would be unfortunate. And Joanne would have drunk herself out of show business for all time. So he hoped she would make it.

It was the third day of shooting. Jeff had just come back to his dressing room before walking over to the commissary for lunch. There was a note stuck in his makeup mirror. "Please call Dr. Cone. Very urgent!"

That was The Doctor. No matter how important, he would never interrupt shooting. When he reached The Doctor he discovered he was on the lot and would like to have lunch, if Jeff was free.

They met in the commissary at the corner table which was reserved for Cone's Cobras, except on days when The Doctor was on the lot; then it was reserved exclusively for him and his guests. By the time Jeff arrived The Doctor was already there, waiting. Cone asked about the young director, about the script, about the rest of the cast. But Jeff knew that was not the reason for this lunch. After they had ordered coffee, it finally came out.

"People," The Doctor lamented. "They think that an actor's life is all booze, money and broads. They don't realize the hard work, the long hours, the grind. They think nothing of imposing."

Jeff knew that preamble well. When The Doctor was about to ask a favor he always blamed it on that vague entity called "people." Jeff wondered what it might be this time. In the last few years, since he'd become a major television personality, he had been asked to do many public appearances. The Doctor himself had prevailed on him to host a luncheon to kick off the United Jewish Appeal only last year. It couldn't be that again.

"You know, if you and I both didn't owe so much to the Old Man, I would have turned them down. Because of him, I said I would at least talk to you."

"What's up?" Jeff asked, impatient with the long preamble.

"Beecher is retiring. Fifty years of service to C.M. and he's stepping down."

"After fifty years he's entitled," Jeff said.

"Also he hasn't been well, slight stroke. Before anything worse happens, they are planning a big tribute, a dinner at the Waldorf. Even his competitors will be there. The boys at C.M. thought, since he's so fond of you, it would be a grand surprise if you would host the dinner."

"When is it?" Jeff asked.

"That's part of the problem," The Doctor explained. "It comes during a shooting week. Just before Thanksgiving. We'll be on a tight enough schedule as it is. And it's one of those weeks when you play the lead. But we could rearrange things a little and free you for forty-eight hours. You could fly to New York, do the dinner and be back on the lot without upsetting the schedule too much."

What it boiled down to, and The Doctor knew it, which was why he had approached the matter so gingerly, was that Jeff would have to leave the studio at the end of a day's work, take the overnight plane to New York, do the dinner and then fly back early the next morning. It would permit him about six hours sleep out of sixty and all to save a few thousand dollars of a tight TV budget. Jeff didn't respond at once, so The Doctor continued.

"Frankly, if I didn't know how you felt about the Old Man, I wouldn't even ask. And, of course, there is the other angle to think about. If the Old Man *is* retiring, and we don't have him for protection, it wouldn't be the worst thing in the world to have the new group like you. It would make them very indebted if you did this."

"Round trip in forty-eight hours. Who'd write my material? What would I have to do?" Jeff asked, putting as many obstacles in the way as he could.

"The speech is no problem," The Doctor said quickly. "I took the liberty of talking to Abe Heller."

"Abe Heller?" Jeff asked, surprised. "To write a tribute to the Old Man?"

"There's a reason," The Doctor said. "You see, part of the problem . . ."

"Part of *what* problem?" Jeff interjected, realizing now that The Doctor had still not made a full disclosure.

"Well, what the boys at C.M. were hoping for was an all-industry tribute, not only their competitors, but all facets of the C.M. operation as well, including the officers of the Auto Workers Union. Their contract is up for renewal and the union officers feel it might weaken their bargaining position if they showed up to pay tribute to the Old Man. What the boys at C.M. think is that if you were there with your long record of labor activity, the union would be more inclined to make a showing.

Jeff resented the fact that The Doctor had talked to Abe Heller about writing the speech even before he knew if Jeff would consent to deliver it. In the first place it meant that he took Jeff for granted, a thought that rankled. And it hinted at a relationship between The Doctor and Abe Heller, which bothered Jeff. Perhaps that was why Abe's idea about countersigning all contracts between TCA and Screen Actors Guild members had quietly but definitely been allowed to die. Perhaps, too, it accounted for Abe's recent affluence.

Annoyed, Jeff decided not to answer at once. "I'll think it over," he said. "Give me a day or two."

"They want to make an announcement in Detroit," The Doctor prodded.

"I have to get back on the set." Though Jeff owed the Old Man in Detroit a huge debt and knew he would go to New York to preside over the banquet, he refused to give The Doctor an easy victory.

By the next morning Jeff decided he would go to New York only if the shooting schedule was switched to give him three full days off. He could use one day to make the trip, one day to rest before the dinner, one day to make the trip back. He enjoyed thinking of the gyrations that the damned penny-pinching TCA production department would go through trying to work it out. But the treadmill of daily television shooting afforded him few enough pleasures, so he felt entitled to this indulgence. He transmitted his conditions through Alise.

Before the day was out, word came back from The Doctor that by switching the show scheduled to be shot and having Jeff do his host bits instead, the three-day break could be arranged.

It wasn't until he was on the plane for New York that Jeff realized the real reason for his resentment. The visit to New York was going to bring back all the pain of losing Charlene. He was sorry now that he'd asked for three full days. The Doctor's suggestion of a hurried trip would have been easier. Maybe he would call Claire Colton, take her and her husband, Irving, out to dinner. He still owed them an invitation after that painful night four years ago. He sat back to rehearse his speech.

What he liked about it was the fact that Abe had managed to praise the Old Man without being phony. He had taken a conciliatory stand toward labor without disguising the bitter battles that had marked the Old Man's steady resistance to the union. Most of all, from Jeff's point of view, it made Jeff himself the symbol of the new age in industry when a man who had been a labor leader himself, as Jeff had been, could become the spokesman for a corporation.

It had a statesman-like quality to it. Abe had outdone himself. And at the same time he had probably earned TCA a fifth, possibly even a sixth year renewal for Jeff's show.

When Jeff arrived at the Waldorf, he found that half a dozen C.M. executives and agency men, including Carl Brewster, had already called to invite him for cocktails and dinner. But tonight he wanted to be free. He would definitely call Claire and Irving. Perhaps they could meet him, even at the last moment. Maybe they would even ask him over. It would be a far cry from his last visit when he had shown up pathetically begging for comfort.

He found his address book, looked up Colton, gave the number to the operator. She called back to inform him that the number had been changed and that she was ringing the new one. A boy answered. When Jeff asked for Claire, he called out, "Mom, for you. I don't know. Some man."

There was silence, then he heard her voice; it was reserved, cautious, "Hello? Who is this?"

"Jeff . . ." he said warmly.

Her first reaction was one of puzzlement, "Jeff?"

"Claire, it's me!"

"Oh, Jeff! What a surprise," she said, though with less enthusiasm than he had anticipated. "Where are you?"

"Just in town for two days to host a testimonial dinner at the Waldorf. I thought if by any chance you and Irving could join me tonight, I would . . ." Something about her silence interrupted him more suddenly than words would have. "Claire?"

"I guess you didn't know. How could you?"

"What?"

"Irving died. It'll be two years in July."

"Good God," Jeff said, startled. "I'm sorry, Claire. I never knew. Can I come see you? Or could you come out to dinner with the boys?"

"The boys have already had their dinner. And I'm just about to have mine. If you'd like to come over and take pot luck."

"Sure, if *you* don't mind," Jeff said.

"No. Come right ahead." She suddenly remembered. "I better give you the new address." It was in the West Eighties just off Central Park.

It turned out to be an older house than the one on East End Avenue. And a smaller apartment. The effects of enforced economies were apparent throughout. But the place was warm and homelike. The boys seemed comfortable in their room which was cluttered with airplane models, jerry-rigged radio equipment, a record player, and many books.

Though they didn't remember him as a visitor, they recognized him instantly as a television star. Even so, they did not seem too impressed. Claire was a little embarrassed as she explained, "We don't let them watch a lot of television . . . I don't. Would you like a drink?"

"You going to have one?"

She seemed to hesitate, "Okay!" She went into the kitchen. Jeff drifted into the boys' room. They started to explain to him what they were doing with the radio equipment. They seemed happy to have a man to talk to. Suddenly Johnny, the blonder of the two boys, asked, "Were you a friend of Daddy's?"

"I knew him," Jeff said. "He was a nice man, a very nice man."

"Yeah," the boy said. "That's what the rabbi said. Daddy was smart, too, he knew all about radios and planes. He knew about everything. When he comes back . . ."

David interrupted, "Mama says he is not coming back."

"When he comes back," Johnny persisted, "he's going to make us a television set. So we can watch whenever *we* want to."

Claire was in the doorway now, a drink in each hand. She gave one to Jeff. "I thought I remembered, scotch and a litttle soda?" He nodded. They almost touched glasses and then drank. "Dinner'll be ready in a minute." She went out to check. Jeff sat down on one of the bunk beds.

In a while Claire was back. "You'll have to let Mr. Jefferson go now, so we can have our dinner." Though the boys protested, she took Jeff by the hand, led him out into the foyer which served as the dining area too. The small table was set for two. Dinner was a chicken casserole, hot and spicy, with a touch of garlic. They ate and talked, mostly about Jeff, his career, his success. She seemed to be avoiding the subject of Irving's death, until Jeff realized that she was doing so deliberately, so long as the boys were awake.

After they finished eating he sat in the small, nicely furnished living room while Claire put the boys to bed. She looked well, better than he had expected. Her face had gained something, in fact. In addition to her clean features, her blond beauty, there was an added strength. And she did not indulge in self-pity. The few times that she had referred to Irving, she had done so with pride and satisfaction, not sadness.

Only when she returned to the room after closing the boys' door, did she say anything mournful. Then it was about Johnny.

"David is fine, as fine as a boy can be under the circumstances, but Johnny keeps expecting he'll come back. No matter what I say, he keeps insisting." That was the only moment when Jeff thought she might cry.

Since she'd brought up the subject, he asked, "How did he die?"

"He worked too hard, drove himself for the boys, for me. They had to have an education fund. And a camp fund. And life insurance, of course. And I had to have a mink coat whether I wanted one or not. They say Jewish men make the best husbands. That would be true, if they lived longer."

"His heart?"

She nodded. "Dentistry is a sedentary profession, but tense. It was his desire for us to have everything, that did it. He left us fairly well provided for, though not nearly as well as he would have liked. I work occasionally. But jobs are scarce now that TV has moved out to the Coast."

"Did you ever think of moving out there?"

"It would mean taking the boys away from their grandparents. And the boys are all they have now. That was the worst part, watching his parents bury their only son. Much as I loved Irving, I think his mother felt it more than I did. All her hopes, all her future, everything was in her son. Now it's in the boys. Besides, I think they'll get a better education here in the East."

He realized that she was finding all the excuses she could to remain. In her way she, too, was refusing to accept his death.

"Have you thought about marrying again?"

"I don't know," she said vaguely. "There'd have to be some man and then I would always compare him with Irving. I just don't know."

"And there isn't any man?" he asked.

"There are men. But there isn't any man. That's what concerns me. I know the boys need someone. You saw how they latched on to you. They need a father, but I don't know if I need anyone."

He nodded. It had been the same for him since Charlene. Girls, many girls, but no woman.

Whatever his motive, his own need, or hers, he found himself suddenly asking, "If you could get someone to stay with the boys would you like to go to that dinner tomorrow night?" She hesitated. "I know it might be boring. Still, you'd hear me make my speech and I'd know I had at least one fan in the audience."

She smiled, and it reminded him of the day after Charlene left when her smile was the only friendly thing he could rely on.

"Please?"

She nodded. "I can get Mama. She jumps at any chance to spend an evening with the boys."

"I'll send a car for you. The dinner's at seven. But there's a small reception and cocktails at six-fifteen. I'll have the car here at six. Or is that too early?"

"No, that's fine," she said, still smiling.

He kissed her gently on the cheek and he left. When he arrived back at the Waldorf there was an envelope in his box at the desk. A duplicate had been pushed under his door. They took no chances at C.M. Both envelopes contained the same material—a list of prominent men whom Jeff needed to mention with appropriate notes about each. Among the names were the Secretary of

Commerce, the Secretary of Labor and the Governors of Michigan and New York. There were also half a dozen four-star generals with whom the Old Man had worked closely during World War II.

Jeff was impressed by the sheer power that would be present on the dais. In going over the floor plan he noticed that there was a table for TCA. Cone and his Cobras overlooked no opportunity, but it would be convenient for Claire to sit there.

The meticulous preparation not only made him feel more secure, it gave him a greater respect for the importance of the occasion. By the time he had finished his notes, rehearsed his speech three more times, once before the mirror, it was almost two o'clock.

The next morning he walked north along Fifth, and, by chance more than design, found himself at F.A.O. Schwarz, the toy shop across from the Plaza. He stared at the window full of animals larger even than life-size and machinery so intricate that only an engineer could master it. He would find something for Claire's boys. With the help of the awed and excited saleswoman, he selected two toys, both extremely expensive. An entire village with functioning figures, vehicles and factories. And a ready-to-assemble two-way intercom which could be used as far away as a city block. He arranged to have the packages delivered by special messenger.

He returned to the Waldorf and found a dozen calls from various C.M. and S.S.D. & O. executives inviting him to lunch. Carl Brewster had called three times. Because he found it amusing to have Brewster fawn on him he called back. Brewster gave him what The Doctor referred to as "The Big Hello." He had held his lunch time open hoping that he and Jeff could get together. He had a table waiting at Twenty-One, upstairs, any time was quite all right with Carl, if Jeff could make it. Jeff allowed Brewster to run through the whole spiel before he refused.

Oh, the joys of being a star again. The little ways of paying back those bastards who had held your destiny so lightly in their hands. If Jeff lived to be a hundred he would never forget how close he had come to failure.

2

The pre-dinner reception, limited to about a hundred of
the most important guests, was already under way when
Jeff came down from his suite. The Governor of Michigan
was there, talking to the Secretary of Labor. The presidents of four of the largest companies in the country
formed a small group. Jeff scanned the room quickly.
Claire had not arrived, but The Doctor and Spencer Gould
stood in a corner of the room near the bar. The Doctor
spotted Jeff and was smiling enthusiastically, beckoning
him over. Jeff started through the room making his way
past little knots of dinner-jacketed men and formally
gowned women who reacted with sudden surprise and awe
when he passed.

Much as he liked that kind of recognition, he always
felt a little cheap about it, as well. It was the rodeo bit
all over again. When he made it to The Doctor's side, he
was introduced to the Senator from Michigan. They had a
chance to chat only briefly, for every guest and his wife
wanted to meet Jeff. So, until the Old Man himself appeared, Jeff was the key figure. Occasionally he looked
around hoping to find Claire.

Then Beecher arrived and the press photographers were
admitted to the room. The Old Man had to pose with every
celebrity present, but he always insisted that Jeff be by his
side. Jeff obliged, remarking to himself how much
older Beecher seemed. He must have had not a slight
stroke but a severe one.

Now it was past time for the formalities to begin. A
thousand guests had assembled in the ballroom and were
awaiting dinner, which could not be served until the
Cardinal of the New York Archdiocese had pronounced
the invocation. Though Beecher was not Catholic, he had

donated so heavily to Catholic charities of one kind or another that the Cardinal felt impelled, as a matter of church politics, to attend and enunciate the blessing.

Except for Beecher, the Cardinal, and Jeff, all the other guests had made their way to their tables. When everyone was seated, Beecher, with the Cardinal on one side and Jeff on the other, entered the ballroom. The Old Man leaned a little on Jeff's arm.

At the sight of the guest of honor the entire assemblage came to its feet, clapping loudly. The three men walked to the dais. The applause mounted. Jeff stood to one side, giving the Old Man center stage, at the same time clapping in such a way that it evoked still another barrage of applause.

As the room quieted, Jeff stepped to the microphone. "May I ask all of you to remain standing while His Eminence invokes the blessings of God on this assemblage and the food we are about to receive." Then he bowed his head, piously.

When the prayer was over, Jeff looked up and saw Claire slip into the room. She must have been politely waiting outside during the long invocation. She was dressed in a simple black gown which contrasted with her blond hair. Her beauty was striking enough for a number of men to stare as she made her way to the TCA table where The Doctor sat, with Spencer Gould, Freddie Feig and their wives.

Jeff caught her eye during the meal. She smiled and it made him feel good. During the meal, between exchanging bits of unimportant talk with the Governor of New York on his right, and the Secretary of Commerce on his left, Jeff scanned his notes, awaiting that moment when it would be time for him to begin the introductions and speeches which were the real purpose of the evening.

Finally Jeff moved to the lectern. Throughout the obligatory speeches The Doctor sat probing, as skillfully as he could, the relationship between Claire and Jeff, not willing to accept that they had not had any contact during the years between the ALUMCO show and now. But it was only an exercise in fighting boredom. Large dinners, speeches, always bored him.

Now it was time for Jeff to deliver the body of his

speech. Abe Heller's material went over well. Jeff could feel it, especially the part about Jeff's having been a labor leader, having led the Screen Actors Guild through good times and bad, having fought industry and worked with it, having come to appreciate what Abe had termed "the men on the other side of the table."

He closed with a personal tribute to the Old Man. When he finished he turned to the Old Man and held out the gold plaque. Beecher stared up at Jeff, but did not move. The pleading look in his eyes made Jeff realize suddenly that either the emotion of the moment, or the limitations forced on him by his stroke, had immobilized him. Jeff leaned over, lifted him to his feet. With one arm around his shoulder he supported Beecher to the lectern. He read the inscription on the plaque, then presented it. The Old Man finally took the plaque, but when Jeff sought to withdraw his supporting arm he felt Beecher's body sag. He obviously needed help, and Jeff remained beside him lending him his strength. It gave the Old Man the security he needed to make his acceptance speech.

"I hadn't thought it was going to be like this. When my time came, I thought I would be resigned, because I am of an age now when I never travel anywhere without packing a dark suit and a black tie. I have friends all over the world, and they are all vulnerable to time, as I am. And how we resent it.

"It's not that a man wants to live forever. But there are always so many people he hates to leave. He would like to arrange everything for those he loves. . . ."

The Old Man continued in that vein, speaking freely about himself, his feelings. And all the while he was leaning on Jeff, being supported and admired by him.

The picture of the two standing so close together, with the younger man supporting the older, with Beecher trembling somewhat as he groped for words had a startling effect on the audience.

There were tears in the eyes of many women who didn't even know the Old Man. And in the eyes of some men who did.

At the TCA table, Spencer Gould, Freddie Feig and their wives sat stiffly ill at ease. Having been in show business so long, they did not know how to react in the face of honest emotion. Claire stared at Jeff admiringly. Beside her, The Doctor leaned forward, his eyes narrow and discerning as he whispered something. No one actually heard what he said. And no one, not Claire on his left or Spence on his right, dared to inquire for fear of breaking the spell that had enveloped the huge ballroom. What The Doctor had murmured was simply, "He belongs . . . he belongs. . . ."

The entire assemblage stood in tribute to the Old Man and Jeff Jefferson who were still locked in a one-armed embrace. The Doctor got to his feet along with all the rest. The word he heard most often as people crowded toward the dais was "Jeff . . . Jeff . . ." People were reaching out to shake his hand, women merely to touch him, but everyone was calling "Jeff . . . Jeff!"

The Doctor stood in place listening to the comments. "Wasn't Jeff great?" "The way the Old Man clung to Jeff." "Wasn't it touching, Jeff and the Old Man."

"Jeff." People who had never been in the same room with him before tonight felt they knew him intimately enough to call him by his first name. He was as familiar to them as members of their own families. And why not, The Doctor thought, they see him every week, which is more often than they see any but the closest of their relatives. Right now they were brushing aside governors, senators, cabinet members to surround Jeff.

Suddenly, as far as The Doctor was concerned, the solution to his problem became very clear.

If people prefer meeting a star to meeting a politician, why bother with politicians? If this man could outshine all the top political figures and dignitaries on that dais, why couldn't he outshine any politician against whom he might have to compete? Think about it, The Doctor said to himself, Jeff Jefferson is seen more often and by more people than the President of the United States!

He remembered words he had spoken to Jeff himself, when he was trying to sell him on television, "The day is going to come when we'll need politicians who look like actors. Or actors who look like politicians."

Well, it was here!

And the people crowding around Jeff were not liberals but good solid Republicans. Jeff Jefferson, whom some had accused of being on the left, belonged with the Old

Man, with his crowd, his politics.

Spot him in the right surroundings and he could be a candidate for Congress, for the Senate, who knows, even for governor! In a state with such an erratic electorate as California anything was possible. And with California now second in population and political power, muscle there would mean muscle in Washington.

As for Jeff's being equipped for the job, someone had once said about him, "He's nobody, so he can be anybody." Who was it? Of course. Lee Mandell when they were discussing Jeff's appearance before the committee.

Mandell was right, The Doctor thought, all one had to do was give Jeff the right lines to speak, surround him with the right people, and he could play a politician of conviction and integrity just as well as he had played all those admirable figures on C.M. Star Theatre.

Without question he could project sincerity. All one had to do was determine what he should appear to be sincere about.

Irwin Cone had found his Republican. And because of this demonstration of Jeff's instant popularity the long, slow buildup would not be necessary. The Big Plan could be accelerated safely.

The Doctor sent Spence's and Freddie's wives home by limousine so that he could hold a midnight meeting with their husbands. They sat in a secluded booth in Peacock Alley at the Waldorf, none of them touching the drinks they had ordered. Spence and Freddie waited. Finally The Doctor spoke.

"Spence, I think maybe from now on you should be spending most of your time on the Coast."

Though the idea did not appeal to him, Spence remained silent.

The Doctor continued contemplatively. "We are going to move into the Republican campaign and with Buddy already an avowed Democrat, he can't make the switch without breaking a lot of dishes. As an outsider to California politics, you can start right off as a Republican with no embarrassment, no explanations."

"And I think," The Doctor added, as a seeming *non sequitur*, "that the bank can now offer that loan to Central Studios. They're about to start shooting a very costly picture. I've read the script. It stinks. They've been turned down by three banks already. Our bank is going to offer them the money. Provided the studio is put up as collateral."

For the first time Spence felt impelled to question, "You said we couldn't move that fast."

"After tonight we can. Within a year we are going to have a Republican senator or governor. And with the muscle we have now in the Democratic camp, I think we're all set."

The last thing The Doctor said, before bidding them good night was, "Don't sell any of your TCA stock. But if you want to give some to your wives or kids, now is the time. A few thousand in gift tax now will save you millions later. Just hold on to the voting power!"

That night Jeff took Claire to Twenty-One so he could unwind. The Stork was too confining for conversation, especially the Cub Room. At Twenty-One one could find a quiet table upstairs. Even so, they were not completely alone, for more than a dozen people who had been at the dinner came over to introduce themselves and offer their respects. But gradually, with the aid of a few drinks, Jeff's tension dissolved.

"I'm proud of you, Jeff," Claire said, "really proud. The way you reacted to the Old Man. That special warm thing that existed between you transmitted itself to the whole audience."

"I can tell you something, then," said Jeff. "I enjoyed it. I mean what you get back from people is worth what you give them. For the first time I know what stage actors mean when they say they want a live audience breathing with them."

When he brought her to her door, he put off saying good night, hoping that she would invite him in. She didn't. So he finally said, "This is a silly thing for a forty-five-year-old man to ask. "May I kiss you good night?"

She smiled and he kissed her, a simple kiss, warm, but not passionate. He could tell from the tenseness of her body that she would not permit any more than that. When he sought her lips again, she turned her face, whispering, "Please, Jeff. I'm a married woman."

"That's a strange thing to say now."

"Until *the* man shows up again that's the way it is."

"Could I be that man?" he asked suddenly.

"You have one thing going for you. Irving liked you."

"And you?"

"We had a lot of likes in common, Irving and I," she said, smiling. She kissed him on the cheek and disappeared inside the apartment. He waited until she had safely locked the door before he stepped into the self-service elevator.

Before his plane left the next morning, Jeff called her. She was up and sounded happy. He could hear the boys in the background shouting over their new toys. As soon as she heard his voice, she said, "Never, never do that again! Those must have cost a fortune, Jeff!"

"What the hell, the money doesn't matter! As long as they enjoy them!"

"Well, I'm sorry to say they do. Now they'll expect that kind of thing all the time! You've spoiled them rotten."

He changed the tone of the conversation suddenly, "Claire, I have to go back now. I wanted to ask, if I can arrange an appearance for you on C.M. Theatre, a featured part, would you come out? The money isn't bad and they pay all your expenses."

"It would mean leaving the boys for a whole week."

"I realize," Jeff said. "Is that too long?"

"It would be the first time since . . ." She didn't have to say anymore.

"Think about it," he insisted.

"I will," she promised.

"Good. I'll call you in a few days to see."

"Do that," she said. Then, suddenly, to prevent him hanging up, "Jeff!"

"Yes?"

"I should explain something to you," she was saying. "Once a woman's been married to the man she's in love with . . . or fallen in love with the man she married . . . she's not very likely to . . ." she was groping for the right words. "She demands more of a relationship . . . an affair isn't enough. Once she's had it all, pieces won't do. So if you had in mind . . . I wouldn't want you to be disappointed or angry with me. Can you understand?"

"I understand," he said softly.

"Okay, then. I'll think about it," she said.

3

As soon as The Doctor arrived back on the Coast, he scheduled two meetings. The first with Al Myers, head of Central Studios. The second meeting was with Walter Craig, partner in a highly efficient but little-known firm of political analysts and advisers. The meetings were set back to back so it was important that the meeting with Myers go off without a hitch to allow The Doctor to meet Craig at Perino's for lunch. It was possible to have a nice long quiet discussion at Perino's without attracting a great deal of notice.

Since The Doctor did not want to spend much time with Myers he adopted his informal friend-to-friend approach.

"Al, we've known each other too long to screw around. Let's talk *tachlis*. Whatever I can do to help I certainly want to do. After all, in a way, we're as dependent on having this studio succeed as you are. It's our home, too. So, shoot!" The Doctor invited.

Myers was a veteran of good times and bad in the picture business. He had seen Central Studios decline from a steady producer of films to a struggling business whose overhead was largely paid by TV. Yet, much as he depended on it, Myers would never accept television as a legitimate medium. It sprawled like a cancer over three quarters of his studio but he lived in the secret hope that one day it would disappear and they could all go back to the old days.

"Irwin," he now asked, "what did you think of our script?"

"I've seen better, but I've also seen worse. Who can tell? I've seen scripts I wouldn't wipe my ass with turn out to be blockbusters!" Cone replied with the appropriate enthusiasm.

"You didn't like it," Myers said.

"What difference does it make what I think?"

"It makes a difference, a big difference, Irwin. I've been going over our position with the accountants. The smartest move now, all things considered, would be to shelve the picture," Myers tested gingerly.

"Shelve the picture?" The Doctor considered.

"You see we have trouble banking it. No bank wants to get involved on the basis of the two stars and the director."

"Then I don't see that you have any choice. Of course, shelve the picture!" The Doctor agreed, too readily.

"I'm glad you feel that way," Myers said. "Because I need your cooperation."

"*My* cooperation? It's *your* studio, Al. You want to shelve the picture, shelve it."

"Well, there's one hitch."

"Hitch?" The Doctor asked.

"Commitments!" Myers said. "The director and both stars. That's damn near half the budget right there. It'll cost almost as much to shelve it as to make it."

"The director and both stars." The Doctor considered gravely. "You got a pay or play deal?"

"In all three cases," Myers said. "You know that."

"I know they're clients of ours, but I wasn't aware of the details of the deal." The Doctor pretended to consider the matter gravely, "Pay or play, that's a serious matter."

"It's as serious as you want to make it," Myers said.

"Me? What can I do?"

"Our attorney suggested that you could induce your clients to waive their rights in favor of a future commitment on another film. Or better still, maybe you could sell them into some other picture so they'd release us altogether," Myers ventured.

"Advise three clients to pass up firm deals? Al, how can I do that and remain an honest agent?" The Doctor pleaded.

"They might be better off in the long run. We might all be better off," Myers suggested, rather than count off the dozens of deals he was aware of in which TCA had double-crossed its own clients to its own benefit.

"Ask me anything, Al, but don't ask me to sacrifice the interests of a client!" The Doctor said righteously.

Convinced that Cone would not budge, Myers resorted to a threat of his own. "We've already been turned down by Bankers Trust. And Bank of America. If we really start shopping around for the money the word would get out that three of your biggest clients together in one picture aren't bankable. What's it going to do to their price next time? Insisting on being paid off now might be the worst mistake they could make."

"I must be honest with you, Al. If they ask my advice, I'll have to tell them in my best judgment they should hold you to the deal," The Doctor said.

Myers rose sadly, started toward the door. Just as he put his hand to the knob, Cone said thoughtfully, "Al."

Myers turned back, for there was a hint of hope in Cone's voice.

"Al, I can't advise my clients to bow out. But there *is* something I might do."

"Yeah? What?"

"I might be able to help you raise the money," The Doctor said, still pretending to wrestle with the problem.

"Where?"

"There's a friend of mine, president of a bank in St. Louis. From time to time he's asked me about getting into picture financing. Maybe if I brought the two of you together . . ." The Doctor seemed to be considering the feasibility of it.

"Call him! Ask him to fly out at the studio's expense," Myers suggested quickly.

"It might be less likely to create talk if you flew to St. Louis. After all, if the deal doesn't go through, why have it known all around the industry?"

"Right. I'll fly to St. Louis," Myers agreed.

"I'll call him and try to set up a date."

"As soon as possible," Myers suggested. "After all, we got a starting date on the picture."

Between the time Myers left his office and the time The Doctor had to meet Walter Craig for lunch, he placed a call to the bank in St. Louis, spoke to the president, who was as much a TCA employee now as Spencer Gould.

"Dick, Al Myers will call you and come out to see you.

You are to advance him eight million dollars on his picture. His collateral must be the studio, all its assets, including the film inventory, *and* the land. The back lot alone must be worth thirty million dollars. If these idiots would only think in terms of land, not films, they'd be richer than they ever dreamed. But once a picture maker always a picture maker. It's a disease!"

When The Doctor hung up he was confident that within twelve months he would own Central Studio. And the best part of the deal was that TCA could say it was not a purchase, it was simply the result of an unfortunate banking arrangement the studio had made to secure financing on a picture that had bombed.

The Doctor was ready now to go to Perino's to keep his lunch date.

Walter Craig turned out to be a younger man than The Doctor had anticipated. He was in his mid-thirties, plump with thick glasses. He looked more like an insurance company clerk than an expert in political management. His unexpected youth caused The Doctor some uneasiness. In addition, Craig had a habit that annoyed him immensely. He scooped out the soft part of the French rolls, made little doughballs which he proceeded then to flip into the empty ash tray.

Over their first drink, The Doctor said, "You're a lot younger than I thought."

"You want me to apologize?" Craig asked. "I've got my Masters in Political Management, and I've been at this game since before I left school. I may be young, but I'm not inexperienced. In fact, I'm the best there is, else you wouldn't have called me."

He tossed another doughball into the ash tray. It bounced out and skittered across the table annoying The Doctor. Dealing so little with people outside show business, Cone was not used to meeting with anyone who did not stand in awe of him.

"Now, you've got a problem," Craig continued. "Shall I guess what it is?"

The question intrigued him so The Doctor nodded, "If you can."

"About every month or so I get this call, from some

man I don't know but whom I've read about. And it usually happens right after he's been written up in *Fortune* or *Time*. He's made his bundle. He thinks he's famous. And now he's ready to devote himself to the public good. Having successfully run a plastics factory or a law firm or an automobile plant he feels he can run anything, government, most of all.

"It never dawns on him that heading a factory and heading a government office might not be the same thing. Now the hell of it is, that in this country most voters feel the way he does. If a man has made a lot of money, ergo, he's very smart, smart enough to run a city, a state or the whole damn nation.

"They don't stop to figure that Washington, Jefferson and Lincoln, three of our greatest Presidents, were all failures in business. That the men who succeeded best at war made our least successful Presidents. They equate success anywhere with success in government.

"So my guess is that you have arrived at that stage in your life when, having all the money you're ever going to need, you've got only two choices open to you. Either you're going to endow something, like a college building or a library, or else you're going to put that money into running for office. Right?"

"Young man, I am delighted to tell you that you're wrong!" The Doctor said. Then he picked up a stray doughball, placed it deliberately into the ash tray, summoned the waiter and ordered, "Another round. And take this goddamn thing off the table!" He pointed to the ash tray. "Now if you're through making diagnoses, shut up and listen!" Then he smiled. For the young man had impressed him.

From that point on each had a higher degree of respect for the other.

"The first thing we should get clear, I do not want to be a candidate. I do not wish to serve in public office. I am quite happy with what I am and what I have. But I represent a man who I believe has the potential for public life. And I want to get your opinion as to whether you think he has a chance."

"You'd put up the money for him?" Craig asked immediately.

"I will see that the money is put up," The Doctor said without committing himself personally.

"Okay. Who's your man?" Craig asked.

"Jeff Jefferson."

The Doctor could not discern Craig's reaction, but if it was unbridled enthusiasm the young man was certainly concealing it well.

"Jefferson, Jeff Jefferson." Craig considered thoughtfully. "He's got a radical background, hasn't he?"

"Not really. President of his Guild for four terms."

"And what about that mess with the congressional committee?"

"He wasn't part of the mess. He was only representing his Guild," The Doctor explained. "The record proves that."

"Proves!" Craig repeated with some contempt. "I don't like candidates who have to explain, or prove or apologize. Besides, I think he's wrong for the times."

"You don't even know him. How can you say that?"

"He's a liberal. Liberals are going out of style. That's because nothing that's run by human beings really runs well, especially government. But the public doesn't know that so they blame the men who run it. It's time soon for the liberals to get their share of blame."

"And if he wants to run as a Republican?" asked the Doctor.

"Republican. Well, that's different. There I think he might have a future," Craig conceded.

"He will run as a Republican!" The Doctor declared.

"It's not that easy," Craig said. "First I have to decide if he has a Republican image."

"He has! I've seen him at it!" The Doctor related the events of the C.M. dinner.

"Sorry I wasn't there," was all that Craig would concede. He was silent a moment. "Look, I'll think about him. And I'll talk to my partner. We might even have to run a survey or two before we come to any conclusions. That'll cost some money."

"How much?"

The swiftness of The Doctor's question made Craig double his price. "Seven or eight thousand."

"You got it!" The Doctor said.

"If we get going, it'll cost a hell of a lot more."

"I told you, there'll *be* a lot more!" The Doctor promised.

Four weeks and two days later Walter Craig was The Doctor's guest for luncheon at the commissary in Central Studio. They sat at The Doctor's corner table, which, from its angle, gave them a view of the entire Green Room, a room actually paneled in fake walnut plywood, but named in the theatrical tradition for that room in which actors relaxed. Only executives, stars, featured players and agents dined here, the menu being more expensive than in the main dining room.

As they talked, Craig did not look at The Doctor but let his gaze sweep the room slowly searching for Jeff.

"Well?" said Cone. "What did your survey reveal?"

Instead of answering, Craig asked, "That table . . . Jefferson and that blond woman . . . who is she?"

"Actress. Friend of his from the East. Claire somebody."

"Oh," Craig grunted, seeming disappointed.

"Why?"

"She's nice-looking. Good image," Craig said.

"She won't be running for office. He will," The Doctor said.

"One of the things we found out is that people remember his divorce. Whenever there's a divorce they always blame the man. Remember what they did to Adlai Stevenson. Even called him queer because his wife divorced him," Craig said.

"Funny thing, people who in their own private lives commit every kind of sex crime you can imagine, demand at least the appearance of purity in their public officials."

"You mean it would help if he was married," The Doctor said.

"It would help if he were married to a woman who looked like that. Of course, her being an actress, we'd have to overcome that," Craig remarked thoughtfully. "Any idea what goes on between them?"

"He insisted she be on the show. We brought her out for a part that we could have cast with a phone call. Of course, I should tell you she's been married."

"Divorced?" Craig asked quickly.

"Widow."

"Good."

"Two kids, though."

"Better. He could stand a family image."

"There's a problem."

"What?" Craig asked, still staring at the handsome couple.

"The kids are Jewish."

"And she's not?" Craig asked dubiously.

"Her husband was."

"Have to think about that. Still, nice-looking couple. They laugh well together. That's good. They enjoy each other. That's even better. Sometimes, politicians in their forties and fifties have been married so long their wives bore them. It's damn near impossible to get them to smile at each other in public. These two have freshness. That's the word, freshness."

"Look," The Doctor interrupted, "I have no idea what their real relationship is."

"I am never interested in what anything *is*," Craig said quite firmly. "Only in what it *appears* to be. And to me they appear to be okay."

He turned his attention to the basket on the table which contained small packaged saltines, flat Swedish brown bread stiff as plastic and the inevitable studio *matzoth*. He picked a piece of *matzoth*, buttered it, salted it. Before he put it into his mouth he reconsidered with concern, "So the kids are Jewish." Then he bit into the *matzoth*.

The Doctor grew a bit anxious. "What else did your survey reveal?"

"People basically don't trust actors. They feel they are late-sleepers, drunks, immoral, overpaid, that they are actors only because they don't like to work at honest jobs," Craig summarized.

"Meaning?" The Doctor asked, expecting a negative reply.

"They don't trust them. But on the other hand, they like them. Maybe because people believe that actors actually do all the things *they'd* do if they only dared. It's a curious mix," Craig concluded.

"Will they accept an actor as a candidate for office?" The Doctor persisted.

"We think, my partner and I, that if we could endow an actor with the right image they would accept him."

"And that image is?" The Doctor asked, becoming somewhat impatient.

"I don't know," Craig confessed.

"You spent three weeks taking a survey, charged eight grand, and you don't know!" The Doctor exclaimed impatiently.

"Mr. Cone," Craig said very indulgently, "Mr. Cone, in our business we live by fundamentals. The first few basic decisions we make determine the course we follow, the image we build, the slogans we create, the ads we run, everything! So we take our time. Because if we make a mistake in our basic concept, no amount of money or effort can overcome it."

"Well, how long will it take," The Doctor began.

"I'd like to see him in front of an audience, a live audience."

"I've already seen him and I told you . . ."

"Look, there's an open date for a speaker at a Community Chest drive in Canoga Park next week. That's a good mix of typical Californians. Not the Hollywood kooks. Just people like the bulk of the voters in this state. If he would accept an invitation I'll see that he gets one."

The Doctor considered that unhappily for a moment. "A small town like Canoga Park? I don't know if I can get him to go."

"I'll make it easier for you. I'll get him an award."

"Award?" The Doctor asked skeptically.

"Sure. Man of the something . . . I'll figure it out. You'll have to pay for the plaque, though."

"Okay. If it makes it easier."

"Nobody ever refuses an award. Meantime, I'll have a speech written for him."

"What'll he say?"

"He'll have some good things to say about charity, brotherhood, and God," Craig said, quite serious.

"Wouldn't you like to talk to him, know what he thinks before you do the speech?"

"I don't give a damn what he thinks," Craig said simply.

"Doesn't it matter?"

"Not to me."

The Doctor couldn't conceal his surprise at such open cynicism.

"You don't ask a doctor to sit in judgment on his patient," said Craig. "Why ask me? I am a professional, a very high-priced professional. One thing you will find out, Mister. I know my business."

Jeff and Claire were getting up from the table. Whether it was the way he held her chair, or the fact that as she rose she smiled at him, Craig said, "Those two are either going to get married or go to bed together. I don't know which."

They had finished shooting Claire's scenes. It was late Friday afternoon. Jeff just had to do his host breaks. At his insistence Claire waited. They were done on schedule, no overtime, and it was not yet six o'clock.

Jeff went into his dressing room. Claire was there, in a simple dress and street makeup. Beside her chair was a suitcase.

"I checked out of the hotel this morning. There's no use paying for an extra day," she explained. He seemed hurt. "If I take the overnight tonight I can be home in time to have breakfast with the boys in the morning. Otherwise it means a whole day spent just traveling."

"I was hoping we'd have the weekend. We've barely had any time together. . . ."

"All day on the set, dinner every evening."

"I mean alone. Away from the pressure of work. Away from crowded noisy restaurants." When he realized that he was making it difficult for her, he smiled. "What my mother would have called 'courtin' time.' "

"I'm sorry, Jeff. But the boys . . ."

"I understand. We'll have dinner, then I'll drive you to the airport. It wasn't fair for me to pressure you."

"Thanks," she said relieved.

Instead of choosing Chasen's or La Rue or the Derby, Jeff decided on a small restaurant over in the Valley where they would not be subject to the stares and speculations of people in the Industry.

They talked about many things, but mostly Claire's reaction to film making. Stage-trained, with her most recent work in live TV, she had never realized how difficult it was to keep an entire performance in focus when it was done in such disjointed bits and pieces. And though she had been subjected to endless hours of rehearsals and run-throughs in live TV, she found them nowhere near as exhausting as the repetitions and the waiting around involved in film making.

"That's what it's like, five days a week, sometimes six," he said. "People think it's a breeze, but it isn't. And it's very lonely work," he said suddenly, making a more personal statement.

"How can you have time to get lonely?" she asked.

"You do," he said sadly. "After work. Having dinner alone."

"You don't have to have dinner alone," she said, referring indirectly to the other women there must be in his life.

"There are women a man will go to bed with with whom he can't stand to eat a meal. Because they have nothing to say, nothing to give. Except the cheapest thing there is in this town." He said it bluntly. It was a confession he had not made before.

"Since I was in New York there haven't been many of those. That's a pretty square admission for a man my age to make. Seeing you there did something to me. Made me realize that deep down, and despite what I know now to have been a lousy childhood, I am a family man at heart. But only to a woman who has something to give. I need encouragement, belief. It's as simple as that. I don't want to be admired. I don't want to be praised. I want to be wanted, I want to know that someone is *with* me, *for* me. Joanne never was. Just as my mother never was. For my father, I mean. She knew he was going to fail. She lived her whole life on that premise. I think she actually willed him to fail."

He hadn't intended to say any of that. Nor had she expected it. But it had been said. There was a long silence. Then he looked at his watch and said, "It'll take almost an hour to get to the airport." He signaled for the check and they left.

The Los Angeles airport at night smelled of stale smoke

and looked shabbier than it did by day. The airline clerks had lost the over-eager daytime smiles for which they were famous. And the passengers all seemed as if they'd been suddenly wakened from a deep sleep. Only the infants who were asleep in their parents' or grandparents' arms seemed not to mind, though there was one child whose crying could be heard throughout the terminal.

They checked Claire's bags and were waiting near the gate.

"I won't be able to get to New York for seven or eight weeks," Jeff said. "If you could come out. I mean TCA does a number of series. Parts wouldn't be hard to find. Maybe you could bring the boys and stay longer."

"I don't know," Claire said. "I'll think about it."

"I'll call you. But we'll have to synchronize schedules. What with the difference in time, my being on the set, your schedule."

"About the time you finish shooting it's nine o'clock in New York. And besides the rates are cheaper," she said quite earnestly.

He smiled. "My mother used to say, 'Watch out for a girl who wants to spend your money, Jeff. But even more, watch out for one who wants to save it. She's the one who's serious.' "

They both laughed. On the loudspeaker a brassy metallic voice, trying hard to be cheerful, was announcing Claire's flight. They started toward the gate.

"It'll be dull without you," he said.

"You'll find things to do," she said.

"Only thing on the schedule is a speech I have to make. Place called Canoga Park. They're giving a Community Chest award for making public service announcements on the show."

"What are you going to speak about?"

"I don't know. I haven't seen the speech yet. Someone's writing it now."

"Well, whatever it is, remember Alfred Lunt's advice to young actors. Just say the words so they can be heard. And don't bump into the furniture."

He didn't even smile. "I'll be wishing you were there."

The passengers were beginning to board. Just before she left his side, she said seriously, "For a man who didn't have any 'time' you 'court' pretty well."

"I do?" he asked, surprised.

"For the last two hours I've been saying to myself, 'If he asks me I'll have to tell him that one of the conditions must be that the boys continue to be raised as Jews,' " she said suddenly.

"Any other conditions?" he asked.

Before she could answer the passenger agent was insisting that she board. She started toward the plane steps, stopped halfway, turned back, shook her head, smiling, no, no other conditions.

Canoga Park was another neon-lit plastic-built California town with a shopping center within sight of the Freeway. It was the kind of town into which you drove only when there was an enforced detour. And when you did, you asked yourself, what the hell do people do here three hundred and sixty-five days a year?

As he left the studio that evening, Jeff Jefferson was picked up by a limousine, charged very meticulously to the promotion and publicity account of C.M. Star Theatre. He unwound from the exhausting tensions of the day with a thermos of premixed scotch and soda. Then he picked up the speech that had been written for him. He had had the chance to see it only once before when he had given his approval. Now he must set in his mind the phrases and sentences he wanted to hit, so that he could look up at his audience at the proper moments. That part didn't trouble him. He was a quick study, a facility he had developed years ago while making pictures on which the writers were only a few hours ahead of the shooting.

But tonight there would be no retakes, and he had to hit it right the first time. He settled back, drink in one hand, script in the other, and started reading. The speech began well enough. Jeff said he was more flattered to be in Canoga Park to receive the award, than he would have been in a large city, for America was truly a collection of Canoga Parks. This was where the values of good Christian charity were practiced in the finest tradition, exemplified by the town's most recent success with the Community Chest. These were the people Jeff thought of when he selected scripts for his show. These people were his audience, and that's why he was proud to accept their award.

The speech went on to touch, only lightly, on a few topics that might be considered political. It made a point of distinguishing Jeff from the other politicians. His posture was, "It is our duty as the people for whom this government exists to rescue it from the politicians. Those who would use it to convert this nation into a laboratory for all kinds of dubious sociological experiments." The use of the word "sociological" was deliberate.

There was nothing in the speech with which Jeff particularly disagreed, though if he had been less tired and more thoughtful he might have.

Everything went with predictable efficiency right from the chicken à la king through the apple pie. Finally the master-of-ceremonies introduced Jeff, thanking him in particular for personally visiting a small town like Canoga Park to receive their award instead of merely writing an acknowledgment. It was a true measure of his warmth and integrity, which the television screen reflected so well.

Ladies and Gentlemen, Jeff Jefferson!

The applause, loud and sustained, grew even louder when Jeff approached the lectern. Finally, he had to plead for silence with a broad gesture of his outstretched arms.

Once he began to speak, though, he was rewarded with such complete silence that he found himself rolling his words to fill the empty air. He slowed his delivery after the first few minutes as he began to enjoy the rapt intensity with which the crowd listened.

In the rear of the room, near the door, sat a man with a lighted clipboard and a pen. He made notes. Jeff was not aware of him and even if he had been, he wouldn't have known Walter Craig. Nor did he meet him that night. Jeff left as soon as his speech was over, pleading his early morning shooting schedule. Plaque under arm, he was relieved to get back into the limousine for the long drive home.

Walter Craig's work was only beginning. Before the dinner he had put down at each place setting, except those on the dais, a card requesting the reactions of the audience to a list of questions. Some of the questions were blinds to conceal the real purpose of the cards. But some were more direct, asking each individual how he responded to Jeff, to his speech in general, and to various specific statements in it. At the end of the evening, Walter Craig collected all his cards, those filled out, those still blank.

Two days later he was in The Doctor's office, waiting patiently as Cone finished a long distance conversation with someone named Dick, obviously a banker. They were discussing the terms of a loan, the security for which involved assets such as studio buildings, film inventory and land, a great deal of land. Since it seemed to have no apparent connection with his own mission, Craig did not listen too intently, though it always intrigued him when men talked realistically about sums in the millions.

Once The Doctor concluded his conversation, he turned his attention to Craig, "Well, what did you learn?"

Craig got out of his chair to strew a handful of cards across the little man's desk.

"What are those?"

"Preview cards. Same as you people use when you test a film out of town. We use them to get reactions. Everything we do is based on reaction. Why guess when it's so easy to find out?"

The Doctor nodded.

Craig picked up a few cards at random, read off phrases and single words which he had circled, "honest . . . sincere . . . speaks his mind . . . right about socialism . . . nice man . . . one of us . . . more like a person than an actor . . . very sincere . . . right, too damn much socialism."

"Of course, some people didn't bother to fill out their cards. But the percentage who did respond was high, very high, indicative of their response to his personality."

Craig reached into his attaché case, brought out some photographs. "I had a man there taking candids." He spread a sheaf of glossies like a card player opening a hand. The Doctor took them one at a time.

"He *looks* like a candidate," Craig said.

"That shouldn't surprise you," The Doctor said.

"It doesn't always work the way you think. Some men look *too* handsome. They antagonize people. People don't trust men who look too handsome. Jefferson has just enough plain features in his face to take the curse off."

"Okay, so what's your diagnosis?" The Doctor asked.

Craig got to his feet, made a rubbing gesture with both thumbs and forefingers reminiscent of the way he had rolled little doughballs at Perino's. "I think you might have a candidate here. With . . . uh . . . unusual qualifications."

"Is that good or bad?"

"Bad if you ignore them, good if you use them," Craig explained.

"Okay. Such as?"

"You see those cards . . . 'friend . . . neighbor . . . real person . . . nice . . . warm . . .'? To them he's real. Not an actor. Not a politician. Just a nice real warm person they believe and trust. We've got to create a new image that he symbolizes.

"The image of a new kind of politician. A citizen-politician. A man who leaves his regular business pursuits to devote himself to the business of government for a limited time.

"To him government isn't as complicated as politicians make it seem. He's got to take the position that basic questions demand basic answers which men with common sense can supply. Government has been in the hands of the politicians too long. The people have to take it back. And he, being one of the people, is the man to do it!"

"What's a party composed of professional politicians going to say to *that?*" The Doctor asked dubiously. "After all, he's got to have a party behind him."

"When the time comes I will take care of the party," Craig declared. "There is no more amenable man in the world than a hungry politician." Then, as though a phrase had just struck him, he said slowly, evaluating it, "A nation made free and strong by citizen soldiers has a right to demand the service, temporarily, of citizen-politicians as well." He nodded slightly, approving his own inspiration. "That's it! That's the key phrase!"

"And the professionals will buy it?" The Doctor persisted.

"They'll buy it, they'll buy it," Craig reassured him, permitting himself to be a bit annoyed that he was forced to answer the same question twice, particularly when his mind was working at top speed on other phases of the problem. "I'm going to want him for a few more trial runs—interviews with political reporters, maybe a TV panel show or two. But all local. We don't dare move on the statewide front until we are absolutely sure what works and what doesn't. It'll take a lot of tracking."

"Tracking?"

"You call it ratings. We call it tracking. What are the people responding to, thinking about, worried by? Mainly, what are they angry about? It changes from week to week so it takes constant tracking. . . ."

"Which," The Doctor interrupted, "takes constant money."

"Exactly."

"Don't worry about the money. Just tell me two things. First, can he be an acceptable Republican?"

"No doubt about it. The people he appeals to are in the middle or on the right. You saw that." Craig pointed to the cards spread across The Doctor's desk. "They're afraid of socialism."

"That's what puzzled me," The Doctor said. "When I read that speech there was nothing in there about socialism."

"There wasn't. But there was one word, a tap word, I call it. If there's a reservoir of anger, resentment or prejudice on a certain issue, the tap word, even if it hasn't anything to do with that issue, will release it. In this case the word was 'sociological.' They went for it. They put their own interpretation on it. They believed that he was coming out against socialism, because they *wanted* him to come out against it. Believe me, he can be a Republican and get quite a share of the dissatisfied Democrats too."

The Doctor nodded, content.

"You'll get the money up?" Craig asked.

"I'll get it up."

As Craig started out of the room The Doctor felt that for the first time in his life he had met a man who was even more cynical than he was. Even Cat's Eye Bastione who was the most practical man he'd ever met was not as cynical as Craig. Craig would do the job. The Doctor had no doubt of it.

He pressed down his intercom to summon Spence. When the nasal voice responded, The Doctor said, "Spence, I want you to draft a letter to send out to a select group of people enlisting their financial aid in the cause of Jeff

Jefferson. On the first list you should definitely include old
man Beecher; also the top executives of any company
large enough to pay substantial taxes to the State of California, even if their main offices aren't here. And, oh yes,
include the name Doris Martinson of Martinson Industries.
Don't specify any sum. Let's see the degree of their interest
first."

"Right!" Spence agreed.

"And don't use TCA stationery. This must be Spencer
Gould, concerned citizen, writing to other citizens patriotic
enough to be concerned, too."

Lincoln Day dinners are occasions on which Republicans
gather to laud Abraham Lincoln in order to raise money
to elect candidates of somewhat lesser stature. The California dinner that year was no exception. Since Los Angeles was conceded to be essentially Democratic territory,
the principal meeting was held in Sacramento. The speakers were a twice-defeated candidate for governor, the incumbent United States Senator whose term was expiring
and whose chance for reelection was somewhat doubtful,
and two state legislators who had already indicated a desire to secure the nomination for governor on the Republican ticket in the election still almost a year away.

Two days before the dinner, tickets for which had not
been selling well, an additional speaker was mysteriously
added to the list—Jeff Jefferson. What part Spencer Gould
and Walter Craig played in arranging that was never
made public. But ticket sales jumped enormously. Several
tables were bought out by anonymous friends whose identity was never established.

Unlike the Canoga Park appearance, and the few which
had followed that one, this time Jeff Jefferson did not travel
alone. Old Beecher had called from Palm Beach and insisted that a C.M. plane fly Jeff up to Sacramento. His
party consisted of The Doctor, Spencer Gould and Walter
Craig. And since Jeff had arranged for Claire to bring the
boys out to visit, she went along too.

Under Craig's meticulous direction, Jeff's group was
last to enter the banquet hall. His appearance inspired the
usual gasps of recognition, followed by a tremor of excitement. Then the inevitable repetition of "Jeff . . . Jeff . . .
Jeff . . ." on all sides. He smiled pleasantly, made his way

to the dais, modestly took his place at the foot of the long table, shook hands with the ex-congressman beside him, sat down, still smiling.

He was pleasant, affable, interested, and ate sparingly during the dinner. When the others spoke Jeff listened with grave concentration in the same manner that he listened to other actors in a scene. For an actor, listening properly is as much an art as speaking properly. So Jeff mustered the sincere, listening pose he had previously used for close-ups.

The speeches which preceded his were not distinguished. Lincoln was lauded. Strained allusions were made to the problems of the day, followed by pledges and promises of courageous policies and eventual victories. Any one of the speakers could have read the speech of any other and no one would have been the wiser.

Toward the end of the evening, just before the main speaker, Jeff was introduced. He responded shyly, trying to separate himself from the other men on the dais all of whom were known politicians. His speech opened with what Walter Craig called the humble bit. Jeff apologized for presuming on the time of such a distinguished audience, and presented himself as a mere citizen and taxpayer, thereby claiming kinship with the entire audience, which no other speaker could rightfully do.

Having thus disarmed them, he proceeded to deliver the heart of his speech which enunciated every concern, fear and resentment that Craig's tracking procedure had indicated was current in the public mind.

Jeff did not try to supply answers, did not even hint at solutions. He ended on a note of sadness and regret which, without a word of accusation, still managed to blame every politician in the state. When he finished there was stirring applause, deep, vigorous. Not the kind of ovation which had greeted him when he arrived but a more serious kind of applause that pledged not adulation but active support.

Craig was secretly delighted. He had made it work. He transformed an actor into a contender, a serious contender.

Craig was not the only one who realized that. Several of the men on the dais, who had spoken before Jeff, knew it too. Even the main speaker of the evening, the incumbent United States Senator suspected it. He was certain of it when his own long address, on which he and his staff had worked for days in order to insure his renomination, turned out to be an anticlimax. The expected interruptions for applause did not occur. All eyes were on the foot of the table, where Jeff Jefferson, listening intently to the senator, was upstaging him every moment.

The reporters present were quick to catch the trend. As soon as the dinner was over they besieged Jeff. At Craig's insistence everyone at The Doctor's table remained seated. He himself moved unobtrusively toward the dais, and stood below the clutch of reporters.

The questions which came in salvos were precisely those which Craig had expected. He was interested in Jeff's answers.

"Jeff, was this the opening gun in your battle to enter the political arena?"

"Are you going to declare yourself a candidate for some state office?"

"Which office?"

"What's a nice liberal like you doing in a place like this?"

Jeff just kept smiling. "Look, fellows, I didn't come here to do anything but make a simple speech. I'm not prepared to answer any questions. In fact in my speech I asked a lot of questions, to which I hope the politicians have the answers."

"Then you don't consider yourself a politician?"

"Definitely not. In fact, that's what may be wrong. Too many professional politicians. Not enough active citizens. Just as this nation was born out of the bravery and sacrifice of citizen soldiers at Concord and Lexington so it can continue to grow only through the sacrifice of citizen-politicians."

Craig recognized, though the press did not, a quote from a speech he had written for one of Jeff's minor appearances. Twice more during the questioning, Jeff resorted to quotations from two earlier speeches Craig had written for him.

When Craig felt that Jeff was running into trouble he mounted the dais. Immediately, the reporters realized they had been right in sensing an event. Craig's protective presence was explanation enough. They had their story.

They were now more interested in writing it than researching any further.

On the flight back to Los Angeles Claire, The Doctor, and Spence were full of congratulations. Craig was the only one who was silent and thoughtful. A man like Jeff, outspoken, uncomplicated, warm, and honest, was exactly what was needed to rejuvenate the Party. Despite the fact that he earned half a million dollars a year, he had convinced the audience that he was one of them, had the same problems, the same concerns about the state and the nation. Above all, he was sincere.

The Doctor's limousine was waiting for them at the airport in Burbank. They all piled in except Craig, who preferred to go home on his own.

On the way back, Jeff's greatest pleasure came from Claire's obvious excitement at his success. This time, before she went back he would ask her to marry him. Feeling the way she did, she must say yes.

She did.

Not quite forty-eight hours after the Lincoln Day dinner, Walter Craig arrived at The Doctor's office. It was the end of the day so Craig, Spence and The Doctor had a drink. Since the meeting had been called at Craig's behest, The Doctor turned it over to him with a simple, "Well?"

Craig reached into his pocket and spread on The Doctor's desk more than a dozen clippings of varying sizes from newspapers in Los Angeles, San Francisco, Sacramento, San Diego and other lesser cities in the state. The headlines were impressive, from two to four columns wide. "JEFFERSON STIRS GOP DINNER." "NEW ROLE FOR MOVIE STAR?" "A REPUBLICAN JEFFERSON? IS IT POSSIBLE?" "NEW HOPE FOR FADING GOP?" "IS GOP MOVING TO THE LEFT?" "NEW GOLDEN BOY FOR GOLDEN STATE?"

The Doctor scanned them, reading the lead sentences of each, then passed them on to Spence. Throughout, Craig remained serious, almost glum until The Doctor looked up at him, and said, "What are you so sour about? Terrific job!"

Craig moved to the bar. Mixed himself another drink.

"Most important fact in those clippings, the thing I

was really searching for, was, would they take him seriously?"

"And they damn well did!" Spence said, enthusiastically.

"Yes. They damn well did! Which presents problems," Craig said.

"You call last night a problem?" Spence asked. "I'd hate to see how you react in the face of failure."

"In my business, failure is the easiest thing to handle. It's over election night. But when you're confronted with success, that's different," Craig answered, leaving his concerns unspoken.

"And when you *are* confronted with success?" The Doctor prodded.

"They took him seriously!" Craig declared. "Now we are going to have to make some decisions."

"Such as?"

"He can't stay on TV much longer or we'll have an equal time hassle."

"I can take care of that," The Doctor promised.

"And convince him to give up all that loot?" Spence asked, concerned about his share of the loss of TCA commissions.

Before The Doctor could answer, Craig snapped at Spence, "Convincing him is *my* business! I'll take care of that!"

"How?" The Doctor asked, curious himself.

"Easy as catching clap. And based on exactly the same principle. Exposure. Expose him to people, applause, hero-worship. He'll catch the fever. He'll become convinced that they not only want him, they need him. Once that happens, he'll be like a fighter who smells the championship. Nothing will stop him from trying. And there's nothing he won't do to accomplish it. The whole trick is in giving him the fever."

"And how do we know if he's got it?" The Doctor asked.

"When it happens you'll know."

If The Doctor had any doubts he did not express them.

Craig turned back to the question that troubled him. "How do we keep him in the public eye once his series goes off the air?"

"How do we keep him in the public eye?" The Doctor

hadn't considered that aspect before. "We'll work on it," he promised, but in such a way as to indicate the solution might not be easy. "Anything else?"

"One thing, the most important thing. He's got to put himself in my hands completely!" Craig proclaimed.

"He hasn't been hard to handle thus far, has he?" Spence asked.

"He hasn't been handled thus far!" Craig shot back. "He's been given a few speeches to deliver. He showed up, he delivered them."

"And Goddamn well!" Spence said.

"And Goddamn well," Craig conceded. He moved to the desk, picked up the clippings and, one by one, read farther down the columns those portions which he had previously circled in red. *"Because* they take him seriously now, they are going to be asking serious questions. They started last night."

"That's good, isn't it?" Spence asked.

"He doesn't handle himself well with political reporters. He's an actor. He responds like an actor. Give him lines he says them. Give him a character he plays it. But on his own, nothing. He did not field the questions well last night. He doesn't know when to duck a question or how. He definitely does not know how to answer reporters who ask, 'What's a nice left-wing Democrat like you doing in a place like this?' "

"How bad is it?" Cone asked.

"It's not fatal. If he cooperates. If he does as he's told," Craig said.

"And if he does?" The Doctor kept driving.

"He's the most inexperienced, most electable man I've ever met."

"You haven't mentioned, for what office?" The Doctor asked.

"Governor, of course! Part of the excitement is seeing how far I can take a man without a single qualification except popularity. Frankly, I can't wait to see how it comes out." He finished his drink and started toward the bar again.

Spence had gone. Craig had gone. The Doctor sat alone in his large office.

"He's nobody so he can be anybody."

"Give him words to say and he can say them. Give him a character to be and he can be it." And that made him eminently electable, Craig said.

What motion pictures had never done, the magic box had accomplished. And why not? A star could make only two or three pictures a year. At most, each picture was seen by between ten and fifty million people. Half of them might see two of his pictures. Perhaps ten million people saw all three of his pictures. But on television he was seen by many more millions than ever saw any feature picture. He became a weekly visitor in their homes. Most important, he was always seen in a highly favorable frame of reference.

A basic change had taken place in the public's thought process. What a man appeared to be was more important than what he was.

The phenomenon had its amusing aspects, too. TCA had a medical series on TV. The actor who played the doctor was flooded with fan mail in which people presented their symptoms, seeking his advice. They had far more confidence in him than in their own doctors. A new era of electronic chemistry had dawned. You could photograph an illusion, project it on a screen and it became truer, more important than any genuine fact.

Cone cautioned himself in his exuberance. There was a risk in putting Jeff forward as a candidate too soon. It would endanger completion of his fourth full season on TV. Every other Republican aspiring to the nomination could claim the right to equal time. The network or any station in the state might be forced to cancel Jeff rather than make equal time available free to all opponents. Jeff would have to be exposed carefully so that he could not yet be considered a candidate.

There was also the other problem Craig had posed. If the time came when Jeff as a candidate was forced off TV, how did one keep his image constantly before the public?

Just before The Doctor left the office he pressed down the button of his intercom. "Spence, I want you to start making discreet inquiries about how much it would cost to acquire Jeff's old films."

"What do we want his old films for?" Spence asked.

"We've got a couple of hundred new ones."

"I'm not saying we want them. I just said to inquire. Casually. Maybe we just want to buy them up and burn them. But whatever we want to do, we don't want to do it so much that we're going to pay a lot for the privilege. Understand?"

"Understand," Spence said, though it was quite obvious he was puzzled, which gave The Doctor a second thought. "Look, better than that. *We* don't want to acquire anything. Set up a dummy company. Let them inquire about those films. It'll be cheaper that way and safer."

Before Spence could ask any further questions, The Doctor clicked off. He was ready to leave the office, having done a good day's work.

The set of news photos now on The Doctor's desk was taken on the afternoon of the quiet, very private wedding of Jeff Jefferson to Claire Colton. In the squib beneath the photos she was referred to as "one-time popular actress but in recent years wife and widowed mother who acts only when it is necessary to support her two sons." Several of the shots were of Jeff and Claire together. There were also some shots of Jeff, Claire and the two boys who had fortunately inherited their mother's light coloring, making a nice natural family group.

As he displayed the photos to The Doctor, Craig said, "We tracked it. Sixty-eight percent of the people like the idea. Seventy-one percent especially like the fact that Jeff Jefferson is going to be a father to those two nice unfortunate kids. The image is perfect."

"Then when are you ready to go into high gear?" The Doctor asked.

"The minute he's finished the TV series," Craig said. "Provided you've got that other problem licked."

"I've got it licked," The Doctor said. "I now own every negative Jefferson has made in his entire career."

"And?" Craig asked.

"The minute he starts running in earnest I am going to sell those films to stations around this state at prices so low they can't afford to pass them up. You'll see him on the late show seven nights a week," The Doctor said, beaming.

"In that case," Craig said thoughtfully, "let's save it for the campaign."

"You're that sure he'll get the nomination?"

"Three more speeches, a half-dozen TV press conferences with the right preparation and there won't be any opposition."

"You sound very sure."

"I told you. We've been tracking."

"You have that much confidence in your phone calls and computers?" The Doctor demeaned.

"Other people have started tracking, too," said Craig. "Party leaders. Potential candidates. And everybody's coming up with the same answer. It's going to take a strong man to beat Jefferson and he's not even a candidate yet."

"*Are* there any strong men around?"

"A few. But Jeff's got the edge right now."

"Despite his inexperience?" The Doctor asked.

"Because of it. He has no legislative record so he can't be confronted. He hasn't taken a strong position on anything so he can't be attacked. There's only one little weakness and I can teach him how to handle that."

"And that is?"

"The Communist hearings," Craig said. "But don't worry about it." He seemed very confident.

"Okay," The Doctor said. "When does he catch the fever?"

"I want to give him a few weeks to get settled into his marriage. Then I've got him booked for two important speeches. But this time I want him prepared, very well prepared, not for the speeches but for the interviews. For the first time in ages the reporters have a subject with some shine to him, some glamour. The more they can bounce their own wit off him the better they're going to look. So he's got to be ready."

"Will he be?"

"I think so," Craig said. "I think so."

"You have to remember that newspapermen are bastards, all of them!" Craig was saying to Jeff. They were seated in the den of the house which Jeff had bought since his marriage to Claire. It was a large room, comfortable, with a huge television screen which every chair either faced or was capable of facing with very slight adjustment. A room of leather and pickled pine, it smelled of both, being freshly decorated.

"Bastards!" Craig repeated. "They are not interested in the truth. Only in headlines. The more startling the headline the more space they get. The more space, the more stature for them. Their job is not to report the news, but to use what you say to further their own personal ambitions.

"Now, you can let yourself be used. Or," and here Craig paused to take another gulp of his drink, mainly for effect. "Or *you* can use *them*. You can play them like a goddamn pipe organ, only letting those sounds come out that you want to come out."

Craig pushed aside his glass, got up to pace the long room. Jeff watched him, wishing he could be as sure about anything as this dogmatic young man was about everything.

"The most important thing, do not engage in discussions with the press. When you are confronted by them, bear in mind one thing: politically, they are your enemies, because they are all left of center. They are not only anxious to use you, but to destroy you as well.

"So you do not discuss anything with the press. You give them cautious, uninteresting answers to all questions. Or, failing that, just a simple 'No comment.' Which gives rise to all kinds of rumors. But I would rather have you responsible for bad rumors than bad quotes. A rumor you can always deny. But what you say one day is tough to deny the next.

"The point is, don't feed them anything. After a while they'll stop pursuing and probing because they will feel, What's the use, he never says anything anyhow. Of course, you can never be rude. You have to be pleasant. But dull."

Jeff leaned back a little. "Pleasant but dull. Won't that be reflected in what they write?"

"Of course," Craig conceded instantly.

"How can that do any good?" Jeff asked.

"Your medium is not the press interview. Just because you go to a meeting and make a speech for some worthy cause is no reason why you have to be the victim of their game. Your medium is television where what you say can't be distorted or editorialized."

"Oh, no?" Jeff protested. "Man, have you ever seen them edit a TV film when they are only forty seconds too long. They can cut syllables if they have to."

"*If* you give them the chance," Craig said, staring down at Jeff.

"You don't have to give them a chance," Jeff responded. "They just do it."

Craig smiled, rubbed his forefingers against his thumbs, then reached into his inside pocket and drew out a neat pack of white file cards. As he spoke, he tapped them against the palm of his left hand.

"They won't be able to do it to you. If you follow my rules. Don't talk freely with the press. Save yourself for the TV cameras. When you spot them, play into them, as if you were doing a scene. And only give them the answers that are on these cards."

Jeff took the cards, flipped through them. Each one held a typed statement. Each statement was of almost precisely the same number of words. Jeff went back to the first. It was a succinct comment on free enterprise.

> Of course, I believe in free enterprise. Provided it is a partnership of free labor and free capital. Working together they can achieve anything. It's what made this country great. And will make it even greater.

Jeff glanced up at Craig. "There's nothing newsworthy about that."

"There will be when *you* say it," Craig said, quite sure of himself. "Jeff, I don't think you appreciate how much people admire you. Whatever you say they'll listen to. And the TV news editors know that. So they'll use you. And because your statements will always be short they will give you forty to fifty seconds of news time, unedited, uncut.

"Of course, if you make long rambling statements like most politicians do, you invite editing. And once they start to edit they distort. That's why every answer to every question has to take less than fifty seconds. I told you. Don't let the media use you. You use them."

Jeff continued to flip through the cards. There were answers to all the questions he had been asked up in Sacramento, including "What's a nice liberal like you doing in a place like this?"

He paused on that answer. Neatly typed were the words:

> I was not only a 'nice liberal,' I was a bleeding heart. Yes, I learned the dangers we're up against and I learned them the hard way. From personal experience. That's one reason I'm here now.

"That phrase 'bleeding heart,'" said Jeff. "Do we have to use that?"

"You weren't a Commie in those days were you?" Craig asked sharply.

"Of course not!"

"Yet they did use you. To protect a lot of innocent actors and writers, you also had to shield a few Commies. There's no use denying it. The facts have been public too long. So, before *they* get the chances to accuse you of being a bleeding heart, call yourself one. It isn't until a candidate confesses some failing that the voters feel they are dealing with a truly honest man.

"So *you* raise the issue. Disarm them! Don't give them the chance to make accusations! Any other questions?"

Jeff flipped through the remainder of the cards scanning each question, each answer. When he was almost done, Craig put aside his drink. He waited expectantly as Jeff scanned the last card.

"What the hell is this?" asked Jeff. "Two cards both with the same question. But each with completely opposite answers."

"What's the question?" Craig asked, knowing full well.

"Are you now a candidate for public office?"

"Oh, yes, that one."

"On the first card I deny it completely. But the second says, 'I have said before if the times comes when the people of this state want a citizen-politician I will have no choice but to be a candidate. I guess that time has come.'"

Craig peered at Jeff through his thick glasses, summoning as great a degree of earnestness as he could. "I never want to tell any man what to do with his life. But as I said before, Jeff, I don't think you realize the effect you have on people.

"In the past few years you've gained new stature in their eyes. Stature you never had before as a movie star. In the past few months just by making a few speeches you've emerged as a man of consequence. The people look up to you. They trust you. They believe in you.

"You keep thinking it's applause for an actor. No! It's adulation for a *man*. The public is like an innocent girl. In good conscience, you can't trifle with her affections. Sooner or later you're going to have to state your intentions. You will have to respond to the public demand. You owe it to the public. Nobody can tell you what to say. *You* have to decide that. You can withdraw. You can say you never were, never intended to be, a candidate for public office. Or you can say that you *are* a candidate. The only thing you can't do for very much longer is equivocate. It isn't fair to the people.

"That's why there are two answers to the question. The choice is yours. All I've done is suggest the words."

Jeff didn't answer immediately, but Craig knew that he had scored his point when Jeff said, "I'll . . . I'll think about it. I'll talk to Claire." Whether it was a favorable decision or not, Craig knew he would get his answer soon.

4

The Glendora High School stadium was damp and cool the night of Jeff's next speech. In the center of the football stadium, Walter Craig stood on the empty red-white-and-blue-festooned dais. He looked around. The people were beginning to enter the gates at both ends of the stadium. They climbed up to their places in the stands, had to wipe the wooden slats dry before they could sit down.

Damn the damp foggy California nights, Craig said to himself. Rain was not out of the question, not even in April. The floodlights from the towers played down on the field, cutting through drifting fog.

Sonofabitch, he thought, why hadn't he settled for an indoor affair in the auditorium? Of course that would have held only fifteen hundred people and it would have eliminated the band. But at least it would have been safe. Now there was no telling how many people would show up. Certainly not the five thousand needed to fill the stadium.

Nervously Craig climbed the platform he had paid to have erected to accommodate the television cameras. He greeted the technical crews, and saw immediately that if there were empty seats in the stands they would show and show badly on camera. To ask the cameramen not to pan the stands would only encourage them to do so, particularly since he had enticed the networks into sending the crews down on the promise that there might be "an announcement of great significance."

Aside from the weather the occasion was promising. The timing was right. The occasion was right. Jeff had been voted the Glendora High School Citizen of the Year Award. Craig looked down at the stands. They were filling, but slowly. People were showing up, some with raincoats, some with umbrellas, but still showing up. Perhaps it wouldn't be quite as bad as he feared.

As Craig reached the parking lot he saw the huge chartered bus pull in. To add to his agony he noticed that its windshield wipers were working methodically. That meant it had come through rain so short a time ago that the driver hadn't yet turned them off. He went toward the bus which was disgorging its cargo of newspapermen. As he greeted them he could tell that the bar and buffet he had provided on the bus had done its work. And a good thing, he observed, as they stepped into the damp night air.

Fortunately the stands were filling up. Those who came were sufficiently protected so that they probably would not desert before the ceremonies were over. Unless the rain came down hard. Craig sought out the school principal to urge him to move swiftly. His only hope was to get to Jeff's presentation and speech before everyone was waterlogged.

The band marched into view. Before they sat down, the principal announced the national anthem. As rehearsed, the spotlights on the field dimmed. Two lights focused on the flagpole at the end of the field. There hung the flag, drooping, heavy from the rain. It was less than an inspiring sight.

The anthem over, the principal called on a local minister to pronounce the invocation. Whether seduced by the presence of the TV cameras or by the largest audience he had ever addressed, the minister proceeded to deliver not a mere invocation but a speech. Craig noticed that the red and blue bunting was beginning to bleed a little, staining the white.

Finally the principal announced the main event of the evening. To the strains of "Pomp and Circumstance" Jeff was accompanied from under the stands out to the dais. He mounted the steps, was greeted by the principal, the president of the Board of Education and the president of the senior class.

Jeff and all those on the dais remained standing while the senior made the presentation. Jeff tried to appear interested, but all the while he kept feeling the collar of his shirt growing damper. And he kept wondering, Will this damn boy orator never shut up?

Finally, long after he had given up listening, they were suddenly thrusting a heavy plaque into his hands.

Just before he began his speech he felt the same surge of panic that he had experienced before all the crucial events in his life—his first scene on film, his first starring role, his first live TV show in New York—those moments when he had thought, Good God, I'll never be able to carry it off!

He was aware of the applause and the cries. They beat against him, but his panic set up a wall that would not let him enjoy the clamor. Only the actor within him made it possible for him to survive the moment.

If the audience was out there you went on. If cameras were on you, you kept going. You improvised. You depended on your instinct. You did anything you could think of to give them a show. Out of the need to survive, or to overcome your own fear you did something.

The cheering was beginning to subside. That was the danger signal. With an audience you did not dare leave accidental pauses. If you couldn't speak you smiled. Jeff adjusted the microphone to a proper height which gave them promise that he was about to begin. He raised both his hands as if to request their quiet and their indulgence. But as he intended, it only served to fan their applause. Then, as if in a gesture of mutual discomfort and in gratitude for their generosity in enduring this wet, dismal night for his sake, he turned up his jacket collar.

A laugh of sympathetic relief swept from the crowd. He had made them react. That encouraged him. His panic began to dissolve just a little.

Though Jeff's gesture was intentional its full effect was unpremeditated. The upturned collar hid his shirt and gave his face the stark, familiar frame of a clergyman's garb. More than his gestures for silence that image did most to quiet the crowd and create an intense air of anticipation.

He could begin now. He had to begin.

With the beams from the light towers spotlighting him, his face wet and glistening, he began to speak. What he said was neither new nor of great note, but the image of

the lone figure standing in the rain, steadfast and dedicated, inspired the crowd and in turn gave Jeff a rising
sense of power. Even Walter Craig, despite his misgivings
about the weather, realized that what he was witnessing
was impressive, magical.

The speech itself was dedicated to young America. The
challenges it faced. The opportunities it would have, if
parents did their best to preserve the American way of
life. When he reached the phrase, "these are our young"
he turned to the band sitting before him only to find that
their uniforms were soggy, their hats drooping comically.
But by now he was totally serious, self-intoxicated. He had
turned panic into power and he was enjoying it.

He was completely oblivious of the news photographers
who kept shooting away at him, enjoying the unusual
composition occasioned by the rain. Even the reporters,
who would much rather have remained on the bus eating
and drinking, were beginning to pay close attention. Tough,
critical, as they were, they were also realists. What was
happening could not be denied. Call it empathy or cha-
risma, it needed no name to endorse it. It simply was. You
could feel it.

In their minds the newsmen were already framing lead
lines and questions.

Claire watched, proud and moved. The Doctor watched
too, fascinated. Suddenly he knew that what Craig had
predicted was happening. Before his eyes, Jeff Jefferson
had caught the fever.

When the speech was over the crowd came to its feet.
People, cold and wet, who had every reason to resent
the moment, flung aside their umbrellas to clap and cheer.
The band struck up the scheduled "Glendora Victory
March" but were drowned out in the applause.

Jeff waited in the rain, collar up, both arms raised in
grateful acknowledgment. An agreement had been reached,
an understanding. The people wanted him. And he wanted
them to want him.

They were crowding around him now, Claire, The Doctor, the reporters. Even Walter Craig was pushed aside
in the rush, though not for long. He reached Jeff's side as
one of the reporters was asking, "Jeff, how do you feel
now about running for public office?"

Before he answered, Jeff's eyes furtively sought the red

lights of the TV cameras. Yes, they were on. And on him. His arm tight around Claire, he said grimly, "I have said before if the time comes when the people of this state want a citizen-politician in Sacramento I will have no choice but to be a candidate."

"You said, *if* the time comes. . . ."

"I guess that time has come," Jeff said, with the proper degree of humility.

At that moment Craig and The Doctor exchanged glances. To himself The Doctor said, That young arrogant bastard was right again.

On the way home, Jeff and Claire rode alone in one limousine, Spence, Craig and The Doctor were in the other.

"He won't back out now," Craig said. "You can talk to him about giving up TV. Or you can wait till some other candidate squawks. I'd do it now, so it doesn't become an issue but an act of sacrifice on his part."

"It's a hell of a lot to give up," Spence said mournfully.

But The Doctor said, "At most he passes up one season. We can always build a new series around him if he loses. In fact . . ." Then he was silent for a time. "In fact, why don't we have a script written for him now? Let him play a crusading governor. No, that's too pat. Let him play a crusading senator or mayor, a real representative of the people. We can use it as the last show of this season. It'll help his image if he runs."

"He'll run!" Craig insisted.

"And it'll automatically be a pilot for a new series if he loses," The Doctor said. "Without risking a dime, we're covered both ways."

The next morning the *Los Angeles Times* ran a four-column photograph of Jeff Jefferson, taken the night before, face highlighted by the rain, collar upturned, eyes penetratingly sincere.

The caption read: "Jeff Jefferson delivering speech last night in Glendora after which he admitted he will become candidate for governor."

On the TV news that same morning every major station in California broadcast Jeff's decision to run. Since the question and Jeff's answer consumed a total of only forty-four seconds it was run intact.

When Jeff had watched the telecast for the third time he realized how well Craig's system of TV exploitation worked. Play to the camera. Keep it short. Don't ad lib. *Use* the medium. Don't let *it* use *you*. Sharp young fellow, that Craig, a man to listen to. He knew his business as well as The Doctor knew his.

They had begun shooting the last show of the season. For Jeff Jefferson, it was possibly the last TV show of his career.

It was going to be a difficult week. It involved not just finishing the series, but the fact that Walter Craig had artfully succeeded in convincing *Look* to cover the event.

The theme of the *Look* piece was the transition of Jeff Jefferson, actor, into Jeff Jefferson, politician. So Craig had arranged for Jeff to conduct a complete campaign in microcosm as well as shooting his last film.

Late one afternoon Jeff was hustled off the set to attend a coffee klatch of Beverly Hills matrons, held in the house of a friend. Of course, Claire was with him. One evening he was driven directly from the studio to a PTA meeting in Westwood, where he posed answering a few questions, then was whipped off to allow the meeting to continue with its scheduled business. One morning, before shooting commenced, he hosted a breakfast for labor leaders in the studio commissary where he stressed his own years of service as a labor executive.

Toward the end of the week he presided over a long lunch meeting with a group of high school editors flown into L.A. by a C.M. plane. He posed for *Look* with individual students in simulated question-and-answer confrontations but the material he used had all been prepared by Craig. Most of his answers would find their way intact into the *Look* article in small boxed nuggets that were extracted from the copy and given special attention.

After the luncheon the students went onto the set to watch Jeff shoot one of his final scenes as the highly principled politician who was being tempted to make a choice between selfish political advantage and personal conviction. He opted, naturally, in favor of his convictions. And in making that choice Jeff never looked more noble, or acted with more conviction.

Craig and The Doctor made it a point to be on the set. Ostensibly Craig was there to aid, assist and suggest advantageous possibilities to the crew from *Look*. But the real reason for his presence was to make sure that the editor and photographer asked no cynical questions. One clever but snide remark could so appeal to them that it might find its way into the copy and destroy an otherwise favorable article. Magazines had come to associate derogatory wisecracks with "truth" and "frankness."

The Doctor was there to admire the expert manner in which Craig had stage-managed the entire campaign to date. He was also there to preside over the final-day-of-shooting party which was a tradition on most shows, but was important in this one which was ending not merely its season but its extremely successful run.

The last shot of the TV drama having been made, Jeff now had only to say farewell to his loyal audience for himself, for C.M., and for all the fine people who had helped produce the show during the past four years.

Although his reading was perfect, the *Look* editor made him do an endless number of repeats, since he felt this was the crux of his entire article—the moment when Jeff Jefferson resigned from one career to enter another.

So while the drinks and sandwiches were being passed around, Jeff struck pose after pose. When it seemed that he might grow irritable out of sheer fatigue, Craig nudged The Doctor and whispered, "Charge him up a little." Craig interrupted to make a constructive suggestion to the *Look* men about a possible additional angle, which gave The Doctor the opportunity to take Jeff aside.

"Just a few more minutes, Jeff-baby."

"Christ, if I smile anymore my face'll crack open," Jeff complained. "This week has been murder. I haven't seen Claire or the boys in days."

"Tomorrow, tomorrow," The Doctor comforted.

"Tomorrow they'll be swarming all over the house to see how I live, as if I live with a *Look* reporter, photographer and lighting man in the house all the time!"

"Easy, kid. One more day. Craig says it's extremely important."

"I know," Jeff relented. "It's being both things at once that's such murder."

"Another fifteen minutes, half hour at most, and that'll

be over," The Doctor assured him.

"There's something else," Jeff said, but he was interrupted as Craig called to him.

"Jeff! Tony would like a few more shots of that part where you say good-bye as host but indicate that you will be coming back to these people in a new role."

"You mean where I say, 'Much as I regret saying farewell to you as host of C.M. Star Theatre, I am doing so to take up the most important role of my entire life. As a citizen of the United States, who feels that public interest is above self-interest.' "

"Right!"

"Okay," Jeff said, moving back into the set, resigned to delivering the same line again for another half an hour.

By now the crew of the show was beginning to disperse. The drinking had ended. The food was gone. The farewells had been said. Only Jeff, Craig, The Doctor, the *Look* crew, and a few lighting men remained. Finally, the crew from *Look* was satisfied. The editor, a tall, heavy-set, young man, with a cigarette constantly in his mouth even when he spoke, stopped only long enough to check with Craig about tomorrow's schedule. Craig walked him out to his car.

When he returned he found Jeff in his dressing room taking off his makeup. The Doctor was standing over him. When Craig entered, The Doctor said at once, "Jeff's concerned about tomorrow."

"It'll be a breeze compared to the rest of this week," Craig said.

"The kids," Jeff interrupted. "I don't want the boys to be used. I don't want them to become an issue. They're not running. I am."

"What do you mean you don't want them to be 'used'? They're there. They're part of your family, part of the household," Craig protested.

"I don't want them to be questioned. They're extremely nice kids and I don't want them upset. That's what I mean!" Jeff said. "I promised Claire."

"Can they be photographed, at least?"

"Yes, but no questions about how they feel about me or how I feel about them. It wasn't easy at the outset. But we get along great now. I want to make sure it stays that way. So leave their religion out of this article! Understand?"

"I'll do the best I can," Craig promised, wondering how to fulfill Jeff's command without antagonizing the *Look* editor, for the boys' religion was one of the main angles he'd used to interest the magazine.

Jeff started out of the dressing room. It was dark out on the huge stage. "Jeff?" said The Doctor.

"Give me a minute," Jeff said.

The other two men walked toward the exit. Jeff heard them open the heavy soundproof door, heard it swing slowly and almost imperceptibly closed. He looked up. Above him, the high scaffolding that supported the lights looked ghostly. He moved back into the set. As host he had used this same fake library for four years.

He looked around, wondering how one said good-bye to half a lifetime. He had spent more than twenty-five years in places like this, sets that seemed so real but were always fake. The whole thing had been an elegant fraud but he had loved it. If anyone had ever told him he would leave acting voluntarily he would have laughed. Yet now he was doing exactly that.

Though, in a way, it was not as great a breach as he had imagined. There was as much fakery in politics as in show business. More. For in show business everyone knew it was fake. And the degree of one's success depended on how real one could make the fakery look. Politics was supposed to be real. Politics dealt with the life and death of people, cities, states, whole nations. Yet in practice it was just as phony.

He had proved it this past week. Faking on the set during shooting hours, faking off the set at interviews. But that was all in getting the job. Once elected, if he was elected, he reassured himself, he would do the job honestly, in the best interest of the people, as he saw it. No deals and compromises for him. He didn't have to make any. If they didn't want it his way, screw them. He could walk out. With the money and assets he had now he was independent.

Then he realized that he was paraphrasing the dialogue from his last show.

He wondered, did the time come when even you as

the actor became so confused between fake and real that you didn't know the difference?

He looked at the set for the last time, started toward the dim red glow that indicated the door to the street.

Outside Craig and The Doctor had been having a hurried discussion.

"Christ, only twenty-four more hours to go!" Craig was saying. "I don't want him to act up now!"

"He won't," The Doctor kept saying, though he was by no means sure.

"That was going to be the climax of the whole bit! It's worth a quarter of a million Jewish votes at least!" Craig protested, angry and concerned.

"I'll talk to him," The Doctor promised.

"Doc, let me tell you," Craig began. It was another of Craig's habits that irritated The Doctor. He didn't mind being called "The Doctor," or just "Doctor," but "Doc" was highly unprofessional and he disliked it. Yet this arrogant young genius kept calling him that. "Doc, if this *Look* article works, and right now it's working, it's the nomination. And this year," Craig emphasized, "this year the nomination is the election. The Democrats are disorganized. They're back-stabbing each other. They've got an incumbent who's tired and unexciting. You want my honest opinion? Any Republican can beat him. So the fight will be for the nomination.

"Now I want that nomination before there's any primary. I want the primary to be a mere formality. I want a unity celebration, not a bitter public fight. The *Look* article can do it. So you better talk to him."

"They'll have to ask questions about the boys, I suppose," The Doctor said sadly.

"Wouldn't you?"

The Doctor nodded.

"Then talk to him!" Craig persisted.

The heavy stage door was opening. As Jeff approached, The Doctor exploded suddenly, to Craig's complete surprise, "I don't care what you think, Walter, I'm going to talk to him!"

Jeff looked sharply into The Doctor's face, prepared for confrontation. The little man moved close, took his arm, spoke confidentially, "Jeff, I *have* to talk to you about this!"

"What?" Jeff demanded.

"Of course, it can't mean as much to you as it does to me."

"What are you talking about?" Jeff asked, puzzled.

"After all, why should it mean anything to you? You're a gentile. You're part of the big WASP majority but I'm not. So it's my duty to talk to you. Finally, after centuries of persecution there comes a little bit of enlightenment . . . even the Catholic Church calls an Ecumenical Council. They're already talking about changing some of the hateful lies in the Bible.

"When that feeling is in the air, and you have in your own home such a beautiful demonstration of loving coexistence, how can you deny the rest of the nation the opportunity of seeing it? Mind you, I'm not saying make a point of it. I'm not even saying let them question the boys. I agree with you about that. But not to let *Look* mention their religion? Why it would look as if you're ashamed of it. And, Jeff, I know that's not like you."

The Doctor paused, but only very briefly, before he said, "After all, I remember that girl from Chicago."

Jeff didn't answer. The memory of Charlene stirred him. And because it did, he resented The Doctor intensely.

"Jeff, it can do enormous good if the rest of the world can see how people of different beliefs live happily together in one household, respect each other, love each other. Enormous good!" he repeated.

Jeff remained silent. Craig seemed about to speak, but The Doctor's eyes forbade it. He knew Jeff too well. Jeff was, after all, an actor. Give him a noble bone to chew on, and he would eventually do what you wanted.

Jeff turned to Craig, asked grimly, "They wouldn't be questioned? Wouldn't have to discuss their religion?"

"Absolutely not!" Craig replied with that degree of over-aggressive sureness that only the unsure feel called upon to display.

"Well, I'll think about it." Jeff turned and started toward his personal parking spot where his new Cadillac waited.

When he was out of hearing, Craig asked, "Well, Doc, will he say okay?"

"He'll say okay!" The Doctor answered. "But do me a favor from now on, will you?"

"I know," Craig anticipated. "Don't call you Doc."

"And one other thing!" the little man said angrily. "Don't make me do your work for you. I despised that little scene I just put on. I don't like to make *Yom Kippur* speeches!"

"*Yom Kippur* speeches?" Craig asked.

"Big tearful appeals. Made the night of *Kol Nidre*. Christ, my father would have turned over in his grave if he'd heard that line you made me give Jeff!"

"You want him elected, don't you?"

"That's what I hired *you* for. Do your job. Don't make me do it for you! Of course I want him elected!"

"I thought you might be cooling off," Craig said, watching for The Doctor's reaction. "I thought now that it looks like the Democrats may own the White House for at least four years you'd lost interest."

"Exactly what does *that* mean?"

"Damn!" Craig said suddenly, snapping his fingers. "Something I meant to tell Jeff about tomorrow." He started to walk toward his car, but The Doctor caught him by the jacket.

"*What did that mean?*"

Craig looked down at the little man through his glasses so that it was difficult to tell whether he was smiling or not.

"It means," Craig said, "that I expect you to make sure I can buy a lot of TCA stock at the issue price."

"What do you know about that?" The Doctor demanded.

"Now that you own the studio, plus several thousand negatives, fourteen shows on the air, and a bank in St. Louis, I understand you've been having discussions with two different underwriting houses in New York."

"How do you know?"

"It's around, Doc, it's around," Craig said. The Doctor released his hold on Craig's jacket. "Just as it's around that only one thing can stop it."

"Yes?"

"An anti-trust suit. That could freeze everything for a couple of years. And if color TV is in strong by the time that suit's over, then your assets'll be worth half of what they are now. From the moment you told me you wanted to push Jeff Jefferson, I couldn't relax till I found out the real reason.

"That's why I thought that now when it looks like the Democrats can do you more good than the Republicans you were beginning to cool on Jefferson."

"I am not cooling on him. I want that man elected."

"Okay. Get his word that he won't make any fuss about his boys in the *Look* article and I can guarantee it."

"When he says to me that he's going to think something over, that means he's going to say yes." The Doctor started toward the studio gate.

Craig watched him go, knowing that he must never again come so close to antagonizing Irwin Cone. If a fix was made in the White House there would have to be a payoff somehow. It might mean running someone else for some office. He wouldn't want to cut himself off from that opportunity. Meantime there was Jeff and the nomination and the election.

Just before seven the next morning, Walter Craig pulled up in Jeff's driveway. Though it was early, perhaps too early, he had to make sure of certain details before the *Look* editor arrived.

He rang the doorbell. Jeff himself answered, smiling warmly despite the early hour. But when he saw Craig, his smile faded.

"I thought it was *Look* a little early. Don't you ever sleep?"

"Between campaigns. Then I sleep a lot, screw a lot, drink a lot. But during campaigns." Urgency and fatigue caused Craig to change the subject abruptly. "Your socks. And your suntan. I went to bed thinking you were set for today, but I couldn't fall asleep. Your socks. Let me see!"

Puzzled, resentful, Jeff stuck out a leg.

"No, no, no! Raise your pants leg. How far up do your socks go?"

"Up to the calf."

"Good!" Craig said, relieved. "Nothing looks lousier in a shot than a lot of exposed leg. Now let me see, got a sunlamp?"

"Yeah."

"Take three minutes, right away!"

"Why not send over a makeup man with some pancake?" Jeff asked.

"Too noticeable. Lamp's better," Craig said, unaware of Jeff's sarcasm. He turned to leave, but Jeff stopped him.

"Why don't you ask?"

"What?"

"What you really came here to find out!" Jeff said sharply. When Craig looked puzzled, Jeff continued, "About the boys."

"Did I say a word?"

Jeff overrode him. "We talked it over. Claire and I. If they aren't questioned directly we have no objection to their religion being mentioned in the article. But no phony posing the boys going to Hebrew school, none of that nonsense!"

Craig, having won more than he had hoped for, nodded emphatically.

"When they get here, I'll tell them! Those are the ground rules!" Jeff said.

Before Craig could leave, the *Look* limousine pulled into the driveway. "I'll stall them," he whispered. "Get some tan!" He started across the lawn, calling, "Hey, guys, let me out first, huh?" Before the editor and cameraman could climb out, the driver obliged by pulling the large car out of the driveway.

Craig started to back down to the road. Then he stopped, got out, and walked over to the limousine. "As we agreed, he's all yours for today. No interference from me. You can get the real Jeff Jefferson."

"Okay," the editor said, wondering why it was necessary to restate what they had already settled.

"Just don't bother the boys about their religion. Say what you want, but no questions. Okay?"

"Okay," the editor agreed, as editors always do when they intend precisely the opposite.

Having done his part by securing, at least in form, the agreement he had made with Jeff, Craig went back to his car and started down the street.

The day went well for the most part. They took pictures of Jeff at the breakfast table studying a speech and

Claire in the kitchen frying eggs for the boys. Her hair was freshly set and she was dressed in a crisp housedress, not the robe she usually wore.

They went through the day taking photographs to foster the Jefferson image. The Jeffersons relaxing around the pool, Jeff taking the boys off to the Tennis Club, Jeff and Claire alone, Claire making calls for a number of charities.

Through it all, Claire posed graciously, wondering if this was what it was going to be like from now on if Jeff were to win. And trying to decide whether she liked it or resented it. Being the wife of a TV star meant being stared at until she had begun to avoid public places. But being the wife of a successful political candidate, would mean no privacy at all. Still Jeff seemed to like it, so for his sake she did the endless number of things that the photographer requested.

The editor got around to the boys during lunch but he never brought up the subject of religion. Instead, he focused on the boys' adjustment to Beverly Hills, their reaction to the difference between living in New York and living out West. Which led him to ask, quite naturally, "How do they get to school here?"

"Bus," Claire said. "Though sometimes when Jeff has a late call at the studio he drops them off. It's rare enough to be a treat," she explained.

The editor turned to his photographer, "Let's get a shot of that right after lunch."

They posed several times. Jeff coming out of the house with the boys, then in the car. While the photographer was shooting, the editor hung back with Claire making idle conversation. After a few minutes he said, very casually, "I respect your feeling about the boys, so I don't want to bother them. But what Temple do they go to? When they go."

"They go. Regularly. It's Temple Israel over on Wilshire. And I appreciate your not asking them."

When their work was over in mid-afternoon, the *Look* contingent departed. On their way back to the hotel, the editor stopped at Temple Israel and had the photographer take a dozen shots of the exterior.

It would have been perfect, the editor thought, to have

the boys posed entering, with those funny little hats on
their heads. But when it came time for the series to be
laid out he would be damned certain to place the pictures
of Jeff driving the boys off to school and the shots of the
exterior of the Temple in such way as to visually indicate that Jeff Jefferson, star and political aspirant, took two
little Jewish boys to Temple every week. It was good,
warm, human interest.

5

Spencer Gould was in charge of the private meeting of California's Republican political powers. Those who lived in and around Los Angeles were driven to the Bel Air Hotel by limousine. Those from outlying parts of the state were flown in by three planes put at Walter Craig's disposal by Consolidated Motors.

The Bel Air had been chosen because it was out of the way, quiet. A meeting there was far less likely to attract attention than at the Beverly Hilton or one of the large old downtown hotels.

When the men arrived they were led into the dining room which had been partially converted into a meeting hall. Chairs were lined up in rows to face a large white screen. On each chair, lying face down, was a copy of *Look*. When a politician picked it up and turned it over he was confronted by a huge close-up of Jeff Jefferson. It had been selected from among more than four hundred shots as most representative of the actor turned politician.

The article itself was extremely flattering, making good use of his liberal background and of his sacrifice in giving up a highly lucrative profession to become a citizen politician.

Small boxed insertions within the text of the article quoted Jeff's feelings on key state issues. Taxes, too high for the average man. Communism, dangerous, a fact he learned from personal experience. Welfare, an unfortunate necessity until the society found jobs for all. Economy in government, a must if the state was to prosper and grow. A number of his stands on other issues were also included, all in the precise words which Craig had written and Jeff had memorized and used so many times he believed them himself.

Before the assembled group had had a chance to read
through the entire article, Walter Craig took his place
by the large white picture screen.

"Gentlemen, first I want to thank you for attending
this morning. Those of you who came out of curiosity.
Those of you who came out of Party interest. And those
of you who came because you represent other potential
gubernatorial candidates."

Craig took a moment to glance about the room. He
spotted the campaign manager for the Mayor of San
Francisco who had announced his intention to run. There
was also a representative of the assembly minority leader
who, though he disavowed all intention of running, nevertheless had "volunteer" groups working for him. Craig
even noticed the supposedly neutral Republican State
Chairman, who secretly represented the United States Senator. The Senator's friends had conceded he could not
sustain another successful campaign for the Senate and
had suggested that he withdraw gracefully by running for
governor.

Certain that all his serious competition was represented, Craig continued his carefully planned speech.

"Now, I don't think that any of you doubt that this
can be a Republican year in California. The Democrats
have only a tired incumbent to offer. And no new platform. The people are disenchanted and restless. They want
a change.

"But we would be fools to think that just any Republican can win. Or that if we have a bloody battle among
ourselves we won't be giving the Democrats enough ammunition to defeat us. We can only turn this election into
a sure thing if we are willing to unite now instead of after a long public brawl in the primary. If we agree here
and in private to support the one man who can be elected,
we would save time, effort *and* campaign funds, campaign funds which could then be used to win the election.
And, gentlemen, I can assure you if the right man is
agreed on, there will be considerable financial backing."

This last Craig said with enormous confidence and
promise. The effect was not lost on the men sitting before
him, holding in their hands the tangible evidence of Jeff
Jefferson's appeal. Craig turned to the screen and the rest
of his presentation.

The computerized results of months of tracking were flashed on the screen as Craig spoke. The figures showed the continuous growth of Jefferson's popularity, as compared with the spotty showing of other potential candidates. In every area Jeff ranked consistently higher than any other Republican contender. He also ranked higher than the Democratic incumbent, particularly in towns and cities where he had spoken shortly after the Democrat.

But the most significant facts the computers revealed concerned specific counties. In normally Democratic areas Jefferson ran almost neck and neck with the Governor, stronger by far than any other Republican. In Republican strongholds he outpolled any other contender. And in the swing areas, of which Republicans had to capture at least seventy percent to win, Jefferson ran ahead of the incumbent ninety-one percent of the time.

"If Jefferson just holds his own in the Democratic strongholds and does as well as the figures indicate in the swing districts," Craig wound up his speech, "he can carry this state by possibly as much as one million votes!"

If his competitors in the audience scoffed at such an ambitious margin of victory, they could not quarrel with Craig's general conclusion.

Now Craig turned to a discussion of the issues. There was projected on the screen print-outs of the tracked opinions of the voters—county by county—on the basic issues, taxes, communism, welfare, right to work, honesty in government. But this time, instead of referring his audience to the screen for corroboration, he referred them to the copies of *Look*. The majority of the audience was beginning to realize that, like it or not, they were being confronted with a political blitzkrieg.

"Now, I'll hold our survey on public opinion on the screen long enough for you to check them with Jefferson's opinions as printed in next week's *Look*. See for yourself how closely they coincide.

"As a candidate he stands for all the things that most of the voters support. No one else has had more exposure, more public acceptance. No Republican can equal him. You have all been present at meetings where he's spoken. Those of you who were invited. And those of you who just dropped in to scout the opposition . . ."

Craig looked at the campaign managers for the mayor and the senator to let them know that he knew.

"When Jeff Jefferson speaks, they don't turn out to hear a politician. They turn out to applaud a Star! They feel an intimacy with him that no other candidate can claim. They've seen him every week. They love him. He's part of their family. No politician in either party can deliver that kind of impact!

"Gentlemen," here Craig raised his own copy of *Look*, "on Wednesday morning this magazine will be delivered to millions of homes in California and across the nation. Jefferson's face will appear on every newsstand from Sacramento to Portland, Maine. Yes, you have here a candidate of national importance!

"The only question before us today is whether he is going to be your candidate *before* a bloody primary battle or *after*? Because he's got the horses. And he can ride them. Money. TV. Popular acceptance. And one other exclusive asset.

"Politically, he's a virgin. He has no record to hinder him. No past to explain. No mistakes to cover up. For the well-to-do, he's rich. For the middle class, he's self-made. For the worker, he's a four-time union president. For the farmer, he's a farmboy from Iowa. Gentlemen, you would be fools to fight him. Because he's going to be your candidate and your governor. I'm asking you to join up now so you can ride the victory train. Only a vain or foolish general commits his troops to a war he knows he can't win. But then, that's up to each of you. Let's break for a drink and something to eat."

His invitation to lunch was intentionally abrupt. He wanted them to start their own private discussions as soon as possible.

The lights came on in the room. The men rose, moved toward the bar where two bartenders were ready with large glasses of prepared Bloody Marys. They took their drinks and separated into small groups. Occasionally a man would slip outside to find a phone.

Craig moved through the room, stopping to accept congratulations on his presentation. Near the door he found Spencer Gould. "The mayor's man has already gone to the phone," Spence said softly.

"The break will come if the senator caves in. When the

Party chairman goes to the phone, that's it," Craig whispered back.

Lunch was already underway when the mayor's representative returned to the dining room. He slipped into a seat at the same table as the Party chairman. Some words were exchanged, accompanied by grave looks. The chairman eased out of his seat just before coffee was served.

He was gone more than fifteen minutes. When he returned, Craig stood up to thank the men for attending the session.

The meeting closed. The politicians dispersed. The farewells were cautious, pleasant formalities. Back in the large dining room two men waited to talk with Craig and Spence. One represented the Mayor of San Francisco. The other was the Party chairman.

He spoke first. The senator would withdraw from consideration for the governorship if Jefferson would back his renomination to the U.S. Senate and help him during his campaign. The mayor's representative said his man would settle for nothing less than second place on the ticket. Spence made it clear that he was in a position to comply with both demands.

As for any other candidates, there would be no deals. Nominal opposition in the primary was needed anyway and that would come from the Assembly Minority leader who posed no real threat. Jeff Jefferson's nomination was assured.

Spencer Gould returned to the TCA office in Beverly Hills. He discovered that The Doctor had left for Washington early that morning, summoned by a hasty telephone call. Spence's good news would have to wait. Instead he called Jeff to report that he and Craig had had an "interesting and helpful meeting" with some of the political leaders in the state and they had been "most friendly and cooperative." Things looked very encouraging. He did not tell Jeff of the totality of their victory. With a primary yet to come, they did not want Jeff to relax, no matter how favorable the odds. Craig had cautioned Spence quite urgently on that point.

His plan was basic. Let Jeff fight the campaign as though he thought he was still the underdog. It was a good image to present to the voters. More important, the exhilaration

Jeff would receive from winning the primary and winning big would give him the impetus to carry him through the rigorous election campaign itself. Candidates had to be handled like prize fighters, Craig instructed.

Or like actors, Spence agreed. They must be brought to the proper degree of insecurity, desire, and nervous tension to deliver their best performance.

During the next two months, Jeff Jefferson delivered. He visited supermarkets, factories, farms, and even busy city street corners. He lunched with important businessmen, attended PTA meetings, and spent his evenings at dinners for one civic purpose or another.

He spoke frequently, always using the same script, with small variations which reflected the computer's latest findings. Where groups had special ethnic or business interests his material was directed at those interests. He was for education, oil depletion, local control, state control, lower taxes, economy, more road building, more schools, more government control over every tax dollar, but less government interference overall.

He never found a less than enthusiastic audience. People liked him before they saw him. Liked him still more when they discovered that he could talk government as well as any politician they had ever heard. He was frank, honest, friendly, clean looking, and too American to create suspicion in anyone's mind. People who were inclined to say, "All politicians are crooks," felt differently about Jeff Jefferson.

Claire delivered her share, too. She spent most of her days at women's clubs, charity affairs, teas, league-of-women-voter meetings. And she had that rare and fortunate quality of being a good-looking woman who did not inspire envy or resentment. Because she had such obvious affection for her husband, such belief in his integrity, other women admired her where they might have envied a less warm and loving person.

The primary went as Craig had predicted, within two-tenths of a percentage point. Even that miscalculation was on the conservative side. Craig delivered more than he had promised The Doctor.

It was a bright day, and clear. Jeff Jefferson was being driven to a rodeo. This time, though, he was not riding alone and sullen in the back of a hooded black limousine. He was in an open convertible. Claire sat on his right and the Mayor of Salinas on his left. And Jeff was on his feet, both arms held aloft, that famous warm Jeff Jefferson smile on his face. He kept glancing from one side of the street to the other at the rows of people who had gathered to watch him ride from the local airport to the rodeo grounds. Walter Craig's advance man had done an outstanding job.

Occasionally someone leaped from the sidewalk to shake Jeff's hand. He obliged in his warm, friendly fashion, seeming both amused and delighted at the tribute.

Ahead of his car with their sirens at a low growl so as to attract attention but not irritate the public, rode six motorcycle policemen. Behind Jeff's open car came two limousines filled with reporters and photographers. Behind them rode lesser city officials and other politicians to whose advantage it was, or would be, to be seen in the Jefferson entourage.

Hearing the crowds scream "Jeff . . . Jeff . . . Jeff!" he thought to himself, One hell of a long way from Amarillo to Salinas. Today there would be no phony rodeo routine, no hokey white cowboy suit, no riding out on a palomino trying to milk applause from the crowd. This time he would not be singing the "Star Spangled Banner" in that flat uninteresting voice of his, hoping the band would cover for him. Instead of having to sit through hours of boring contest between man and beast, merely to go through the formality of awarding a prize, this time there was his speech to deliver, an important speech. The campaign was reaching its peak and the Democratic incumbent was beginning to realize how badly jeopardized were his chances. He was particularly enraged in recent weeks by the appearance on TV of a continuous stream of late late shows featuring Jeff Jefferson. Despite the protests of County and State Democratic Committees the practice continued. One County Chairman appealed to the Federal Communications Commission for an equal time ruling. But since none of the films had any political content or were personally laudatory of Jeff Jefferson as a candidate, the FCC decided not to intervene.

Even the threat of court action did not move them. Finally, when the Chairman of the Democratic State Committee did bring action, the case was thrown out and it became obvious that to go to the U.S. Supreme Court would mean there would be no resolution until long after the election.

Thus, night after night, seven nights a week, in addition to the TV spot commercials that both parties used with comparable frequency, Jeff Jefferson could be seen for several hours in his old films.

To make the incumbent's position even worse, Jefferson's heroic image was almost invulnerable. He had no political record. And no lapses or shortcomings, so long as he confined himself to Walter Craig's carefully prepared speeches and responses. This he did, with the faithfulness of a well-prepared, well-directed actor.

It was at this target that the Governor, out of sheer desperation, had decided to level his attack. His polls had revealed that much as people loved their TV and screen idols, there always lingered a feeling that actors were less than completely stable citizens. So gradually, but with increasing concentration, the Governor focused his criticism on Jeff's profession and on his lack of actual experience in government. This campaign culminated during a TV appearance when a newsman was primed to ask, "Governor, do you seriously contend that an actor is not, and could not be, qualified to run this state?"

The Governor smiled, ready with his answer even before the question was completed, "Jack," he said sure as always to address every newsman by his first name, "Jack, let me put it this way. My opponent is every bit as qualified to be governor of this great state as I am to be the star of a television series." Having drawn the newsmen's smiles, he went on to add, "Don't ever forget it was an actor who assassinated Lincoln."

The furor which followed was so great not only among Republicans but among the actors' contingent in the Democratic party that even the Governor's apology could not quiet it. A new and dramatic issue had to be found to divert the public displeasure which had been aroused by that injudicious bit of humor.

The new attack took the form of an exposé pretending to enormous gravity. In a speech covered by television the Governor held up copies of print-outs of Walter Craig's computer-processed information.

The Governor also revealed "certain mysterious events" that had taken place "at a certain unnamed hotel" on a "certain day . . . a black day for the Republican Party . . ." in which such computerized print-outs had been used to deny "the registered voters of the Republican Party the right to exercise their primary vote."

Within twenty-four hours the Governor gave the press, piecemeal as his advisers suggested, additional bits of information all of which he had possessed from the outset. First, he mentioned the name of the Bel Air Hotel, then the date of the luncheon meeting. Finally he issued a list of those who attended. Each revelation pretended to be a new discovery confirming the original information and giving the story longer life and increased press coverage.

In his speech three nights later, the Governor finally presented all the facts, in detail, and made his most condemnatory charge. Jeff Jefferson was a tool, a manufactured candidate, created and brought to his present state of prominence by a campaign based on computerized information which treated the public as a brainless entity to be punch-carded into groups by age, sex, race, religion, job, income. The electorate was being manipulated by machines. Its tastes, preferences, and opinions were sought not to be respected but exploited!

This, the Governor charged, was a cynical perversion of the democratic process! He ended his speech saying, "They haven't told us yet what happens to a voter who chooses to vote differently than the computer tells him he's supposed to. What do they do, take his vote away? Are we witnessing the end of truly democratic representative government? That is the real issue before the people of this state next Tuesday!"

Coming so close to election day, it was a highly effective charge. The fact that it was supported by copies of Walter Craig's print-outs gave it great force and effect. How the Governor had secured such information was not known, but any bribe of sufficient size could have produced it.

That speech served not only to dispel the stench of the Governor's ill-conceived remark about actors but made the first real inroads into Jeff's steadily growing popularity.

Within twelve hours Craig's figures reflected the effects of it. He considered them serious enough to scrap Jeff's planned speech at the Salinas Rodeo and prepare a totally new one.

Now, as Jeff Jefferson maintained his balance in the moving car, he was concerned more than a little by the fresh material which rested in the black binder which Claire held. For Jeff had grown to like Craig's reliable phrases. He particularly liked those speeches in which he knew where to expect his laughs. He had learned to use those reactions as natural punctuations. His facial gestures were geared to them. This new speech would not afford him that practice and confidence. But Craig insisted, with election only a few days away, it had to be made and made at once.

They were approaching the arena now. This time no changing into the phony white cowboy outfit. This time the gates were opened wide. The convertible moved through them, up the concrete ramp and onto the field itself. The band struck up a march and preceded the limousine as it started to circle the field. Drum majorettes in skintight satin outfits displayed their breasts and buttocks as they maneuvered skillfully before Jeff's car. This time, too, as he neared the pens and the chutes, the cowboy contestants did not smile deprecatingly but cheered.

The mayor's introduction was overly florid ending with the inevitable "Our candidate for the highest office in this state and your next Governor, Jeff Jefferson!"

The cheering, the whistling, was long, enthusiastic, sustained. Craig had told him once that there comes a moment in every campaign when the public smells the winner, and they applaud him not so much because he represents what they believe but because they want to be on the side of the champion.

Just before Jeff felt that the applause might weaken, he made his first attempt to quiet the audience. Smiling, gesturing helplessly in the face of such an ovation he turned to those on the platform as though saying, "I'm doing my best but as you see they won't quit."

A few moments later, he made his first real effort and the crowd was finally still. Jeff paused a long moment, as he always did, to create the proper sober atmosphere.

Then he usually began with a joke. This time just before he could begin speaking one of the Brahma bulls let go a belligerent bellow.

Instantly discarding the first line of his speech, Jeff adlibbed, "Take it easy, Governor, I'll answer you if you give me a chance."

The applause began again, this time louder, stronger than before. Finally the clapping, the laughs died down. Now the crowd leaned forward anticipating combat. That bastard Craig knows how to pick the right audience, thought Jeff. Of course, a rodeo where conflict is the purpose of the day. Any contest would be welcome here today. Well, he would give it to them.

Spurred on by the expectation of the crowd, Jeff welcomed the new speech that he had previously viewed with concern. He began by thanking the crowd for listening. "I feel honored that you let me join you in your favorite sport and mine!"

There was applause, of course. People always applaud politicians who laud them.

"Now, I would not expect the Governor of this state to be here today. Nor would I expect him to appreciate genuine folks like you. Or to understand your problems. Or try to deal with them. No, he is off in Los Angeles or San Francisco addressing some group of coffee-house beatniks and liberals who criticize the free way of life because they feel superior to it. They feel that freedom, about which they talk so much, is meant for them alone, not for the likes of you and me."

There was more applause, interlaced with boos for the Governor.

Jeff continued, "Or maybe the Governor is meeting with his political cabinet to invent some new vicious lies, to make it seem that the Republicans have plotted in secret to manipulate the people of this state.

"Well, let's take up his accusations! For God's sake, let's finally have the truth!"

Jeff delivered that last on a rising crescendo. The crowd responded just as he expected. He counted twenty-four long beats before they would let him continue. Man, they were really with him.

"The Governor has charged that there was a secret

meeting of Republican politicians in a secret place at an unannounced time. Well, as to the secret place, it was a public hotel in Bel Air. You, your wife, your children could drive up to that hotel, go in freely, have lunch or get a room. I don't call that a very secret place. Do you?"

A loud rolling "Nooo!" echoed from the stands.

"Now as to whether it was a secret meeting, I have taken the trouble, since this charge was made, to investigate. And I have discovered in addition to the forty-seven guests who attended there were present eight waiters, two assistant managers, six busboys. And, oh, yes, two bartenders. We Republicans like a little drink before lunch."

That evoked the laugh that it had been written to secure.

"Well, with eighteen outsiders in a group of forty-seven I wouldn't exactly say it was a secret meeting. Would you?"

Again a loud, sustained "No!" from the crowd.

"Now as to its being at an unannounced time, the invitations to that meeting were issued by simple note through the U.S. mails to all the men who attended—not exactly the way one carries on devious activities, is it?"

Another pause, another loud, "Nooo!"

Now Jeff changed mood, displaying sincere indignation and anger as he had played it many times before the movie camera. His face gradually lost its smile. It seemed leaner, as though anger had tightened his muscles. Then he launched into the most meaningful part of his speech.

"Now, much as I resent these sly accusations, I resent far more one accusation that is aimed not only at me, not only at my staff, but at *you!* The Governor thinks that *you* are too naive, too easily used, or just too damned stupid to vote intelligently!

"Yes, that's what it comes down to! When he holds up a batch of papers and says they are copies of secret polls we have taken and that we use them to fool you, he is saying that he believes you are stupid, that what you think doesn't matter, and *shouldn't* matter.

"In other words, he feels that you should be ruled, taxed, educated, and governed by men who don't know what you want. And what's more, that they should not even be allowed to ask you what you want! Well, I say *that* is not democratic government!"

Applause broke out, sharp, belligerent.

"I say that the Democratic Party has grown lax and overconfident in the last thirty years. They have forgotten how democracy started in this land, when citizens gathered in town meetings, discussed their problems, then arrived at solutions. And the town officials were there, heard those ideas and acted accordingly! That was the democratic process!

"And it is what *I* have always believed democracy should be. So when I, new to this game of politics, agreed to run for office, I was just fool enough to say, I would like to know what the people think. Because if I don't think as they do, then I don't deserve to be their governor!"

There was a wild burst of applause.

"So I set out, in my simple way, to do what they did in the old town hall—listen to what the people have to say, listen to their needs, their desires, their dreams!"

The applause was beginning to anticipate him now, scarcely giving him time to get out all his words.

"For that purpose I have a staff of loyal people who get on the phone each day and ask between one and two thousand of you what you think about the issues in this campaign. Then the next day I have a report of what the people of this state think. What they want their next Governor to *do* for them! In other words, we are applying every day the old process of the town hall to today's politics where millions of lives are involved, not merely hundreds!

"I want to restore the democratic process to California politics! I want to be responsive to the needs, desires, and opinions of the people of my state! And I'll be damned if I am going to let any hack politician stop me!"

The applause was now overwhelming. Campaign skimmers, programs, and empty popcorn bags sailed into the arena in tribute. People leaped to their feet to applaud. Finally the entire crowd was standing and cheering.

Unable to achieve quiet, Jeff almost shouted into the phone, "If the Governor of this state no longer has faith in the democratic process, if he no longer cares what the people think, then I say he has been Governor too long!

"It's his kind of government, led by a small band of self-anointed liberals that's stripped our treasury bare, made our taxes insufferable, and produced turmoil in our schools. The Democrats have left the average man and woman, like you and me, hopeless and defeated! Well, you are only defeated if you let yourself be. You can still fight! Join me on election day and we can make California once again the Golden State!

"For myself," Jeff concluded, "I am going to keep on asking the people what they think. I am going to keep on reading those reports! Every day during this campaign! And I promise you I will continue doing so after next January first when I become your Governor!"

The crowd went wild. Jeff stood proud and happy, with a sense of power that he had never quite achieved before. He reached back, groping for Claire's hand and brought her to her feet to stand alongside him.

Listening to the deafening ovation he thought, This is not the capricious hero-worship that people lavish on movie stars. This is real affection, and more. He wasn't speaking *to* the people. He was speaking *for* them. They didn't *like* him. They *loved* him. They didn't *want* him. They *needed* him. The transformation from actor to politician was complete.

6

On the day of that Salinas speech and for the entire weekend immediately preceding the election, Irwin Cone was in Washington, staying at the Shoreham Hotel.

Normally The Doctor would have had Buddy Black accompany him on such a trip because of his Democratic connections. But this time he had come alone, to be met by his eminent counsel from New York, Merwin Appleman, who by virtue of his association with past Democratic Presidents and his present power in state politics, had the political muscle to arrange a private meeting between The Doctor and an important member of the White House staff.

They arrived separately at The Doctor's suite. First the leonine lawyer. Then the White House aide, close friend of the President, close as well to the Attorney General.

The ostensible reason for this meeting was that Doctor Irwin Cone, a friend of Appleman's, had heard rumors that his firm was being investigated by the Justice Department. Naturally Cone was greatly concerned. He was not aware of having broken the law, but if he had done so, he would like to resolve the matter as swiftly and quietly as possible.

No one, no matter how suspicious, could object to such an exploratory meeting.

The three men said little through lunch, for there were constant interruptions by the waiter, an eager little Italian who strove unendingly to make sure that his patrons were totally satisfied. But once lunch was over, it was possible to relax over a good cigar without being overheard.

Even before being asked, Roger Wittinger, the White House assistant, a portly young man, who mouthed his cigar with almost sexual satisfaction, observed softly, "I

479

have looked into the matter. There's a good deal of truth to what you heard."

The Doctor did not respond with either interest or alarm. He knew that those in power only used that threatening approach when they came prepared to bargain. At such times no trouble was small, no favor easy. So he would let this young man play out his little drama.

"I took the liberty to go over to the Justice Department myself. Quite a file!" Wittinger raised his hand high above the table top to indicate its thickness. Turning to Appleman he said, "When you first called me I had no idea . . . no idea . . ."

That's right, The Doctor said to himself, build it up, sonny! He probably is aware we intend to go public as soon as this is cleared up.

"It seems," Wittinger continued, "it seems that there have been a number of complaints. From TCA clients. As well as from one TV network. And from several advertising agencies. There has been too much pressure to sell TCA shows, too much trading off. And then there's that matter of owning a studio, producing films, and representing talent, all at the same time. Justice says it's worse than the old days when studios owned their own theaters. They're really steamed. They're going to move on this! Soon!" Wittinger puffed again, before he said, "I just hope we're not too late."

This last comment was injected to give Appleman a chance to present his case and start the bargaining.

The elderly lawyer leaned forward in his easy chair. "What aspects of the matter concern the Justice Department most?"

"Several," the young man said, not willing to weaken his position by concentrating on any one issue.

"For example?" Appleman tried to lead.

"Well, acquiring the studio," the young aide said.

Appleman looked to The Doctor who put aside his cigar. "We acquired that to help out a bank that had loaned eight million dollars to the studio to make a picture! Unfortunately the picture did not come up to expectations."

"I heard it was a disaster," Wittinger said.

"Yes, it was. So there was the bank stuck for eight million with only a studio and some land for security. Plus the negative of a picture that wouldn't earn back its print

THE KINGMAKER

481

cost. They foreclosed. But if picture makers are having trouble running a studio these days, what chance has a bank got? So we bailed them out. We took over the studio."

"And the land."

"And the land," The Doctor had to agree. "And we have been paying the bank at the rate of two million five per annum. With interest."

"Mainly by selling off the land in small pieces," the young man prodded.

"There're two payments left to make," The Doctor said, not choosing to become embroiled in any further discussion about the land.

"And when those payments are made you'll still own the studio, all the equipment and most of the land," Wittinger observed.

"Fortunately, the value of the land has gone up considerably since we took over. I guess if the bank had been smarter they might have held on and tried to do the same thing," The Doctor admitted, making the whole deal seem to be an extremely fortuitous development.

"What bothers the Justice Department," the young man said, "is that TCA and various of its officers and relatives have a controlling interest in that bank."

There was a pause. Young Wittinger had just shoved a stack of troublesome chips into the center of the bargaining table.

"The Department has also collected statements from a number of key network executives to the effect that TCA exercises what they call 'undue' control over the networks in some situations."

"That's a laugh!" The Doctor said. "Coming from the networks! Talk about monopoly!"

But young Wittinger was insistent. "There are more than a few instances in the files where network executives testified that TCA refused to make certain of their stars available unless TCA received not only its commission on the stars' salaries, but a substantial payment on top of that for non-existent services called 'supervisory fees,' and the like. Justice considers that commercial bribery."

"And what," The Doctor demanded, "do they call it when the networks take a half interest in a show before they let it go on the air? What do they call it when there

THE KINGMAKER

are only three networks and you're dead unless you pay off one of them?"

"They're aware of that. But right now they're concentrating on TCA," Wittinger persisted.

To change the temper of the meeting, Appleman asked, "Is that the basis of their complaint?"

"One thing more," the young man said, "the worst offense seems to be that TCA represents talent in one room and buys it in another in the very same office. *That* is a flagrant conflict of interest."

"We obtained the permission of all the Guilds in advance!" The Doctor declared righteously.

"It's gone so far," Wittinger continued, "that an individual—Heller, I believe his name is, Abe Heller—who used to be executive secretary of the Screen Actors Guild, is now vice president in charge of negotiations for TCA."

Whether the young man had discovered that connection accidentally The Doctor did not know, nor did he feel it wise to probe deep enough to discover.

"Yes," Wittinger continued gravely, "the files are replete with complaints from people which TCA represents who feel that they have been cheated, forced to work at low rates, and in some cases have been kept out of work until they capitulated."

"Young man," The Doctor interrupted, smiling indulgently, "have you ever dealt with talent? Do you know the kind of crazy hallucinations that go through the mind of an actor without a job? Or a writer whose script has been rejected by everyone in town? Or a director who's been removed from a picture? They blame everybody in the world except themselves."

Wittinger did not respond, because it was obvious from The Doctor's intensity that he had not finished.

"Gratitude!" The Doctor exploded. "We began producing film more for their sake than ours! We made a full disclosure to the Actors Guild. They voted us their permission. And now they turn on us this way." The Doctor shook his head sadly. "Young man, did you ever hear of the Doctrine of Informed Consent?"

Wittinger nodded. "The Justice Department is fully aware of how you got the permission."

"Look here, young man . . ." shouted The Doctor.

Because Appleman feared that his client was dangerously close to losing his temper, he interceded, "Suppose, without prejudice to my client's interests, we were to admit all of these charges just for the sake of argument. What would the attitude be of the Justice Department? How can we settle this matter so that all alleged violations are cured to their satisfaction and TCA is allowed to continue in at least some phases of its activity?"

"You mean a consent decree of some kind?"

"That might be one way," the lawyer agreed, though he meant it would be the only desirable way.

"That," said Wittinger, "I would have to investigate and discuss."

The Doctor, having had time to recover from his anger, said, "Before you do, let's take a calm look at the whole situation. Is TCA going to produce motion pictures and TV film or is it going to represent talent? If it's going to produce TV films and pictures then there is nothing wrong in owning the studio where they make their pictures. Right?"

Wittinger did not respond either by word or gesture. The Doctor continued.

"As to the possible conflict of interest, what if TCA gives up, voluntarily and for all time, representing talent? Then there's no possible problem. And since we would no longer control any stars we'd have no more muscle to exact these extra payments you claim we get."

The Doctor paused, letting the young man evaluate the deal he was proposing. "I haven't talked with my associates yet, but I will personally guarantee to withdraw TCA from the talent end of the business. If that's what the Justice Department insists on. I think it's unfair. I think we're being pushed to the wall on the basis of irresponsible complaints but I am willing to go that far!

"After all, I didn't spend a lifetime in this business to be branded a criminal. My job is providing entertainment, not fighting the Government of the United States!"

Appleman looked at Wittinger in such a way as to rebuke him for having hurt this gentle little man. Then he pushed back his chair, breaking the tight circle, "I think my client has stated his position fairly and honestly. Why not speak to whoever is handling the matter and see what his reaction is?"

"It's the Attorney General himself," the young man

said, having saved this blockbuster to close the meeting. Even Appleman was shaken by the revelation.

"Well, if that's the man you have to talk to, talk to him. After all, you're no stranger to him."

Whereupon the lawyer rose from his chair. "Gentlemen, I promised the Chief Justice I would drop by and say hello before I left town." He shook hands and departed.

Once the old man had closed the door, The Doctor leaned forward in his chair, looked into young Wittinger's dark, fleshy face. "You know, you surprise me. Not about the charges. But *you!* What is a young man as bright as you doing in government? What can they pay you at the White House? Twenty-seven-five?"

"Twenty-four," the young man admitted, sheepishly.

"Twenty-four thousand dollars a year?" The Doctor echoed almost in pain. "Is it worth it? I mean, where does it lead? What's the future? Even if this Administration stays in power another term, what does that mean to you? Five years from now you first have to start making a career for yourself. You married? Got kids?"

The young man nodded.

"Don't you ever think about *their* future? Look, I hate to see a young man short-change himself and his family just because he's been bitten by the public-service bug. Let me tell you something. Sometime within the next four months, no matter how this wrangle with the Justice Department comes out, we are going to float a public issue of TCA stock. It'll come out at ten. I will personally see that there will be ten thousand shares waiting for you. And I can promise you that within six months the price will go to forty. Or higher. If it doesn't I'll buy the stock back from you myself. That's how confident I am!"

He pretended to be struck by an afterthought, minor to him but of possible importance to the young man.

"Look, if there's any problem getting up the money for the stock, that can be arranged," The Doctor assured him.

"No. I think I can manage that on margin."

"Good! Good!" The Doctor seemed delighted.

Then as if to change the subject Wittinger asked, "How does it look in California? The election, I mean."

"I think the Republicans are going to take it."

"I've seen projections. Some of them say by over a million votes."

"Possible. Very possible," The Doctor agreed.

"An actor! Who would have thought it!"

"We handled him, you know."

"I know," Wittinger said, but with far greater significance than The Doctor had attributed to his own statement. "I've heard all about it."

"No secret. We handled him as long as he was in show business."

"Even when he was president of the Screen Actors Guild, I understand. But what I meant," the young man explained, "is that I've heard all about the terrific job that Walter Craig and Spencer Gould have done with him."

"Oh, yes," The Doctor agreed vaguely, as though Craig and Spence operated independently of him.

"Very impressive!" Wittinger said. "Especially for California. Weird state politically."

"Yes, they did a hell of a job," Cone agreed. Suddenly he remembered, "Say, you're from California originally, aren't you?"

"Born and spent most of my life there."

"Ever thought of going back? When you get fed up with Washington."

"In my business you never rule out any options," the young man said.

"Not even running for office?"

"It's been suggested."

"There's a man at TCA you should get to know. Buddy Black. Strong Democrat. In fact he's as committed a Democrat as Spencer Gould is a Republican."

"I know," the young man said. "I'm familiar with his contributions to the State and National Committees."

"Oh, are you?" Cone asked.

"Yes, I am," Wittinger said without blinking.

"You two ought to get together. I mean, California is going to be looking for a new senator two years from now. Something to think about. Buddy would know. Yes, you two ought to get together."

"I'm due to be out there on White House business in about twelve days."

"I'll arrange it!" The Doctor assured him.

They shook hands. The young man left. The Doctor opened the windows to let the heavy smell of cigar smoke escape, saying to himself, So that's what he wanted. And I thought it was the capital gain on the stock. The Doctor realized he could have had the deal more cheaply than he had anticipated. It was not often that he was out-bargained, even by accident. But this time, because of the high stakes, he didn't particularly regret overpaying. The main objective was to have that consent decree signed, and thus be free to issue TCA stock with a view to putting it on the Big Board.

For The Doctor, election day was an anticlimax. It was like opening a show that had gotten good reviews in New Haven, Boston, and Philadelphia. There was always a slight sense of doubt that something might go wrong, but no real concern. Craig's print-outs showed a clear margin in almost every county and The Doctor had come to have utmost confidence in them.

They were sitting in the living room of Jeff's election-night suite. Three television sets were on, the one that belonged in the suite and the two others that had been brought in for the evening. By nine o'clock California time all three networks had predicted Jeff the winner by a sizable margin. By ten-fifteen, an unusually early hour for such a move, the incumbent Governor conceded. Sooner than was expected, Jeff and Claire had to freshen up and go down for the victory speech. The suite emptied except for The Doctor and Walter Craig.

The Doctor sat soberly watching the television sets. Craig reached for one of the drying turkey sandwiches, not to eat it but to play with the bread. Cone was too intent to become annoyed or even notice.

When Eric Severeid came on to do his wrap-up from the East Coast, where it was now one-thirty, The Doctor turned down the sound on the other two sets. Looking more dour than usual, Severeid found no unexpected surprises in the national picture as reflected by the state and local returns.

"But," Severeid continued, "the fact that there have been no surprises tonight does not mean that we have not seen some events of remarkable national significance. The most important of which has occurred in California, where a complete political novice has been swept into the State House with an overwhelming plurality. From now on, no contender for the Republican nomination for President can expect to win without the approval and cooperation of Jeff Jefferson who, until yesterday, was an actor and a political virgin. But who from this night on must be regarded as a power in the Republican Party. And, if a deadlock should develop at the Republican convention, Jefferson could well emerge as the only strong compromise candidate available. Thus in one night a handsome, seemingly sincere, but completely inexperienced figure emerges full-blown on the American political scene. And if he has presidential ambitions, who can deny him the dream? This is Eric Severeid in New York."

The Doctor leaned back in the armchair, mute, concerned. Somehow it always happened. Even facts he knew well took on added gravity and importance when Severeid said them. In that way at least The Doctor was like any American television viewer. He turned to Craig.

"I guess that's possible, isn't it?"

"You can't elect a President without California. And for the next four years he's California," Craig said.

"I mean the possibility of his actually becoming a candidate for the Presidency," The Doctor replied, thoughtfully.

"Scares you, does it?" The Doctor never bothered to answer obvious questions. "Remember, I told you once. In my business defeat takes care of itself. It's success that creates the problems. Now you know what I mean."

The Doctor nodded. Suddenly the network cut to the victory scene downstairs. There was Jeff smiling broadly, waving to the crowd. Alongside him was Claire, and just to the side of her were both boys. They were all waving. Jeff used his now familiar gesture to plead for silence, but the band and the crowd only became noisier. Finally the noise subsided. When Jeff started to speak, The Doctor picked up his coat and started out of the room without even saying good night to Craig.

Ten days after the election, there was a lengthy official meeting at the Justice Department in Washington

between a representative of the Anti-Trust Division and
Attorney Merwin Appleman. The Doctor insisted on being
present, for when important matters were involved he
did not rely on even the most competent and highly priced
lawyers.

In that meeting it was finally agreed that the Justice
Department would proceed to make formal charges against
TCA as a company and Doctor Irwin Cone as an individual and that indictments would be handed down. The
indictments would be limited to those infractions which
could be cured by a consent decree in which TCA agreed
to cease representing talent in any and all fields. Hence-
forth, TCA would limit its activities to producing, distribut-
ing, owning, and leasing film, and carrying on only those
activities as were in furtherance of such production, to
wit, owning studios and adjacent land, banks, and other
enterprises of a like nature.

The decree implemented every single provision of The
Doctor's Big Plan.

Once the decree was signed, the large Wall Street banking firm, which had been ready for months, proceeded
to issue ten million shares of stock in TCA, Ltd. at ten
dollars a share, based on assets which included the studio,
equipment, land, a majority interest in a bank in St. Louis,
and an inventory of more than four thousand negatives of
half-hour and hour television films.

The stock began to rise immediately and climbed steadily for five weeks until it reached sixty-one dollars a
share. Then it fell back gradually to a stable price of fifty-
four dollars.

The Doctor's interest in TCA stock at the end of the
five-week period was valued at one hundred and twenty-
seven million dollars. In gratitude for his sudden good
fortune, he decided to make a charitable contribution of
sizable proportions, tax deductible, of course.

Since cardiology had been the specialty that had appealed to him, and since his father had died of a coronary
infarct, he decided to donate a complete cardiac unit to
the Bethel Hospital of Los Angeles. It would be dedicated
to the memory of his beloved father.

The only moment of hesitation he suffered came not
when he had to sign the check for four million three hun-

dred thousand dollars but when he had to decide on the inscription for the bronze plaque to be affixed over the entrance to the wing.

He wrote out several. The first read "The Samuel Cohen Intensive Care Unit, donated in loving memory by his son, Doctor Irwin Cone."

He struck that out in favor of "This Intensive Care Unit donated by Doctor Irwin Cone in memory of his father, Samuel Cohen."

But the anomaly still persisted. Finally, he wrote: DONATED BY DOCTOR IRWIN CONE IN MEMORY OF HIS BELOVED FATHER, SAMUEL. This neatly avoided the question of what old Samuel's name had been at the time of his death.

Eventually the installation would come to be known to everyone as the Cone I.C.U.

7

The voice of the Chief Justice echoed through the rotunda.

". . . and that I will well and faithfully discharge the duties upon which I am about to enter."

And Jeff repeated, "And that I will well and faithfully discharge the duties upon which I am about to enter."

After which Jeff Jefferson kissed the Bible as his mother had taught him to do years ago whenever she made him take an oath. Then he kissed Claire. The crowd started to shout: "Jeff . . . Jeff . . . Jeff . . ." though he was no longer their TV Star but their Governor.

The ceremony was followed by champagne. While the press photographed Jeff, The Doctor slipped away unnoticed, except by Walter Craig whom he had signaled to join him. They started down the steps of the Capitol together.

"Good job. Excellent!" said The Doctor.

"Thank you," Craig said, knowing that the little man had not summoned him merely to offer such unnecessary congratulations.

"Of course, now that I've got a governor I don't need his muscle."

"You will," Craig said. "One thing I've learned in this business. Power never goes unused."

"What happens to him now?"

"Sometimes the man takes over the office. Sometimes the office takes over the man. I guess with him it'll depend on whether he's *playing* a governor or *being* one."

The Doctor glanced at Craig to see if he was joking or just being his own cynical self.

After a moment Cone asked, "I was wondering what

you would do if someone asked you to take on a senatorial candidate."

"U.S. or state?"

"U.S."

"Republican or Democrat?"

"Democrat."

"Democrat . . . next time?" Craig evaluated. "I think there'd be a good chance for a Democrat next time."

"Okay!" The Doctor said. "And don't worry about the money. When the time comes, it'll be there."

Craig nodded. The agreement was firm. He knew The Doctor was a man of his word. For the little man had been educated in a tough school. He honored his promises, paid his debts.

Cone got into his limousine, gestured good night. Craig started up the steps to rejoin the celebration that was still going on in the rotunda.

Though Craig usually lost interest even in a victorious candidate once the election was over, it was the last official duty he had in connection with every successful campaign.

The big new scorcher
by the sensational
bestselling author
of FIRE ISLAND...

ACAPULCO
by Burt Hirschfeld

Acapulco—where the super-rich of the world
gather . . . where a ruthless movie producer, a
self-destructive sex queen and a brilliant, tormented
writer are locked in a savage triangle of greed,
lust and betrayal . . . Where millionaires and
mystics, abandoned hedonists and dedicated artists
seek their salvation and find their ultimate corrup-
tion—in the biggest, boldest, most blistering novel
of the year!

"Smooth, sophisticated, erotic!"

—*New York Times*

A Dell Book $1.50

From the publisher who brought you
The Sensuous Woman
The Sensuous Man
and
The Happy Hooker!

SCORING

by DAN GREENBURG

SCORING is the frankest and funniest sexual memoir written in our time. The title comes from the most popular national pastime where First Base was a goodnight kiss and Home Plate too rarely reached. Dan Greenburg is a compulsive scorekeeper. He keeps a record of every girl he has ever necked with or petted above the waist and every girl he has ever scored with. A harder-working necker, grappler, pincher, petter, and finally, scorer never survived to write about it. SCORING is riotously funny, disarming, candid, touching and true. It is Dan Greenburg's story, but it is yours, too—whether your coming-of-age occurred in the 40s, 50s or 60s. Some things just don't change.

A DELL BOOK $1.50

If you cannot obtain copies of this title at your local bookseller, just send the price (plus 15c per copy for handling and postage) to Dell Books, Post Office Box 1000, Pinebrook, N. J. 07058.

"A sizzler! You won't be able to put it down."
—*San Francisco Examiner*

LANA

THE PUBLIC AND PRIVATE LIVES OF MISS TURNER

by Joe Morella and Edward Z. Epstein

Part of her life has been an incredible success story—the teenager who became the sweater girl of the screen, then Hollywood's super-star.

Part of her life has been scandal—the husbands, the lovers, the shocking rumors, the tragic involvement with Johnny Stompanato and his slaying by her daughter Cheryl . . . the younger men she turned to . . .

Now for the first time her whole life is revealed, in a book that is unblushingly candid, yet never less than fair to the complex and driven woman who is Lana Turner.

"Fascinating . . . It's all here!"
—*Detroit Free Press*

A Dell Book $1.25

If you cannot obtain copies of this title from your local bookseller, just send the price (plus 15c per copy for handling and postage) to Dell Books, Post Office Box 1000, Pinebrook, N. J. 07058.

The hottest heist since
The Anderson Tapes ...
by the author of
Miami Golden Boy.

MILLIONAIRES

by HERBERT KASTLE

The place was Bay Island, connected to Florida
by a narrow bridge. On it were twelve luxurious
homes, each one occupied by a millionaire. Even
the President of the United States, a frequent
visitor, was just another guest in the company
of the super-rich.

Walter Danforth "Bucky" Prince came to the
island with a distinguished family name, a reputation as a super-stud and a handpicked crew of
helpers. His purpose was simple: to take over
Bay Island and loot it. . . .

"Steaming sex, violence and suspense!"
Library Journal

A DELL BOOK $1.50

If you cannot obtain copies of this title from your local bookseller, just
send the price (plus 15c per copy for handling and postage) to Dell Books,
Post Office Box 1000, Pinebrook, N. J. 07058.

How many of these Dell Bestsellers have you read?

1. **IN THE SHADOW OF MAN**
   by Jane Van Lawick-Goodall $1.50

2. **THE GIFT HORSE**
   by Hildegard Knef $1.50

3. **THE WASHINGTON PAY-OFF**
   by Robert N. Winter-Berger $1.75

4. **BRIAN PICCOLO: A SHORT SEASON**
   by Jeannie Morris $1.25

5. **THE HAPPY HOOKER**
   by Xaviera Hollander $1.50

6. **THE MAGICIAN**
   by Sol Stein $1.25

7. **ACAPULCO**
   by Burt Hirschfeld $1.50

8. **THE NEW CENTURIONS**
   by Joseph Wambaugh $1.50

9. **DELIVERANCE**
   by James Dickey $1.25

10. **THE DISCIPLE AND HIS DEVIL**
    by Valerie Pascal $1.25

11. **THE MS. GIRLS**
    by Cheryl Nash $1.25

12. **MYSELF AMONG OTHERS**
    by Ruth Gordon $1.50

13. **THE JANE CASTLE MANUSCRIPT**
    by Philip L. Greene $1.25

If you cannot obtain copies of these titles from your local bookseller, just send the price (plus 15c per copy for handling and postage) to Dell Books, Post Office Box 1000, Pinebrook, N. J. 07058.